"Engaging . . . The unfolding of events feels mostly realistic on a macro scale; things progress in a way that makes sense as the story advances. Varley is a master of pacing—even the slower, more introspective moments feel packed with urgency. That urgency is what makes for a true tautness in a thriller . . . A captivating page-turner that offers one man's look at an alternative end of the world. *Slow Apocalypse* will satisfy fans of science fiction, literary thrillers, and mysteries alike."   —*The Maine Edge*

"A page-turner . . . [Varley's] prose style is accessible without being slick or dumbed down; this is a literary novel with a potboiler plot, easily digested but not insultingly simple. He builds a thought-through, realistic world, then explores how his cataclysm would change it."   —*The A.V. Club*

"An entertaining postapocalyptic thriller."
                                   —*Genre Go Round Reviews*

PRAISE FOR JOHN VARLEY

"John Varley is the best writer in America."   —Tom Clancy

"My life-experience of John Varley's stories has been that the great majority of them are literally unforgettable."
                                                —William Gibson

continued . . .

BOOKS BY JOHN VARLEY

The Ophiuchi Hotline
The Persistence of Vision
Picnic on Nearside
(*formerly titled* The Barbie Murders)
Millennium
Blue Champagne
Steel Beach
The Golden Globe
Red Thunder
Mammoth
Red Lightning
Rolling Thunder
Slow Apocalypse

THE GAEAN TRILOGY

Titan
Wizard
Demon

The John Varley Reader: Thirty Years of Short Fiction

SLOW APOCALYPSE

JOHN VARLEY

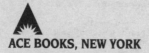

ACE BOOKS, NEW YORK

THE BERKLEY PUBLISHING GROUP
Published by the Penguin Group
Penguin Group (USA) Inc.
375 Hudson Street, New York, New York 10014, USA

USA | Canada | UK | Ireland | Australia | New Zealand | India | South Africa | China

Penguin Books Ltd., Registered Offices: 80 Strand, London WC2R 0RL, England
For more information about the Penguin Group, visit penguin.com.

SLOW APOCALYPSE

An Ace Book / published by arrangement with the author

Ace Books are published by The Berkley Publishing Group.
ACE and the "A" design are trademarks of Penguin Group (USA) Inc.

For information, address: The Berkley Publishing Group,
a division of Penguin Group (USA) Inc.,
375 Hudson Street, New York, New York 10014.

ISBN: 978-0-425-26213-9

PUBLISHING HISTORY
Ace hardcover edition / September 2012
Ace mass-market edition / July 2013

PRINTED IN THE UNITED STATES OF AMERICA

10 9 8 7 6 5 4 3 2 1

Cover photos: rusty background © Piotr Tomicki / Shutterstock;
rusty car door handle © Hemera Technologies / Thinkstock;
old car door handle © iStockphoto/Thinkstock.
Cover design by Judith Lagerman.
Interior text design by Laura K. Corless.

This Los Angeles book is dedicated to our Los Angeles friends, Jon Mersel and Marion Peters

PROLOGUE

The sound of automatic weapons firing made everyone look up.

Dave Marshall was standing on the sidewalk on Hollywood Boulevard with a hundred other gawkers. They had all been looking at the front entrance to the W Hotel, where half a dozen men in black armor, combat helmets, heavy equipment belts, and military assault rifles were blocking the doors. They didn't wear any kind of insignia or identification of rank, no bright yellow FBI printed on their backs, no Homeland Security patches, no LAPD.

A few minutes earlier three black armored personnel carriers had roared up and these anonymous heavily armed men poured out. They quickly cleared the small plaza around the subway station, and a dozen of them had entered the building just as Dave was leaving it.

He was as curious as everyone else, and maybe a little worried, so instead of doing the prudent thing—if this was a bomb report or a hostage situation—which would have been to get as far away as possible, he'd lingered to see if he could find out what was going on. Regular LAPD patrol cars arrived without sirens, half a dozen of them almost simultaneously, and the officers had blocked off the street and gave orders for everyone to move along. That's when they heard the gunfire.

He looked up. One of the big panes up there had shattered. Shards of glass glittered in the sunlight as they twisted and turned on their way down. Before they had gone very far a human figure followed them, falling backwards, his arms flailing.

Dave could tell the man was bald. He could see bright redness on the back of his white shirt. He even fancied he could see a stream of blood arcing away from the falling body, though that might have been his imagination.

Then he lost sight of him behind other bystanders, and there was the sickening thump as the man landed very close to where Dave had been standing only seconds before. It was much louder than he would have expected. He actually felt the impact with the concrete. There were shouts and screams of horror.

The cops quickly got a lot more serious about moving people along. He was jostled and almost lost his balance because he kept looking back over his shoulder and trying to count the floors. It wasn't until he was across the street and could stand still for a moment that he was able to get a good look at the hole in the side of the building where the big glass pane had been. One of the black-clad commandos was leaning out, looking down at the dead man below. Dave was now sure that the man had fallen from the eleventh floor.

Something else he was sure of was that, no more than ten minutes ago, he had been talking with the dead man in the man's apartment.

Suddenly, he was more frightened than he had ever been in his life.

It had all started a little over twenty-four hours before . . .

CHAPTER ONE

Hollywood and Vine. The Walk of Fame, the boulevard of broken dreams.

Dave Marshall was standing on Carmen Miranda's terrazzo and brass star embedded in the sidewalk, in front of the Hollywood and Vine subway station.

The place bustled with activity at midday. Noon, by Dave's watch.

He was looking for a man who lived in the W. The concierge told him his quarry had left over an hour ago, and had said something about needing a drink.

Where would you go if you needed a drink at noon on Hollywood Boulevard?

On the southwest corner was what used to be The Broadway. All that was left of that was the sign on the roof. It had been converted to condos, and the ground floor was a trendy restaurant and nightclub called Katsuya, frequented by wannabes and some actual celebrities. The drinks there would be expensive, and it wasn't open, anyway. Almost across the street from him was the fabulous old art-deco Pantages Theater, home of the Academy Awards for eleven years. Several small businesses were squeezed in along the theater frontage, and one of them was the most likely spot to find his man: the Frolic Room.

Dave made his way over there.

Everybody in Hollywood knows the Frolic Room, though most residents have never been inside. Its exterior has been in countless movies and television shows. There's something about the neon outside that evokes the 1940s, and sleaze. Every other month or so the sidewalk is blocked with big reflective screens and camera dollies, and the curbs are full of the grip trucks and Winnebagos that signal a movie shoot. But not today. When there's no shooting going on, the front door is usually open, as it was now.

He entered and stopped to let his eyes adjust. It was a small room, quite dark, a lot longer than it was wide. To the left was a bar with a dozen stools, and to the right was a counter with more stools, beneath a black-and-white mural of Hollywood scenes done in the style of Al Hirschfeld. The bar got some of its business from tourists, movie buffs, and people waiting to get into the Pantages next door, but most of the people who drank there were regulars, many of them relics from an earlier Hollywood. Three of these serious morning drinkers were seated at the bar near the door, and all the way back was the short and scrawny figure of Colonel Lionel Warner, USMC, ret., hunched over and scowling down at his drink.

He didn't look up as Dave took the seat beside him.

"I guess the sun is over the yardarm somewhere," Dave said.

Warner scowled down at the bar, then killed the last of his drink, which had probably been a Jim Beam. Warner was about seventy, but you wouldn't want to tangle with him. Bald as a cue ball, with a face weathered by desert and jungle, he still communicated a wiry strength that said he could toss a man twice his size through a window, and had done so many times. His hands were scarred, with thick knuckles. He was a spit-and-polish Marine down to his boots, his clothes always freshly pressed, his bearing upright and military. But today he was hunched over his drink, and he looked a lot older than he had two days ago, when Dave had last seen him.

"That yardarm business is navy talk," Warner said. "Marines drink whenever we want to." He signaled for another. The bartender looked dubious.

"Maybe you ought to wait a bit, Colonel," he said.

Warner lifted his head and glared at him.

"Do I look visibly intoxicated to you?" He turned to Dave. "Marshall, do I look drunk?"

Dave had to admit that he didn't, though he knew he must be.

"Then set me up again, and one for Mr. Television Writer here. You guys know each other? Stan, this is Dave Marshall. Dave, meet Stan."

Being a writer carried no particular weight in the Frolic Room. Hollywood is lousy with writers. Some of them even work now and then. Stan poured for both of them. Dave took a sip of the bourbon and looked at the colonel.

Lionel Warner first saw combat in Vietnam and seemed to have been at least peripherally involved in every American conflict since then, right up to and including the beginning of the Iraq War. But many of the things he had done were off the books. There was a lot he claimed he couldn't talk about. Beginning in the early eighties he had been involved with intelligence work for agencies he had never named. Dave wasn't sure that some of them had names. He'd been talking to Warner for just over a month, looking for ideas, for stories he could tell, and had gotten the distinct impression that what he'd heard was just the tip of the iceberg, that 90 percent of what Warner might have told him was just never going to be told.

That was a shame, because while some of the stories the colonel had been free to relate were interesting, none of them had really grabbed Dave. But he kept plugging at it, because he knew there would be something there eventually, and because he rather liked the old buzzard.

Dave had met the colonel at a wrap party for a picture about the Gulf War. He hadn't been involved in the picture, but he knew somebody who knew somebody, and found himself with an invitation. Warner had been the military advisor. They found themselves thrown together more or less at random, and when the colonel found out Dave was a writer he said he had a lot of stories to tell, and then told some of them. They were fascinating. Dave had never done a war picture, but there was no need to tell the colonel that, and he didn't seem to care. Dave was looking for ideas, and the colonel was a fountain of them. At the end of the night they had an informal agreement to meet and see what they could develop.

He hadn't expected to hear back—all sorts of ephemeral deals are cooked up at parties like that, and they seldom survive the night—but Warner called the next morning and wanted to get together. That led to their first meeting for lunch in the restaurant at the W, where he was surprised to learn Warner had a two-bedroom condo. Dave knew the insane prices apartments sold for in that building, and he knew Warner couldn't have made that kind of money on a colonel's salary. But if half the stories he'd told him the night before were true, he'd had plenty of opportunities to pick up a little here and there, under the radar. If you are involved in the "takedown"—his word for assassination—of a Colombian drug lord, for instance, who was going to complain if you pocketed a few of the stacks of hundred-dollar bills guys like that liked to keep around for bug-out money? That, or bags of jewels, or raw gold. Dave hadn't asked Warner where his money came from, but when the right time came he planned to. There was very likely a good story there, if he'd tell it.

The colonel had been studying him for quite a while. Now he spoke.

"What would you do if you knew the world was going to end?"

"What? Like, today? Next week? Next year?"

"I guess that would make a difference," Warner allowed.

"Are you talking about the planet blowing up, something like that, where nobody could survive? Or just a major catastrophe, like an earthquake?"

"Smaller than the planet blowing up. Bigger than an earthquake. Let's say it's not the end of the world, but it's the end of the world as we know it." He frowned. "Isn't there a song about that?"

"R.E.M.," Dave said, surprised that the colonel had heard it.

"Don't look at me like that. I listen to the radio. My men in the Gulf War liked that song. And don't forget, my generation invented rock 'n' roll."

"So you did. Are you telling me you're getting drunk because you think the world's going to end?"

Warner considered it.

"It might. I'm not saying it will. But I think there's hard times ahead."

"Tell me about it."

And he did.

It took several hours, and more drinks. Colonel Warner paced himself instead of tossing them back, but he was pretty out of it by the time he was through. Dave had made his first drink last for most of the story, so when Warner began to show signs of passing out, Dave was able to navigate him out onto the street, across it, and up the elevator to the eleventh floor of his building. He found Warner's keys, got him inside, and poured him onto the nearest couch, where he fell instantly asleep. Dave pulled off the man's shoes, and stood for a moment looking down on the old warrior.

Quite a story he'd told him. Could any of it be true? He frankly doubted it, but it didn't matter. It was the story that counted, and he finally had what he wanted.

Dave thought about it all the way down in the elevator, then on the escalator down to the Hollywood and Vine subway station. He could see it all falling into place as he stared up at the thousands of empty film reels that decorated the ceiling of the station, and it got even better as he boarded the train and found a seat. The train sped through the long tunnel under the Cahuenga Pass, and soon reached the end of the line in North Hollywood.

When he first started interviewing the colonel he'd parked in the structure behind the W, but it was outrageously expensive. There was plenty of free parking within an easy walk of the North Hollywood station. He told himself that it left him well positioned to pick up his daughter in Burbank after the meetings, but the truth was, he was pinching pennies. A year earlier he would never have given a twenty-dollar parking fee a second thought. Hell, he'd been known to hand a twenty to the parking valet.

Not any longer.

He found his five-year-old Cadillac Escalade. According to his wife, Karen, it was already an antique, ready for the scrap heap. She was ashamed to be seen in it, which is why she was driving the newer Mercedes these days, even though the Caddy had been her idea.

He was still early to pick up his daughter, Addison, at the equestrian center. He drove down Lankershim, then Riverside, then Alameda to Bob Hope Drive and found a place to park the beast in the shade at Johnny Carson Park. Right across the street were the NBC Burbank Studios, where he had labored for seven very lucrative years.

Three years ago.

He had written for a lot of different comedies at first, none of them very memorable, but all of them paid well, thanks to the

Writers Guild minimum basic agreement. It changes your life, getting on staff at a successful sitcom after six years of scrambling as a freelance. Karen and he had been living in a studio apartment in North Hollywood when Addison was born, and the rent was overdue. They managed to scrape by, and then, almost without warning, they were well-off, living in a two-bedroom high-rise in Mid-Wilshire.

Then came the big break. He wrote a pilot called *Ants!* It was about three exterminators waging war on a race of alien insects who were living among them. But it wasn't *X-Files* material, it was a little *Coneheads* and a little *Slackers* and a little *Men in Black* and a little *Ghostbusters*. He had based one of the characters on the John Goodman character in *Arachnophobia*, another on the Jenna Elfman character in *Dharma and Greg*, and another on . . . well, on several characters, all of them played by Adam Sandler. The pilot was picked up, and the first season was a smash. The show never made number one in the Neilsons, but was usually in the top ten.

They had a seven-year run. During the second year Dave and his family moved into a five-bedroom house in the Hollywood Hills. Then the show was canceled, and he'd been scrambling ever since.

He got some money from syndication rights, residuals, but that market was not what it used to be. A lot of stations preferred to sell their off-peak time to infomercial companies instead of spending money to run an old show. He had written three sitcom pilots, but none of them had been made. During the last year he had even tried to get back as a staff writer on another show, any show, but got nowhere. He was about to turn forty, over the hill for a sitcom writer. You have to be tuned in to those absolutely latest trends, and even if he felt he was, he was *perceived* as being an old man. At thirty-nine. A one-hit wonder.

In desperation, he was trying to write a feature movie, something he had never done. And he was using the same formula that had worked so well with *Ants!* That is, find out what's popular and do that, only more. In other words, copy.

What was most popular right then was war films based on video games. So his research had to be in two parts: games, and war. The first part was easy. Even if he was a living fossil of almost forty, he could buy and play games just like anyone else. He felt he had a good handle on that stuff. But he'd never served in the military and all he knew about real war was what he'd seen in movies or read in books. Colonel Warner had been consulting for studios and gamers for years. Dave had winced when he learned how much Warner's per diem was, but he paid it. And so far it had been a bust, he'd not heard a thing that inspired him toward a story line.

Until today. And oddly enough, the story line didn't have anything to do with war.

He realized he was woolgathering, switched on his iPhone, and started dictating everything he could remember about the colonel's unlikely story while it was still fresh in his mind.

That occupied him for a little over an hour, and he realized he'd better get going or he'd be late picking up his daughter.

There is a neighborhood in the Valley where most people own a horse.

It's east of the Disney Studios, west of Dreamworks, partly in Burbank and partly in Glendale, just across the Los Angeles River—actually a concrete-lined ditch most of the year—north of Griffith Park. It surrounds the Los Angeles Equestrian Center. Drive through it on Riverside and you'll see that instead of bike paths, there are horse lanes. Take any of the side streets and you might see blacksmith trailers parked in driveways, with the smiths busy shoeing horses. Most of the houses, and even a lot of the apartment buildings, have stables in the back. The area is crisscrossed with riding trails, and bridges connect it to the much bigger network of trails in Griffith Park itself.

This is where Dave's daughter had stabled her ten-year-old warmblood gelding, Ranger, since she convinced Dave to buy him two years ago. Ranger was a move up from her first horse, Hannah, an even-tempered Appaloosa mare that he had been assured was a suitable mount for a ten-year-old. Back then she wanted to be a rodeo rider. Now she aspired to dressage and jumping—which she would not do as long as she was a minor living in his home. Bottom line, Addison was a horse person and enjoyed anything about riding. Including, Dave had to admit, currying, feeding, and mucking out the stable.

They say a boat is a hole in the water into which you throw money. Dave was neither a nautical nor an equestrian person, but he had learned in the last four years that a horse is a money pit, too, especially if you live in the city. There was the expense of the animal itself: $15,000 for the nag she was currently riding, which was in the low-end range. There was the cost of feeding and stabling, which was more than he used to pay in rent. There's all the tack: bridles and bits, stirrups, halters, things he'd never even heard of, like breastplates and martingales. A good English saddle could go for $2,000 and up. And don't forget riding lessons. You can't just get up on the back of a horse and teach it dressage. You have to have someone show you how. A good riding coach doesn't come cheap.

One day soon she'd be wanting a mount with better bloodlines. He wasn't looking forward to that conversation. And, of course, she would want to keep Ranger. Dave was facing the possibility of owning two horses. Right then, he couldn't afford just the one. He was wondering how he was going to break that to Addison.

He parked and walked over to the ring where she and a few others were putting their mounts through their paces. He had to admit, his heart swelled every time he saw her sitting there on her English saddle, wearing her white jodhpurs, gray coat, top hat, and shiny black knee-high riding boots ($600 a pair), her blonde hair tied up in a bunch at the nape of her neck. His little girl was growing up. He watched her trot the horse toward a low obstacle—two feet six inches high, the tallest he'd allow her, and he had to close his eyes every time she took one.

Then she spotted him and smiled and waved, and for a moment the poised young woman went away and was replaced by the tomboy she had been until a few years ago. Sometimes he wished she'd stuck to the rodeo dream. He thought he might rather see her barrel racing in cowgirl boots and jeans and a shirt with pearl buttons than so erect and dignified and in control. He wasn't always sure he knew this new girl.

Dinners could be a bit stifling at the Marshall household recently. Karen and Dave were not getting along well. She had been stubbornly ignoring his ever-less-subtle hints that they were going to have to curb their spending. A showdown was coming. He had considered having the uncomfortable conversation that evening after Addison went to bed, but the colonel's story had changed all that. Now all he could think of was wolfing down the dinner Karen had grudgingly laid out for them and heading to his office to write the whole story down.

They had had to let their cook/housekeeper go the previous month, the gardener the month before that. Now they had no help at all, and help was something Karen had come to believe she was entitled to. She seemed to have deliberately forgotten all the culinary skills she had when they were newlyweds living in the Valley. Tonight the menu was scooped out of plastic containers from the Whole Foods down the hill. Last night it had been delivery Chinese. Tomorrow he expected pizza. He knew he was being punished for being a bad provider. Karen picked at her food. Addison ate in silence, well aware of the tension between Mom and Dad.

Not a happy home. Addison loaded her dishes into the dishwasher, gave him a kiss on the forehead, and retreated to her room, saying she had a paper to turn in at school tomorrow. Karen just glared at him as he got up. He knew there was no point in telling her he thought he had a way out of their financial crisis if he could nail this story and sell it to Universal or Paramount. At that point, he didn't think she would have believed him.

So he went to his office with the million-dollar view of Century City and West Hollywood, booted up the computer, and started to write.

CHAPTER TWO

THE PROMETHEUS STRAIN

A motion picture treatment by Dave Marshall

The people who worked there called it Area 52, when
they called it anything at all. Officially, it didn't exist.
It was an inside joke, Area 51 being the airbase in the
Nevada desert where the aliens from the Roswell
UFO crash were allegedly taken. The people who
worked there didn't even know where they were. They
were flown in and out on jets with no windows. They
worked on projects funded from the unaccountable
Black Budget, and the money supply was almost endless. Ask for a new piece of scientific equipment, and
it would show up within a week.

Eddie Parker didn't care where the place was,
never even thought of it as Area 52. He simply thought
of it as the Lab.

Eddie did not work well with others, never had,
and he knew that he would never rise very high in the
rat-maze bureaucracy and backstabbing atmosphere
of most research establishments. Luckily for him,
interacting with his fellow humans was not high on
his list of priorities. At least that's what he told himself, until he met Jenny.

The security people would have preferred keeping
the scientists at the Lab all the time. But they had tried
long-term sequestration and found that it tended to drive
the researchers a little crazy. Since many of them were
borderline crazy already, it didn't take much of a nudge
to push them over the edge into uselessness. A certain

amount of R&R was needed. Two weeks decompression every three months was deemed about right.

Eddie did not want R&R very much, as it took him away from his toys. But rules were rules. They asked him where he wanted to go and, picking a name out of the air, he said New York City. He'd never been there.

They put him up in a suite in a fine hotel and he spent most of the first week at his highly secure laptop, communing with the supercomputers back at the Lab. But eventually he did venture out. He took in a movie, ate a hot dog at Nathan's, but mostly he just walked.

She was good. He would think he had lost her, then spot her wearing a different hat, with her coat reversed. She was there as both bodyguard and watchdog, and it seemed silly to him. He wasn't going to talk about his work and he wasn't going to run away. So he approached her and told her he knew what she was doing. She admitted it, and they had coffee together. After that, she stayed by his side. Her name was Jenny.

She was no raving beauty, but she was pretty enough, and smart. He found it easy to talk to her.

Then one evening as she was putting him to bed for the night, she kissed him, and though he was never sure just how it happened, he found himself in bed with her. It was his first time, and she seemed to know it—later, he realized it was probably in his dossier, which she would have memorized—and she was gentle and supportive of his awkwardness. That night, as sleep eluded him, he knew he was in love.

The next day he had to return to the Lab. They parted at the airport with kisses and made plans for their next meeting in three months.

His work suffered for a while, but it was all he really knew, and soon he was back into the project he had left behind. But for the first time he began to entertain notions of a life after the Lab. Perhaps even of quitting the Lab entirely, going to work in the private sector. He tossed ideas around, ideas he planned to share with Jenny when he returned to New York and met her for breakfast at Windows on the World, at the top of the North Tower of the World Trade Center.

They never found enough of her to identify. He stood all day just outside the police lines, inhaling dust and grit, until his new handler gently led him back to the hotel, where he informed them he was ready to return to the Lab. For a few days he hoped for a phone call— *missed my train, the taxi broke down, oh my God, Eddie, when I think of how close I came to being there* . . . but it never came.

He felt the same frustration all Americans felt in the aftermath of the atrocity. *How do we get our revenge on nineteen dead men?* Killing Osama bin Laden would not be enough. The wars in Afghanistan and Iraq gave him no satisfaction. Gradually he came to focus on the nineteen. Two things about them immediately stood out. All of them were Muslim. And fifteen of them came from Saudi Arabia.

Why are we bombing Iraq? Why aren't we bombing Saudi Arabia?

He was not the only one who harbored such thoughts about America's erstwhile ally in the newly declared "War on Terror," but Eddie happened to be the only person who was equipped, personally, to do something about it.

Someone once said "Revenge is a dish best served cold." Eddie was in no hurry. His field was bacteria, those tiny bits of living material that descended from the very first life to appear on Earth, around 4 billion years ago. It was quite likely that he knew more about bacteria than anyone else alive. It was certain that he knew more about methods of manipulating, cloning, and even creating them than anyone, because no one else in the world had the facilities available to him.

Bacteria are the ultimate survivors, mutating quickly in response to antibiotics, able to thrive at high levels of radioactivity, acidity, and at temperatures up to 270 degrees Fahrenheit.

Eddie had worked on the development of bacteria targeted on oil spills. But in recent years he had been concentrating on ways to use bacteria to recover more oil from proven reserves. The problem was that though there was still oil underground, the easy oil had been pumped already. The days when you could poke a hole in the ground and stand back as the black gold gushed out were long gone. The oil reserves remaining on the planet were increasingly hard to get at. Most of the oil in fields currently producing, including those in Saudi Arabia, could only be recovered by increasingly exotic means.

Eddie had been working on a bacterium that would enable the crude in existing wells to flow more easily, or to naturally increase the underground pressure. It was called the Prometheus Project.

He focused on the largest oil field in the world, the Ghawar, a strip 175 miles long by 20 miles wide, 100 miles due east of Riyadh, in the Empty Quarter of Saudi Arabia.

The most common technology for getting the remaining oil out of a field was to inject water into the ground. But when you pump water in, you get some water back, and the percentage of oil to water is called the "water cut." Fresh wells produced almost 100 percent oil. With older fields, you got back more and more water until it was not worth the cost of injecting it. For some years now, the water cut at the Ghawar fields was on the order of 60 percent, and it would only continue to rise.

The Saudis wanted someone to do something about it. They wanted a magic bug that would turn the more sluggish fractions down in those wells into something that would flow like springwater, if not quite so sparkling.

Eddie told them he was their man. Everyone was hoping for results in a matter of months, but it took years. It was a real challenge, because he had to produce something that showed promise as a crude-oil liquefier while at the same time hiding his work on the real bacterium he had in mind.

This bug would freeze Ghawar solid as a coal seam. Try pumping *that*, you murderous bastards.

He finally perfected an organism he officially called the Prometheus Strain. It performed to perfection, stripping away enough hydrogen from the crude-oil fractions to produce pressure, and leaving the residue liquid enough to pump.

But he didn't tell anyone about the culture for a while. He had more work to do. He produced a second culture, Prometheus Two, a variant of the first. It was amazing what a difference a few little genes here and there could make.

When the second culture was ready, he announced that he had found the solution to the depleted-oilfield problem.

He demonstrated Prometheus in the lab, and it performed perfectly. Bandar bin Sultan, the Saudi prince sent to witness the demonstration, was impressed. He wanted to try it in the field.

Eddie boarded the windowless plane with Prince bin Sultan and they flew to Washington, where they boarded the prince's private A-380, a two-story airborne palace with a staff of twenty and only himself and the prince as passengers. Eddie ate a fine meal, and then slept soundly in a large bedroom.

He woke when the plane was descending into Dubai. He saw the gleaming spire of the Burj Khalifa, the tallest man-made structure in the world, and almost empty. He could make out the outlines of the gigantic Palm Jumeirah and the even larger Palm Jebel Ali housing developments, gigantic artificial islands, huge landfills in the shape of palm trees dotted with resort hotels and mansions.

All built not on sand, but on oil. Take away the oil, and those people down below would still be fishing from dhows and traveling on camels. They wouldn't have much time to raise fanatic young terrorists willing to fly airplanes into buildings. They wouldn't even have the airfare to get aboard.

The next day, Eddie was taken to the Ghawar field and, with little ceremony, added Jenny Two to the slurry being pumped into the ground.

Two weeks later, the Ghawar field exploded.

Dave thought it was his own snoring that woke him up. He was leaning back in his ergonomic chair, and when he slept in that position he could wake the dead.

The sun was turning the sky pink in the east. Most of the lights were still on in the towers of Century City, below him. A marine layer of low clouds had moved in over Santa Monica, as it usually did that time of year. Much of yesterday's smog had dispersed to wherever yesterday's smog goes, and today's batch wasn't brewing yet. The streets he could see were almost deserted.

He was stiff and sore all over. Not as easy to pull an all-nighter when you're almost forty as it was in college. He started a pot of coffee and sat back down to read what he had written.

Six pages, seventeen hundred words. It sounded good to him.

It was partly extrapolation. The truth was, at that point he was far from sure "Eddie Parker" even existed. The colonel had not given him a name, Dave made that up. He was just "one of the big brains at a very secret lab." But that didn't matter, as the whole story was highly unlikely, but good enough for a movie.

His cell phone rang. It was the colonel.

"Get your ass over here, right now," he growled.

The colonel let him in, and then looked up and down the hallway before shutting the door behind him. He threw the lock and set the chain, then gestured Dave toward a glass-topped table near the front window, looking out over Hollywood Boulevard to the Pantages Theater. On the table was a laptop, a partially disassembled semiautomatic handgun, and a cleaning kit. He gestured him toward a chair at the table.

"Something to drink?"

"A little early for me," he said.

"Me, too. I got coffee, tea . . ."

"Nothing, thanks."

Warner's apartment was minimalist, almost Spartan, with very little to give it that lived-in feeling. There was no artwork on the walls, no military mementos, no personal touches at all. A few beige leather couches and chairs in the living room, a gas fireplace, a wall-sized flat-screen television. No DVDs, only a few books in a small bookcase. It was the room of a man who had lived in barracks all his life and kept all his possessions in a duffel bag, ready to move in five minutes.

There was a pair of large gun safes. The doors of one of them were standing open, and he saw rifles, shotguns, and handguns, all looking well cared for. He didn't know a lot about guns, but he knew some of them were military weapons that he wasn't sure were actually legal. But that was none of his business.

"I'm ashamed to admit that I don't remember a lot about yesterday, beyond a certain point," the colonel said. "I do have the distinct impression that I ended up saying a lot more than I should have." He grimaced. "I've spent my whole life keeping my lip zipped. I'm pretty good at it. But you've had me talking on this project of yours . . . about things that I'm authorized to talk about, mind you." He stopped, and shrugged. "I guess I got in the habit of talking to you. Things got out of hand."

"I got the impression that you were pretty shaken up," Dave said.

"You can say that again. Before yesterday, I was just getting rumors. You've noticed the stock market lately?"

"It would be hard not to. Up, down, up again. Mostly down."

"Driven by oil prices, and futures," Warner said. "Oil's over two-fifty a barrel, and still rising with no end in sight. The big investors are getting worried. Especially now that they're getting wind of some of the rumors I've been hearing for the last couple of weeks."

"Frankly, Colonel, that's what makes that story you told me yesterday kind of hard to swallow. How could all this be happening and nobody knows anything about it?"

Colonel Warner picked up part of the disassembled pistol lying on the table. He began running a cleaning rag through the barrel. He sighed, and looked at Dave.

"Obviously people know about it. But as soon as the shit

started to come down in Saudi, they clamped a national security lid on it as tight as any I've ever seen. In the first week the secretary of state paid a visit to Riyadh, and so did the leaders of the oil-producing countries in the region. I don't have any idea what they decided to do about it. But the top people at Saudi Aramco were sworn to secrecy, and told they could be arrested and have a major extraordinary rendition put on their ass, flown off to some shit-hole country where they could be shot without a trial. Saudi Aramco, if you didn't know, is the state-owned oil company. It's the most profitable company in the world. They own Ghawar, the biggest oil field in the world, and Safaniyah, the biggest offshore field, in the northern Persian Gulf. Plus dozens of smaller fields. They produce 15 million barrels of crude every day.

"Or, let's say they used to."

He moved his chair to sit behind his computer installation and gestured Dave over to sit beside him.

"Here's Google Earth looking down at the Ghawar field," the colonel said. Dave leaned forward, trying to figure it out. Warner moved the cursor around quickly.

"Lots of sand. Not much to see unless you know what you're looking for. You can pick out roads here, and here. The big black squares are towns for oil workers. These black dots are wellheads. Thousands of them. Here's a pipeline.

"But look at the date. Google is great, but it's not current. Now, let me show you what that same area looked like yesterday."

He moved to another keyboard, another twenty-four-inch flat screen. He typed quickly. A password window popped up.

"I'll have to ask you to look away for a minute," Warner said. "This is classified satellite data from the National Reconnaissance Office. I'm still authorized. Technically, I shouldn't let you see these images, but I don't know any other way to prove to you that you have to leave this stuff alone. You don't want to play with these boys, believe me."

The password box turned red, and they saw the message:

YOU ARE NOT AUTHORIZED TO DOWNLOAD THIS DATA
NRO DIRECTIVE 98

"Damn it," the colonel fumed. "I got on yesterday. Let me try another . . ."

He entered another URL, got a password request, and typed something in as Dave looked away. Warner leaned back with his arms folded.

"God knows what they're doing in the White House, the Pentagon, all the intelligence offices. They've kept a lid on this thing for a few weeks, but you can't keep it a secret from people on the ground in Saudi. It's too big. They can *see* it. There have been leaks—hell, that's how I got it, somebody told somebody, who told somebody else, who told me."

"Somebody at Area 52," Dave said, without thinking.

"Area what?" He scowled at Dave, and then the light dawned. "You've already been writing about it, you silly son of a bitch. Area 52, that's rich."

"I had to call it something."

Warner ran his hand over his bald head, glanced at his computer screen, which was still displaying the hourglass icon, and leaned intently toward Dave.

"There will be more leaks. This whole thing is going to come out in the next ten to twenty days. God knows what they'll do then. But you have to deep-six whatever you've written about it, because right now, they're scared, and when these people get scared, they play rough. They're going to be dead serious about keeping it all top secret until they figure out which way to jump. They *will* shoot you if they think you know stuff you're not supposed to know. They're still thinking of this as a problem to solve, instead of the all-out disaster it's going to be. Do you understand what I'm saying?"

Dave said he did, though he still wasn't sure the man wasn't exaggerating, or even if he had the right information. Warner saw his doubt, and sighed.

"Already some wise guys, the billionaires, the banks, the stock brokerages, have begun to get wind that something's wrong out in the Saudi desert. The cover story is terrorist sabotage at a few dozen wells, they'll have it all under control in a few weeks, a month. All those big financial institutions and investors are running scared. They can't figure out what to buy and what to sell. You noticed, gold is shooting up, oil-company stocks are tanking—"

The computer screen had caught his eye, and he broke off and turned toward it.

A THUMBPRINT IS REQUIRED TO ACCESS THIS SITE

The colonel grinned at him from one side of his face, as if to say, *See, I'm still connected.* He pressed his thumb to a small scanner. After a second, the dialog box went away and a new screen came up.

NRO SATELLITE IMAGING
AUTHORIZED USERS ONLY
ENTER DATE, ASSET, AND LOCATION

He typed in yesterday's date, the satellite designation—Keyhole 13/8—and latitude and longitude numbers. He'd mentioned the Keyhole program in their previous talks when Dave asked him if it was really true that U.S. spy satellites could read a license-plate number or a newspaper from space. He said plates yes, newspapers no, that the Keyhole satellites had optics that could see objects down to ten centimeters.

"Here we go," he said. "Ghawar, yesterday."

Dave leaned in close and immediately saw that things were different. White streaks now pointed to each of the wellheads.

"What am I seeing here, Colonel?"

"The wellheads are on fire. That's steam you see blowing off to the northeast. Smoke and steam, actually. A lot of them are burning."

"I thought crude oil made black smoke when it burned." Dave was remembering the awful pictures of the burning oil fields of Kuwait when the Iraqi Army set them afire during their retreat at the end of the Gulf War.

"It does. It's not the oil that's burning. That's still deep underground. But that bug that was supposed to make the crude more liquid, it turned it into thick sludge instead, like I told you. What you see burning is the hydrogen that was liberated when the bug ate the crude. When hydrogen burns, it combines with oxygen to make water."

"Okay, you've made me a believer."

"There's more. This would be a catastrophe, but I've known about this for almost a week. What I saw yesterday, that's what made me want a drink." He manipulated the mouse. They zoomed out into space, and began traveling to the north. When they reached the northern Persian Gulf Warner zoomed in again, but not quite as close.

"Offshore rigs in the Gulf. Most of them are burning. These are over the Safaniyah field."

Dave was starting to sweat. It was one thing to hear this ridiculous story over drinks in the Frolic Room, and something else again to see it illustrated before his eyes.

"Could it . . . I mean, could it have traveled underground? Could it all be one big field over there? Not one big pool of oil, but moving along a seam in the rocks, or something like that?" He shook his head. "I don't know enough geology to even ask the right question here, I guess."

"And I don't know enough to give you the right answer. But I don't think so. I thought of that, and at first I was hoping that might be what's going on. I mean, if we lost all the Persian Gulf oil, it would wreck the world economy, it would be a disaster bigger than anything the world has seen since the Second World War, but we could adapt, I guess. Conserve fuel, drill in Alaska, offshore in Florida and California. I think even the environmentalists would shut up when they saw just how bad a world without petroleum energy would be. And there's oil in Russia, Indonesia, Venezuela, Nigeria. But like I said, there's more."

He moved the map again.

"That's Iraq. Iran. More fires. See? There, there, and there?"

Dave saw. Still, it was all in the Middle East. But now the colonel pulled way back, so that they saw all of Asia, and once more they traveled to the northwest.

"We're in Russia now. The Khantia-Mansia Autonomous Okrug, east of the Urals, in the Western Siberian Lowlands." Dave saw a land with a lot of green, laced by a meandering river and pocked with a lot of lakes. The colonel moved the cursor around. "That's the northern fork of the Ob River. This town is Nizhnevartovsk, here at one of the bends. Sixty below in the winter, ninety-five in the summer. Fifty years ago there wasn't much there but mosquitoes and reindeer. Then they struck oil, and now it's the richest town in Russia. North of it is the Samotlor oil field, one of the biggest outside of the Middle East. Take a look."

He zoomed in, and it didn't take long for Dave to see it. The area was laced with white dots and white lines that he assumed were wells and pipelines. Some of them crisscrossed the lakes. It was pretty, actually, and the white streaks blowing southwest from some of the wells would have made it even prettier if he didn't know what they were.

"There's no way those fields are connected. This is twenty-five hundred miles from Saudi Arabia. The damn bug is airborne."

"But that doesn't make sense, according to what you told me. You said the guy wanted to get back at the Saudis for 9/11. Why would he want to have it spread to Iran and Russia?"

"I don't think he did want that. I did a little research on bacteria the night before last, and I learned they can mutate pretty fast. God knows how fast a tailored strain like this one can change, but it looks like it doesn't take long."

They were both silent as they looked at the disaster unfolding in central Russia.

"Do you know anything more?" Dave asked. "Like what became of the guy who did all this?"

The colonel snorted. "May he rot in hell. No, I don't, and I'm not going to try to find out. I can guarantee you he's buried deep and, dead or alive, will never see the light of day again. What I hope is they have him at work on something to stop this bug."

"You think he can?"

"I have no idea."

There was a soft ping from the computer that was showing the satellite pictures, and a window popped up.

YOU ARE NOT AUTHORIZED TO ACCESS THIS SITE
YOU ARE IN VIOLATION OF FEDERAL LAW
DO NOT TERMINATE THIS SESSION

Dave was alarmed, but the colonel didn't seem too concerned. Ignoring the command, he logged off the site by the simple expedient of turning his computer off. He looked at Dave a bit sheepishly.

"That wasn't actually my password I used," he said. "Borrowed it from a friend. Looks like they're narrowing access, which means they're even more scared than they were a few days ago." He paused, and looked thoughtful. "Look, Dave, this might get a little sticky if they can trace this all back to this computer.

I don't think they can, it was routed through two cutoffs, but you never know what new capabilities they've got. It might be best if you went on home now. I wouldn't want to get you involved. In fact, it's probably best if we don't meet again. I don't give a damn about your movie with this going on. I don't think anybody's going to give a damn about *any* movie for a long time. We're all going to be too busy. I've got a lot of thinking to do, a lot of plans to make. You should do the same."

"What do you suggest we do?"

"Take care of your family. That's all that counts now."

Those were the last words he heard from Colonel Warner.

CHAPTER THREE

He was shaking as he got on the Red Line train, and still shaky as he got off in North Hollywood. Seeing the colonel fall again and again. You see things like that in movies all the time, but it looks completely different in real life.

He sat there in the Escalade, sweating, trying to come up with a plan. What he wanted to do was go get Addison, and find Karen wherever she was. Gather his family together and get the hell out of town.

Could they connect him with Colonel Warner? Had he left a fingerprint? He was glad now that he had refused the coffee.

He started the Escalade, and headed up and over Laurel Canyon.

He lived on Mockingbird Drive, right on the extreme western edge of the expensive part of Hollywood, in the hills. In fact, he was so close to the Beverly Hills Trousdale Estates that he could stand on his back patio and throw a baseball over the city line. That baseball would land at the bottom of a ravine, and on property worth about twice as much per square foot as his because of the Beverly Hills address.

The neighborhood didn't have a formal name, but his family always called it Birdland, a name Addison came up with when they moved there, when she was five. Some of the streets around them were Thrush, Kinglet, Robin, Swallow, Oriole, Thrasher, and Skylark. The house was very near Blue Jay Way, where George Harrison once lived, though actually getting there involved over a mile of driving through the spaghetti maze of streets in the canyons.

He found himself looking for helicopters as he climbed

Doheny Drive. When he got to Mockingbird he turned cautiously, all his senses on alert. There were no military vehicles parked near the house, no soldiers with black uniforms and rifles. He turned into the driveway, activated the electric gate, drove through, turned off the engine, and listened to the silence. After a while he got out and cautiously entered the house.

Built in 1972, the house had five bedrooms, six and a half baths. Five thousand square feet in two stories, and that was not counting the guesthouse. Four-car garage, swimming pool, and something not many houses up in the hills had: almost a quarter acre of lawn. The southern end was a large deck that ran to the edge of a forty-five-degree downslope covered in ice plant to hold the soil in place. The whole thing was white, boxy, and modern, with a lot of glass walls facing south and very few windows facing the street, which was standard practice for people living in the hills.

It was way too much house for the three of them. Dave had grown to hate it in the last few years. It was an albatross around his neck. He had paid what seemed an insane amount for it at the time, then watched as his investment doubled, then almost tripled, then fell over the edge with the popping of the housing bubble. If he sold it, he would walk away with a few thousand dollars.

His office was the guesthouse. The top floor was used for storage. The bottom floor was one large room with a galley kitchen, a gas fireplace, the obligatory media center, and a large conference table. When he was flying high in the situation comedy business they would often hold story conferences at that table.

The south wall, like the south wall of the main house, was all glass. The view ranged from Hancock Park to Mar Vista, with Century City, the Miracle Mile on Wilshire Boulevard, Baldwin Hills, and of course downtown Beverly Hills in between. At night he could see the long lines of headlights and taillights on the I-10 and the 405, and the planes lining up to land at LAX. It was a killer view, and he had arranged the series of long oak tables he used for a desk to face it. He sat down in his chair and powered up one of the three computers on the desk. He brought up the views from the three street-side security cameras.

All was still quiet on Mockingbird Drive.

He saved his treatment onto a flash drive. Then he shredded it, and files of his interviews with Colonel Warner. There was nothing he could do about the bank records of the checks he had written to him. And who was he kidding? If those people thought he had seen data he shouldn't have seen, there was a waterboard or a bullet somewhere out there with his name on it.

Once more he went back over the events of the last two days in his mind. Was there any other possible interpretation than what Colonel Warner had shown him? Up until that morning Dave had been leaning toward the theory that he had simply been spinning a tall tale, or maybe exaggerating some rumors he had picked up from some of his friends still in government. How was it possible that something of that magnitude was going on, spreading around the globe, and it wasn't all over CNN? Was that plausible?

Well, maybe just. Keeping the secret in the Arabian desert would be the easiest. Nobody lived out there except oil workers, and they could be sequestered. The visible evidence—the smoke during the day and the flames at night—reminding him of the biblical pillars that guided the Israelites—could be explained as accidents or sabotage, for a while.

It would be harder to cover up in Iran, Iraq, and Russia, but not impossible. For a while. That seemed to be the key here: for a while. Weeks? A month? He didn't know how long this had been going on, so it was pointless to try to figure out how much time might be left until it all came out. Because it would have to. Surely the people living around Samotlor knew something beyond sabotage was going on. You can prevent people from traveling, cut off electronic communications, but you can't cover all the bases. Word will get out. In time, even the *absence* of news from the region becomes noteworthy.

So he decided the story was plausible. But plausibility was not truth. If it *was* all true, he should be doing something about it. Even if only a part of it was true, there were probably things he should be doing. Things like stocking up on food and water. Things like—worst-case scenario—buying a gun.

But what? What would be prudent, and what would be panicky?

He realized he didn't have enough information. First he needed to answer the basic question: What would things be like in Los Angeles if there were no gasoline? What would they be like in the state of California, for that matter? What would they be like in America?

He went online to try to find some answers.

In a few hours he was much more frightened than he had been before.

"Did you know that Los Angeles has about a sixty-day supply of water?"

Karen looked up from her plate of take-out Thai food and frowned.

"You mean with the drought? We've already cut back to watering the plants once a week. What more do they expect us to do?"

He wasn't going to tell them the story of the last two days until he was sure of a few more things. But his mind was swimming with recently learned information, and he wanted to share it.

"We get almost half our water from the Los Angeles Aqueduct. It's a hundred years old now. It brings water from way up north in the Owens Valley and Mono Lake. It's downhill all the way."

"No it's not," Addison said. "There are mountains between here and there."

"The water is siphoned over them," he told her. "There are no pumps needed. Doesn't cost much to run it. Not that the people of the Owens Valley have ever been happy about it. They were bamboozled by William Mulholland back in 1905. Without that water, Los Angeles could never have developed the way it did."

"Didn't we see a movie about that?" Karen asked.

"*Chinatown* was based on the water wars. The thing is, the people way up there in the Sierras have never really forgiven L. A. for it, and in fact, the way they figure it, we're *still* stealing their water. And we keep wanting more. I was just thinking, if they ever got angry enough, it would be easy to sabotage that big pipe. You know how many people the Los Angeles metro area could support without the water we bring in?"

Karen didn't even look up, already bored with the subject. "How many, Daddy?"

"Nineteen out of twenty people who live here would have to go somewhere else."

Neither of them had anything to say about that. Dave figured he might as well give them the rest of the story. It's not as if conversation had sparkled around the Marshall dinner table lately.

"Most of the rest of our water comes from the Colorado and California Aqueducts. That water has to be pumped." And pumps need electricity or fuel to operate. But he didn't add that. "Only about 10 percent of our water comes out of the ground."

"That's fascinating, Daddy."

He could tell she didn't really think so, but Addison had always been tactful. He smiled at her.

"So, would you like to hear about our power supply?"

Neither of them did.

In trying to answer that basic question—what would Los Angeles be like with little or no petroleum fuel?—he had found some interesting and alarming facts.

He was surprised to learn that L.A. got about half its electricity from coal-fired plants, some of them in the city, some in the neighboring states. Another quarter came from burning natural gas, 10 percent from nuclear plants, and around 5 percent from hydropower, mostly from Hoover Dam. But all the coal for the plants in Arizona and Utah was brought in by trains that ran on diesel fuel.

How would Los Angeles, perhaps the most gasoline-dependent city in the world, react to a severe shortage?

He had an idea that it wouldn't be pretty.

The next day after taking Addison to school Dave dropped Karen off at the Burbank airport for a flight to San Francisco. She was attending a conference there. He wasn't sure what it was about. He felt guilty about that, but he had a hard time keeping up with her causes at the best of times, and this was far from the best. He couldn't stop thinking about Colonel Warner and the burning oil wells.

He decided to go on a shopping spree. But first he decided to make a list. What would he need to survive with limited or no gasoline? He went down to the basement to see what he had.

It was under the guesthouse/office, and reachable only by an outside stairway going down the hill, almost overgrown with vines. The door was sturdy steel with a strong padlock. He hadn't been in there in ages.

His earthquake supplies were good for only the recommended three days, and it was all years old. The first-aid kit was a joke.

Against the east wall was a hodgepodge of stuff that most people accumulate.

When Addison was six and joined the Girl Scouts, Dave thought it would be fun if the family camped out together. So he bought a tent, a camp stove, a giant cooler, cots, air mattresses, all top-of-the-line, and they set out like pioneers on the Oregon Trail for the wilds of Lake Tahoe—where you have to make reservations several weeks ahead, and pay $75 for a three-day weekend. He had pitched the tent among a horde of forty-foot RVs. The Marshalls were the only tent people at the campground.

They lasted one night. Karen complained of the cold, hated bacon and eggs cooked over a propane stove, and was eaten up by bugs. They checked out, and checked in to a luxury hotel, and spent the rest of the weekend in the casinos or lounging by the pool. Addison asked one time about a month later if they could do it again, and her mother said no. The camping gear had sat in the basement ever since.

He couldn't blame it all on Karen. He wasn't all that wild about sleeping on an air mattress himself. Addison seemed to enjoy the experience, but she knew better than to pressure her mother about it.

He ran a finger over the rolled-up tent, which was covered with dust. He recalled it had cost him about $600, and had been set up once. The old propane stove was still there, too, but he had no bottled gas for it. He put that on his shopping list.

Alongside the old tennis rackets and boxes of books were three bicycles that were also gathering dust. When they'd lived in the Valley, in the flatlands, they'd actually used them as a family, riding the bike trails on weekends or evenings. Then they moved to the hills, and after a few trips down and back up, pushing them the last quarter mile, they put them in the basement and never used them again.

It made him sad to look at them. What did they do as a family anymore? He'd spent most of the last decade in the high-pressure world of comedy writing, about as insecure as any job can be. Karen had flitted from one to another of her transient passions. He didn't think Addison was actually *neglected*; they were involved in her school—Karen more than him—and she always seemed a happy little girl. Let's just say she was encouraged to be self-sufficient, and she was good at that. Now he found himself wishing he'd asked her if she really *wanted* to be self-sufficient.

Addison had been five when they moved. Her bicycle was now much too small for her. All three of them were good bikes, with fat tires and light aluminum frames. In his youth it was all ten-speeds. He squeezed one of the tires and wasn't surprised to find that it was flat, but the rubber also felt flaky from age. He made a note of the sizes and put that on his shopping list, along with a new bike for Addison.

By the time he left the house he had a long list.

For once he was happy with the cavernous interior of the Escalade. He descended on Costco in Burbank like Crazy Horse on the Seventh Cavalry. For the first time he used one of the flatbed shopping carts, and he filled it up with bottled water, cases of canned meat, tuna, veggies, and whatever else struck his fancy. For good measure he bought lots of toilet paper. He figured, if it's the end of the world as we know it, the toilet paper was going to have to last awhile.

When he had it all stowed in the back, he realized he was breathing hard, and felt like he was on the edge of a panic attack. He used to get them when they were writing to a deadline, and lately he'd had a few when he contemplated his financial situation. He knew that what he'd just done was more like a hysterical reaction than true prudent planning. He had not been able to talk this over with anyone, and the pressure of that was getting to him. He had seen a man killed. He had heard the most frightening story he'd ever heard, and he'd seen what looked like proof that the story was true, or at least partly true. And so what was it that he was most worried about at that moment? Why, it was telling Karen about all this. He was sure she would think he was crazy. And it would be hard to blame her.

When he picked up Addison she looked in back. She raised one eyebrow at him.

"Doing a little shopping?"

"No, I found all this sitting by the side of the road."

"Neat. Spam?"

"Never know when a case of Spam might come in handy."

"I've never actually eaten Spam."

"And you probably won't, unless we have a big earthquake."

"Ah. Earthquake supplies." That was really all the explanation needed for a girl who grew up in Southern California.

He spent that evening and into the night surfing the Net.

First he looked for stories about the murder of Colonel Warner. There was nothing. Not in the *Times*, not on CNN, not anywhere. It was such a blank that he began to worry if merely searching for his name might alert someone in a secret government agency. He quickly deleted his search from memory.

It wasn't hard to find other stories. The oil-well explosions and fires at Ghawar, and in Iran, Iraq, Kuwait, and Russia was the big story of the day, though it was being reported as if it had just happened. Coordinated terrorist attacks on the oil fields, most likely by Al Qaeda, though Hamas and Hezbollah were suspected, too. The National Guard was on alert, patrolling the oil and natural-gas fields in Texas and Louisiana, and the wells and pipelines in Alaska. The Coast Guard was protecting the offshore platforms in the Gulf of Mexico. The Royal Navy and the Norwegian Navy were on duty in the North Sea. Firefighting crews from Texas were on their way to or already in place in Saudi and Kuwait.

The stock market had taken its worst three-day beating since 9/11.

There was a story about oil tankers that had gone missing in the Indian Ocean. Some of them had been seen to explode, some of them had simply fallen off the radar. Somali pirates were being blamed, though no one had said how they would make a profit sinking tankers.

The most interesting stuff was on the blogosphere. The online population was confused, suspicious, and angry. As usual.

The same people who figured Arabs weren't smart enough to fly airplanes into skyscrapers, that the Twin Towers had been brought down by charges placed inside them by their government, naturally thought these oil-well fires were a conspiracy. Who was behind the conspiracy was a matter of some debate, but that it *was* a conspiracy was a given. Ironically, Dave thought, they might not be far from the truth this time.

Other, more rational voices seemed mostly frustrated. They agreed that the terrorism angle was probably a lie, but that left the question of who benefited from this whole business? The obvious suspects—big business, big oil—seemed to be panicking, and hemorrhaging money, from all anyone could tell from the outside.

The insider blogs, opinion pieces from people who might be in a position to know, sounded flat-out frightened. These were government insiders, reporters, policy makers. No one was telling them anything. Whatever was going on, real knowledge of it was the most closely held secret anyone could remember. The top presidential advisors, cabinet secretaries, congressmen heading key committees and their staffs looked like they weren't getting a lot of sleep. A few had even disappeared and couldn't be found.

The next morning he opened Quicken and scanned through his financial data. It hadn't magically improved since the last time he checked. If they were going to have to hunker down, he would want to lay in even more supplies. If they were going to move, he'd want to be as liquid as possible.

There was no point in trying to sell their cars, with gas prices the way they were. Selling the house in the current market would be a disaster, and it might not move at all, but he could possibly get a loan on it.

The best news was that his family had not yet reached the

point where they had maxed out their credit cards. He still had a few thousand of what was to have been their savings in the bank. He had cashed in all their investments to make ends meet, so it was all in low-interest checking. That would come in handy. And the balances on their four platinum cards were low. None of them had a credit limit. He could buy pretty much whatever he thought they might need, and worry about paying for it all later.

An army surplus store in the Valley sold olive drab five-gallon metal jerry cans that might have been left over from World War Two for all he could tell. There was a lot of empty shelf space around the ones they had left, which was eight. He bought them all and earned a dirty look from a guy who came in the store as he was paying for them.

The Target store at Santa Monica and La Brea had sold all their plastic gas containers. He called around to some other stores and found they were out, too. But at another surplus store on Hollywood Boulevard he found another dozen metal containers. He bought them all. Then he found a Shell station on Sunset and got in a line with six cars ahead of him. He killed the engine and waited.

When he got to the pumps he first filled the Escalade. Then he opened the back and started in on the gas cans. As he topped off the third one an attendant approached him. He had bought gas there before and never seen the attendant leave his post behind the counter.

He said, "Sir, we're asking customers to only fill two containers, plus their gas tank."

"Why is that? It just makes it inconvenient for me, I'll have to find another station and wait in line again."

"I don't really give a damn." He looked hassled and frustrated. "It was up to me, I'd sell you all the gas you wanted. But I got a call from the distributor, and he said that's what we gotta do." He shrugged. "It won't matter pretty soon, anyway. I'm gonna be dry in about another hour, and the tanker don't come by till day after tomorrow."

"Just one more can?"

"You already done three."

He was right. Dave could see the people behind him were impatient, so he closed the rear gate and set off in search of more of the precious fluid that he'd taken for granted all his life.

He found a station with only two cars in line and managed to fill the rest of his cans. On the way home he passed a station with a sign out front that said NO GAS.

He unloaded the full gas cans and stored them away in the basement.

On the way back to the Valley he did something he had thought about all day. He called up the members of his posse and invited them over for a friendly game of poker.

He didn't remember who first started using "the posse" when referring to his writing team on *Ants!* It wasn't all that original, but they all liked it better than "the team," or "the group." Who wouldn't? There were five of them, all but one of them first-timers at working together as a comedy-writing team.

The exception was the oldest, Bob Winston, who had worked on three successful shows before Dave's, and became a sort of mentor to the rest of them. The sad fact was that Bob was a bit of a burned-out case. He had lost what the rest of them called his comedy mojo, though they would never say it to his face. They respected him, he knew the ropes, how to handle the fickle and demanding higher-ups. Though Dave was the titular leader of the posse, Bob was the father figure, and naturally the one he turned to that day.

It took a little convincing, but Bob agreed to contact the others when Dave told him how important it was. Naturally, Bob assumed it would be about a new project, which he wasn't all that interested in, being pretty much retired and well-set for life with residuals coming in steadily. He had invested well when he was one of the hottest writers in town. He had a big house in Holmby Hills that backed up on the Los Angeles Country Club, in the same neighborhood as the Playboy Mansion and the Spelling estate.

"Can you give me some notion of what your idea is?" Bob asked.

"It's not really . . ." Dave decided it might be easier to assemble everyone if they did think it was a story idea.

"It's not a comedy," he said. "More of a continuing drama."

"Give me a hint. Are we talking *The Sopranos*? *Law and Order*? Or more in the neighborhood of *Lost*?"

"Stranger than that," Dave said.

Bob promised he'd do his best to get everyone together, Dave's place, seven o'clock until whenever. Dave hung up and pulled to the curb outside Valley Scooters, which he'd found after a brief Internet search.

He walked down a line of scooters parked on the sidewalk. They were bright and shiny as new pennies, and as colorful as a basket of Easter eggs. A salesman approached him.

"Get 'em while you can," he said. He was a young, thin guy with tattoos around his neck and a ring in his left eyebrow.

"Selling a lot of these things?"

"I wish I could get two or three hundred more of them every month. But the factories can't turn them out fast enough. You checked the prices at the pump these days?"

Dave admitted that he had.

"Up another five cents for premium this morning. This one gets eighty miles to the gallon."

Dave knew he shouldn't look like he was too eager to buy, but the fact was he'd already decided he was going home with one. Possibly two.

"I live on a hill. Would that be a problem?"

"I wouldn't recommend this one for climbing hills. Motor's too small. I'd recommend you move a step or two up in horsepower." He patted the black vinyl seat of a machine that looked a little heftier. "You don't take these things on the freeway. Fifty is about right for a top speed, cruising around the city. Take a look at this one over here."

He took a ride on a white 150cc Vespa LXV 150, and he liked it. He put it on his credit card and then stowed the scooter in the back of the Escalade, where it fit easily.

He went home and did a search on Craigslist, and got lucky. He found another Vespa, this one 90cc, with an asking price of $1,900, just down the hill in West Hollywood. The man he talked to on the phone said it belonged to his partner, who had a new job that was too far away to commute by scooter. Dave told him he'd be there in an hour, stopped by the bank and took a large cash advance on another credit card, pulled into the driveway of a nice little bungalow on Laurel Avenue and quickly concluded the deal. The scooter was a bright pink, and the seller tossed in two deep purple helmets.

CHAPTER FOUR

The posse gathered in the office for poker that evening. As they got started, most of the chatter was about the sad state of the industry. He knew they all needed work except Bob, and felt a bit guilty knowing that they expected that he would be outlining a new writing project.

They didn't play for pennies, but it was not a high-stakes game. It cost five dollars to get in, then raises were limited to ten dollars. They had never had a single pot over three hundred dollars. Dave was down about thirty dollars and Bob was the big winner when somebody called for a break.

"You know, Fearless Leader, the poker is fun and all, but we all know you brought us here to talk about a new show. So how about it?"

That was Jenna Donovan, five foot two, flaming red hair she could never keep under control, about a billion freckles. She was the youngest of them, twentysomething moving in on thirty, and she had the most twisted sense of humor of any of them.

"Not a series idea," he said.

Dennis Rossi frowned at him. "Bob said that's what was happening."

"I said I thought so," Bob said. "Dave didn't actually say that." He was the gray eminence, hair gone completely white, a face carved out of reddish granite, chewing on his empty pipe. Dennis was curly-haired and hyperactive. He often went for broke in the poker games, and usually proved just what that expression meant.

Dave decided to treat it like a pitch meeting. They all had plenty of experience with those, trying to sell an idea to executives at a studio. It would start them off on familiar ground, then maybe he could ease them into the notion that it was much more than a story idea.

"It's not a comedy," he said.

"Not a problem with me." That was Roger Weinburger. Where Dennis was always on the verge of an explosion, hurling ideas left and right as he paced and sweated, Roger was calm and quiet. He listened to the rest of them and waited until they wound down, then tossed out a line that had them all hysterical, a line that almost always ended up in the final, shooting script.

"Say there's this top secret government laboratory out in the desert somewhere," he began. "Say . . . I don't know, say, Nevada."

"Area 51," Bob suggested.

"Let's call it Area 52."

He took them through the story as the colonel had told it to him. Then he brought in two new characters: a writer in Hollywood and a former military technical advisor he was working with, hoping to develop a story.

"The writer is dubious about all this," he said. "But he thinks it's a good story idea, and when he tells the colonel this the colonel realizes that he's said too much."

Confusion on the faces around the table now, but he had their interest.

"The colonel takes the writer to his apartment. Say, it's in the W on Hollywood and Vine. He uses his computer to access some real-time spy satellites that the public never gets to see, but the colonel is still able to access. He shows the writer that oil wells all over the Middle East and in Russia are burning."

"Hey, wait a minute," Jenna said. "Oil wells *are* burning all through the Middle East and Russia."

"Which will make it all seem even more plausible," he said, plunging ahead. "The colonel tells the writer that the business of the fires being started by terrorists is a cover story. Meanwhile, rumors start to surface. Lots of chatter on the Internet, lots of theories, most of them bogus. The stock market, the futures markets, they all start to fluctuate wildly as the big investors try to get good information."

"You can't be serious," Dennis said, for once seeming to be frozen in position with none of his nervous tics.

"I'm serious as cancer," he said, abandoning the fiction once and for all.

There was a long silence around the table as they all shifted mental gears.

"You're saying all this happened," said Roger. "It happened to you."

"I'm saying the parts about the colonel and the writer happened. I am the writer. The colonel was Lionel Warner."

"Is this on the news?"

"No, which is scary in itself. But I was there, and I saw him shot, and fall eleven stories to his death."

"You've got to be kidding."

"I wouldn't do that to you."

"What about all that other stuff? The Area 52, and the crazy scientist?"

"I can't vouch for that. I'm not even sure if Colonel Warner was certain of the details. But I can tell you what I saw. There were *way* too many oil wells burning for it to have been a terrorist act."

Dennis seemed to want to reject the whole thing. Bob was frowning. Jenna kept her own counsel, and Roger was inscrutable. But he had a question.

"So why are you sharing all this with us?" Roger asked.

"Because I had to talk to somebody about it, and you guys are the only people I could trust not to reject all of this out of hand."

"What about Karen?" Jenna wanted to know.

"I wanted to run it all past you guys first."

"Well," said Dennis, standing and stretching and walking toward the glass wall that framed his million-dollar view, "I think that old man pulled a fast one on you."

"Then why did they kill him?" Jenna asked.

"That part I don't know," Dennis admitted, "but I don't think it had anything to do with some crazy superbug that eats crude oil."

There was a short silence. Dave certainly wasn't going to ask for a vote on the matter, but he hoped the others would weigh in.

"I'm reserving judgement," Roger said. "I'm not saying it's impossible, and I'm having a tough time figuring out any other reason these storm troopers you speak of would kill the man . . . but this is the real world, Fearless Leader."

"I've had the same problem," Dave admitted.

Bob had a suggestion.

"How about this?" he said. "Let's take it all as a starting point for a story, instead of as a story in and of itself. Let's bat it around a bit, like a story conference."

"I don't get it," Dennis said. "How does that help anything?"

"How does it hurt?" Bob countered. "Let's just say, for the purposes of developing this story, that it's all real. That people in Washington and other capitals around the world are doing their best to cover it all up because they don't have a clue about what to do next. Let's postulate that, very soon, this whole country is literally going to run out of gas. So . . . number one, what happens next? And number two, what would a prudent individual do to prepare for it?"

Dave could see the interest growing as Bob spoke. They were story people, they were used to taking a situation and running with it.

"Here's a bit of data for you," he said. "Los Angeles gets enough rainfall every year to support about 5 percent of our current population."

"You've been researching this," Bob said.

"I have. Where do you think we get our electricity? Half of it comes from coal-burning plants in Utah. But the coal is brought in by diesel-powered trains. They won't be running if this scenario is correct. "

Dave let them ponder that for a while. Jenna spoke up.

"Food, water, power," she said. "We take all that for granted, but we shouldn't. Los Angeles is a desert. It's only transportation and water that's made it possible to live here. Without that, we all dry up and blow away. How long do you think the food in stores and warehouses would last, if no more was coming in?"

"I have no idea," Dave said. "I wasn't able to find any data on that. Maybe nobody's even considered it."

"What about the people who plan for the Big One?" That was Roger. "Surely they must have an estimate of food resources when transportation is disrupted."

"They probably do," Bob said, "but remember, all their planning is assuming one thing we can no longer assume. They figure that, no matter how big the Big One is, we won't be on our own. Help will come from outside. The Red Cross, the National Guard. But the thing about this disaster is, no help will be coming. *Everybody* will be without fuel. No rescue helicopters, no truckloads of supplies. Nothing."

"So what would our prudent, forewarned writer need to do to provide for his family for an unknown time?" Roger asked.

"Lay in supplies, obviously," Jenna said.

"I've done that."

"Bulk staples. Flour, cornmeal, rice, sugar . . ."

"Coffee," Dennis suggested. Dave doubted Dennis could survive very long without coffee.

"Lots of booze," Bob said, to general laughter.

"See?" Dave said. "I'm glad I brought you here. I've bought a lot of stuff like canned meat and tuna. I didn't think of flour, because I'm not a baker."

"You'd have to learn to be one," Jenna said. "Buy a lot of carbs, that's my suggestion. It'll last longer. I'd be buying twenty-pound sacks of rice by the carload. It's cheaper than canned food, too."

"I'd be cleaning my weapons," Roger said. That was greeted by another silence.

"I don't have any weapons," Dennis said.

"Neither do I," Dave said.

Jenna said she had a pistol that she'd never used. Bob had quite a collection of rifles and shotguns.

"How long does it take to buy a gun in California?" Dennis wondered.

"Too long," Bob said, dryly. "There will be civil unrest. Can you envision how bad it could get when parents see their children starving?"

"Starving? Isn't that a little extreme?"

Bob shook his head.

"Follow this scenario out to its end, and it gets really frightening. The gasoline and diesel is running out. The store shelves are empty. Nothing is coming into the city. There isn't room or time to grow anything here. Where do you go to put food on your table? The central valley? Sure, but you'll have to walk, and it's a long ways, and there isn't much water along the way. And one other thing. What makes you think we'd be welcomed in the valley? I suspect they'd be inclined to save the food they're growing for their own children."

They batted it around a little longer, and came to an unpleasant conclusion. The best course of action was to get out of town, right now. Head for someplace in the country where food was grown and stored. Head for a place that got most of its electricity from hydro plants.

When they were gone Dave sat at his desk, looking out over the city, brooding. Tomorrow would be a busy day.

"Daddy?"

He jumped, and turned around. Addison had come into the office.

"What is it, honey?"

"Were you just making all that up? Is it all a joke, or is it true?"

"How did you hear that?"

She came down and walked over to one of his cluttered bookshelves. She moved a pencil cup to one side and revealed something that he didn't recognize at first.

"You rascal! How dare you! You've been spying on me!"

She looked frightened for a moment, then realized he was kidding.

"It's that old baby monitor. We brought everything along from the old house when we moved, and me and my friends used to use it when we played. Then I used to put it in here sometimes when your writing group was here because I liked to listen to you guys when you're making up stories.

"When I heard you calling Mr. Winston I brought it back in here and hid it on that shelf. Because . . . well, Daddy, you've been acting kind of strange."

Dave got up and took her hand and led her over to the couch. They sat side by side and he put his arm over her shoulder. She snuggled up against him.

"Addie . . . It's not a joke. I don't know how much of what you heard is true, but at least some of it is."

"You really saw that man get shot and fall out of that building?"

"I really did."

"That sounds awful."

"It was. It was about the worst thing I've ever seen. And the fact that he was accessing classified information that it seems the government didn't want him to see, and the fact that they *did* kill him . . . all that makes me think what he said was true."

"But what does it all mean? You were talking about getting guns and stuff."

"Well, some of them were. They think it might get violent."

"Will it?"

"I honestly don't know. I can see how it could. I'm just glad we've got a little advance warning. For most people, what's coming is going to be a big surprise."

She was quiet for a while.

"What you said . . . if people can't buy food for their children . . . they probably won't just sit around quietly, will they?"

"I wouldn't."

"What would you do?"

"Addie, let's not get into that. That's a problem for another day."

She wasn't having any of that.

"Are you going to buy a gun?"

"I don't know. I might."

"If you do, will you teach me to shoot it?"

Dave began to wonder if, in some ways, Addie might be well ahead of him in thinking about this. He kissed her on the top of the head, and she looked up at him with a shy smile. He knew at that moment that he'd do pretty much anything to see she was safe and fed.

They got up and went to the window.

"I wish you had told me when you learned about this," she said. "I may not be an adult yet, but I'm not really a child, either."

"No, you're not. I'm sorry, and I won't do it again."

"So . . . when are you going to tell Mom?"

"She's due back day after tomorrow. I'll tell her then."

Addison sighed deeply.

"That's going to be interesting."

* * *

The next day was a busy one.

Addison was helping him gather information, and the more they learned, the more they were sure they were in for hard times ahead.

The president of the United States appeared at a press conference. He still wasn't admitting anything beyond the fact that there were going to be shortages of gasoline, diesel, and home-heating oil. He advised people in cold climates to look into converting to electric, natural gas, or even coal, and he proposed a tax credit for those who did, and urged Congress to pass the bill quickly.

Then, to no one's surprise, he announced a national program of gasoline rationing. Details were still being worked out, but it was to begin in a week. All Americans would be getting ration books or cards or stamps, just like in World War Two. And just like then, not all of them would be getting the same allotment.

"Police, firefighters, doctors, and other emergency workers will have first priority," the president said. "Farmers will get more than factory workers. Citizens of rural areas will get more than urban dwellers. We will endeavor to make the distribution of gasoline as equitable as possible, but it will inevitably entail hardships for many of us. We will take any measures necessary to get us through the coming winter and into next year, when we feel confident that this crisis will have passed. Luckily, it's still summer, and we have some months to prepare."

He then announced a long list of conservation measures. Car pooling would no longer be an option, it would now be mandatory. Every seat in every vehicle would have to be occupied during morning and evening rush hours, or you would not be allowed on the freeways. This, too, was to begin in one week, so people had time to organize it as best they could. States and cities were instructed to set up connection boards on the Internet. For those who didn't find some neighbors willing to share a ride, their only option would be to drive to a freeway entrance, leave their car there, and get a ride with someone who needed another passenger to fill an empty seat. Walking or riding a bicycle to a freeway entrance was an even better idea.

The president took a few questions, but refused to address the increasing rumors that all was not what it seemed. Which only fueled more rumors.

While Addison continued gathering information on her computer, Dave started calling around. It didn't take long to find what he was looking for.

The doorbell rang a few hours later. Dave hurried outside and around the house and through the door in the privacy wall. Waiting outside was the dealer.

His name was Marcus. He was a grip at one of the studios. Dave didn't know him well, but knew Marcus was the go-to guy if you needed something in a hurry and maybe not strictly legal. He didn't look like a drug dealer. He was in his thirties and dressed in chinos and a polo shirt, with a good tan and wild blond hair. They got into his black van with the darkened windows. It was all tricked out like a traveling Nevada whorehouse, with shag carpet, mirrors, a small bar, and a red velvet bed that took up half of the back.

Marcus sat in a chair and he lifted the mattress, propped it up, and opened a recessed compartment. Dave could see metal gleaming.

"What you into? Handguns? Rifles, shotguns?"

"I want a good revolver—medium-sized, not a cannon—and a shotgun."

Marcus tried to sell him a rifle with a spotter scope but Dave held firm, and ended up with two Smith & Wesson .38 model 19s with four-inch barrels and an old but well-preserved Remington 870 Express 12-gauge.

He was about to call it quits when he spotted something else.

"How much for that one?"

"The Ithaca side by side?" Marcus gave him a price that Dave suspected was double what the gun was worth, and Dave took it. He thought he could cut it down into something Addison could handle. A double-barreled shotgun didn't take much aiming.

Actually, he hoped Daddy could take care of any necessary ugly business before his little Addison had to shoot at all, but you could never be sure.

* * *

Dave stowed the hardware in a place he was sure even his nosy daughter didn't know about. Then he went back to the main house and found Addison still hard at work on her computer.

"Mom called," she said.

"Yeah? What did she have to say?"

"Just that she would be back tomorrow, but she had to take a later flight. I wrote down the flight number." She handed him a Post-it, then smiled up at him with wide, innocent eyes. "I didn't tell her about the guy in the black van you spent so much time with. Or about the things wrapped in blankets you brought into the house. I presume they were golf clubs?"

"Golf clubs are lethal weapons if you know how to handle them. Did anyone ever tell you it's not polite to snoop?"

Her smile just got broader. "Politeness is highly overrated. And besides, I may snoop, but it's not sneaky if I tell you I did it, is it?"

"I'll have to think on that one. Addie, I'm going out for a while, there are a few things I need to do."

"Can I borrow your credit card?"

"What for?"

"Don't worry, I won't gamble all your money away at a Honduran Web site or subscribe to a lot of porn sites. I found some books that we can get FedExed that I thought might come in handy." She had printed out a list, and she handed it to him.

It all looked like useful stuff, from how-to books to survival manuals to something called *The Anarchist Cookbook*, which taught you how to make bombs from common household chemicals. As he looked over the list, he was struck by just how little most people know about so many basic things, things our pioneer forefathers probably did routinely. How do you dress out a rabbit, or a deer? Clean a fish? How do you make cloth, or soap? What wild mushrooms and berries are edible? Who knew if they would need any of this stuff, but he agreed it was best to have it on hand. At some point they might not be able to Google it up.

"Okay," he said, "but anything you win in Honduras, I get half."

On his way out, Dave stopped and studied his house in a way he had never done before. Every man's home is his castle, they say.

It had always been a figure of speech, but how did this house stack up, as a literal, defensible castle?

There was no moat or drawbridge, but other than that, it was a lot better than most American homes. The architect had never considered that anyone might have to defend himself inside but had taken something else into consideration: the penchant of Hollywood hill dwellers for privacy. Many houses were built on tiny lots that were the next thing to vertical. Most people built right up to the curb on the street side, with only a door and a driveway entrance.

On the street side of his house there were just two windows on the second floor, and they were narrow. What you saw from the street was that bit of second floor looking over an unbroken eight-foot wall of thick, stucco-covered brick, painted white, broken only by a solid metal electric gate. The street door was right next to the driveway gate and was just as sturdy. His wall joined his neighbors' walls on both the east and the west. The east side of the house had no windows on the ground floor, and just two more on the second, which looked out over his neighbor's sprawling ranch-style house, patio, and pool. The stucco wall continued on the west side of the property and down the hillside for about fifty feet, to the edge of the property on the next street down. The south side of his property was pretty much wide open, but if he were a Goth, Hun, or Vandal he'd think twice about storming the castle from that side. A six-foot retaining wall kept his patio and pool from sliding down the hillside, and at the bottom of the wall it was a slope of forty-five degrees, held in place by thickets of ice plant. There was no path to the bottom.

He wouldn't want to approach the house from that direction if he were intent on doing the residents harm. The entire time they had lived there no one had ever ventured down except gardeners, and they didn't go very often. At one time there had been more substantial plantings on that slope, shrubs and a few small trees, but he had had them all removed one summer when there was a big fire scare. Now there was nothing growing anywhere near the house, as the LAFD advised. The flat roof was concrete, with a small array of electricity-generating solar panels, and surrounded by a low parapet trimmed with red ceramic barrel tiles.

He decided that the east boundary was the most vulnerable side. The slope was not quite as steep, and the ground cover not as thick. But someone in one of those two upper windows with a shotgun could make it very uncomfortable for anyone coming up the street from that direction, and once an invader got to the top, he wouldn't have achieved much. There was a narrow gap between the north wall of the house and the street wall, and Dave would be filling that in if things got nasty.

CHAPTER FIVE

He couldn't put his finger on it, but when he got down out of the hills things felt a little different. It was a hot day, so maybe that accounted for some of it, but it seemed to him that a lot of people were driving more aggressively, less politely, than usual. On the other hand, traffic was fairly light. He made his way across town easily, but he did notice that the parking lots of all the grocery stores were at capacity and beyond. There were lines of cars in the street, waiting to get inside.

The gun shop he visited was crowded, and some of the patrons were angry. A guy behind the glass counter was raising his voice.

"No guns today!" he shouted. "Everything you see has a red tag on it, which means it's been sold, and the owner is waiting for the background check. I'm expecting a shipment in two days, handguns, rifles, and shotguns, but I'm not taking orders. Come back later and see what we have. Meantime, all I have is ammunition."

There was some grumbling, but most of the people left, though others kept arriving to replace them. An assistant was writing a notice on a piece of cardboard to tape to the front door. Dave moved up to the counter and told the man what he needed. He started pulling boxes from the shelves behind him.

"How long has it been like this?"

"About a week." The man shrugged. "Same thing happened right after 9/11, though it wasn't this bad. It was *real* bad after the Rodney King riots. Every now and then something happens, gets folks scared. Like a Democrat getting elected to the White House. That's always good for business. If I could legally sell machine guns and bazookas, I'd make a fortune."

He wouldn't sell Dave as many 12-gauge shotgun shells as Dave asked for, but he felt lucky to get what he had. He bought several boxes of .357 cartridges after the guy told him they were the same caliber as regular .38 ammunition but packed a lot more punch. He paid for it all with a credit card.

He had to buy a canvas bag to put it all in. All that lead was amazingly heavy.

He went to the bank and withdrew his limit on all of his cards, and closed his account. He had a thick stack of twenties and hundreds when he was done. What would it buy in a week? A month? A year? Even if the worst fears didn't come true, it seemed certain the country was headed for very bad economic times. Buy gold? Last time he checked it was very expensive, and going up as people grew more worried. He was no economist; he didn't know which way to jump. Best to lay in real wealth in the form of food and fuel, and then see how things developed.

He stopped at the Home Depot on Sunset and Western and loaded up on the cheapest grade of quarter-inch plywood they had. It wouldn't stop a bullet but it would slow down an intruder scaling his castle walls. While he was there he realized that many of his tools were electric. He bought an old-fashioned hand drill and an assortment of saws, then picked up a small gas chain saw and a wood splitter.

When he got home there was a big flatbed truck backed up in his driveway. He screeched to a halt and hurried to the open gate. When he got through he saw two large fellows unloading bales of hay.

"What the hell . . . ?"

Addison was standing by the garage, looking nervous but determined.

"Addison, did you—"

"Yes, Dad, I did. I . . ." She stopped, and glanced at the workmen, then came to him and pulled him by the arm. She stopped at the edge of the retaining wall, well away from any listening ears. She spoke softly.

"If we're not going to have any gas," she said, "well, we're not going to get over to Burbank every day to take care of

Ranger. I'd worry about him. And besides, a horse is a good way to get around."

"This is what the credit card was about."

"Yes, plus the books and other stuff. I'm sorry, Dad, I know I shouldn't have tricked you . . . but you can see we can do it. We have two spare stalls in the garage, and I'll clean up after him, and the hay and grain is pretty cheap, really."

He followed me home, Daddy. Can I keep him?

He sighed. "I guess we better move him today. Do you know if we can rent a trailer at the equestrian center?"

"We could, but I have a better idea."

Addison had her arms wrapped around her father as he cautiously descended the hill to Sunset. It had been a while since he had driven a motorcycle, and the scooter was a lot smaller and less powerful. He didn't entirely trust the brakes, so he kept it very slow.

Actually, he didn't entirely trust their ability to get the horse from Burbank to the Hollywood Hills safely, but he figured they'd better start getting used to doing things in a different way. He made it to Sunset without incident, then east to Cahuenga and along the 101 freeway, past the Hollywood Bowl, and up and over Cahuenga Pass. Soon they were in Burbank and he swung the scooter through the entrance to the Equestrian Center and on to the building that housed Ranger's stall. Addison hopped off and ran to her horse, who seemed glad to see her.

They filled a canvas bag and the small pannier on the scooter with what gear they could carry, tack and brushes and a pair of riding boots. Addison saddled the beast.

Ranger handled the traffic like a pro, as if he did this every day. There were a few people who honked their horns, even though horse and rider were not blocking anything on the wide streets, but most drivers seemed delighted at the sight of the girl on the horse. They got lots of smiles and thumbs-ups.

He stayed behind them as they crossed the freeway and Ranger ambled down Ventura Boulevard. Then they crossed over and began to climb. The streets up there were narrower, and winding. In most places there wasn't room for two cars to pass. He got ahead of Addison and putt-putted in front of them to each curve and waited there.

It is a complicated and winding route up from the Valley, across the hills and valleys and down to the house on Mockingbird. It took them half an hour to reach Mulholland Drive. Addison dismounted. Dave turned off the scooter's engine, and they both walked for a while. There was quite a bit of forage up there, though you had to be careful not to let the horse eat somebody's valuable plantings.

They reached Sunset Plaza, and before long they could look down the hill and see the house. A pitcher with a good arm could have landed a baseball on their roof. It looked as if they were almost home, but it was an illusion. They had to descend Sunset Plaza almost all the way to Sunset Boulevard itself before going up Rising Glen, down Thrasher, and finally up Doheny and into their neighborhood, a total of three and a half miles. Walking or riding a horse gave you a whole new perspective on distances.

At last they arrived at the house and Addison took the horse into the empty garage stall. Dave helped her move a bale of wood shavings into the stall, which they spread across the concrete floor, and she got out a bale of hay and gave Ranger about half of it. He moved a few items to form a crude barrier between the horse and Karen's Mercedes, then found a tub and filled it with water. He tried to imagine the scene when Karen arrived home the next evening to find that part of their garage had been converted into a stable.

Dave and Karen didn't speak much when he picked her up at the airport. That had become the new norm in their relationship.

When they got home Dave kept trying to start a conversation about the current political and social situation, the uncertainty everyone was feeling, but it was hard to get her interested in current events. She might very well go to work for a group whose purpose was to obtain extra gas allotments for poor people who were unable to get to their jobs, but she seemed oblivious to the fact that rationing was going to make big changes in her life, too.

As they were finishing their dinner there was a loud neighing sound from outside. Karen frowned, and started to get up.

"That's Ranger," Dave said. Karen stopped, and sat back down.

"And what is Ranger doing here?" she asked.

"Well, it's a long story, and sort of complicated, and not all that easy to believe," he admitted.

She gave him a long, hard stare.

"You probably think I haven't noticed some strange goings-on around here," she said, evenly. "Well, whatever it is you're trying to hide from me, I guess now's the time to get it all out."

"I wasn't hiding it, exactly. Well . . . maybe I was. I was hoping for a better time to tell it all to you. Because, I admit, it's a lot to swallow."

She rested her chin on her fist and gave him a flat stare.

"Please do go on," she said.

Her eyes were hard as nails, and he had the sinking feeling that he was doomed before he even started. But she was right, it was time to get it all out in the open.

"It begins with Colonel Warner," he said, and talked nonstop for half an hour.

It might not have been the best pitch he ever gave, but it was the most heartfelt, and the audience was tough. Karen's expression never changed throughout the story. She said nothing for a long time. Addison kept looking back and forth between her parents. When Karen spoke there was no hint of emotion in her voice.

"And what do you propose to do about this?" she asked.

That was not what he had expected, and he hoped it was a good sign.

"Well, I've stocked up on gasoline and a lot of other essentials, in case food might be hard to get for a while. How long do you think the food in markets and warehouses will last if the trucks and trains don't keep rolling, bringing it all in from all around the country?"

"I'm sure I have no idea."

"Well, I don't have an exact time, either, but I suspect it would be only a few weeks. Maybe less."

"Again, what do you propose to do about it?"

He took a deep breath. He hadn't told Addison about this, nor anyone else.

"I originally thought we'd hunker down, sit it out right here. We could last for months with what I've put away. But if people are getting hungry, if people are *starving*, as I suspect they soon will be, then we would have to defend it all. So I think the best idea is to get out of here while we can. Los Angeles will soon become untenable."

"Get out of here," she said, in the same quiet voice. "And go where?"

"What we need is a place with fertile land, adequate rainfall, and hydropower. And that means, to me, the Pacific Northwest. Oregon and Washington, Idaho. British Columbia, if they would take American refugees."

"Refugees." Her expression still hadn't changed. "You really think Americans are going to become refugees."

"I was thinking, we could go visit your brother. Martin has a big house, most of their children moved out. We could stay with him until we got settled."

He was suddenly feeling very tired. He had said all he had to say until he heard something from her. Which wasn't long in coming. She stood up, calm as could be.

"I can't begin to imagine why you have manufactured this silly story," she said. "I think you may have cracked under the pressure of not finding work. I don't want to think there's a more sinister motive. I might be able to shrug it off, take it as a bad joke, but you seem to have infected our daughter with your paranoid fantasy, and I can't forgive you for that. I'm moving out, right now, and I'm taking Addison with me. Come with me, Addison, and we'll pack."

Addison glanced at him. He didn't move. This was up to her. She folded her hands and looked at her mother.

"I'm staying here," she said.

"Addison, I'm not telling you again. Get out of that chair and come with me."

"No, Mom." There was a catch in her voice, but she held her mother's eyes.

Karen's eyes were cold.

"I see," she said. "I can't physically force you to come with me, but both of you should know that my lawyer will have something to say about all this. He'll be contacting you tomorrow. I can't wait to hear you tell your little story in court. Which is where I'll see you next." She turned and stalked out of the room. Dave could hear her going up the stairs. He looked at Addison.

"Well," she said. "That went nicely, don't you think?"

Karen came back down carrying a suitcase. Dave followed her to the door.

"Karen, don't do this."

"Get out of my way."

He closed the door behind her. He felt numb, and more than a little shaky. It felt like one part of his life was over and another was beginning, and he wasn't ready for it. He had known for some time, even before the crisis, that this day would come, in one way or another. He still loved her, or maybe he still loved the woman he thought was somewhere inside this hard, detached Karen who had replaced the woman he married, but he doubted that she loved him any longer, not even deep down.

Addison joined him. He put an arm over her shoulder. He thought she might cry—he would have, if it had happened to him at her age—but she didn't. He thought that, of the three of them, she might have been the strongest.

Addison answered the phone. She listened a moment, and then handed it to her father.

"It's Mom," she whispered. "She's crying."

He couldn't immediately make out what she was saying; it was an incoherent mixture of words and sobs. But she finally pulled herself together.

"I've never been so humiliated in my life," she said. "I went to the hotel and gave them my credit card . . . and it was *refused*! What have you done to us, Dave? That desk clerk, the way she looked at me . . . and they kept the card, David! As if I had stolen it!"

"I'm so sorry, Karen. I have some cash, if you want it. You can go somewhere else. Where did you try to check in?"

"The Beverly-Wilshire." He knew the Beverly-Wilshire's rooms went for around $600 per night. "I suppose you want me to live at the Motel 6."

"No, but there are good accommodations that are cheaper than the Beverly-Wilshire. Just come back here and I'll give you the money. We'll work something out."

"I can't. I wrecked the car."

"Karen, are you all right?"

"Of course I'm not all right. But I'm not injured. I was so upset . . ."

"Tell me where you are, and I'll come get you."

The car was at the curb on Santa Monica Boulevard, on the edge of Beverly Hills. Karen was sitting in the backseat on the left, and at first he couldn't see anything wrong with the car. He parked behind her and got out onto the sidewalk, leaving Addison inside. Then he could see that the right front fender was crumpled and a lot of paint had been scratched off on that side. The doors on the right side were also caved in. Karen got out of the car and stood looking at it.

"What happened?" he asked her.

"I was crying, and reached for my purse. I hit a parked car."

"Where's the car?"

"Gone. He came out of that shop there. He was angry. It was a silver Porsche. We exchanged insurance information and he drove off."

Dave squatted down and took a closer look at the fender.

"My beautiful Mercedes," she said, and started crying again. Addison appeared at her side and put her arm around her mother.

"Karen, it's no big deal. I don't think those doors will open, but the fender's not touching the tire. We can drive it home."

"Are you sure?"

"I don't see why not. We'll start her up and drive it a few blocks and see how that goes. Okay? Do you want me to take you to another hotel?"

She didn't answer at once. He didn't know if she realized she had been overdramatizing, but he found himself wondering, with a bit of hope, if she had used the excuse of the "totaled" car to backtrack on her announced intentions.

"And pay with cash?"

"They do still take it, you know. They might want a deposit for phone calls and other room charges."

Still she said nothing.

"I think there's a hotel a couple blocks south of here. The Carlyle, something like that." He happened to know the room rates were more like $150 per night. He had Googled it. She looked like she was thinking it over.

"It's a Best Western, isn't it?" she finally said. It broke his heart, the hopelessness in her voice when she said it, as if he were recommending a flophouse.

"Nothing wrong with that. Or, I could take you back home. I'll move into the guesthouse, you'll hardly have to deal with me. It'll be better all around. You can still call a lawyer in the morning."

She looked around her, as if she'd never seen Santa Monica Boulevard before.

"Come on, Mom," Addison said.

Karen sighed, and he held the door of the Mercedes open for her.

"I'm not driving that car again," she said.

"Fine. I'll drive it. You take the Escalade."

They saw very little of each other during the following weeks, though every time they did run into each other in the course of the day, her expression was a little more smug than it had been the last time, and he was sure he looked like the nervous wreck he was becoming as the days went by and things settled into the new normal.

The school year ended. Aside from feeding Ranger, and cleaning up after him, Addison spent as little time as possible at the house. Dave could hardly blame her. He had bought her a new bicycle. She and her friends were getting used to cycling to places their parents used to take them in their soccer-mom SUVs. At first, Addison would arrive home in the evening exhausted from the hard climb up Doheny, but after a week she was doing a lot better. Even some of her friends from the flatlands came by to do whatever it is fourteen-year-old girls do, giggling behind closed doors with their iPods and their cell phones. They took turns riding Ranger on the steep streets, so the big horse got enough exercise to stay in shape.

Dave suspected boys were discussed, now and then.

He had made one last trip in the Escalade, stocking up on staples like flour and rice and cornmeal and sugar. He was now leaving the house only every third day, puttering along on his little scooter, shopping for items he had forgotten and taking the pulse of the city.

What he saw, though far from apocalyptic, was alarming enough. Grocery-store shelves were looking barren. Staple foods were sold out, and when a new shipment arrived at Ralphs or Vons, lines formed outside to get the one twenty-pound bag of rice or flour allowed to each customer.

The army surplus stores on Hollywood Boulevard and on Vine were shuttered, sold out to the bare walls. There were no more guns to be had, except on the street, at ruinous prices.

He spent some of his time cobbling together a scooter trailer from plywood and the wheels off an old wagon he had bought at a garage sale, using plans he found on the Internet. It wasn't a pretty thing, but it would do to carry home any treasures he managed to snap up in his prowls of the supermarkets, Costco, and Home Depot.

There was the expected chaos on the Monday when both gas rationing and mandatory carpooling began. To no one's surprise, the rationing system was far from ready on the first day. Some ration cards had gone out, but many millions nationwide had not received them, and thus were not able to purchase gasoline. The uproar over that was immense, to the point that the president had to go on television and announce a week's delay. Until then, everyone could continue to buy all the gas they could afford.

With prices fluctuating wildly between eight dollars and twelve dollars per gallon, that often meant less than a tankful.

All the cities and towns along the vast freeway system posted police at each freeway entrance, and simply didn't let any car enter unless it had a full load of passengers. Commuters arrived and had the option of parking their cars on the city streets or getting in line to take on passengers. The next day the newspapers and blogs were full of stories of how people actually had a good experience with what was, in essence, hitching a ride with total strangers. For once they had people to talk to, and they often found that they enjoyed it.

Once on the freeways, of course, the real benefit of the gas shortage became obvious. The commute had never gone more smoothly. The parking lots downtown were three-quarters empty.

Metro riders had the worst of it. The buses and trains were jammed far beyond capacity, running late, and the bus stops and train stations overflowed. Talk radio hummed with outraged callers, and the majority of them were riders on the Metro. The mayor appealed to school-bus companies, and after they did their morning rounds thousands of them roamed the Metro routes, picking up people who were already late for work and not happy about it.

To the surprise of many people, the city muddled through a hectic week.

It turned out that 90 percent of public-school students who had been taking buses could reasonably be expected to walk to school, though that was sometimes as much as three or four miles. Parents objected, overweight students objected, and the school district shrugged. This is how it is, the superintendent said. There will be no buses. Deal with it.

But the gasoline tankers continued to roll along the interstates and delivered their loads to the neighborhood service stations, defying Dave's gloomy predictions. Gas could be had, just not as much of it as they were used to.

People bitched. People moaned. People vowed never to vote for the mayor, the governor, the president, and all the Congress ever again.

But as the days went by they began to adjust.

Dave had to admit that he was conflicted. He had invested pretty heavily in a doomsday scenario. Everything he thought he knew had pointed to it. It had all seemed reasonable, it had seemed impossible that things could simply carry on, though at a much reduced level. He had bet the farm—or what pitiful acreage he had left after three lean years—and he was beginning to think that he'd made a terrible mistake. He was feeling like a millennialist end-of-the-world prophet on January 1, 2000. He was besieged by doubts.

Karen went out frequently, at first. One thing that can be counted on in a rationing regime is that a black market will develop, and that there will be those willing to pay premium prices for somebody else's gas allotment. Many of Karen's friends were quite wealthy, and were not about to let a gas crisis crimp their lifestyle. One or another of them would call on her most days, in their BMWs and Mercedes SUVs, and they took off to the Polo Lounge or Spago or Urasawa for lunch. Dave had taken to leaving hundred-dollar bills here and there where she would find them. It was easier than getting into a row by forcing her to ask him for money.

One day in the middle of the second week of their official estrangement, the ladies stopped dropping by. The phone stopped ringing. Addison, the confirmed supersnoop, informed him that she had listened as his wife made a few calls of her own, and it was clear she was being cut off. Like sharks scenting blood in the water, they had sensed that she could no longer afford to run with them. Karen got the message eventually. She stopped making calls and took to her bed with a massive migraine. She hadn't had one in years. This one lasted four days.

It was three weeks into their estrangement that something finally happened that seemed to confirm his worst fears.

CHAPTER SIX

Dave was sitting in his office contemplating the wreckage of his finances. The bills for his spending spree had come in, and even though they were not yet overdue, he was getting calls from the credit-card companies asking when they could expect payment on the over-limit balances. He was thinking he had made a big mistake.

He was jolted out of his dismal thoughts by a shock wave that rattled the windows in front of him.

It was an exceptionally clear day, about an hour from sunset. Beyond his windows, smoke and debris was rising from a wide area just over six miles due south of him. He knew the distance because he had measured it on a map. It was the Doheny oil field, erupting like a volcano.

The field was one of the reasons people came to Los Angeles in the early part of the twentieth century. Over the years the city had grown up around it, and now it sat between Culver City and Baldwin Hills. La Cienega Boulevard cut right through the middle of it, and on each side you could see hundreds of pump-jacks, big iron beams on fulcrums that had always reminded Dave of some strange bird pecking slowly and rhythmically at the ground. What they were doing was pumping oil, a hundred years after the original wells had been sunk.

He watched, awestruck, as large chunks of earth and metal rose slowly into the air, finally reached an apogee, and were relentlessly pulled back to the ground by gravity. He knew they were much larger than they looked, to be visible six miles away. Where they hit, they sent up secondary showers of debris. It took him a moment to realize that beneath some of that falling wreckage were homes. People would be sitting down to dinner, mothers and fathers and children.

He raced outside, digging in his pocket for his phone. He was punching buttons with his thumb as he entered the main house. Karen was just coming down the stairs, looking confused.

"Was that an earthquake?" she asked.

"No. The oil field just exploded."

The screen said *Dialing* . . . then Addison answered.

"Daddy? Did you feel that quake?"

"It wasn't an earthquake, Addie. It was an explosion. Where are you?"

"I'm at the Beverly Center."

That put her two miles closer to the inferno than he was. Karen was watching the huge rising column of smoke and flame, looking stunned.

"Where is Addison?" she asked.

"She's okay. Listen, Addie, I want you to stay on the line." The Beverly Center was at La Cienega, between Beverly and Third. There were five aboveground levels of parking, and three levels of retail sitting on top of them. Access from the parking levels to the shops was by a series of external escalators.

"I want you to go to the escalators and take a look outside, and to the south. Can you do that?"

"Sure." She sounded a little frightened, and she hadn't even seen the fire yet. He was worried because some of that debris seemed to have landed a mile or two from the column of flame that was still growing. Could it reach four miles? Should he try to go get her in the Escalade? He suspected her best bet for getting back to him quickly might be on her bike, but he didn't feel good about that.

Even as these thoughts were churning through his head, there was another bright explosion, silence for a few seconds, and then a third. He backed away from the windows, which soon rattled from the shock waves. These blasts seemed even more powerful than the first one.

"Daddy, I'm outside, and I can see a lot of smoke and fire down south. What's happening? I'm scared!"

"Just stay calm, Addie. It's an explosion at the oil field."

"Like in Iran and Russia and stuff?"

"Yes, like that. I didn't think about all the oil we're sitting on here in Los Angeles. I mean, it's nothing like Saudi Arabia . . ." He shook his head. That was more detail than she needed. He was pacing, mostly looking at the fire. He did notice that Karen was going back upstairs.

"You're a long ways from it," he told her. "Back here at home we'll be even safer. What I want you to do . . . Hello? Hello? Addie, stay on the line."

But she was gone. The call had been dropped. Cursing, he dialed again, and the call went straight to voice mail. "Addie, come right home!" he said, and dialed again. This time she answered.

"I lost you, Daddy. You didn't hang up, did you?"

"No, honey, and don't you hang up, either. I think the cell towers are overloaded with people making calls about the explosion. We may get dropped again, so listen. I want you back here."

"So do I."

"I'm coming for you. I want you to wait for me on the San Vicente side, okay? I'll be coming that way. I want you to stay up there on the second parking level, and if you hear more explosions, I want you to move to the center of the parking lot. I'm worried that some debris might be falling down there. Can you do that?"

"Yes. This far away?"

"I really doubt it, but I don't want to take the chance. I'll be there in . . . fifteen minutes. You stay on the line. If we get cut off again, don't try to call me. I'll be calling you." Something else occurred to him. "Is anybody with you?"

"Laurie was, but she took off."

Good. He wouldn't have to take any of her friends home. He ran out to the garage, holding the phone to his ear.

They were cut off again as he backed the Escalade out of the garage. He kept thumbing redial as he barreled down the street, but couldn't get a connection. He wanted to do eighty, ninety miles per hour but he forced himself to slow down. There are a lot of hairpin curves on Doheny. It wouldn't do Addison any good if he rolled the car.

Traffic was still light as he made the left on Sunset. He turned on the radio as he crossed and sped down the hill. Incredibly, most of the stations were still playing music or idiotic talk shows. He kept thumbing the dial until he arrived at KPCC, public radio, which had switched to crisis mode. But they didn't have much to report yet beyond the fact of the explosion itself. In fact, he knew more than they did from having observed it from his backyard. Reporters were on the way.

He made the right turn on San Vicente and as he was rolling down the hill again he found K-EARTH 101. They had reporters on the way, too, but theirs were closer. They also had people calling in from Culver City and Fox Hills and Ladera Heights, very close to the oil field.

"A lot of stuff fell out of the sky," one guy was saying. "Something big landed on my roof, and something landed on my neighbor's house and it's on fire. Now this black stuff is coming down, and it sticks to everything. I'm getting my family in the car, and we're . . . Come on, Shirley, we've got to move! I don't know . . . the street is covered in this stuff. My shoes are sticking to the ground."

"Sir, you hang up now and take care of your family," the disk jockey said. "Now we've got . . . Mike in Culver City. Go ahead, Mike."

"Chris, the smoke is black as ink, and it's blotting out half the sky. It looks like it's blowing south, toward Westchester and LAX. We had a—"

"Let me interrupt you, Mike. We have confirmed that all flights, that is *all flights* leaving LAX have been canceled, and all arriving flights have been diverted due to the smoke that has almost completely obscured the airport. Visibility is near zero in that area. So if you have loved ones arriving, call the airport information line and find out where they're going. Flights are being diverted to Ontario, Bob Hope Airport in Burbank, and John Wayne Airport in Santa Ana. Now, go ahead, Mike."

"Like I was saying, Chris, first we got a shower of what was mostly dirt mixed in with something that looked like chunks of asphalt. Then we got this goo falling, like hot tar on the road. It sticks to everything. I don't know how we're going to clean this shit up . . . Sorry about the language."

There was more, but Dave turned it down as he arrived at the Beverly Center.

He pulled off to the right and looked up along the opening of the second-floor parking lot, and there was Addison. She was waving to him. He gestured for her to come down, and she nodded. He got out of the car and looked south again. It was terrifying, it looked like the end of the world. The sun had just set but there was plenty of light yet to see just how large the smoke cloud had grown. As he stood there yet another explosion flared bright orange, the sound arriving a few seconds later.

Addison came spiraling down the ramp and onto the sidewalk, braked, looked both ways, and crossed over to him as he opened the back of the Escalade. He could see she had been crying.

"I'm scared, Daddy."

"I know, Addie. It's scary." He gave her a big hug, and they both jumped as they heard another explosion. He put her bike in the back, got into the driver's seat, and waited a moment until she was buckled in. Then he made a U-turn and started back up San Vicente.

Addison called her mother to tell her she was okay, then she turned up the radio volume.

"This just in. The Los Angeles and Culver City fire departments have issued a mandatory evacuation order for a wide area. This is because of the danger of the many fires spreading, and also the smoke. Currently the wind is blowing to the southwest between five and ten miles per hour. The smoke is not known to be toxic. Let me repeat that, so far as is known now, the smoke is not toxic, but it is not healthy. Those with respiratory problems are in immediate danger, and even healthy people should avoid breathing it, especially the ash and fine particles of what seems to be tar that are in the smoke. Face masks are recommended. You can improvise a mask from a piece of cloth. Winds are expected to shift, so the evacuation area extends to the east and south as well as to the southwest. Here are the boundaries of the mandatory—let me say it again—*mandatory* evacuation area."

It was a huge area, a monstrous area. There had to be half a million people within it. It was bounded by Venice Boulevard to the west and north, Jefferson Boulevard to the north, Crenshaw to the east, and Century to the south. It included parts of Venice, all of Marina del Rey and Culver City, Baldwin Hills, Windsor Hills, and most of Inglewood. Loyola Marymount University was within that area.

"We don't know where to tell you to go at this point, friends," the disk jockey was saying. "I assume somebody's setting up temporary shelters, but for now, the best advice is simply to *get out*. Drive to the east, if you can. If you have friends outside the area, try to get to them. If not, just drive out of the area and park somewhere and keep listening. I'll fill you in on all the latest information as soon as I know it myself."

"Do we know anybody in that area, Daddy?"

"I'm trying to think. Nobody's coming to mind."

He turned on Sunset, then on Doheny, and started up the hill. Addison was looking back, and he could see the orange light on her face.

"This is the worst thing I've ever seen, people," the disk jockey was saying. He choked up, and couldn't go on for a moment. "I'm watching it on television, and it looks like the world is coming to an end. I've had no reports on deaths or injuries, but it seems certain that there's going to be a lot of them. As Mayor Giuliani said after 9/11, probably more than we can bear. If it was terrorists who did this . . . well, we'll just have to wait and see. How somebody could do this is beyond me. It looks like an atomic bomb." He paused, and Dave could faintly hear somebody shouting.

"I'm sorry about that, listeners. Let me be clear here. We have no information that it was a nuclear explosion. The LAPD is not reporting any radiation. I repeat, there is *no* indication that this was an atomic bomb. At this point, we don't know what caused this terrible thing, but what we do know is what I said before. Get out, my friends, just get out. Don't bother to load anything into the car but your family and your pets, and drive as far as you can, as quickly as you can. And stay tuned for further information."

Dave turned down Nightingale and pressed the remote for the gate, swung into the driveway, and put the Escalade in the garage. They got out, walked around the garage, and stood looking at the spectacle. He felt Addison put her hand in his and squeeze. He put his arm around her.

"Do you think a lot of people are dead, Daddy?"

"I'm afraid so, honey. Let's hope it's not too many."

She nodded, then headed for the garage. Ranger needed tending every day, even if the world seemed to be falling apart.

It was now dark enough for the patio lights and the lights in the pool to come on. Dave looked up at the second floor of the main house, and saw that Karen's lights were on but the drapes were closed.

Dave had a six-inch Meade refracting telescope. He went inside and rescued it from its corner, took it out, and set it up on the concrete at the edge of the pool. He got it focused on the conflagration and panned across it. He could see houses burning, and columns of fire and smoke rising into the night. All around it were the flashing red lights of fire trucks and ambulances and the blue lights of police. When he aimed at north–south streets he saw no taillights at all, only headlights coming his way, in all lanes. They didn't seem to be moving much. The I-10 freeway was a parking lot. He hoped the DJ was telling the truth about the smoke's not being toxic.

He went inside. As he switched on the television his phone vibrated in his pocket. He checked the number, saw it was Dennis Rossi.

"You missed the chance for some serious money," Dennis said, when Dave answered. "I was ready to bet you $1,000 that your little story was bullshit."

"Believe me, I'd have been happy to lose that grand."

"Yeah, I know." He sighed. "I didn't bother to tell Ellen about this when you laid it all out. Didn't take it that seriously. But I've been telling her now, and she wants to hear more. Plus, you must have quite the view of what's going down. Are you up for some company? I'll bring the beer."

"Sure, come on over."

As he hung up he saw Addison standing on the patio looking south, outlined by the towering orange flames. He felt a deep ache inside. He wanted more than anything in the world to protect her from all this. But all he could do was watch, and await developments.

He knew the families of Bob and Dennis, though not well. They had all spent so much time together under the pressure of writing that they didn't feel the need to see each other outside of work. Every year when the series was renewed for another season they would all gather at Bob's Holmby Hills estate for a barbecue, and that was about it. Jenna was not married but usually brought a boyfriend. Roger was divorced and Dave didn't know his ex-wife at all. He knew Roger had two children and that the ex had custody.

Dennis arrived a half hour later with his wife, Ellen, and son, Dylan, who was eight. Addison was there to greet them in Karen's absence. They pulled up into the driveway and she shut the gate behind them. The three got out of their Explorer and walked slowly to the edge of the yard.

"We got glimpses of it coming off the Cahuenga Pass," Dennis said, softly. "But we couldn't see just how . . . huge it is."

There was another bright flash of light, and a few seconds later the thunderclap of a new explosion. Dave heard Ellen gasp.

"It's so awful," she said. "It's so awful."

Dylan was tugging at Dave's pant leg.

"Could I swim in your pool, Mr. Marshall?"

So much for the end of the world as we know it. Dave had to remind himself that Dylan was only eight. He might not have understood the gravity of the situation himself, at that age. Also, looking a little closer, he could see that the child was scared.

He had put the cover over the pool weeks ago, to keep it from evaporating in the summer heat. He planned to use it for drinking water if things got bad, and it looked like they were going to.

"Sorry, Dylan," he said. "The pool-cover motor is broken." Addison started to say something, then caught his gesture and kept mum. Dylan shrugged, and devoted himself to his iPod, where an action movie was playing on the two-inch screen.

"You think it's growing?" Dennis wanted to know.

"It's grown to the west since I started looking," Addison said.

"You can see several fires to the east," Dave said. "I figure those were started by burning debris from the first explosions."

"Those would be houses, right? In . . ."

"Baldwin Village. Windsor Hills. Maybe Crenshaw."

"I don't know those places very well."

"Mostly middle-class homes."

They couldn't see how far the fire had spread to the south, but Dave knew debris must have landed there, too. The flames coming from the center of the oil field seemed maybe a little less intense.

"Would anybody like something to eat or drink?" That was Addison, valiantly trying to be the hostess during her mother's indisposition.

"I couldn't eat," Ellen said. "But I'd like a soft drink, if you have one."

Dave was grateful for the chance to look away from the fire for a bit as he helped Addison find beverages and put out bowls of peanuts. It seemed to calm her down to have something to do. As she served, he brought the television outside on a rolling cart. The helicopter views of the conflagration told them a lot more than they could see themselves. Dave channel surfed compulsively, and no one objected.

Bill Danvers, KCAL, channel 9. He was jogging along, his cameraman trying to keep up. It was a chaotic picture that only stabilized when he paused for a moment to let the camera pan over the flames ahead of him:

"It's pandemonium here on the east side of the fire. I'm trying to make my way toward it, and every street I've tried is filled with cars that are not moving. They have nowhere to go, it's gridlock. Some have driven up into yards, but they can only get so far, and the yards are now gridlocked, too. Many people have abandoned their vehicles and are walking away from the flames, which I can see towering in front of me. In the last block I saw several elderly people sitting on the curb, unable to go any farther, at least for now, and one man who looked as if he was having a heart attack. There was nothing I could do for him. I had to move on."

Melanie Worth, KCBS, channel 2, posed against yellow police tape, flames leaping into the air behind her:

"The heat here is incredible, I don't know how much longer we can stay in this position. Just across the street from me there are a dozen structures on fire, and behind that, I'm told, are literally hundreds of homes burning. There is only one fire engine that I can see. I'm told more are on the way, but it won't be easy to get here. I hear sirens in the distance. I hear a plane approaching . . . There it is, one of those smoke-jumper planes just dumped a load of orange fire retardant on the edge of the flames. I'm afraid it's not doing much good. The fire here is just too broad, too intense. The fire chief has just made an announcement with a bullhorn. He said something about a firestorm. Bob, do you know what a firestorm is?"

Bob, back at the studio, was unsure. Dave switched stations.

Three men sitting at an anchor desk in a frantic newsroom, KNBC, channel 4. One of them seemed to be a fire expert:

"Firestorms are most often seen in big forest fires. If there's enough fuel, and it's spread over a large enough area, the fire begins to create a wind. It blows in from all directions to the center of the storm. These winds can blow up to sixty or seventy miles per hour, perhaps even more. That's gale-force winds, all blowing toward the center of the fire. People nearby can have breathing difficulties as the oxygen in the air is used up. Temperatures can get so intense that trees or buildings at a considerable distance from the storm will ignite just from radiant heat. You can suffer severe burns, even if you're not near the center. Tornadoes of flame can form, called fire whirls, and these are especially dangerous, as they can hop around and spread the fire even farther."

"Do we have a firestorm here, Roger?"

"From what I'm seeing from the helicopter shots, there have been several near the epicenter of the explosion. I'm not sure if they're likely to form in the residential areas that are burning. Some of it will depend on the type of vegetation in those areas. Eucalyptus trees, for instance, can actually explode when the oil inside them is heated enough, and that spreads the fire."

"But you said these storms happen in forest fires."

"Not only there. It all depends on how much fuel there is, and how hot it burns. There is a high fuel load in crowded neighborhoods, and the ones that are burning look crowded to me. Firestorms can happen in cities. Dropping a nuclear weapon, as in Hiroshima, creates an instant firestorm."

"But this isn't a nuclear weapon."

"So we've been told, and I don't see the characteristics of such a bomb. But urban firestorms predate Hiroshima. The Great Fire of London, the Chicago Fire of 1871, and the fire that followed the San Francisco earthquake of 1906 are examples. And during World War Two there were a dozen firestorms caused by conventional bombing. Firestorms killed maybe fifty thousand people in Dresden, and over one hundred thousand in

Tokyo. The most recent urban firestorm I'm aware of was in Oakland in 1991. Only twenty-five people died there, because there was enough time to evacuate."

Dave thumbed the remote. KTLA, channel 5. A helicopter view, with a man and a woman at an anchor desk in a box down in one corner:

"This story has been developing faster than we can keep up with it. We will continue to do our best. We are now a little over two hours since the first explosion. What you're seeing from our channel 5 eye in the sky is the Hollywood Park racetrack. That's about five miles south of the site of the explosion."

"Kathy, do we have any information yet on what caused this?"

"Dale, we've got Jackson Morris, our City Hall reporter, standing by downtown for a news conference by the mayor, which has already been postponed twice. He just told us that none of his sources seem to have any solid information. We can only guess at what the mayor will have to say."

"Kathy, we've just received word that the president of the United States will address the nation in about an hour. We've been told that he is on his way to California, and may make his speech from Air Force One. Has that ever been done before?"

"Not to my knowledge, Dale. But these aren't normal times."

"You said it. First the fuel shortage, and now this."

"They have to be related, don't you think?"

"Well, I don't subscribe to any of the wilder conspiracy theories floating around, but yeah, oil wells burning in Russia, Saudi Arabia, Iran, oil wells burning in Los Angeles. But we never had any video on those earlier fires. All those countries were able to keep a pretty tight lid on the news. All we got were some grainy satellite shots, and no reporter ever penetrated the security cordons around the fires. I just hadn't been aware of how . . . of how *cataclysmic* it all was."

"None of us were, Dale. There are a lot of things we haven't been told, and I don't mind saying, I think we've been lied to by our government. I think it's about time—"

The little box in the corner disappeared, and the larger helicopter shot turned into a maze of those squares that are what static looks like on digital television. Dave was about to click away when the image stabilized again. This time the helicopter shot was the PIP and the anchor desk filled the screen.

Kathy and Dale sat perfectly still for a moment. They seemed to have run out of things to say. Then Dale cleared his throat and glanced down at a sheet of paper.

"Ah . . . Kathy, we're getting a live report from Susie Mihashi at Hollywood Park. Go ahead, Susie."

Dennis leaned toward him in his lawn chair.

"I think Kathy and Dale just got slapped down, big-time."

"I think you're right. You think it was the government or the station management?"

"You think there's a difference, now?"

Susie Mihashi didn't look so good. She was wearing a pantsuit that had started out the day white, but was now streaked with black soot and what looked like globs of tar. Her hair and face were no better. She was being buffeted by a high wind.

"Kathy, Dale, it's getting pretty windy here at Hollywood Park, and the wind is erratic. A fire marshal just told me that there are firestorms to the north of us, and air is being sucked toward them. That's doing battle with the westerly wind we had before. So we never know just what's going to be coming down. Several times . . . Uh-oh, here it comes again."

She held a scarf to her face as a cloud of ash blew around her, tugging at her clothes. More black goo landed on her. She was seized by a coughing fit.

"She should get out of there," Addison said. Dave looked over at her. Her lower lip was trembling. He got up and put his arm around her and she buried her face in his chest. There wasn't much he could say to her, but he murmured encouragement.

"Okay, okay, I'm all right," Mihashi was saying. "As I said, the wind has been shifting. Authorities have established a command post here at the racetrack. Medical personnel have set up a triage center, and I've seen hundreds of people brought in on stretchers. Many more have walked in. I'm told all the hospitals are full. There are a lot of elderly with respiratory problems. They are being given face masks and loaded onto buses, when they are available, and driven away from the fire. Police and rescue are working against great odds, what with the traffic jams and the sheer number of people who are hurt. There have been some severe burns. Doctors have put out emergency calls. If you were a paramedic in the military, they need you down here. I'm told that there are only a few hundred beds in local burn centers. In the past they did drills simulating a nuclear attack, and it was clear even back then that all our facilities would be quickly overwhelmed. And that's exactly what has happened."

"Susie, we've been instructed not to use the word 'nuclear.' " That was Dale, and he sounded furious.

"Sorry, I can't hear you. Anyway, many of these burns are really nasty, very painful, caused by a hot, tarlike substance like you can see on my clothes. It sticks like napalm, and it can keep on burning right into your flesh."

Somebody was honking a horn out on the street. Dave broke away from the group and went to the gate. Outside was Jenna's little red Smart Car. He opened the gate and she drove in and quickly hopped out.

"This is it, isn't it?" she said. "This is what you were talking about."

"I'm afraid so."

"The president is going to be talking to us, is what I heard. That's going to be more bullshit, isn't it?"

"I wouldn't be surprised."

Jenna looked south, and put her hands to her mouth. As they watched, a large area to the east suddenly blacked out. Dave thought it was West Adams and University Park, around the USC campus.

"Power failure," Dave said. "A big one."

"Daddy, I think the wind is shifting."

He had thought the brightness of the flames had been dimming because the fires were burning themselves out, but now he could see that Addison was right. A lot of the black smoke seemed to be coming their way, obscuring their view. Little strings of black tar began drifting down, featherlight like some kind of evil spiderwebs. When he inhaled, he got his first whiff of smoke.

"We'd better move inside," he said.

It didn't take long to relocate, and shortly after they were all inside, the smoke wrapped around them like fog, and pulled a curtain over the awful show they had been watching.

CHAPTER SEVEN

"My fellow Americans . . ."

The president sat behind a desk that could have been any-where, but which they had been told was aboard Air Force One. Behind him were the usual American and presidential flags, but what was unusual were the four generals standing to each side of the flags. They were ramrod straight, eyes forward.

The president looked shockingly bad. He seemed to have aged twenty years since his last press conference. There was a bandage around his head, and Dave was pretty sure he was wearing heavy theatrical makeup around his left eye, as if to cover up a shiner. His right hand was wrapped in a thick bandage.

"Early this morning an attempt was made on my life."

He paused for a moment.

"My wife and I were awakened by the sound of gunfire outside our bedroom. A Marine guard and at least one Secret Service agent betrayed their trust and mounted an armed attack within the White House.

"Marines and Secret Service agents loyal to this country fought a pitched battle with the assassins and killed two of them. During the fight, I am sorry to tell you that two agents and one Marine lost their lives. At this time the head of my Secret Service detail cannot be sure if more conspirators are still alive, holed up in the West Wing. For that reason, I have left Washington and am on my way to a secure location.

"The attempt on my life was only part of a conspiracy that stretched across this great country. It was nothing less than an attempted military coup, organized by the former Chairman of the Joint Chiefs of Staff, General Walter McCoy. Last night, in attacks coordinated with the assassination attempt, a handful of officers at military bases from California to South Carolina attempted to take over the command structure of the United

States military. As of this moment, most of these insurrections have been put down and the conspirators arrested. But fighting is still going on at several sites. I am sad to say that there has been great loss of life among troops loyal to this country.

"As you might imagine, there has been much confusion among the officer corps as regards just who is loyal and who is not. It has sometimes been hard to determine which orders are lawful and which come from the leaders of the coup. We are doing our best at this time to reestablish order and the legitimate chain of command.

"No one should have any doubt: The officers responsible for this outrage will be arrested, or killed if they do not surrender immediately. If arrested, they will be charged with treason and given a court-martial and treated as if their offenses were committed under fire, in combat. If found guilty, they will be executed under a special executive order I have just signed. These executions will be televised to all United States Armed Forces personnel at home or abroad. General McCoy has already received his court-martial, before I boarded Air Force One."

The president paused, and took a drink from a glass of water.

"These loyal Americans you see standing behind me are four of the other Joint Chiefs of Staff. Two of them, Admiral Zenger and General Gomez, were approached this morning by General McCoy and asked to join his rebellion. They refused, and immediately contacted the White House, to find that the attack was already under way. The other two, General Cruickshank and Admiral Baker, had no knowledge of the plot, and have reaffirmed their loyalty to the constitutional chain of command whereby I am the commander in chief of all United States military forces."

There was another pause, longer this time, and Dave began to wonder if the man would be able to go on.

"General McCoy's motives for fomenting this conspiracy may never be entirely known, but a precipitating factor was a disagreement that has been brewing in recent weeks concerning the ongoing petroleum crisis. A split has developed among my advisors, both civilian and military, as to how to proceed in dealing with the situation.

"I must reveal to you now that you have not been told the truth about the origins of the disasters in the oil-producing countries of Asia. Every occupant of this office has told you less than the truth from time to time. A nation must have its secrets. Presidents usually do this only reluctantly. And it was with great reluctance that I allowed a story that I knew to be at least partially false to be communicated in regard to the oil-well explosions.

"But it is now time to tell you the truth, to level with you, the American people. General McCoy was opposed to what I am about to do. I know that at least one of the men standing behind me, Admiral Cruickshank, is also opposed, but he did the right thing. He expressed his opinion, he made his case, and when he was overruled by my executive decision he followed lawful orders, as a good soldier should."

The president wasn't reading from his prepared text when he said that. Dave got the feeling that he was still stunned that a general in the United States of America would *not* follow a presidential order. Well, so was Dave.

"Not a good speech," Dennis commented.

"He hasn't had time to polish it," Jenna agreed. "Too many big words, too many long compound sentences."

"I don't think his speechwriters had their hands on this."

The president looked down at the papers in his hand, back on script.

"We told you that the explosions at the wellheads were the result of terrorist attacks. The fact is, that may be true, but it may not. We withheld what we knew because of the unique nature of these explosions, which were not caused by bombs or any other conventional form of sabotage. We have known since shortly after the wells began to explode that it was the result of the action of a biological agent."

He paused to let that sink in.

"Someone, somewhere, using advanced bioengineering techniques, made an agent, a bacterium, that attacks crude oil and renders it useless as a source of the many things we extract from oil, including gasoline."

"Liar," Dennis said.

"They're still not coming clean," Jenna said.

Dave kept quiet. The plain fact was he thought it unlikely the American people, or he, himself, would ever know if the story the colonel had told was true in all its details. And, at this point, did it really matter? Somebody had made the Prometheus Strain, in a secret high-tech facility.

Maybe some future congressional committee or journalist or historian would find the true source, rooting through old records, but Dave doubted it. If it had come from an American government site, he would expect that anyone who discovered that truth would have a very short life expectancy. This was the sort of secret that would stay buried, not least because it would bring down governments if exposed.

So all he really cared about was what the president was about to say, or what he *hoped* the man would say, which was *what are we going to do about it?*

And he was missing it, sitting there woolgathering while the city burned.

". . . have been unable to determine the source of this plague. There are those—and General McCoy was one of them—who are convinced that one or another of our enemies was responsible. But they have been unable to agree on just who that might be. The initial attacks were made in Saudi Arabia, not on our own soil.

"It would be madness to release this thing on the world, knowing it would spread. That would seem to point to the involvement of one of the more fanatical terrorist groups operating around the world, some of which have a great hatred for the Saudis.

"However, our scientists tell me now that the original bacterium, the one introduced into the great Ghawar oil field on the Arabian Peninsula, would have been able to spread only underground. But bacteria mutate very quickly, and it seems that a strain capable of spreading through airborne spores evolved. It was carried, by the wind, on aircraft, on the clothing of oil workers, and wherever it landed, it found its way to the pumping machinery of oil wells and down to the oil deposits themselves. You have seen the explosive results.

"All our attempts to limit the spread of this plague have so far been to no avail. Oil fields in China, in Indonesia, and many other places have been infected, and have exploded.

"The American government, in cooperation with most governments around the world, has limited press coverage of these events in the hope of avoiding panic, but events so large cannot be hidden forever. The story was beginning to emerge, and it was my judgement that more harm would be caused by continued efforts at information suppression than by a clean break, by finally telling the people just exactly what it is they are all up against.

"As the disaster unfolding right now in the great city of Los Angeles demonstrates, the bacterium has now arrived on our shores. I regret to tell you that oil fields in Alaska have also been destroyed. There have been explosions in California's Central Valley, from Bakersfield to Coalinga. We are certain that the great oilfields of Oklahoma and Texas are next. People in affected areas should follow the instructions of their local authorities."

There was more, but Dave TiVoed it and began channel-hopping again.

Three hours passed without any further explosions, and it began to seem that the fire might be at least contained, though there was little hope of putting it all out anytime soon. They were all glued to the TV. They began to hear distant, smaller explosions with no bloom of flame preceding them.

Jim Weston, KABC, channel 7:

"I've never seen anything like this before, friends. The fire has been spreading relentlessly to the south and east, leaping over streets. Unlike people who live in the hills or on the edges of the metro area, these people on the flats never imagined that an out-of-control inferno could touch them. So shrubs and trees are right up against houses, and the houses and apartment buildings themselves are tinderboxes. All it takes is a burning ember landing on a roof, and soon the whole structure is in flames. There just aren't enough firefighters to stay ahead of the new fires that start up as far as several blocks away.

"But the fire department is now drawing a line, and what a line it is. The fire chiefs won't discuss it with the press, but I've seen it with my own eyes. The entire neighborhood has been evacuated. Police are going door to door, ensuring that no one remains in the homes and apartments. They are breaking down doors or windows if necessary. They have cleared a street, and are now . . . they are blowing up the houses in an attempt to create a fire line.

"The only way this fire is going to be stopped is to deprive it of fuel. This is done all the time in forest and brush fires, but to my knowledge, it has not been done in a city since the great earthquake and fire of 1906 in San Francisco. There, firemen dynamited whole blocks, turned them into rubble. It was the only way to stop the flames from consuming the whole city, and it worked.

"But try telling that to a homeowner whose house has been selected as one of those to be destroyed so that his neighbors downwind can be saved. I've witnessed heartbreaking situations. I've witnessed dangerous situations, too. Some few owners have refused to leave, even though it's obvious that if they stay, they will perish in their own homes. These homes are doomed, from either fire or explosion, but some are reluctant to admit that."

The scene switched to recorded video of a man standing on a lawn, cradling a shotgun in his arms. Police bullhorns told him to drop his weapon. He gave them the finger. He looked like just an ordinary guy, dressed in a golf shirt and khaki shorts, but he was making his stand. Dave's heart went out to him, though he knew the man was impeding the firefighters, and he hoped it didn't end badly. He looked over at Addison, who was transfixed by the sight. He went to her and hugged her, and tried to hug her face to him, but she was reluctant to look away; she kept peeking with one eye.

"This is your last warning. Put down the weapon or we will be forced to remove you." The guy looked a little uncertain for a moment, but then shook his head. Dave thought he was about to raise his weapon, which would have been certain suicide. There was a series of loud popping noises and the man jerked a few times and landed on his back. He could feel the dampness of Addison's tears on his shirt.

But the guy was sitting up. He didn't reach for his shotgun, lying beside him.

"Rubber bullets," Dennis said.

"Beanbags. I think the LAPD uses beanbags. He was too far away for a Taser."

"It's okay, Addison," Dave said. "He's okay."

"That's going to hurt like the devil for a few days," Jenna said. The police hadn't bothered to handcuff him, they were in too much of a hurry. Two cops simply grabbed him by each arm and pulled him to his feet and dragged him away.

The view switched back to the live camera, and the reporter.

He was moving furtively through a hedge. Reporters can sometimes have an inflated sense of their own drama, but Dave had to admit that it was possible the guy would not be welcome where he was going, that stealth might be necessary. Such stealth as could be achieved with bright camera lights shining in his face.

The picture was very jerky as the reporter pushed his way through some dense shrubbery. He fell down once, but scrambled quickly to his feet.

"I've been ordered out of this area," he was whispering. Call it a stage whisper. "But I think you are entitled to see what's going on, even if it's not good for the city's public relations. We're going to kill the lights here . . ." The picture got a lot darker.

"We're switching to night vision now. I don't know if you can see it, the row of houses across the street from me. From where I'm standing, the fire is behind me, no more than ten or fifteen minutes away at the rate it's been traveling."

The picture was now various shades of green, the sort of picture you sometimes saw from reporters embedded in combat units. The houses looked very different, as they were now seeing by infrared light. Dave could see no movement.

There was a distant shout. The entire row of houses exploded in brilliant flashes. Dave could see debris arc into the air and land in the small front yards and the streets.

The wind blowing toward the firestorm quickly swept the dust away, and figures in protective gear ran into the picture. There was the noise of a loud engine, then another. Moving into the picture from the right were two huge bulldozers. They began to push the rubble away from the street. Streams of water arced into the picture.

"I don't know if this will do any good," the reporter was saying. "But the 'dozers seem to be pretty efficient, they're already moving the stuff into piles of—"

There was a shout, and two police officers hurried up to the camera, which suddenly became very jerky.

"Hey, get your hands off my camera! You can't do that!"

But they were doing it. Dave didn't hear anything about them being under arrest, but it was clear the cops meant business. The cameraman stabilized his picture and turned around just in time to capture a nightstick swinging at the lens. The picture went black.

Back in the studio, the anchors were momentarily speechless.

"Well, you saw it yourselves, ladies and gentlemen," said the female part of the team, Amber Goldman. "Tempers are running high in the danger area ahead of the fire. We'll try to reestablish contact with our on-the-scene reporter, Arnold Tylcr."

"Guy's asking for another one of those 'technical problems,'" Dennis said.

"Do you think it will stop the fire, Daddy?"

"Let's hope they know what they're doing, honey."

"All those homes. People's houses. Where are all those people going to go? I'll bet there's hundreds of families that are homeless now."

More like thousands, Dave figured, but why bring that up?

"I know the city has shelters," he said.

"If they don't have enough shelters, maybe we could take in a homeless family. For a while. You know?"

"We'll see, Addie. Some of those folks will have friends or relatives they would prefer to stay with. I'm sure the Red Cross and the Salvation Army will be there soon."

"I just want to help."

"We'll do what we can."

Around midnight they all admitted that they were hungry. They had emptied a bowl of trail mix and several cans of soda pop and beer, but they needed something more substantial. Addison and Dave went into the kitchen to put something together.

Normally he would have fired up the grill and put on some steaks or chicken, but that didn't feel right to him. A cookout was a festive occasion, and how could they be festive with such a horror just outside the windows? He suggested they keep it simple, and Addison agreed.

That idea happened to jibe well with his current mission of cleaning out the freezer. The power might not be reliable soon. There were about a dozen frozen Costco entrees left. He picked a penne pasta and a kung pao pork and popped them into the microwave.

Addison busied herself with making a salad from the last of their lettuce and tomatoes. There was nothing else to put in it but some seasoned croutons. Fresh produce was getting hard to come by.

Jenna left about two in the morning. Dylan had sacked out on the couch right after dinner. Dave invited Dennis and Ellen to spend the night in the guest room, and they agreed. Addison hurried upstairs to see to fresh towels and toothbrushes. Dave was happy to see her so busy.

Dennis put his wife and child to bed, then came down and joined Dave. Earlier they had listened to the rest of what the president had to say. None of it was good.

The bottom line was, the country was running on fumes, and they should not expect more deliveries of crude oil. Not from other countries, not from Alaska, not from Texas. No more crude, period.

"Ships carrying crude oil to our shores have either gone missing, or are known to have exploded. The bacterium causes the crude oil to expand as it solidifies, and we must assume that the missing tankers split open and went to the bottom of the sea.

"For some time now, we have been pumping oil from our own wells and refining it into gasoline and diesel fuel as quickly as we can. The bacterium does not attack refined petroleum products, only crude oil.

"We have also been tapping into the Strategic Petroleum Reserve in Texas and Louisiana and refining that, too."

"What's the Strategic Petroleum Reserve?" Dennis wanted to know.

Dave paused the TiVo. He had learned about the SPR during his research on America's energy resources and consumption.

"They store petroleum in salt domes underground. They hollow the domes out with water, pump out the salty water, and pump in crude. It's all along the Gulf Coast, at Baton Rouge and Lake Charles in Louisiana and two little towns in Texas."

Dave switched the president back on.

"It is that fuel that the nation has been running on for the last few months. There is still some oil in the reserve, but we fear the bacterium will get to it, too. For this reason, I now have to announce even more stringent rationing measures than those the nation is currently struggling under."

There would be no more gasoline sales to private parties. All gasoline not already in the tanks of private cars was now nationalized. The president then called on the governors of all fifty states to mobilize the National Guard to protect the gas in underground tanks at service stations.

Police were urged to park their cruisers and take up foot and bicycle patrols.

Emergency responders were told to limit vehicle response to the direst emergencies. Again, paramedics were to use bicycles whenever possible, and deliver treatment at the scene.

"That's gonna ruffle some feathers," Dennis said.

"No kidding." It didn't sound like a good time to have a heart attack.

"What about the fire department?" Dennis gestured to the fire outside. "How many engines you figure are down there working that fire? What happens when they run out of gas?"

Dave looked out once more at the fire. The center, the oil field, was no longer the realm of towering orange flames. Everything flammable in there had burned. But now there were hundreds of pale blue jets shooting into the sky, like the flames of monstrous acetylene torches. At the ends of these jets were billows of white, painted orange by the flames beneath: the liberated hydrogen from down below combining with oxygen in the air to produce water.

It was hard to be sure, but he thought the structure fires hadn't spread much more to the east in the last few hours. Maybe the fire department was getting a handle on it all, maybe they had managed to establish a perimeter.

But how would they fight future fires without gas for their trucks?

CHAPTER EIGHT

For the next three days they mostly lived in front of the television set. Aside from one trip down the hill, and what he could see from his backyard, Dave's only information about the world came from the TV and the Internet.

Things were happening almost too fast for anyone to keep up with it all, and stories that might have grabbed headlines in previous months were relegated to one-minute summaries. The regular networks ceased all entertainment programming and went to twenty-four/seven news coverage.

Stock trading had been halted on the day of the presidential assassination attempt. The market had already lost 75 percent of its value by then.

Inflation was a matter not of monthly price increases, but daily. Everyone was trying as hard as they could to rid themselves of paper money, which was rapidly becoming worthless, but few were accepting it. The nation had moved to a barter economy in only a few days. Gold and precious stones were accepted in trade. Food was even better. Water was getting expensive. Gasoline could be had on the black market. Payment in gold, thank you, none of those worthless greenbacks.

The great American economic engine—still the biggest in the world—was shuddering to a stop. All around the country people were finding it difficult to get to work, though there were some surprises. People who had a twenty-mile commute each way often found they could cover that distance on a bicycle in roughly the same time it used to take them in their car, on freeways suddenly almost free of vehicular traffic.

A lot of people found that a twenty-mile bike ride when you are not accustomed to it, even on level ground, was not to be taken lightly. There were heart attacks, and emergency response time was averaging two hours. Morgues became crowded with the bodies of overweight businessmen picked up at the side of the road.

But if you survived the bike ride to your job downtown, you often would find that's where your troubles really began. The chances were about fifty-fifty that your job was no longer there. Many professions had become useless, including Dave's own. There was precious little demand for comedy writers.

Millions of Americans were discovering that what they did for a living was no longer something anyone would pay them to do. Stockbrokers were the obvious example. Bankers came to work, but were told they would have to work without salary until the crisis was over. Many other professions were told the same.

Basically, the entire economic house of paper and electronic impulses in computers came to a standstill while everyone waited to see if the government could somehow prop up the currency.

The insurance industry collapsed overnight. Some of them tried to use almost valueless dollars to pay out on policies covering the neighborhoods from Culver City to Crenshaw, where the fire was finally brought to a halt. The government nationalized the banks, then the insurance industry, and froze all transactions. From day to day announcements came from the Treasury and Commerce Departments, from the Federal Reserve, from the Federal Trade Commission, from any and all agencies charged with keeping the economy rolling. They all added up to very little. We have a plan. We'll announce details tomorrow.

But by the third day, hardly anyone was listening to the government at all, only to its representatives in uniforms, and then only at the point of a rifle.

Dave didn't really pay a lot of attention to the economic news. He had nothing in the bank and no investments. He had a mountain of debt that no one was trying to collect. He had spent most of his small hoard of paper money when it began to go south. Technically, he didn't own the house, but no one seemed likely to come around seeking back payments, and no sheriff was likely to show up to evict them. He owned two worthless vehicles. Other than that, all his wealth was now squirreled away in the basement in the form of food, gas, water, and equipment that he hoped would be useful for survival in hard times.

Because hard times were surely coming.

* * *

Soon, the only source of news from abroad was the Internet. And it wasn't the Internet they were used to. There were gaping holes in it. Some countries took total control of cyberspace and imposed a blackout. Web sites vanished, never to return. A lot of what was left was obviously managed. But the Internet remained too anarchic for any institution to totally control, and bits and pieces of information that hadn't been vetted by some government agency intent on preventing panic sometimes filtered out.

There was news of revolutions, violent demonstrations, and widespread panic in the streets of foreign cities. There were bits of video here and there, mostly taken with inconspicuous cell phones and uploaded to transient sites that popped up as quickly as the authorities shut them down.

In many of the former oil-producing countries, anarchy reigned. In countries that imported a large part of their food, hunger was beginning to be felt. Dave saw video of soldiers firing into crowds, of large parts of cities burning, from Cairo to Calcutta.

There was saber rattling in Russia. The new Russian president blamed the West for sabotaging oil fields, and spoke openly of declaring war.

By the end of the first week, it became so hard to get any reliable news from overseas that Dave was unable to confirm reports of a nuclear exchange in the Middle East. Some Web sites said Tehran and Tel Aviv had been bombed, and he saw video of widespread devastation that could easily have been the result of a nuclear weapon. But Israel and Iran both denied it, and showed footage from those cities proving that they still existed. Who could tell if it was old footage? Dave assumed that the people in power, in Washington and London and Tokyo and other world capitals, knew the truth, but they weren't saying much, and even if they had, no one was believing much.

As predicted, the oil fields in Texas and Oklahoma and Canada and many other places blew up in a string of catastrophes that hopscotched across the continent. Now that there was some forewarning, few of them were as deadly as the one in Los Angeles. Geologists knew where the oil was, and they knew where the people were, so over the next several days there were mass evacuations, sometimes just ahead of the explosions.

What most people hadn't known was just how much oil there still was underground in the United States and Canada, and in just how many places. Because they had long been importing foreign oil most people had assumed that America had pumped its own resources dry. That was very seldom the case. There was still oil beneath the surface at Titusville, Pennsylvania, where the first American oil well was drilled. Not a lot of it, compared to other places, but enough to come bursting to the surface and make a huge mess.

The worst loss of life was in and around the Midland-Odessa region, the "oil patch" in Texas. The evacuations were in progress when the still-vast deposits of crude beneath the Texas plains erupted to the surface. Fires ignited, many times larger than the Doheny field. Many people were caught on the jammed highways.

Some became so heavily mired in the sticky goo that shot into the air and rained down on them that they couldn't move their cars, and when they got out, they found they couldn't even walk. Last time Dave heard of it, the authorities in Texas were still trying to rescue thousands of people stranded in cars that looked like they had been dipped in a tar pit. Then the news reports from Texas and Oklahoma dried up.

Before Texas became a news black hole the towns of Winnie and Freeport blew up. These were the communities that sat over the Big Hill and Bryan Mound salt domes, respectively, two of the repositories of the Strategic Petroleum Reserve. Both domes were down to about one-quarter of their capacity, but that was enough, when the bug got to them, to create a massive explosion that wiped out the towns. The good news was that both places had been evacuated the day before. Similar explosions happened in the Bayou Choctaw dome below Baton Rouge and West Hackberry under Lake Charles, Louisiana, and the Spindletop area in Beaumont, Texas.

At one point a television station showed a satellite picture of North America taken the day before. Much of the continent appeared to be on fire. That station experienced "technical difficulties" shortly after that, but the image had been captured on thousands of computers and quickly went viral.

The mayor worked with the Red Cross and the Salvation Army in helping find temporary homes for the thousands of displaced. When Addison heard about that, on the fourth day after the fire, it led to their first expedition down off the hill.

Dave debated going on bicycles, but they planned to cover quite a bit of ground and he figured that, while Addison might be able to handle it, he needed a little more exercise before he was ready to ride a bike all day. So they got out the twin Vespas, the white one for him and the pink one for Addison, and he checked her out on hers.

"We'll go down slowly," he told her. "You don't want to ride the brakes, but you have to be careful not to get going too fast."

"I'll be careful, Dad."

They made it down to Sunset without incident.

"This is spooky," Addison said.

He had to agree with her. That part of Sunset, the strip, was crowded, often jammed, all day long. It was even worse at night, when the trendy clubs came alive with the beautiful people and wannabes. The cars were often bumper-to-bumper, and barely moving.

Today there was nothing. Literally no traffic, not a single automobile to be seen, either being driven or parked at the curb.

But it was not a ghost town. There were people walking. There were far more people on bicycles. They saw one fat, bearded guy in dirty denim with some kind of gang colors on his back, riding a big Harley.

But it continued to be spooky. They drove up to Hollywood Boulevard. Things looked even stranger there. There was not a tourist in sight, and very few people at all. There were no cos-tumed performers in front of Grauman's Chinese Theatre, whose marquee was dark. Farther down the street, very few shops were open. Nobody seemed interested in going to Ripley's or the Wax Museum. Frederick's of Hollywood and all the other stores sell-ing platform boots and outrageous lingerie were all closed.

"Nobody shopping at Whores R Us," Addison said. "I guess there's not a lot of pole dancing going on these days."

* * *

Back on Sunset they heard a siren. They saw a gasoline tanker truck approaching. Dave signaled to Addison to pull over to the curb, and they sat there as three vehicles went by. The first was an LAPD motorcycle cop. There was a shotgun lying across his lap. Then came the tanker with a nervous-looking driver. Behind him was a military Hummer carrying five or six National Guardsmen. One stood behind a .50-caliber machine gun. Other weapons were sticking out the windows. They looked ready to shoot at anything. There had been attacks on gas stations.

It was the same story in the Silver Lake neighborhood, a few people walking the streets, some bicycle riders. The streets had become broad pedestrian promenades.

Next was Echo Park, and that was a little different. Echo Park was one of the older Los Angeles neighborhoods, an easy walk from downtown. At its center was a long lake surrounded by a narrow ring of parkland, a block from Sunset. It used to be almost exclusively Hispanic. There had been a lot of gentrification recently, but there were still plenty of brown faces around. Before the crisis, you would hear a lot of Spanish spoken, and there were tiny carts selling bacon-wrapped hot dogs with sautéed onions and jalapeños, and others with stacks of peeled fruit on ice.

There were no hot-dog vendors that day, but a farmer's market had been set up in the parking lot of the Walgreens on Sunset.

"Let's go look, Daddy," Addison said. They parked and locked their scooters and chained them to a tree.

Dave had no idea where the produce came from, but a lot of it was the sort any self-respecting greengrocer would have tossed in the trash. There was lettuce with brown leaves, apples with blemishes that might or might not have contained worms, sickly-looking onions and squash. The only things that seemed plentiful were oranges, lemons, grapefruit, and limes.

There were a dozen horse-drawn carts that looked like they had been hastily slapped together from cut-down trailers, some of them still painted in U-Haul or Ryder colors. Others were even more primitive, just some plywood nailed together, chicken wire stretched from posts, and automobile wheels welded to axles and bolted to the bottoms.

That market was where they saw their first wood-burning truck. It put all the other improvisations to shame.

It was drawing a crowd. The owner, a small Hispanic man, looked to be in his fifties. He was explaining how it worked, but it was in Spanish.

It was a flatbed, stake-sided Ford. It had led a hard life. The paint was deeply oxidized, and there were dozens of dents in the fenders. There were no bumpers. It looked as if it had sat out under a tree on flat tires for quite a while. It had only one door, on the driver's side.

On the other side was a thing about the size of a home water heater, welded to the frame of the truck. The bottom was a fifty-five gallon oil drum. Clamped to the top of that was an inverted aluminum trash can. The bottom of the can had been cut away and replaced with the lid, which was hinged so it could be swung open. Closed, it left a gap of a few inches all around. Near the top of the oil barrel a pipe about four inches wide was welded to a hole in the barrel's side. Silver galvanized ducting lead away from that hole and made a couple of bends before entering another fifty-five-gallon drum from the top. A similar pipe emerged from the other side and went to the engine, which had some plumbing that led right into the carburetor.

Most of the welds were sloppy, there were dents here and there where things had obviously been bashed with a hammer until they fit, and there was duct tape all over it. The man who was talking about this was as proud as Henry Ford himself, pleased at the attention, and eager to show off his secrets.

He removed the trash can from the top of the assembly and set it on the ground. He removed the lid, and they could all see it was about half-full of wood chips. It was easy to see that gravity would feed the chips down into a smaller chamber in the oil drum beneath. He called it a *despida la camera*, or something like that, which Dave translated as fire chamber. Suspended beneath the fire chamber was an ordinary, large, stainless-steel mixing bowl with a lot of holes punched in it. On the side of the drum was a crank that, when the man turned it, clanked against the bowl and shook it.

"Para las cenizas," the guy said, with a smile.

"Ashes," Addison said. "I think he said that bowl is for the ashes."

Dave had forgotten that Addison's Spanish was much better than his, both from two years of classes and from having a few Hispanic friends in school. And it did look like ashes were falling through the holes in the bowl.

The guy opened the second drum, which was divided into two chambers, both of them filled with wood chips that were rather darker than the chips in the trash can. Addison was concentrating on what he had to say.

"Something like, the gas comes through the pipe and into the filter," she said. "It . . . cleans the impurities so it won't clog the . . . something."

He could see that the hot gas produced by burning the wood chips would be forced down through the wood chips on one side, then back up though the other.

"Can you really run a truck on wood?" Addison asked.

"Looks like it."

In response to urging from the crowd, the man reassembled the contraption. He stuffed a wad of newspaper into a hole, and lit it. In a few minutes wisps of smoke curled out of the top of the trash can. The man turned a crank that seemed to get a flow of air entering the fire chamber, running some kind of blower, but he didn't keep at it long. It seemed that, once you got it going, it would be self-sustaining. Wood chips would fall from the hopper into the fire chamber on their own.

A second man, much younger, inserted a crank into a slot that hadn't been on the truck when it left the Ford factory. The truck was old enough that there were no electronics under the hood.

The younger man turned the crank and the engine coughed, and didn't catch. With a second crank it coughed again, made a wheezing sound, and then began to turn over smoothly. The whole Rube Goldberg assembly clattered like bedsprings in an earthquake, but it was definitely running.

Everyone around burst into applause.

It wasn't until he got back home and logged onto the Internet and did a search that Dave fully understood the wood-burning truck.

He hadn't known that, during World War Two, when gasoline was scarce to unobtainable, over a million vehicles in Europe were powered by wood-burning engines. They were bulky and balky, but they worked. In Denmark, 95 percent of trucks, boats, tractors, and electrical generators were powered that way.

The process was called gasification, and it worked with wood or coal, peat, lignite, or charcoal. Gasoline first has to be turned into a vapor in an engine. An engine will burn coal gas or wood gas as readily as gasoline.

For once, it seemed that FEMA, the Federal Emergency Management Agency, had been on the ball. They published a sixty-six-page booklet, available for free online, that detailed how to make a gasifier from parts you might find lying around your garage. If not, any hardware store could supply you with what you needed.

Dave wondered about the efficiency of a wood-burning car. It wasn't hard to find out. One ton of wood equaled about one hundred gallons of gas. That meant that twenty pounds of wood would take you as far as one gallon of gas. Which sounded like a lot, until he found out that gas weighs about six and a quarter pounds per gallon. So you had to carry about three times as much wood, by weight, as you would have carried in gasoline.

Weight wasn't the most important factor, though. Volume was the problem. You didn't shove logs into the gasifier, you used wood chips, which were bulky. And the wood had to be dry. Powering a small passenger vehicle was probably going to be more trouble than it was worth, but there was little problem with a large hopper of wood chips on a medium-sized truck. And the heat from the burner was used to dry out wood for tomorrow.

It looked like they were headed back to wood- and coal-burning technology.

Leaving Echo Park, they went down Figueroa and passed the Original Pantry, which had opened in 1924 and boasted that it had never closed since then. It was dark, and a chain and heavy padlock had been threaded through the door handles. Karen and he had eaten there many times during their scrabbling days, and the leftovers would usually feed them for two more meals.

Nearby was L.A. Live, the entertainment complex that had

been built around the Staples Center and the Convention Center. The Nokia Theatre was there, along with a Regal multiplex, the Grammy Museum, lots of restaurants, and the Ritz-Carlton and Marriott hotels. It featured huge electronic signs that were usually bursting with color and noise. Today they were all dark and silent. They puttered through it, almost alone, until they reached Staples. There, the streets were blocked off with plastic barriers. There were National Guardsmen standing by their Hummers and they had their weapons in their hands, but they weren't stopping anyone from walking through.

Inside, they saw hundreds of bikes and dozens of scooters all parked behind a long counter. They walked their Vespas up to a female police officer and she tied baggage claim checks to them and showed them where to park, then tore off part of the checks and handed them the stubs.

"There been a lot of thefts?" he asked her.

"Like you wouldn't believe. Don't ever leave those things unattended."

Dave thanked her for the advice, and she directed them past a tunnel corridor that said it led to Sections 7, 8, 304, 303, 102, and 103. Addison paused.

"Are the people in there, do you think?"

"Probably."

"Can we go take a look?"

They came into the arena about halfway between the expensive seats down below and the cheap seats above. Below them was the big rectangle that could be frozen over for Kings hockey games, where they would install the wood floor for Lakers basketball. It was bare concrete now. On the side opposite there were rows of folding tables. Sitting behind the tables were maybe a dozen men and women. Behind them were long lines of people shuffling along with papers in their hands.

They went down to the floor and were directed to a table at the end. The line there was a little shorter than the others. They got at the end of it. These were the people volunteering to take in the homeless. They didn't have the exhausted and frightened look of the people in the other lines.

Eventually they sat in metal folding chairs facing a woman Dave judged to be in her mid-fifties. She had white hair, slightly disheveled, and a kindly face. She reminded him of his third-grade teacher, Mrs. Wyatt. She removed a form from a clip-board and replaced it with a fresh one. She looked up at them and smiled tiredly.

"I'm Polly Sessions," she said. "I'm a welfare case worker for the city of Los Angeles."

"Dave Marshall, and my daughter, Addison."

"I'm pleased to meet you, Dave, Addison."

"We wanted to see about taking in someone who is homeless from the big fire," Addison said.

"Well, bless you. It's a great thing you're doing."

"It was Addison's idea," Dave said, and she blushed.

"You must be very proud of her."

"Couldn't be prouder."

She turned the clipboard around and handed him a pen.

"What I need for you to do first is fill out this form. And I'll need to see some identification from you, Mr. Marshall."

"Why don't you do this, Addie?" he said, and dug in his pocket for his wallet.

"We will of course have to run a routine check on you. We can't legally place children in a home without checking the criminal databases. I'm sure there will be no problem."

Dave hoped they didn't do a credit check. He didn't want Addison to know just how deeply in debt they were. He didn't see what bad credit would have to do with their ability to provide shelter for a homeless family, but with the bureaucracy you never really know.

Addison finished the form and handed it to Polly. The social worker scanned it, and then frowned. Had he missed something? Were they deficient in some way?

"The confirmation process is running slow," she said. "Normally, we would be able to approve you and send some people out to you that very day. But we have a problem. Not your fault, I assure you. But you live in the hills."

"Why is that . . ."

"Transportation. With the fuel situation there's very few buses, and there are none that run anywhere near your home even when they *are* running. Almost no cars, most of our clients are on foot. We don't expect you to provide food for your guests—though we hope you would share your cooking facilities—which means they will have to come into one of our emergency food-distribution stations every few days. There are no stations within five miles of your zip code. The children would need to go to school, and many of the parents would need to get to work.

"Mr. Marshall, we've placed over five thousand people so far, and we have about ten thousand to go. So far, we've been able to place most of them on the flats, and much closer to their old neighborhoods. I don't know how much longer we'll be able to do that. The public response has been good, but already some are beginning to suffer from what we call 'sympathy fatigue.' People are realizing that this temporary situation could go on for a long time."

"Like it did in New Orleans."

"Exactly. We're also starting to see an attitude of 'every man for himself.' Fewer people are coming in to volunteer. What I'm going to do is put your names on a waiting list. Some of your neighbors in the hills are already on it. If and when we run out of suitable homes down here, we will call you. Okay?"

Addison said okay, but he could see she was frustrated. Dave had to admit that he had mixed feelings, himself. He truly did want to help out. But he was not as starry-eyed as his good daughter, not eager to share his home with strangers, and most of all, he was feeling the 'every man for himself' syndrome more with each passing day.

Addison wanted to see more of the relief operation, so when they were done they walked around Staples to the Convention Center behind it.

There were several large tents erected in the small plaza along Figueroa Street. The odors of cooking came from inside, and a long line snaked from the Convention Center entrance and into the tent. On the other side, tables had been set up, and they were jammed with people eating. As soon as they were through, they were hustled along to dump their paper plates and plastic sporks into overflowing Dumpsters. People eyed them suspiciously as they passed.

"Are they angry with us?"

"Angry with the world, I suspect," Dave said. "I think it's starting to sink in that this may last a long time."

"How long, Daddy?"

"I wish I knew."

Addison had lost her enthusiasm for exploration. Dave knew how she felt, as if they were gawking at these people's misfortune, but he wanted to see inside the Convention Center before they went. He thought most residents of the city still didn't know just how bad the situation was, and he wanted the best information he could get.

They climbed two flights of shut-down escalators, walked across a terrazzo floor that had constellations inset against a blue night sky. A glass atrium crisscrossed with massive white girders towered over them. It was his first time in the center, and he realized it was huge. There was lots of trash swept hastily into piles against the walls.

At the end of the atrium were rows of doors, all of them standing wide open. People were coming and going in both directions, and they saw lines leading into the restrooms. They could smell the restrooms, too, and dirty diapers, and the odor of stale human sweat.

They went through the doors and were in a vast, high-ceilinged room. There was no way for them to get a real idea of just how many people were in there, because some of the moveable walls that were used to separate exhibitors when a large convention was there had been placed to form small rooms. Elsewhere blankets and sheets had been draped over lines tied between these walls. It gave a little privacy, but not much.

They walked along the edges of the vast temporary indoor city, looked down the lanes between rows of rooms. They couldn't see the ends of the lanes. People were doing laundry in buckets and hanging it out to dry on poles, which probably accounted for the dank humidity in the place. It smelled worse in there than it did outside. He saw some chess players and of course there were children playing, but most of the adults were just sitting around with very little to do.

"Let's get out of here," he said. Addison nodded. Her eyes were moist with tears.

They reclaimed their scooters and drove away.

CHAPTER NINE

Dave was eager to get home, but they still had some daylight left and since he didn't expect to be coming down off the hill very frequently, he decided to take a different route home. So they detoured through Chinatown and over the Los Angeles River—all but dry, as it always was in the summer—and onto San Fernando Road. Things were much the same on this side of town as they had seen elsewhere: gas stations guarded by the military, no automobiles, a lot of bicycles and pedestrians, and a few motor scooters. They turned down Los Feliz and crossed back over the river and then made a right into Griffith Park.

Immediately they heard the roar of chain saws.

There were city trucks parked all along Crystal Springs Drive, the main road through the park. The gas-powered chain saws were being used to bring the trees down. Once they were on the ground, other workers moved in and began cutting the branches into manageable lengths. There were men splitting chunks of wood, and several wood chippers howling as the downed trees were fed into their hungry mouths.

"Daddy," Addison shouted, "they're ruining the park!"

"I know, honey, I know. It's just something we're going to have to get used to."

They came to a line of white sawhorses and not far beyond them was a huge flatbed truck, the kind used to carry big cranes to construction sites. A section of chain-link fence had been taken down and a second huge truck had been driven over the dirt and set up with hydraulic braces out at the sides to keep it from tipping over. On the truck was a crane big enough to lift a locomotive. And that's exactly what it was doing.

They were just north of Travel Town, the outdoor railroad

museum. It was another place his family had gone when Addison was younger. It was a collection of old railroad equipment: about a dozen engines from various eras, and maybe twice that number of rolling stock—freight cars, passenger cars, and the like. Most of it had seen better days, with wood crumbling, glass broken, metal rusting.

A man noticed them and came in their direction, smiling. He was in his seventies but walked with a spry step. He was wearing denim pin-striped overalls and a matching hat with the SANTA FE logo on it, and looked the very picture of a railroad engineer.

"Afternoon," he said, with a tip of his hat.

"Same to you," Dave said. "What's going on here?"

The smile grew even wider.

"You could call it a resurrection, I guess. We're just about ready to load old Number 3025 onto this truck and bring her back to life."

"No kidding?" Addison said.

"I wouldn't kid you, young lady. And what's your name?"

"I'm Addison."

"Nice name. I'm Burt Henrikson."

Dave introduced himself and shook the man's hand.

"The last time I was here," Addison said, "I remember that all the engines looked kind of . . . rusty."

Henrikson laughed.

"More than kind of. There's holes in the boilers and the fuel tanks and just about everywhere else. But holes can be patched, and we figure we can probably get seven or eight of these old ladies back on the tracks."

"These are wood burners?" Dave asked. "Coal burners?"

"Some of them started out that way, but they were converted to oil a long time ago. But there's nothing to stop us from converting them back. One of the jobs we hope to do when these engines are working again is hauling coal. Did you know that Los Angeles gets half its electricity from burning coal?"

"As a matter of fact, I did know that," Dave told him.

Henrikson eyed him narrowly.

"Not many people do. You've been doing some research, I'll bet, because those idiots on television aren't talking about things like that. I've even called them up, tried to tell them some of it, and they say they aren't interested."

"Some people think they're being censored."

"Could be. Would you like to see what we're doing, little lady?"

"I sure would!"

"Well, come on, there ain't nothing secret about it. Watch your step."

It was quite an operation, getting the old locomotive off its dead-end siding and onto the waiting flatbed truck. There were a dozen men working at it, and the crane operator moved it very slowly.

"Old Southern Pacific Number 3025," their new friend said, with satisfaction. "Built in 1904, over a hundred years old. She came here in 1952. Considering all that time in the sunshine and rain, she's in pretty good shape. Seventy feet long, 115 tons."

People seldom realize just how gigantic the old steam locomotives were until they stand next to one, and this was a behemoth. She looked even larger, somehow, dangling at the end of massive chains.

"Those four driver wheels are some of the biggest ever made, eighty-one inches high. With a full head of steam, she could hit a hundred miles per hour on the coast route to San Francisco."

"I gather you're a railroad man, Mr. Henrikson."

"Just Burt's okay. Yeah, I'm a retired engineer, but I never got a chance to handle anything like this baby. Luckily, we still have some old-timers around who know steam; otherwise, we'd never try to repair those boilers."

"I hope they know what they're doing," Addison said. "Couldn't they blow up?"

"They sure could. But I trust these guys, they're going to make these things stronger than when they were new. And at last, I'll be able to drive one of them. Somebody's got to do it, or Los Angeles is going to run out of coal in a week."

The rest of Travel Town was also abuzz with activity. Many men, most of them Burt's age or older, were swarming over half a dozen of the big black engines. There was the blue glare of acetylene torches, the screech of saws cutting metal, and the clang of hammers. They could see someone pounding the end of a metal bar glowing white-hot, and then plunging it into a barrel of water. Dave didn't doubt that they'd get at least some of them up and running. It was a labor of necessity, but also a labor of love.

"I hope you folks have laid in a lot of supplies," Burt said, seriously.

"We're doing okay."

"And you better have some way to cook, other than electricity. I'm as proud as can be of these old steamers, but they're not going to be able to bring in a tenth of the coal we'll need to keep everything running."

Burt suddenly didn't look so happy.

"We're going to be shipping food, too, but I doubt we can keep up with the demand." He sighed. "There's over two hundred railroad museums in California, but only a few of them have much in the way of steam engines. The state museum in Sacramento has twenty engines that are pretty much ready to roll, but most of the others have only one or two, or not even that many."

"What about those diesel-electric ones they use today? Can they be converted to coal or wood?"

"Guys are working on that right now. I'm dubious, but I wish them luck. Of course, they're going to need some of the coal we haul in from back East, too. Bottom line, there's just not going to be enough of anything to go around. I'd say get out of Los Angeles, but it may already be too late."

Burt's words kept repeating themselves in Dave's head as they got on the Vespas again. Any way he looked at it, getting out of the Los Angeles area seemed like the smart thing to do. There were just too many people, not enough arable land to support a tiny fraction of them, and not enough water to grow enough food.

But was it too late already? He decided to make one more plea to Karen when they got home.

They went south through the pass on West Cahuenga Boulevard. At the beginning of Mulholland Drive they crossed over the freeway because Dave wanted to see the state of Lake Hollywood, which, along with Castaic Lake, supplied Los Angeles with its drinking water. But just around the first curve of Lakeridge Place on their way up the hill they encountered a roadblock manned by National Guard troops. They were told that only residents were being allowed through. They thanked them, and went on down the road to Hollywood, and then home.

Addison went off to feed her horse and Dave stood there in the early evening looking south over the devastated city. Wisps of black smoke still rose from the Doheny fire. Much farther south he could see three large fires burning. When he turned on the television he could find no mention of them. Censorship? Or were there just too many other stories to report?

That evening Dave made a last trip in the Escalade, with a list of things he hoped to find. He stopped at Vons. It was like a tornado had hit the store. Entire sections had been wiped out: canned goods, cake mixes, baking needs, beverages. Frozen-food lockers were turned off; there was nothing inside them. Dairy cases were empty. Toilet paper, paper towels, napkins, paper plates, plastic forks, all gone. Dog and cat food, the same. Some small amount of produce had been available, but as soon as a stock boy brought out a box of apples people filled their carts. There was a long line, as only one checker had shown up for work.

His route back to the street took him past the loading dock at the back of the store. He saw two men wearing VONS badges passing cardboard boxes to some rough-looking guys with a truck. They stopped and looked at him for a moment. He pointedly looked away. None of his business.

In the morning Dave went out on the edge of the patio with his laptop. That way he could look out over the city as he bounced around on the Internet.

There had been outages every night since the fire. Many of them he could see from his perch in the hills, others he heard about on the news from more distant parts of the Southland. They were "rolling blackouts," dictated by lost generating capacity. His neighborhood in the hills had only suffered two blackouts, and they were brief. Some nights it looked to him as if some areas of the city were not getting power all night long. But the lights of the downtown skyscrapers blazed as brightly and as wastefully as they ever did before the crisis. At night the city had become a vast, irregular checkerboard, with squares that were lighted and squares that were almost completely black.

The local news was good only for the large, obvious stories that couldn't easily be swept under the rug. For any other news he had come to rely on blogs. Many of them came from disgruntled, angry, or frightened city workers who knew things that they felt the general populace should know.

It was from an anonymous blog that he heard that natural gas was coming into the city fitfully, if at all, from Texas, Louisiana, and Utah. He didn't know too much about the relationship between crude oil and natural gas, but he knew they were bound up together in some way. Wikipedia told him that the essential difference between a natural-gas field and an oil field was that one had a lot of gas and a little oil, and the other had a lot of oil and a little gas. They both came from the same source, which was anaerobic decay of ancient organic matter, far beneath the earth's surface. It seemed likely to him that, if all the Midwestern oil fields had blown up, as they had heard, collateral damage had probably destroyed gas wells and pipelines, too.

This wasn't good news for power generation, as Los Angeles got a quarter of its electricity from burning natural gas. It wasn't good for consumers, either. The morning of their trip downtown he had turned on the stove to fry some eggs and nothing had come out of the burner. It had stayed off all that day, and all that night, and the next morning it was still off. He made a note to set up the propane stove, and fixed himself a bowl of cold cereal with powdered milk.

Addison joined him on the patio with her own breakfast, two pieces of toast and a jar of sugarless fruit preserves.

It was eight fifteen in the morning.

The umbrella on the pole that went through the center of the heavy wrought-iron circular table began to sway back and forth. The coffee in his cup jiggled, and then some of it slopped out onto the glass tabletop. Off to his left he saw an undulation of the water in the pool, beneath the cover that he had been keeping in place to prevent evaporation.

"Earthquake," Addison said, in a reasonably calm voice. He found himself on his feet, not quite remembering standing. Addison came to him. He put his arm over her shoulder. If it got any worse, he'd get them down on their hands and knees.

"What about Mom?" she asked.

"She knows what to do. Best stay out here."

The shaking stopped.

Addison was hugging his waist. The waves in the pool made a few more laps, but the cover soon damped that out. It was very quiet. Then Karen screamed.

He hurried into the house and bounded up the stairs, trying to imagine what he might confront when he got there.

Karen was sitting on the bed, in her nightgown. Her head was thrown back and she was taking a deep breath, ready to let out another scream. She seemed completely unhurt. He went to her side and sat, put his arm around her, and instead of screaming she dissolved in tears.

"Dave, make it stop!" she cried.

"Hush, hush," he whispered, and kissed the top of her head. He noticed that she didn't smell very good. "It's over. It stopped."

She continued to cry. Addison appeared in the doorway and he gave her what he hoped was a reassuring thumbs-up. She nodded, and backed away.

"You're not hurt?"

She shook her head. He kissed her hair again.

"No big deal, honey. No big deal. I'd say it was a 5.5. We've ridden out worse than that."

She nodded, but still didn't say anything.

"Maybe you'd like to come down and join us for breakfast," he ventured.

There was a long pause, and then, "Maybe I will."

He felt unreasonably happy. It would be her first trip downstairs in a week. Addison had been bringing meals up to her, and bringing them down mostly uneaten. They hadn't talked about it, as one doesn't talk about the crazy old aunt hidden away in the attic. When she turned to face him, he was shocked. She was wearing no makeup and her hair was a mess. There were dark circles under her eyes, which were alarmingly red. Her cheeks were hollow. He thought she had lost weight. Her lips were trembling, and she swayed slightly as she tried to get up.

"Just let me freshen up a bit . . ." she said, vaguely, and started off toward the bathroom, taking small, careful steps.

Addison was looking in the open door.

"Is she all right?" she asked, timidly.

He got up and put his hand on her shoulder, steered her out of the room, and pulled the door partly closed behind him. He guided her toward the stairs.

"No, she's not," he said. There seemed little point in lying about it. They didn't say anything more. Over the last weeks they had become a team, so not much needed to be said, much of the time. One of the things they didn't say, but Dave was sure they both knew, was that it would be a much stronger team if they could just get Karen to suit up for the game.

Some books and various bric-a-brac had been shaken off the shelves. It didn't take long to sort that out. In the kitchen some of the cupboard doors had opened and some canned goods had rolled onto the floor. One jar of peaches had shattered.

While Addison and he were cleaning up the breakfast dishes there was another mild shock. Karen had settled herself in front of the television, but didn't seem to be seeing much, and the sound was muted. She got to her feet and all three of them stood silently for a moment, waiting to see if this was just the beginning of something big, or merely an aftershock. When nothing had happened for a bit over a minute, she sat back down.

Karen had showered, washed and combed her hair, and applied some light makeup. Addison and Dave sort of tiptoed around her, neither of them quite daring to start up a conversation, and she didn't seem inclined to talk to them.

Eventually he went outside. It was 10:35 A.M.

Something out there was not right.

Helicopters were now a rare sight over the Los Angeles Basin, but two were hovering in the middle distance. They were due southeast from him, little gnats circling silently. They were about three or four miles away, which put them around the Park La Brea area.

Park La Brea is an interruption of the orderly north–south east–west grid of streets down on the flats, situated just north of the Miracle Mile on Wilshire. It covers 160 acres. The streets are laid out in a diamond pattern. To the west are two-story apartment blocks, and to the east are eighteen or twenty mid-rise apartment buildings. Just to the north was the Hollywood Farmer's Market, where he had had many a lunch with his posse and his family, and The Grove, a high-end shopping complex. To the south was the Los Angeles County Museum of Art. Just to the east of LACMA was the place that often came as a surprise to out-of-towners: the La Brea Tar Pits. Many people have heard of the tar pits, of course, but most don't realize that they are right in the middle of town, on busy Wilshire Boulevard.

Now there was the George C. Page Museum, which displayed the bones of mammoth, mastodon, giant ground sloth, saber-toothed tiger, and American lion—all the big animals that had thrived in the area.

The Page Museum was like an earthen bunker, partially underground, with sloping grass-covered sides. In front of it was the largest tar pit, looking deceptively calm and inviting beneath a few inches of water. You could easily see how animals would be lured there, to bog down hopelessly in the sticky goo beneath. There was a sad life-size tableau on one edge of the pit: a family of Columbian mammoths, the male half-buried and struggling to escape, while the mother and baby cried out to him from the shore. In the middle of the pond, swamp gas bubbled constantly to the surface.

Something looked out of kilter.

He got his telescope and brought it to bear on the buildings of the art museum. The one farthest to the east was an irregular shape, and housed the collections of Japanese art, including a fine selection of tiny netsuke that he loved. To the west of that was the Hammer Building and the Ahmanson Building, and across the entrance plaza was the Broad Contemporary Art Museum, and LACMA West, housed in the old May Company building at Wilshire and Fairfax.

The Ahmanson Building was leaning. The west side looked to be a lot higher than the east side. There was a big gap between it and the Broad, and it looked like part of the ceilings of both buildings had collapsed. On the other side of the plaza, the Broad was leaning in the other direction. It was as if something big was trying to force its way to the surface right beneath the plaza.

He moved the scope and zeroed in on the big tar pool just off Wilshire Boulevard. He couldn't find it. Where it had been, a black cone, like a volcano, had formed and spilled over into the street and covered much of the lawn between the Japanese pavilion and the Page Museum. The life-size mammoth sculptures had vanished. As he watched, the huge heap of tar heaved, heaved again, and spit out a thick black goo that ran down the sides of the new formation in all directions.

He became aware that Addison was standing beside him.

"Can I see?" she asked, quietly.

He moved aside and let her look through the telescope.

He didn't know why the destruction of LACMA should shake him so, but it did. It couldn't compare to the tragedy of people killed and left homeless by the explosions and fires from the Doheny field. But there was something about the accumulated treasures of the human imagination being engulfed by a substance that looked like primordial ooze that was profoundly disturbing. It was something he had never seen. It struck him as something new and unprecedented, like watching the collapse of the Twin Towers on 9/11. Cultures from all over the world were represented in those big buildings down there, and it looked as if it were all being swallowed up.

He found some television coverage.

"The police are trying to prevent people from entering the damaged buildings," a reporter on the ground was saying, "but there are not enough of them, they're spread too thin, and most of them are exhausted from endless double shifts, and the whole force is depleted from resignations and inability to get to work, as I revealed here in a special report two days ago. And, frankly, I get the impression that they just don't care that much. One cop told me he had more important things to do than to protect works of art, and—his words—'idiots who run into a collapsing building.'

"Museum staff are risking their lives, carrying priceless works of art out to waiting trucks. There are also quite a number of volunteers. Frankly, it's hard to say if all of them are . . . well, there is some suspicion that looting is going on, right under our noses. I spoke to a curator a few moments ago, and she was in tears. She said they were only able to save a part of the paintings collection. Most everything else—statues, pottery, furniture, things like that—has already been destroyed or is too heavy to move without special equipment, which they don't have and wouldn't be able to move into these precarious buildings anyway."

He went on like that for a while. Then Addison shouted.

"Daddy, it's falling down!"

He could see it on the television, probably better than she could. The reporter was running and the camera was jolting, but he could see another wall of the Ahmanson collapsing, right into the street. Everything was enveloped by a dust cloud for a moment, and then the shattered building loomed out of the dust.

"It's really happening, isn't it?"

Karen had caught him off guard. She was standing off to one side and a little behind him. Her arms were crossed in front of her as if she were cold.

"Really happening?"

"What you said. That crazy story about the man who wanted revenge, and made something that would destroy all the oil in the world."

"We'll never know if that story was literally true," he said. "But real? It's happening right in our backyard."

They watched in silence for a while. When she spoke she still didn't look at him.

"I volunteered down there at LACMA. Remember?"

"I think so." The truth was she had worked for so many causes over the last few years that he hadn't been able to keep them all straight.

No, that was not fair. He hadn't really been paying attention to her projects. The fact was that for a long time he had been a workaholic, largely absent from her life. He had been coming to the reluctant and painful realization over the last months, thinking about how their relationship had fallen apart, that he was at least as responsible for that as she was.

"I've been very depressed," she said.

"No. Really?" The dry understatement was the sort of thing the old Karen would have caught, and probably even appreciated. But she gave no sign she had noticed.

"I haven't really been here," she went on. "Not for you, not for Addison. The last few weeks have been sort of a blur. I think I slept a lot."

"That's what I do when I'm depressed. I guess everybody does." Once more, it was as if he hadn't spoken. He decided just to listen.

"And then, looking out the window just now. The museum is falling into the earth. Just like those mammoths so many years ago. All their dreams and aspirations, swallowed up in blackness." He didn't point out that the museum was being raised up from below. He understood her analogy. "I remember once looking at that tableau of the mammoths at the Page. I almost cried. Silly, I guess. But that mammoth, slowly sinking into the tar. Do you think he had dreams?"

"I can't speak for mammoths," he said. He cautiously took her hand. He realized he was treating her like a recovering mental patient, treading carefully. "I've heard that elephants try to tend to their sick or wounded. Maybe mammoths did, too. And many animals care for their young, will fight for them against great odds if they have to. I guess that qualifies as a dream."

"He didn't know it, that mammoth," she went on, "but his whole race was doomed. Before long there would be no more mammoths. And I wondered, was it some consolation to him that his mate and his child would go on? Even if the race of mammoths was soon to die out?"

He didn't like where this was going. He gently turned her to face him.

"Karen, this is a great tragedy, but it is not the end of the world."

"It isn't? It sure looks like it."

"I know it does, but there's hope. We will not die out, the human race will get through this. The big question for me lately has been, will *we* get through it? Me, and you, and our child. Our family."

"I haven't really been a part of the family lately."

"No. You haven't. But that was then. All it takes now is for you to . . . I know this isn't as easy as it sounds, you can't just turn off depression, but . . . honey, we *need* you. Addison and me. We need you to buckle down like I know you can. If we work at it, we can survive this. I know we can. But we have to have your help."

When she finally looked at him there were tears in her eyes.

"I'll try."

"That's all I ask."

"I guess there are two things I need to do then." Karen sighed.

"I'm eager to hear what they are."

"First . . . do you think it's still possible for us to drive to Oregon?"

"I think it would be difficult, but I wouldn't say impossible. Not quite like crossing the Donner Pass in a covered wagon in the winter."

She looked at him to see if he was kidding. The truth was, of course, he didn't know if it was possible.

"I've heard some communities have been setting up road-blocks on Interstate 5," Dave said. "A lot of towns feel like they've already taken in all the extra people they can handle. But they might not be hostile if we could convince them we'd just be passing through."

"Do you still think going to Oregon is a good idea?"

"It's hard to say. It's the trip that worries me. I don't think there's any question that being in Oregon right now would be better than being here. They've got plenty of water and they should have plenty of electricity. They've got more arable farm-land, and the farmland is closer to the population centers."

She sighed.

"The time we should have left was back when you first suggested it, wasn't it?"

"No question."

"My fault."

"Well, Karen, I could say yes and beat you up about it, I guess. But I've thought about that a lot, and I can't say that if the situation had been reversed, if *you* had come to *me* with such a crazy story and no real evidence to back it up, I might not have believed you, either. It's as if I'd told you we were about to be invaded by Martians. So, I think it's best if we just pass over all that and deal with the situation we have now."

"I will if you will."

He wanted to hug her, but she was still keeping a physical distance from him and he wasn't sure she was ready for that.

CHAPTER TEN

Karen called her brother in Oregon to ask if they would be welcome, assuming it was possible to get there at all.

It took her a while to get through. Phone service had been getting spotty, especially the landlines. But cell service was a bit more reliable, and after several attempts she got her brother Martin on the line. She put him on the speakerphone.

Martin and Karen were not close. He was eleven years older than her; she was an unplanned baby. Martin had been a high-school and college basketball star, almost made the NBA, and had worked as an assistant college coach and then as head coach at a Portland high school. He lived with his wife of twenty-seven years in a large home on two or three acres about twenty miles east of the city. The area was semirural, with some larger spreads where actual farming was done.

Martin and his wife, Brenda, were deeply religious, born-again Baptists. Three of their five children had scattered to distant colleges in the East, while their youngest daughter continued to live at home. Their contact with Karen and Dave was largely limited to exchanging Christmas cards.

Dave was counting on Martin's sense of Christian charity to allow them to squat in one of their spare rooms until he could work out a way to make a living. He was hoping that Karen could sell that proposition.

Martin and Brenda were sick with worry about three of their children. The eldest, who had been working for her master's degree in Seattle, had made it home just before the gas rationing began.

The other three were undergraduates in New York, Atlanta, and Columbus. The situation in Georgia and Ohio was not good—it wasn't good anywhere in the country—but things were still more or less under control. Both those children, a boy and a girl, had been in contact in the last few days.

Jenny, the daughter in Ohio, wanted to come home and was trying to get a ride on one of the buses the Ohio State engineering department had been adapting to burn biodiesel, ethanol, or coal. These refugee vehicles had been setting out regularly during the last few weeks on circuitous routes aimed at getting students back to their homes, but there were not enough of them yet.

Herbert, who was a junior at Georgia Tech, was electing to tough it out in Atlanta. It seemed he had a local girlfriend whose family had taken him in, and he still believed that education could go on at some level during the crisis, though most people were dubious that classes would begin in the fall in most places in the U.S.

They were worried about both of them, but nothing like they worried about their son Ben, twenty-five years old, who had just completed his first year of postgraduate study at Columbia University in New York. They hadn't heard from him in over a week.

"Phone service is out all over Manhattan," Martin said. "I've been trying to get news from New York City. Have you heard anything?"

"Nothing at all."

"We've heard that the bridges and tunnels to New Jersey are blocked, either by the National Guard or local people. Same thing with the roads to upstate."

"We've heard the same thing about the communities to the north of us. They say the locals have blocked the interstate. It's easy to isolate Los Angeles from the north, because there's very few roads through the mountains."

"Well, if you hear any—"

They were cut off, and it took Karen another ten minutes to get another connection. When they got him back, Martin cut to the chase.

"I suspect you didn't call to hear about our woes, Sis," he said. "I'm sure you have troubles of your own. I see no point in making you ask, so am I right that you're calling to see if you could come live with us until this crisis is over?"

"It seems a lot to ask, Martin," Karen said. "I should tell you that Dave thinks this . . . crisis . . . will last quite a long time."

"Martin," Dave said, "I learned a few things before this all even began. I don't think it's wise to talk about it on the telephone, even though it hardly matters now, because . . . well, the government has been saying one thing and I have reason to believe the truth is something else."

There was a silence, and Dave wondered if they had been cut off again.

"Say no more," Martin said. "I don't know about down there, but up here a few reporters have sort of mysteriously vanished. A radio station that was critical of the federal government lost its license, and a television station that had been questioning some of the things we were being told suddenly had a whole new staff and isn't reporting much of anything except government handouts. I've got a friend who knows somebody who works there, and he says it's been taken over by the National Guard. So if you have something you think might be dangerous to talk about, wait until we meet face-to-face."

"If we can meet face-to-face," Karen said.

"The answer is yes. You're more than welcome to stay here."

"Martin, thank you so much," Karen said. "I know we can make ourselves useful. I'm a hard worker, and—"

"Let me finish," Martin said. "You say you might have a problem getting out of Los Angeles. I'm afraid that's only where your problems begin. Oregon has sealed the border. All the roads leading into the Pacific Northwest from the south are closed. People are being turned back."

"Who's turning them back?" Dave asked.

"The National Guard. The governor is in charge of it now, and he's pretty much ignoring anything from the feds. We haven't actually seceded from the Union, but that's only because there's been no formal declaration. Oregon and Washington, and I'm pretty sure Idaho, are virtually sovereign states now."

"So no one is getting in?"

"Not *everyone* is being turned back. I don't know how long that will last. I'm pretty sure that having a brother here would get you in. What I'll do is write a letter confirming that you are my kin, and fax it to you. I'll also send you a copy of my driver's license to prove I'm a resident. You should be sure to bring all the ID you have, especially your birth certificates."

"I have all that," Karen said.

"Good. But let me caution you. I'm not absolutely sure you can get in. My understanding is they are concentrating on the main roads north from California, the 101, Interstate 5, 199 from Crescent City, 97 and 139 to Klamath Falls, and the 395 from Reno. Your best bet would be to enter Oregon on U.S. 95, which would take you to Burns and then to Bend. What everybody's worried about is the masses of people coming in from California. But very few people are trying to get in from the east. Folks from Idaho are content to stay there. Plus, Eastern Oregon is not such desirable real estate."

"I see what you mean," Dave said. "But that would mean going all the way—"

"Yes, Interstate 80 to Winnemucca, then a bit over one hundred miles to the Oregon border. It's two or three hundred miles farther than the direct route up I-5, but I really think you might have a lot more trouble on the interstate."

"Martin, I don't know if I have enough gas to go that route."

"Well, the decision is up to you. If you can possibly make it that way, I'm sure it would be the best."

They talked a little longer but everything that needed to be said had been said already. As soon as they hung up Addison came to her father, looking very worried.

"Daddy, how are we going to get Ranger to Oregon?"

"We'll have to look into it tomorrow, honey."

But he had spent some time figuring out how much gas they would need to get to Oregon, and the numbers did not look good.

Karen needed to get up to speed on everything that had happened while she was depressed and in denial.

He took her down to the basement and showed her the things he had stockpiled. She was impressed, and apologetic that she hadn't been available to help.

"Why all the bleach?" she asked, looking at the dozen big plastic bottles.

"A few drops will sanitize a gallon of water."

"You've been reading your Boy Scout Manual."

"And a lot of other books. I'll show them to you."

"When I think of all the things that will be in short supply . . ."

"Food is the big one."

* * *

They started picking out what they could pack into the Escalade, stopping every once in a while to watch the tar-pit disaster unfolding both on television and with their own eyes. The underground pressure exerted by the expanding pool of tar had moved north and had now destroyed most of Park La Brea. He could plainly see some of the apartment towers leaning out of true. The TV news showed people streaming away on foot, leaving their homes behind. More people who needed shelter, more mouths to feed.

They were both a little amazed and bemused at how little they owned that was truly valuable, in any sense, either in terms of being sellable or tradable, or things with sentimental value.

They had one photo album that held only the oldest original prints from both their families, some of them going back almost a hundred years. These seemed to them to fall into the category of historical artifacts, and when they began scanning their photo-print collection into the computer they had kept these old, yellowed or color-faded snapshots. Everything else was now on a few DVDs, the originals thrown away.

He had wondered if they would have any trouble with Karen's wardrobe. It turned out he was worrying for nothing. Her mind had apparently not been idle during her depression. She had realized that almost everything in her closet—bigger than the bedroom in their first apartment together—was useless. Later, she told him that realization was something that made her depression even deeper, to look at those racks and racks of designer clothes and know all that money had been wasted.

"Well, you got enjoyment out of them at the time," he pointed out.

"You could have said the same if it had been a cocaine habit instead of a shopping habit," she said. "And I would have had just as little to show for it."

Both of them wished she had been more interested in jewelry, as gold and diamonds were sure to retain their value in the coming times. She had some, and of course they packed it. Almost all her pieces had come from him as birthday presents.

In the end, they got all the clothes the three of them would be taking into two large suitcases and one medium-sized one.

After that, everything got painful.

He pulled the Escalade out of the garage and opened the back. He had long ago removed the last row of seats. Now he removed the seat behind the front passenger seat, leaving only the one behind the driver.

What had looked cavernous before now looked all too small.

The manual said the cargo space with just the back row of seats removed was 90 cubic feet. Take out the second row and you had a staggering 137 cubic feet. Keeping one seat in the second row he estimated they had somewhere around 100 cubic feet of usable space to pack.

His thoughts turned to the western pioneers setting out on the Oregon Trail in Conestoga wagons. What did they bring? For food they would have brought staples: flour, cornmeal, sugar, dried beans. It had to last a long time. For his family, he figured that if they weren't in Oregon in a week, they were probably never going to get there. They could eat mostly out of cans.

The pioneers would have expected to hunt wild game along the way. That meant gunpowder and shot, or bullets. He certainly intended to bring his small arsenal, but he didn't figure he'd be plugging any bunny rabbits along the way.

He thought they could count on Martin and his family to have everything needed to furnish a home. So they packed their propane stove and as many lanterns as he could fit in, and only basic cooking things.

But first things first. Priority One was taking all the gasoline he had stockpiled.

He started from the back, lining the cans up in rows. They ended up taking about a quarter of his available load space.

They packed only as much water as they thought they'd need on the trip north. Once out of the arid Southland, he didn't see that water would be a problem.

Next came the food. He let Karen select it, and he packed. He wanted to take all they could, but he didn't stack it all the way to the roof.

Then Karen and Addison devoted themselves to filling in the blanks. They stuffed in blankets and sheets and towels and even pillows until all the space between the food and the ceiling was filled. Anything lightweight and foldable. Why not? It wouldn't be heavy enough to affect the gas mileage.

He tackled the problem of the bikes and scooters. He wasn't about to leave them behind.

He had decided early on that irregular shapes like that would take up entirely too much space inside the Escalade. But he had a lot of rope.

After hours of struggling and much sweat and scraped knuckles and having solved geometrical problems that might have challenged Einstein, he had all the bicycles and two of the suitcases secured to the luggage rack on top. He wasn't sure he would ever be able to untangle them again, but he was satisfied they wouldn't shake free during the trip.

The only place he could figure out for the scooters was hanging over the sides. He made slings of rope and tied them to the rails of the luggage carrier, then ran ropes under the vehicle and pulled everything tight.

The sun was going down when they were finished. The three of them stood back and looked at it. Two things came to mind. Karen beat him to the first one.

"Those scooters look like lifeboats hanging off the sides of an ocean liner," she said. And then he heard a sound he hadn't heard in a long time: Karen laughing. He looked at her, standing at his side, hair disheveled, dusty and sweaty, and was flooded with love for her. For a while there he didn't think he'd ever get her back. He still felt cautious, but maybe she *was* back.

"What it looks like to me," he said, "is the Joad family's car, on its way to the promised land in California. Except they didn't have an eighty-thousand-dollar Cadillac with a DVD player, OnStar, a rearview camera, and a heated steering wheel."

"Yeah, but they had Henry Fonda."

"That would help," he admitted.

The next day the television people were calling it the Tar Bubble. There indeed seemed to be some sort of bubble, a swelling underground that was causing the surface to bulge up in a ridge about two miles long by half a mile wide. All the towers of Park La Brea still standing were tilting madly.

The Tar Bubble was easy to see. In the center it was now two or three hundred feet high. All the buildings of LACMA had collapsed. The Page Museum was no longer visible. During the night three of the apartment towers had fallen over.

After breakfast of oatmeal with reconstituted milk, brown sugar, and some walnuts, the three of them went into the basement and looked over the piles of stuff they would be leaving behind. They needed trade goods, so they tried to figure out what people would be looking for most urgently. There were two extra kerosene lanterns. He hated to part with them, but they already had two. Kerosene, he had learned, was usually refined from crude oil, but it could also come from coal, oil shale, and wood.

They all agreed he had bought too much Spam, since none of them liked it. He had chosen it because he thought it had a high protein content, as it was made from pork and ham. He should have read the label. Most of Spam's calories came from fat. It was heavy with cholesterol, and had an amazing amount of salt.

"I should point out," he said, "that when food is in short supply, you have to look at it differently. Fat is a bad thing when the supermarket shelves are stocked and the main thing you worry about is gaining weight. But when your circumstances are different, when you aren't getting your twelve hundred calories per day, fat is a good thing. It concentrates a lot of energy. I'll bet that cavemen fought over the fattiest meat."

"And we're still taking quite a bit of Spam with us," Karen pointed out. "If we get to the point of living in caves and hunting bears, I'll eat all the fat you bring home. Meantime, we'll eat the canned meat sparingly." Good enough.

They unpacked the Escalade, then had a brief dispute about who should go to Burbank to look for a horse trailer. He suggested just Addison and himself, while Karen stayed behind to organize things. She wouldn't have it.

"You're a screenwriter, Dave. What always happens just after somebody says, 'Let's split up'?"

"Somebody dies. You're right. We'll all go."

She had some more good advice, too.

"I think you should bring a gun."

He thought about it, then went back inside and got the Smith & Wesson from the safe, where he had stored it. He started back to the car, then turned around and got the Remington shotgun and a box of shells. He put the revolver in the waistband of his pants, where it felt uncomfortable, alien. He supposed he could get used to it, but he wished he'd bought some sort of holster for it.

Outside, he handed the shotgun to Karen through the window.

"You remember how to use this?"

"I think so." She thumbed three shells into the magazine.

"You know how to shoot, Mom?"

"My father insisted all his kids learn how to shoot."

"I didn't know that."

"There's a lot of things you don't know about me, Addie. I didn't always live in the Hollywood Hills."

It was Karen's first look at how spooky the city had become.

"Somebody broke into that store," Addison said.

She was right. It was across from the huge Guitar Center on Sunset. Broken glass was strewn across the sidewalk, and a few caved-in guitars. A man was sitting in a folding chair in front of the store with a rifle cradled across his lap. He watched them go by, and he didn't smile.

They passed several other stores that had obviously been looted, but this wasn't the mass anarchy that prevailed during the Rodney King riots. It looked more opportunistic. Dave figured it was people breaking in at night, knowing the police would be putting a low priority on property crimes. They didn't see that any fires had been set, either. These seemed to be pragmatic looters, without the rage that prevailed after the King verdict. They saw several more guys that he assumed were owners, patrolling their closed shops with weapons prominently displayed.

There was more activity at the Equestrian Center than he had expected. Horses having recently become a much more valuable asset, the Center had been turned into a clearinghouse and trading post dealing in feed, tack, and the animals themselves. He parked the Escalade and they drifted through the impromptu bazaar. A bale of hay was going for three times what Addison had paid for the stuff in the garage, and there wasn't a horse there selling for less than the price of a good used car.

Luckily for them, there wasn't much of a market for horse trailers. There were a few dozen of them sitting around. Some of them had price tags, and phone numbers.

They looked at several of them, and settled on a no-frills Delta, with wood-slat sides and a canvas top. The metal fenders had quite a bit of rust and the canvas had seen better days, but the tires and axle looked okay, and that was all he really cared about.

Addison opened the back and wrinkled her nose.

"We can hose it out at home," Karen said.

The trailer had been marked down from $750 to $500. Dave had $400 cash in his pocket and he'd be happy to get rid of it.

He got out his phone and punched in the number on the trailer. He got two rings, and then a man answered.

"Calling about your horse trailer for sale," he said. "Would you consider $400?"

"No sir, I wouldn't. In fact, I wouldn't take hardly any amount of greenbacks. If I need to start a fire, I can use newspapers. Where are you, sir?"

"I'm standing beside the trailer."

"I'll be there in five minutes."

He made it in three. He shook hands with Dave and introduced himself as Irving. He was a short man wearing a knit shirt and designer jeans, not at all the picture of a cowboy. He looked more like an accountant.

"I was going to take that sign down," he said. "I've got more paper money at home than I can use, and money in the bank that's probably worthless."

"But is it still for sale?"

"For swap, I'd say." He stared for a while at the line of trailers, some of them capable of carrying eight horses, as big as city buses with living quarters in the front. "I guess it's no secret that these damn things aren't worth too much these days. Who has the gas to pull them?" He looked over at the Escalade, then back at Dave, implying a question, but he wasn't going to talk about gasoline.

"What do you want to trade?" Dave asked.

"What do you have?"

Karen stepped up. "What do you need?"

Dave faded away quietly as Irving and Karen began to dicker. Addison took another look at the trailer, opening and closing the squeaky gate.

"You think Mom can make a deal?" Addison whispered.

"There's a lot of things you don't know about your mom, Addie. She's been paying retail for years, but when you were young and we had to stretch a dollar, she could outdicker an Arab rug merchant."

The final deal included all the Spam they had brought, with some other items thrown in. Irving looked happy, and Dave felt happy, too.

It had been a while since he towed a trailer, and he didn't like the jerky motion as he started out, but he got used to it quickly. The trailer squeaked and rattled, but it seemed sound enough.

Thirty minutes later he was backing it up the driveway toward the garage. It took him four tries to get it right. With any luck he wouldn't have to back it up again until they got to Oregon.

Addison got Ranger into the trailer easily enough.

"There's room for half a dozen hay bales up there, Daddy. Should we pack them? If they're too heavy, or something, we could just take some grain and then we can stop and let him graze along the way?"

Since he wasn't optimistic about getting the horse to Oregon, it didn't matter too much if they pulled a little extra weight for a while. He was pretty sure they would have to swap him somewhere along the way, for gas if possible. But he didn't tell her that, he just said she could pack the bales. She backed the horse out of the trailer and returned him to the garage, then got the hose and a bucket and some soap and started cleaning.

While she did that Karen and Dave got busy loading the Escalade again.

The day had been hot, and they were all dusty, sweaty, and thirsty when the sun went down that evening. With any luck, it would be their last evening at the hilltop house, and tomorrow would be their first day on the road.

CHAPTER ELEVEN

He had put off calling the posse until he was sure they would be leaving, but it was time.

Roger's number went to voice mail, and he didn't leave a message, figuring he'd call back later. He wanted to say good-bye, if he could. But Jenna picked up.

"Hi, Jen. How are you doing?"

There was a long, heavy sigh with a hint of a tremor at the end.

"Not so good, Dave."

"Tell me about it."

"Well, we haven't had the fires and all that here in the Valley, but food is getting scarce. Real scarce. The gangs are running wild, all of them trying to expand their territories. I hear gunshots every night, and I haven't seen a police car in three days. I think they've all gone home. You want more?"

"No, that'll do. I called because we're taking off for Oregon tomorrow morning. We're carrying everything we can, but we don't have a truck, just the Escalade, and maybe enough gas to get there. What I'm saying, we have more food than we can take with us, and I'd like you and Bob and Dennis and Roger to have what we have to leave behind."

"Jeez, Dave, that's so . . . I don't know how to thank you. But there's a problem. I have exactly zero gallons of gas for the car, and no idea where to get any more."

"Do you know anybody who has a car and can help you?"

She thought about it.

"There's this guy I've been dating. Nothing serious, or at least it wasn't serious until everything started going to shit. But I've been reevaluating some things. I'm worried that a single girl is going to be at a big disadvantage in the days to come, you know what I'm saying?"

"I think I do."

"The world is changing, Dave. I never needed a man to protect me before, but that was when there was a cop five minutes away, all day and all night. We're falling right into anarchy here, people are looking sideways at each other, I see people walking around with pistols in their belts and rifles in their hands. Pretty soon it's going to be every man for himself . . . and where does that leave a single woman?"

"Looking for somebody to protect her, I guess."

She sighed. "Okay, Dave, thank you again, thank you a thousand times. I'll be there tomorrow. I hope it'll be in a car with this dude driving. I'll have to split it with him, but it's better than nothing. But one way or another I'll be there, even if I have to walk and take what I can carry in a backpack."

That would be a walk of maybe fifteen miles, one way, much of it up and down steep hills. Dave didn't think much of that idea.

"Hang on a minute, Jen. I need to think about something." He found Karen in the living room, catching up on the news.

"Karen, I've been talking to Jenna, and she's in bad shape. No food at all, and it's getting violent in the Valley. She's got no gas for her car, so she may not be able to come and take food back to her place, like we talked about."

"Why take it back?" she asked. "This is about to be a big, empty house. Tell her to bring what she can carry of her stuff and just stay here. It couldn't be any worse than that awful apartment she lives in.".

Dave smiled at his wife, and gave her a thumbs-up.

"Jen, why don't you pack a suitcase, whatever you can carry, or get that guy to give you a ride over here. And then just stay."

She was silent for a moment.

"You mean live in your house?"

"It's going to be empty. Why not?"

"If you're serious, then yes, I'd love to do that. I'll be there tomorrow, even if I can only carry a change of clothes."

He told her how to find the semiconcealed entrance to the basement, and where he would be leaving his spare key. She thanked him again, and they hung up.

He got Dennis on the first ring. He was not as bad off as Jenna, but just as thankful to take him up on his offer of free food. He still had enough gas in his car to get to Hollywood from his home in Glendale, and probably enough to get back home.

"How are things out there?" Dave asked him.

"Tense," he said. "I've heard gunfire at night, coming from the direction of Forest Lawn. There's a couple neighborhoods just a few miles from them that are Mexican gang territory. On the good side, we've got a neighborhood watch going. I was surprised to find out how many of my neighbors have guns."

"Do you?"

"I didn't, but you got me worried and I found somebody. I bought a piece-of-shit .32 automatic. But I fired it once, and it works, and I feel a lot better having it."

"Be careful, coming over."

"Oh, I will. We'll be there before sunup, if at all possible. I don't feel like I dare leave Ellen and Dylan behind."

"I think that's wise. And you might think about not going back home."

"What do you mean?"

He explained the deal they had offered Jenna, and said it was open to his family, too. Dennis thanked him, and said he would talk it over with Ellen.

Another call to Roger was as fruitless as the first one. He called Bob's number, got a busy signal, called again and got an eerie whistling noise, like some sort of message from deep space in a cheap fifties sci-fi flick. The third time Bob picked up.

Bob listened to Dave's offer.

"I think getting out of town is probably your best bet," Bob said. "I think you're going to need a lot of luck, but it's still the best option for you. As for your offer to split up the things you're leaving behind, I'm very grateful, but the fact is I was about to call you and make a different offer.

"My guess is that I have more food and fuel than you do. I thought a lot about what you said that day, when you laid out your fantastic story. By the time I got home I'll admit I had pretty much dismissed it.

"But I woke up in the middle of the night with the sudden conviction that everything you said was true, and that I'd better start doing something about it."

"I'm glad I convinced somebody."

"You didn't, actually. I think it was my paranoid subconscious that did the trick. And I'll also admit that when I got up the next morning the strength of my conviction had faded somewhat."

"The harsh light of day will do that. Believe me, Bob, I had the same problem."

"In the end, I did what I should have done before even going to bed that night. I told the whole story to Emily."

Bob's wife, Emily, was one of Dave's favorite people in the world. She and Bob had been married for over forty years. They had started out with nothing but a car and a typewriter, drove to Los Angeles from some little town in Alabama, and Bob started freelancing. He hit it big with two sitcoms and a cop show in the seventies, another hit in the eighties, and his last big one in the nineties. They had bought their house in Holmby Hills, invested well, and had six children. Somehow, Emily had managed to remain down-to-earth in spite of her neighbors. When Dave was in doubt as to how to handle a crisis with Addison, he had often turned to Emily.

"Emily asked me if you seemed crazy," Bob continued. "Like had you gone off the deep end. I said no, you seemed sane enough to realize that what you were telling us *sounded* crazy."

Dave had to laugh at that one.

"So she asked me what's the downside of acting as if what you said was really happening? What's the worst that could happen? We'd end up with a basement full of canned food. If it turns out you're nuts, come Christmastime we donate it to the Salvation Army. Tax deductible. So I've laid in truckloads of stuff."

"Good for you."

"Well, I owe you, Dave, because it's already worse than I ever thought it could be, and something tells me we haven't seen the worst of it yet."

"I think you're right."

"So that's why I was going to call you to say that your family is welcome to come down off that hill and stay with my family. Lisa is here, and Mark, and Marian, and we expect that Teddy will make it here from San Diego on his bicycle soon, and *still* we have spare bedrooms. I want to tell you that the invitation stands, and is open-ended. For however long this madness lasts."

"I don't know quite what to say, Bob. I'm incredibly grateful."

"But you're going to Oregon."

"I think that's our best bet."

"I do, too. And we may end up following you. The family has voted, and so far we've decided to stick it out here. Of course we will wait for Teddy. But after he gets here . . . the more I think about it, the more sense it makes to move to the Pacific Northwest."

They wished each other luck.

He tried once more to get Roger, with no luck. He decided to try him once more in the morning, then to tell Dennis or Jenna or Bob to try to make contact with him.

They managed to crawl into their separate beds a little before eleven. Dave wanted to be as rested as possible for an early start the next morning.

He was startled by his bedroom door opening. Karen was standing there. The faint reflected glow from the hall lamp they always left on all night outlined her body beneath her nightgown. She was still as slender as she had been on their wedding day. His breath caught in his throat. How long had it been since he'd seen his wife like this?

"I can't stop crying," she said.

He sat up and swung his legs over the side of the bed.

"Don't get up," she said. "I want to get in bed with you."

"I'd love to have you here with me," he said. "I've been lonely."

"I don't want to make love, okay? I just want you to hold me."

"Whatever you say."

She closed the door behind her. The only light in the room came through the high window from a distant streetlight. She was a pale ghost floating toward him. At the side of the bed she shrugged out of her nightgown, put one knee on the bed on the side opposite him, and slipped under the sheet. He got in with her and she came into his arms. It was impossible for her not to notice his arousal.

"Maybe this was a bad idea," she said.

"Don't worry, I can handle it. As long as it doesn't bother you."

In response, she hugged him tighter. He smelled the shampoo in her hair, breathing deeply.

"I'm so scared about tomorrow," she said.

"I'm nervous, too."

Without his even thinking about it, his right hand had strayed down the smooth curve of her back. She didn't protest, so he gently rubbed her back. He wanted her so badly. He wondered how she would react if he offered to massage her. He would start with a foot rub . . .

They held each other for a time he couldn't measure, and then the bed started to shake. They both sat up quickly. They were bounced around, but not violently. It was mostly a side-to-side motion. He could hear things rattling in the bathroom, but no sounds of bottles smashing. The drapes were swaying, and he heard boards creaking in the walls and floor.

"Tremor," he said.

"Should we get outside?"

"It doesn't feel like a big one."

Suddenly the bedroom door flew open and Addison was standing there in her nightgown. The bright shaft of the hall light pinned Dave and Karen like convicts escaping prison.

"Daddy, I woke up and the room was shaking . . ."

She trailed off when it registered that her mother was in the bed with him. Karen pulled the sheet up to her chest.

"It's okay, Addie," Karen said, and patted the bed beside her. "Come sit with us and calm down. It's going to be okay."

"Oh, that's all right, Mother," she said, backing out of the room. "It wasn't a big one, and it's over. G'night." She started to shut the door, then turned back. "I love you," she said, and smiled.

Once more back in the dark, they both lay back side by side and laughed.

"I thought the earth was supposed to move at the *end* of lovemaking," she said.

She was lying on two pillows with her arms above her head. He took the edge of the sheet covering her and pulled it down to her waist. She made no objection, so he pulled it all the way off her. She kept looking at him as he gently put his hand on her flat belly and slowly, slowly moved it down into the fine blonde hair.

She moaned softly, and rolled over on top of him. She straddled him, holding herself up on her arms, and they looked at each other from a few inches away. Then he rose to her lips and they kissed. Karen knew how to make a kiss do the work of a whole bottle of Viagra. Not that he needed it.

They pressed close and began to move, and a little while later the earth moved, again, but this time it might not have registered on the UCLA seismometer down the hill, though it must have been a close thing.

CHAPTER TWELVE

People often say, afterward, that the earthquake "sounded like a freight train." They say the same thing about tornadoes, too. Dave could testify that it *hit* like a freight train. If there was a warning, a slight shimmy or shake, he slept through it. What he recalled was waking up in midair.

He didn't think he actually fell back onto the bed. It was more a case of the bed rising to hit him.

It happened in absolute blackness. The power died in the early seconds.

He bounced again, totally disoriented, unable to tell if he was on his back or facedown until the bed hit him again, on his right side. He reached out and felt Karen, tried to grab her, lost her, flailed wildly, and found her again. He held on to her arm and pulled her to him. She was screaming, but he could barely hear her for all the other sounds. She clung to him and they were hurled to the floor.

He had a blanket in his other hand and he tried to pull it over their heads as Karen clung to him with her arms around his waist. They were being pelted with objects thrown from the dresser.

He could hear the closet doors banging against the walls. The shelves in there collapsed, spilling many years' accumulation of junk on top of the clothes that had fallen to the floor.

He heard glass shattering from the direction he assumed was the bathroom, and figured it was the big mirrors in there crashing to the tiled floor.

All these more distinct sounds played out against the background of the entire house groaning in protest, as every nail in every board squeaked and squealed inside the walls, above the ceiling, and under the floorboards. It was almost as if the house were being twisted, back and forth, as well as bounced up and down and shaken side to side. Everything was moving in every direction it was possible to move, and it simply *would not stop*.

It felt like it went on forever, but they later learned it was just over two minutes. The moment the motion slowed down, Karen tried to get to her feet.

"Addison!" she cried out.

Dave held firmly on to her arm and she fell back at his side.

"Just hang on," he said.

"But Addison—"

"I know, I know, but you won't help her if you trip over something in the dark and break your leg. I can't see a damn thing."

"I can't either."

"So help me find the bed. I think it's over this way . . ."

They groped around and quickly found it. He moved alongside until he came to a lamp lying on the floor. His knee dug painfully into something sharp, but he ignored it and felt his way to the nightstand, which was lying on its side. He found the drawer, which had slid open at some point. He felt around on the floor until he found the 4-cell Maglite he always kept there. He found the button and pushed it, and the beam hit him in the face. He blinked, and turned it away.

They were both silent for just a few seconds, taking it all in. The chandelier had gouged a big hole in the mattress. There was a crack running along the ceiling, and several pieces had fallen out. There was a crack in one wall. Half the contents of the closet had managed to make it into the room. It looked as if the closet had been put on spin cycle, like a washing machine, and anything that would fit had been thrown through the door.

Neither of them lingered. He got up and grabbed his pants and pulled them on quickly, found his slippers and stepped into them.

"Don't go out there barefoot," he cautioned Karen. "There's going to be a lot of broken glass."

"I came in here last night without any shoes."

"Then let me clear the way. It's only been a minute; Addison is going to be all right." He made himself believe that, as the alternative was too awful to contemplate.

The beam of light from his flashlight was like a solid object, as if a film crew had fogged the room before the cameras rolled. It was dust, coming from everywhere. He had to step up onto an overturned sideboard and then down on the other side. Addison's room was impossibly far away, at the end of the hall.

"Shine a light on the floor back here," Karen said. He did, and she picked her way through the debris. He gave her his hand and pulled her up on the sideboard.

"You're bleeding," she said, pointing at his knee. There was blood soaking through his pant leg, and he could feel some trickling down his shin.

"It's not bad."

"Shine it in there." He stopped and did as she said, illuminating her bedroom, which was even more a shambles than his. But there was a pair of shoes close to the bed. They were high heels, which was ridiculous, but better than nothing with all the sharp edges lying around. She slipped them on and followed him down the hall.

Addison's door was jammed shut. He put his shoulder to it, and it didn't budge.

"Addison! Addison! Are you all right?"

There was no answer. Karen began shouting her name as he hit the door again. It moved slightly. Once more, and it slammed open. He'd been afraid something had fallen to block it. But it was just the door frame that had been twisted out of whack.

He swept the flashlight beam over the room.

Addison had long been a trinket collector. Two whole walls of her room were shelving he had put up to hold her various collections. Much of it was glass or china, most of it breakable, and all of it was on the floor in multicolored heaps.

Instead of just pinning or taping posters of Miley Cyrus and Zac Efron and the other usual teenage suspects to the wall as Dave had done at her age, Karen had insisted they be professionally framed, complete with glass, and hung. Every one, perhaps two dozen of them, was on the floor now.

Addison's bed was a frilly white thing with a canopy. It was still standing, undamaged. Her dresser was overturned, clothes spilling out of it.

Dave saw all that in a few seconds. What he didn't see was Addison.

"Bathroom?" he suggested. Karen hurried off in that direction, calling her daughter's name. He went to the closet and looked in there, saw chaos similar to his own closet but with a lot more clothes and tons of old toys. Again, no Addison.

He left the closet and turned around in time to see her crawling out from under the bed. She looked dazed and her face was pale, but she wasn't crying.

"Karen, here she is!" he called out, and knelt beside her.

"Honey, are you hurt? Let me see your eyes." He didn't see any obvious damage, but he was worried about concussion. Her pupils looked normal.

"Daddy, you're bleeding," she said. Karen was beside them now, and they hugged each other. Karen was crying. He felt like crying, too, but he didn't have time for it. The room started to move again.

"Let's get under the bed!" Addison shouted. "It's safe under the bed!"

He was actually thinking about it, though he wasn't sure it was a good idea, but the shaking lasted only a few seconds, and was not severe.

"Aftershock," he said.

"I think I'd like to go see if Ranger is all right," Addison said, and burst into tears.

The horse was badly shaken, but Dave ran the flashlight over him and didn't see any major injuries. It looked like he had been knocked down, and a few bales of hay had fallen on him. A lot of it was clinging to his back. Maybe it had kept him down, or maybe he was just unable to get to his feet while the shaking was going on. He was stalking in circles within the confining space of the garage, looking wild-eyed. Addison started to go to him, but Dave held her back.

"Addie, I want you to be absolutely sure he's not going to panic and hurt you before you try to get close to him."

"I'll be all right, Daddy. He knows me."

"I'm not sure he does, right now."

"I'll be careful."

They watched as she moved toward the horse in small steps, talking quietly to him. Each time around he eyed her, but he didn't seem ready to go to her yet.

"I need to get a halter and lead rope on him and get him out of here," she said. "I think he wants to be outside as much as we do."

He couldn't argue with that. Stepping outside the house had been an amazing experience; he hadn't realized just how tense he was until there was no longer a roof over his head. It felt so good to stand on the patio—which had a crack running through the concrete toward the pool—and look up at the moon.

He manually opened the driveway gate and stepped out onto the pavement. There were no lights on anywhere on Mockingbird Lane. The big houses loomed in the moonlight, everything eerily silent except the quiet trickle of running water. He aimed the light down and saw one of the gutters was filled with water that was carrying a lot of debris in it, both natural and man-made.

He smelled pool chlorine and realized what had happened. Somewhere up the street somebody's pool had cracked, and it was all running out to the street.

He went over to the west, looked down into the valley at Beverly Hills. It was filled with dust, but he could see the flicker of a fire in one of the houses.

He pointed the light downhill to the east but it was still dusty and he couldn't see anything. He went back up the driveway and saw that Addison had a rope on Ranger and was walking him in circles.

"He's calmed down a lot," she said. "Can I take him out on the road? He really wants to keep moving."

"I'd rather you didn't. At least not until we find you another flashlight."

"That's what I'm after," Karen said. He found her beside the Escalade, which was partially buried in garage junk. The whole vehicle had crept along the concrete until the driver's side was banging against the garage wall and the rear had crunched into the garage door, buckling it outward.

Unable to reach and open the tailgate, Karen had opened the right rear door and was pulling out boxes, trying to get to where they had stored two lanterns. She had already removed the other 4-cell Maglite from under the seat and set it on the floor beside her. She was an incongruous sight, dressed in a nightgown and red high heels, bent over and burrowing through their carefully packed gear.

She glanced at him, and then at the flashlight on the floor.

"Give that one to Addison," she said. So he took the light to his daughter and waited until her circling brought her near him.

"You can take the horse out onto the street, but don't go farther down than the Greenbergs' house, and don't go so far around the curve uphill that you can't still see our house. *Walk* him, don't ride, and keep that flashlight on the ground. No telling what might be in the street."

She nodded, and went down the driveway and then down the street.

He turned away and walked back to the patio. He encountered Karen crossing from the garage with an electric lantern.

"I'm going inside to get some better shoes and clothes," she said.

He swept his flashlight beam over the outside of the house. He was surprised to find that only two of the big glass floor-to-ceiling windows that faced the patio had broken. Both of the sliding doors had sprung, but they would probably go back in their tracks easily enough.

He headed toward the southern edge of his property, at the edge of the hill, intending to look at the city.

His first thought: the plains of Mordor.

Dust still hanging in the air obscured everything on the flatlands except some of the tall buildings on Sunset, farther south on Wilshire, and west in Century City. Not a single light shone in a single window in any of them. If not for the bright moon hanging in the west he probably wouldn't have seen them at all.

Beneath the dust there were hundreds of orange lights flickering, like lava boiling up from the ground. At first he thought it might *be* lava, that the earth might have opened up along the fault lines and was now spewing molten rock directly into the city. But it was nothing as cataclysmic as that, though it was bad enough. It was houses on fire.

With the electrical grid so erratic, and in some places almost nonexistent, people had looked to other alternatives. Those who had kerosene lamps and the fuel to put in them used them. Others used candles.

Karen joined him at the edge of the hill.

"Dave, Addison says we should . . . My God, there's fires everywhere. Where are all those people going to go?"

"Sleep outdoors, I guess. I'll bet a lot of them won't be too eager to sleep indoors for a while, anyway."

"I know I wouldn't. Um . . . Addison says there's something we should see."

"Is she—"

"She's okay. She came back with the horse and gave him something to eat."

They started for the driveway. Karen was now dressed in a pair of white Reeboks, a pair of loose slacks, and a blouse that looked far too fancy for the situation, but everything she had of a practical nature—which was only a few changes of clothes— was packed away.

"What is it, Addison?" Dave asked.

"Just come and look, Daddy."

They followed her out the gate and down the hill. Five houses down, almost where Mockingbird Lane intersected Doheny, Dave began to see what Addison had wanted them to see, looming out of the darkness.

The ground had cracked and slid, with their side now about three feet lower than the other side. There was a gap about two feet wide. It ran the width of the street and into the lawns on either side. On the north it ran beneath a house, which had shifted badly. On the south side the crack had missed the house there, running along the east side of it and then out onto Doheny, where it looked like it crossed the road, but his flashlight wasn't powerful enough to see that far. He couldn't be sure, but it looked as if there had been a landslide there where the crack entered the hillside. He suspected there would be more, both uphill and downhill.

He cautiously moved toward the edge and shined his flashlight down into the crack. It was not too terribly deep, and narrowed the farther down it went, but it was deep enough.

"I guess you know what this means," he said.

Karen sighed. "It means we won't be leaving today."

From up the street, they heard a woman screaming for help. They hurried in that direction. Rounding the corner, they passed several houses on their way uphill. A man came from his driveway. Dave knew most of his neighbors downhill, at least to say hello to, though they didn't socialize. Uphill he only knew his immediate neighbors, and he didn't know this man.

"Is your family okay?" Dave asked him as they got nearer.

"Yes, thank God. There's a lot of damage, but all we have is a cut where my wife stepped on something on her way out. Do you know the people at the end of the road? It sounds like it's coming from there."

"No, I don't, but I guess we'd better go see."

"I've got to take care of my wife first. I just located the first-aid kit. Have you got any phone service?"

"I haven't even tried. I'd be surprised if we did."

The man looked very worried.

"I need to get in touch with my son in Pasadena," he said. "I need to see if he and his family are all right. I don't think I have enough gas in the car to get over there. You wouldn't happen to have any gas for sale, would you?"

"Sorry," Dave said. They left him and kept going up the hill. The woman had stopped screaming, but Dave could hear voices up ahead.

"Dave!" Karen gasped. "Dave, look!"

She was pointing off to their left. They had been hugging the right side of the road, stepping over cracks in the pavement here and there, nothing like the monster down below but enough to trip over if you weren't careful. Now he joined his flashlight beam to Karen's, and saw a big bite had been taken out of the pavement.

"Don't go too close to it," she said. "It might collapse under you."

"I'll be careful," he said, and moved toward the brink in small steps. He edged around the huge hole and stepped up onto a broken piece of sidewalk. From that vantage he could look down, and it was only then that it hit him that a house had been where this chunk had been taken out of the hillside.

"Addison, don't go there!"

"I'll just stand beside Daddy."

She took his hand and they both looked over the new cliff. The house had slid a long way, and was nothing but matchsticks now. It might have landed on another house down below, but he couldn't be sure about that. Daylight would reveal the extent of the damage, as it would certainly reveal so many other things.

"Did you know these people?" he asked his daughter.

"Just by name. The Solomons," she said. "Remember Judy

Grainger? She lived next door to them, but she moved away a few years ago. Mrs. Solomon gave us cookies when she was baking. They're in their sixties or seventies. He worked at Paramount doing something in the art department, Judy said. I hope they weren't at home."

"Me, too."

There was nothing for them to do, and he could see flashlight beams in the canyon. People down there were looking for survivors. They hurried on up the street.

At the very top there was a small traffic circle. There were houses to the east and the west, and a third one up against the hillside to the north. Behind it was scrubland much like the area must have been before the developers came. No houses loomed up there, and part of the hillside had been planted in ground cover intended to keep the hillside in place. But they were recent plantings, and they hadn't spread very far. The house was an ultramodern box, put up only a few years ago. Dave remembered it, as all the Mockingbird Lane residents did, because of the constant truck traffic back and forth during the year and a half it took to build the place.

He assumed it had been built to earthquake code and probably would have still been standing, but a big part of the hillside had shaken down onto the flat roof, and crushed it like a wooden matchbox.

There were four people near the wreckage. He didn't know any of them. One man was down on his hands and knees in front of a gap where the roof had not quite touched the sidewalk when the building collapsed. He was shining a flashlight into the gap, which just might be high enough for a man to wriggle through.

A woman in a torn nightgown saw them and zeroed in on him. She looked to be in her forties. She grabbed him by the arm and pulled him toward her ruined home.

"My husband is in there," she cried. "Please, please, help me get him out."

He looked around at the two other people, a man and a woman who stood close together, probably a man and wife. The man shrugged helplessly. Dave reluctantly got down beside the other man. He looked through the gap, and saw that it ended maybe ten feet farther in. It was possible that the gap continued

SLOW APOCALYPSE **139**

to the left or right, but there would be no way to tell unless you crawled in there.

"I haven't heard a sound," the man said, quietly. "What's your husband's name?"

"Phil. I was downstairs watching television, I couldn't sleep, that's all that saved me. I ran outside and the whole hill came down . . ." She lapsed into tears again.

"Phil!" the other man shouted. "Phil, can you hear me?"

There was no reply. They got up and went around the house to the west. One window had survived almost intact, and Dave shined his light in there. He realized it had been a second-floor window, and it was now almost on the ground.

"I can see part of a room in there," he said.

Karen had climbed up to join them. She tugged on his arm.

"Dave, you aren't going in there, are you?"

"Not unless I hear somebody," he admitted. If he heard someone crying out for help, he would have to do whatever he could to get him out. But he wouldn't risk his neck crawling through a place like that, with aftershocks sure to come, without a damn good reason.

"My name's Joe Crawford, by the way."

"Dave Marshall. This is my wife, Karen."

They returned to the street and gave the woman the bad news. She glared at them, then headed up the hill herself, still calling her husband's name.

"I hope she doesn't go in there," Joe said. "Should we stop her?"

"It's her right, I guess. But nobody could be alive in there."

"I agree. How did your house hold up?"

"Pretty good," Dave said. "There's cracks here and there, and some ceiling fell down. But it's habitable."

"Sounds like my house," Crawford said. "Not that I plan to sleep in it tonight."

"Daddy," Addison said. "I think we ought to go house to house and see if anyone needs help."

He looked down at her and smiled, thinking he should have been the one to come up with that.

"Good idea, Addie. Let's start at the top here and work our way down."

They spent the next few hours knocking on doors. Many of the residents were already outside, all of them showing one degree or another of shock and disorientation. Dazed and confused, some just sat down on the street to await the coming of daylight.

Most of the rest of the people answered their doors promptly enough. Some of the houses were known to their neighbors to be empty, their occupants having fled in the last weeks to anyplace they thought might be safer than the big city.

None of the houses were as badly damaged as the one at the top of the hill, but many had shifted off their foundations. These tended to be the older homes, built to different earthquake standards.

Dave estimated that, in normal times, at least half of the houses they visited would have been deemed total write-offs. Just bring in the bulldozers and finish what Mother Nature had begun. Now, of course, they would remain standing. Even in normal times, this was the sort of event that bankrupted insurance companies, the sort of event that would have soon brought government intervention. Today, he wondered if the government would show up at all.

They came to the crack in the road and all had to peer down toward the bottom. It sobered everyone. Seeing destroyed or badly damaged houses was bad enough. Seeing the very earth cracked open made one feel very small, very vulnerable. If the ground you walked on was no more stable than this, where was there any stability?

Dave was beginning to think the neighborhood had escaped with only one probable death and two possibles, when someone from the search party thought he heard a cry for help from a house just on the west side of the crack. It was on the north side of the street, a two-story structure built in the traditional mission style, with adobe walls and red barrel tiles on the low, peaked roof. They approached the house, and their flashlights soon revealed that the east end of the roof had collapsed. It was from that part of the house that the cries were coming.

"That second-floor window," said one of the men.

"I guess we go in," someone else said.

Nobody looked too eager to do that, but they all knew it had to be done. They were all getting a new appreciation for the many rescuers they had seen on television, braving aftershocks to pull survivors from the rubble in Haiti, in Turkey, in China and Indonesia. He followed Joe Crawford onto the porch and watched as he tried the door handle. It didn't budge.

They looked to one side and saw a multipaned window with several panes cracked. Dave used his flashlight to knock one pane out, and cautiously stuck his hand through the gap and sprung the latch. The window eased open on its own, then almost fell onto the porch. There was room for Dave and Joe to squeeze through.

The living room they entered was a shambles, as they had by now come to expect. The residents had a lot of books, a lot of bric-a-brac, much of it quite fragile. All of it was on the floor in a jumble that made it almost seem a bomb had gone off in the room. Dave moved his flashlight beam around and saw a stairway leading up to a railed balcony overlooking the large open-plan living room. He gestured toward it. Joe nodded, and they picked their way carefully through the debris.

At the top of the stairs they heard the cry again. It was actually more of a whimper, and Dave was sure he would not have heard it from outside the house.

"Over that way," he said. Joe followed him as he made his way toward the part of the house that had fallen in.

They swept their flashlights into each of three bedrooms as they passed them, then into the fourth. Dave could see a lot of broken red barrel tiles, and big, splintered ceiling beams. It took him a while to realize that the biggest heap of debris in the room had a king-sized bed beneath it. He continued sweeping his flashlight beam, passed over what looked like a heap of clothes, then brought it back.

"Oh, man, I think that's a person, Joe."

They picked their way over a few roof beams and then crouched. It was a woman, completely covered in dust. She was only visible from the waist up, clad in a nightgown. Dave gently brushed dust and bits of plaster from her face. Her eyes opened.

"Can't move," she said.

"Don't worry, we'll get you out."

"Hurts."

"We'll get you out."

Joe had been exploring down where her legs should be. He lifted pieces of plaster away one by one, set them aside.

"My husband," she said.

"Shh. We'll find him. You just hold on." She squeezed Dave's hand, but weakly.

He watched as Joe got down far enough to see what the problem was. Joe gestured, and Dave craned his neck to have a look, not wanting to let go of the woman's hand. One end of a big, heavy beam had fallen on her leg, just above the knee. A jagged point had driven into the flesh. Joe put his hands under the beam and lifted. It didn't budge so much as an inch.

"Should I give you a hand?" Dave asked. Joe slowly shook his head, and leaned over to whisper in Dave's ear.

"There's way too much weight on it. I don't think we can shift all that stuff. We might be able to cut through the beam."

Dave leaned closer to the woman's ear.

"Ma'am, do you or your husband have any tools in your garage?"

"Tons of them," she whispered. "Whatever you need."

"Okay, I'll go—" The woman squeezed his hand much harder. "Please don't leave me."

He glanced at Joe, who nodded.

"I'll take a look." He got up and headed for the door.

"Joe, wasn't there a woman down there who said she was a nurse?"

"Used to be, she said. Name was . . . Milly."

"See if she's willing to come up here. I'm in over my head."

"Got it."

Alone with the woman, Dave leaned as far as he could over the pile of debris and aimed his flashlight down at the woman's leg.

"What's your name?"

"Dave. Dave Marshall. I live about—"

"I think I've seen you. You drive an Escalade? You have a little girl, and a pretty wife, she's usually in a Mercedes?"

"That's Karen. Addison is my daughter."

"My name is Roberta. Bobbie to my friends."

"We'll have you out of here soon, Bobbie." He looked at her face, realized that with all the dust and dirt and sweat that was running down it, he couldn't estimate her age within twenty years. She might be thirty, she might be mid-fifties.

"Dave, you have to look for my husband."

He didn't know what to tell her. He had finally got a good view of her injured leg, and he didn't like what he saw. There was no gushing blood that would indicate a severed artery—she would certainly have bled out before they even got there if that was the case—but blood was definitely flowing.

"My husband," she said, and then had a coughing fit.

"I haven't seen him."

"He was in the bed. I was thrown out."

Dave explored again with his flashlight. Everything was so chaotic, the flashlight beam throwing such hard-edged shadows, it was hard to tell what anything was. So much debris, absolutely no order to it.

"I can't see him from here. I haven't been able to check the other side of the bed. That's probably where he is. What's his name?"

"Ralph."

Dave called his name. There was no response. He tried again, mostly for something to do to take his mind off his helplessness to free Bobbie.

Joe showed up with Millie behind him. He had a handsaw, and she had a first-aid kit. They made their way over to where Bobbie was pinned. Millie took over the hand-holding duty, while trying to examine her at the same time. Joe was looking over the beam, coated with decades of dust and cobwebs, trying to determine the best place to start cutting.

The beam pinning Bobbie was resting at a forty-five degree angle, part of it still in the attic, the other end pressing on her leg. A jumble of stuff that must have been stored in the attic had fallen on the bed. Judging from the boxes that had split open, most of them had contained books. A lot of books, a lot of weight.

Dave gathered a handful of the spilled books and threw them into a corner, then another, and another. He cleared off most of a sheet of plywood that was lying almost level, pressing down on the fragment of roof beam. And once more it took him a while to realize the dusty, plaster-covered thing he had uncovered was a human head and shoulders. The top of the man's head was crushed, gray matter leaking out. His eyes were open, but coated with dust.

Dave hurried back the way he had come and made it almost to the end of the balcony before he leaned over the railing and vomited. He started back toward the bedroom. He was met at the door by Joe, who took his arm and led him a few steps back the way he had come. He spoke quietly.

"If I cut that beam, the rest of the ceiling will collapse."

Millie joined them, looking grave.

"She's in and out of consciousness. Even if we can get her out, she's going to lose that leg. In fact, the best way of getting her out would probably be to amputate it."

"Can you do it?" Joe looked at the saw in his hand. Tears were running down Millie's cheeks, making trails in the dust.

"I'm sorry, guys, I just don't think I'm up to that." When neither man said anything, she got angry. "Look, damn it, I worked in a hospice, I have no experience of trauma care. I wouldn't know where to begin."

"Nobody said you should," Dave said. "We were just asking. So what do you think we can do for her?"

"Hold her hand, I guess."

So they went back into the room and Millie knelt beside her. But she was only down there for a moment, holding Bobbie's wrist. She stood up.

"She's passed," she said.

Joe sighed, and threw the saw across the room.

They crossed the crack in the ground and checked the last few houses. All the residents were okay except for the normal bumps, bruises, and minor cuts, which they had already treated. They came to Doheny Drive and met another party making their way down the hill. Everybody exchanged information. Doheny dead-ended against the hillside about a quarter of a mile up, and there had been a major slide up there, which had buried two houses. Three others had totally collapsed, no sounds coming from any of them. They estimated six or seven dead up there. They also had three bad injuries, including one that was critical. The good news was that two doctors lived up there.

They met another group coming up the hill.

"We need to stand together as a neighborhood," one of them said. His name was Richard, and he said only one room of his house on Doheny was habitable. It was agreed that those who wanted to would meet at an address almost on the flats, a few streets up from Sunset Boulevard, a home that was largely undamaged. Dave thought he knew the place. The time of the meeting would be at noon.

"What time is it now?" someone asked.

Several people got out their cell phones, which were showing no bars but still had working clocks.

"I have seven thirty."

Dave had noticed that it had gotten lighter, that they were no longer groping around in total darkness, though the flashlights were still useful.

"That can't be right," another person said.

But it was. The sun never really came out that day. They had all gotten used to the amazing crystal blue skies of Los Angeles with hardly any gasoline engines pouring pollution into the air. That day the sky was black.

CHAPTER THIRTEEN

Dave and Karen walked back up the hill and through their open gate and stood on the edge of the hill looking out at a nightmare.

It looked as if every city block had a fire. That was probably an exaggeration, but there were certainly hundreds of them, perhaps thousands. And the smoke was all black. He knew that when firefighters poured water on a blaze the smoke usually turned white. There was not a single plume of white to be seen. The LAFD was out of commission, out of gas, probably out of water with broken water mains. These fires would have to burn themselves out.

Which could take a long time if they spread to neighboring houses, and jumped streets. Dave didn't see any reason why they wouldn't. The only good news was that there was no wind.

By far the largest fire was in one of the triangular towers in Century City. It looked like it had started down low, on the third or fourth floor, and had by now engulfed the whole structure. Dave thought it was unlikely that anyone had been in the building, then wondered if cleaning staff had still been working. They might have made it out by the stairway on the side opposite the fire. He hoped so.

He turned away and looked at his house. With a little light, it all looked even worse. He knew he should be grateful that the house was standing at all, but it was a difficult situation in which to count one's blessings. He started to go inside.

He hadn't gotten far when the ground began to rock again. It was not nearly as strong as the main quake, but that had been a monster, certainly the largest ever felt in Los Angeles. If he had to guess, Dave would have estimated this aftershock was around a 6.0. He set his legs apart and listened to more items falling inside the house. He was surprised there was still anything to fall. It continued to shake for fifteen or twenty seconds.

"Honey, don't go in there," Karen called out. "I don't like you in there." She was coming toward him. "We'll sleep outside tonight."

"You want some breakfast?" Addison asked.

They sat down at the picnic table to a meal of cold canned hash and oatmeal and instant coffee heated over the propane stove.

Addison brought over a pan of biscuits, which were soft on top and black on the bottom.

"They're supposed to be baked in the oven," she said, looking unhappy. "Maybe I should throw these away and try again."

"Don't worry about it, Addie. We'll eat our mistakes for now, if we can, and I know we'll get better. I don't want to waste any food."

"Maybe if I cover them next time."

"That should do the trick." He scraped the worst of the carbon off the bottom of four biscuits and spread boysenberry jam on the tops, and they went down okay. He refilled his coffee cup and drank half of it.

"Daddy, there's an area over there to the west I've been looking at. It doesn't look like there's any fires there. I wonder why that is?"

Dave got up and went to the edge with his daughter and looked where she was pointing. Sure enough, there was a swath of land that didn't seem to have any flames in it. It was hard to judge how wide it was, but it had to be at least five or six miles long, reaching to where he estimated Wilshire Boulevard would be. Then he noticed that there were some columns of white smoke rising from that area, as if the fires there had been doused by water. That would be around UCLA, Westwood, Holmby Hills. He thought he could make out the Los Angeles Country Club, sitting on the eastern edge of the fireless area. Could it be that people down there still had enough water pressure to fight the fires? Did the remnants of the LAFD concentrate their equipment over there? North of that area, where he couldn't see, would be Bel Air. Expensive real estate, all of it, including Bob Winston's home. So once again the rich seemed to be getting special treatment.

Then he realized he was wrong.

"I think a dam might have broken, Addison," he said.

"Which one, Daddy?"

"Probably Stone Canyon. That's the biggest one."

"You mean the water put out the fires over there?"

"I think that's what happened." He didn't add that the water might have done a great deal more than that.

The hills were a series of canyons running mostly north and south. The biggest was Cahuenga, where the Hollywood Freeway cut through. Then there was Runyon Canyon, Nichols Canyon, and Laurel Canyon to the east of him. To the west, Coldwater Canyon was a mile away, and just beyond that was Franklin Canyon. There were two dams in Franklin, one small one nearly at the top, and a larger one just above the flatlands. Dave didn't think there was enough water in either dam to spread as far as what he was seeing, and besides, it would have been a lot closer.

But three miles away was Benedict Canyon, then Beverly Glen Boulevard, which ran just over the hill from Stone Canyon, which contained a dam and reservoir even bigger than Lake Hollywood. If that dam had collapsed, the water would have roared down the steep canyon walls, sweeping away hundreds of houses and everything else in its path until it crossed Sunset Boulevard and might have begun to lose a little of its force as it spread out over the flatter land of UCLA and Westwood

Without even thinking about it, Dave dug his cell phone out of his pocket and flipped it open. Then he felt foolish. What were the chances he could get a signal?

But when he looked at the screen, he had three bars. Could that be right?

He scrolled through his stored numbers and thumbed the one for Bob Winston. He expected to be unable to get a call through. Surely whatever cell tower was still operating would be overwhelmed.

He heard it ringing. He counted twelve rings and was about to hang up, when someone answered, sounding suspicious, as if he thought he might be getting a pitch from a telemarketer. It sounded like Bob.

"Hello?"

"Is that you, Bob? It's Dave! I'm amazed I got you. My battery is low, and there's no telling when we might get cut off. So let's don't waste any time. From up here, it looks like the Stone Canyon dam broke in the quake."

"The dam did break. The house is damaged, but standing. We didn't get the worst of it. We got a five-foot wall of water. The first floor flooded. Outside, the street is full of debris. We moved up to the second floor and watched the trees and parts of houses flow by. When the water went away we had six inches of mud covering the first floor."

Bob lowered his voice.

"There's a dead body half-buried, almost in my front yard. We haven't even had time to take care of him yet. We've got his ID, license, credit cards, so when somebody comes looking . . ."

He couldn't go on. He took a deep breath.

"How did you—"

"The house held up," Dave said. "Lots of broken glass, some cracks in the wall, but basically solid. We have at least three dead that we know of, probably two more."

"Lord, I haven't even had time to see about the neighbors," Bob said.

"At least the fires around you got put out."

"Mark wants to go south a ways, see how far this mess goes, but I'm not happy about that idea."

"Why not?"

"We've heard gunfire from down that direction the last few nights. Even during the daylight, yesterday. I don't know who's shooting at who. I'm worried about mobs forming, coming in here because they think the rich people still have food. The thing is I *do* have food, but I doubt my neighbors stockpiled as much as I did. What I'm afraid of is hungry people looting houses. All the stores have already been cleaned out."

Dave heard Bob sigh heavily.

"So, are you still planning to head north?"

"I can't at the moment, Bob. Our street is cracked wide open just a few houses down from me. I guess I'm lucky it didn't crack right under our house. I haven't even been down as far as Sunset, but I wouldn't be surprised if there are more obstacles on the way. It may be a while before we can leave."

"I'd put it off as long as I could, if I were you. I've got a feeling this is just the beginning. I think we're on the edge of anarchy. I've been listening to my CB radio every chance I get, and I don't like what I'm hearing."

Dave felt like kicking himself. Why hadn't he thought of

buying a Citizens' Band radio? It had never occurred to him. It was an old technology. People had grown so used to e-mail, Skype, and most of all, cell phones.

"I had to dig the damn thing out of a box in the attic. There's not a lot of talk out there. I tell you, Dave, I've swept the AM and FM bands from one end to the other, and there's not much out there. No FM, and only two AM stations I could find, and they don't have a lot of information. No television at all, that I can find. No cable down here. Have you tried to connect to the Internet?"

"Not yet. I don't see how it could still be operating."

"Dave, my friend, I'm scared. I feel so isolated. Thank God most of my family is here. I picked up a man broadcasting out of San Diego, and it felt like I'd contacted Borneo. Our world is contracting, day by day. We've retreated to the second floor, because it's more defensible. My family is . . . we're standing watches, Dave. Armed watches. This morning I put up a sign in the driveway that said trespassers would be shot. And I *meant* it. Or, at least I thought so. But I can't picture gunning down a hungry family. I just can't picture it. Gangs of looters? Yeah, I think I could shoot. But women? Children? What has the world come to?"

"I've thought of that, too, Bob. It wouldn't be easy even to send them away. But I have to feed my family, too, and I have a finite amount of food."

"How is your situation up there . . . I mean, about defending yourself?"

"I'm armed, like I told you. The neighborhood may be coming together. There's supposed to be a meeting down the hill soon. I think the guy organizing it is thinking about things like that."

"Listen, if you don't feel safe, my offer still stands. You can come join us down here. The more people we have around us, the better I'll feel. So if—"

The signal was gone. Dave looked at the screen, and the battery was dead.

He told Karen about the call. She said she would feel safer there in the hills, at least until they had a better idea of what was going on down below. Dave agreed. They decided he would go alone to the meeting down the hill while his wife and daughter tried to set up something to live in. He got on his bicycle.

But he was only a short way down Doheny when he saw a computer-printed notice stapled to a palm tree. It said the neighborhood meeting had been postponed until noon the next day, because most people needed more time to get their own houses in order, as best they could.

The three of them spent the rest of the day assessing the damage and figuring out what to do about it.

"I suggest that we move out of the main house and into the guesthouse," Dave said. "The main house is too damn big. I'd like us all to be closer together. Also, there's less area for me to board up."

"I like that," Addison said.

Karen shrugged, then nodded. The guesthouse had two rooms upstairs: a bedroom and a front room, which Dave had never quite figured out a use for. There were couches and chairs in there. It was a good place to sit and look out over the basin, but you got the same view from the big room downstairs which he had always used as his office. There was a stairway that led to a railed balcony, about ten by fifteen feet, and under that area was a galley kitchen with a small refrigerator and stove. Dave didn't recall the stove ever being used, and there was nothing in the fridge except bottled water and some beer. He and Addison went around picking up all the useless stuff that had fallen and broken, putting the soft items in black plastic garbage bags, the hard and jagged stuff in the wheelbarrow to be carted to the most distant corner of the lot and dumped there. Before long they had a mountain of debris.

While Dave and Addison excavated their new home, Karen started a salvage operation in the old one.

She retrieved anything useful and undamaged that they had elected to leave behind when they planned the Oregon trip. Sheets and blankets, towels, bath soap, lots of extra clothing. She brought it all down and set it on the patio. Toilet paper and paper towels, pots and pans and silverware and other basic kitchen equipment, what food and spices were still left in the kitchen. She was like a survivor on the beach salvaging the remains of a shipwreck. You never knew what might come in handy, and she took everything that might have even the slightest use, since she had a whole guesthouse to put it in, didn't have to pack carefully, and she intended never to go back inside the wreck of her old home again once she had finished.

The three of them struggled to bring an undamaged mattress down to the patio, intending to put it in the guesthouse for Addison. But once they were down there, Karen looked at both buildings and shook her head.

"It's not going to rain tonight," she said. "I don't want to sleep inside."

"I know what you mean," Dave said.

"The ash is still falling, Daddy." It was true. The many fires had released a storm of gray ash into the air, and it had been slowly drifting down. Though it was nothing like it had been in the first hours after the quake, all three of them were filthy just from standing around outside.

"I'll set up the tent. We've got cots down in the storage room."

The girls followed him down the narrow steps to the small threshold of the underground storage room.

It wasn't as bad as he had feared. Most of the food he had bought was in metal or plastic containers. Stacks had tumbled and boxes had split open, but they didn't lose very much. Karen looked at it all, a bounty she would have scoffed at as a foolish waste of money not very long ago, and put her arm around Dave's waist.

"You've taken good care of us," she said, quietly.

"It doesn't feel like it."

"You got the early warning. I screwed that up."

"I think the best idea is to forget about that, okay? I'm not angry. Addison's not angry. Addison, are you angry?"

"I'm not angry, Mom. And I think Dad's right, let's just not dwell in the past, we have enough to do to deal with the future."

Night had fallen before they were through. It was a starless, moonless night, the sky seeming blacker than any sky had any right to be. Living in the city with its constant glow had not prepared any of them for such inky darkness. They turned on a battery-powered camp light, which only made the shadows seem to press in closer. Dave didn't want to use the lamp any more than he had to, so he took his ax and broke up a few dresser drawers brought out from the main house.

"Pretty expensive fire," he commented. "How much did we pay for that dresser?"

"Too much," Karen said. "I wish we'd bought gasoline instead."

"Me, I wish we could burn than flat-screen plasma TV. At least the dresser is useful now. What is it, sixty years old? Seventy, something like that?"

"I don't recall. It does make a nice fire."

Huddling near the fire was much different from sitting around the harsh light of the fluorescent camp lantern. They were all glad when that was turned off. The darkness was still just as intense, but the flickering shadows cast on the walls of the house and the perimeter wall seemed comforting rather than threatening.

They opened a can of corned beef and one of refried beans. Karen improvised a flat griddle over the fire, and made tortillas out of cornmeal and flour. They folded beef burritos with a little salsa spooned from a big plastic jar, with a side of canned corn. Dave was so hungry he ate three, chiding himself, knowing they were going to have to go on short rations sooner or later. But Addison downed two of them herself, and so did Karen. No one talked. Dave felt like they were a real family for the first time in too many years. It was a good feeling.

They looked out over the basin, where fires still burned, but not nearly so many. Most of them had finally encountered some obstacle and were guttering.

Dave barked his knuckles twice setting up the tent, and didn't feel he'd done a very good job of it, but it would do for now. In the morning, when he could see better, he'd straighten it out.

Karen put the empty cans in the fire and scorched them clean.

"No trash pickup," she said. "Even if we bury this stuff, if might attract raccoons. Or rats."

"Good idea," Dave said. "There's something else I want to talk to you both about. I do intend to bury our garbage, and I'll tell you why." He paused.

"This is hard, but I might as well just say it. Karen, Addison, I don't want our neighbors to know how much food we have."

He let them digest that. He was pretty sure it wasn't going to go down well with his daughter, and also pretty sure that Karen, newly practical again, would understand his reasons.

"I'll throw it open for discussion," he said, "but my feeling is that the old rule of 'share and share alike' doesn't apply when survival is at stake. The plain fact is that some of us here on the hill have a lot of food, and some of us surely don't."

He waited for a reaction. Addison was looking down at the picnic table. This was the girl who wanted to open their house to strangers, who would have been on the serving line at the soup kitchen at Staples Center if Dave had let her.

"Won't food be coming in again, when they get those big train engines going again? The ones we saw in the park?"

"I hope so, Addie. I really do. And maybe it's coming in already. We'll find out more as the days go by. But things were bad enough before, and they're likely to be a *lot* worse with this earthquake. I imagine the roads and rails are torn up. What I want to ask you to do is, if anyone asks you if we have any food, you tell them to come talk to me. Can you do that?"

Addison didn't say anything.

"Addie, please, can you just do that?"

"Okay. I guess I can."

Dave decided not to push his luck on that point. He didn't know enough himself, though he hoped to learn more at the neighborhood meeting the next day. There must be others who had CBs or ham-radio equipment. He had a feeling that would be their best source of news for the time being.

The fire had burned down to embers, and the three of them entered the tent and got as comfortable as they could on the cots. Dave was so tired he expected to drop off quickly, but it took at least an hour.

The sun never quite made an appearance the day after the quake, either, but there was a bit more of a sense that it was up there somewhere. There was a light breeze from the Pacific, which blew off some of the lingering black haze, but the air was hot and close and tasted bad. The ashfall had lessened, but with any breath of wind, ash that had already fallen stirred up and covered everything.

Dave ate his breakfast of bottled orange juice and canned corned beef hash standing up, looking out over the devastation.

Karen was trying to bathe in a few gallons of water. They had a large amount of water in the pool, but it wasn't infinite. The cover would slow evaporation, but could not stop it. Water was the thing that worried Dave the most. You could live a long time without enough food. Without water, you were dead in days.

Karen had strung a rope at about her chin height in a corner of the patio, tying it to the fence on one side and the frame of a sliding door on the other. She had hung a blanket over the rope. Dave could see her head and her feet in shower clogs as she dried herself off. He set his dirty plate on the picnic table and went to meet her as she pulled the blanket back. She was dressed in a clean blouse and pants, and was tying her hair back. She smiled at him.

"That feels better, though I think I'd prefer the spa down at the Beverly Hilton."

"I'll see what I can do."

"Addison went first," she said, gesturing to the gray, soapy water in the large galvanized tub. "Do you want a fresh tub, or will you make do with thirds?"

"If you can handle seconds, I can do thirds," he said.

"I left some clean clothes on the little table in there. Throw me those you've got on when you start."

He went under the rope and pulled the blanket across, shucked off the filthy clothes he had slept in, and threw them to Karen. She had put a canvas camp stool there beside the tub.

"There are so many things I have to rethink," she said. "We're so used to automatic washers and dryers."

"Drying should be easy."

"Yeah, I can string a clothesline. But washing . . . Women used to use washboards, and hand wringers, didn't they? Did you get a washboard?"

"I'm sorry, I didn't think of that. Tell the truth, I wouldn't have known where to look for one."

"Same here."

"I'm sure I could make one in the workshop out of corrugated sheet metal—"

"That would be good."

"—if I had any corrugated sheet metal."

They both laughed. Dave wondered once more what all he had forgotten, and if any of it was more critical than a washboard.

It felt good to scrub the grit off himself. He felt layers of sweat and ash and plaster dust flowing off his skin. He was amazed at how black the water had turned. He used a dab of shampoo on his hair. Then, once he had soaped up, there was the problem of how to wash the soap off himself. Well, he figured the water Karen had used hadn't been much less soapy, so he splashed himself until he felt a little less slippery, then toweled dry and put on the clean clothes. He found he felt 100 percent better.

Karen had put all their dirty clothes in a laundry basket. Addison went to the tub and looked down at the water, made a face.

"You want to dump this, Daddy?"

"No, no, no. That's what RV people call gray water. You can't drink it, but it's not sewage. I want you to pour it into buckets and take it into the downstairs bathroom. I'm hoping the toilets still work. What you do is, after you've done your business—and I don't mean taking . . ."

"Taking a pee?"

"Urinating. Don't flush after that. But after . . ."

"Number two?" She was laughing.

"Yes. Dump some of this gray water in. It should flush. At least for now. The longer we can do that, the less we have to worry about disposing of poop."

"Poop, Daddy?"

"Don't you laugh at me. Anyway, limit your use of toilet paper, too. We've got a stockpile, but don't expect we'll have any more."

Addison frowned. "What do you use when we run out?"

"Well, honey," Karen said, "back on the farm in Iowa, we used corncobs."

"Corncobs? Eeew!" It took her a few seconds to see her leg was being pulled, and all three of them laughed. Karen had grown up in Iowa, but she'd never been on a farm.

"So what do we use?" Addison persisted.

"People did use corncobs," Dave said. "Or the Sears, Roebuck catalog."

"You think the Neiman-Marcus catalog would work?" Karen asked.

"Don't see why not. They probably use a better grade of paper."

"And that's about all it's good for, now," said Addison.

Addison wanted to go down the hill to the meeting, but Karen vetoed the idea, saying there was still too much to do to get their new home ready for occupancy. None of them was delighted with the idea of sleeping indoors again anytime soon, and with the tent and the unlikelihood of rain that time of year in Los Angeles, they wouldn't have to. But things had to be stored away, including most of the things still packed in the Escalade, and Karen refused to think of the guesthouse as her home until the clutter was cleared away entirely and at least some cleaning had been done.

Dave got his bicycle out of the garage and headed down the hill as slowly as possible. Soon he came to the big double hairpin turn. He was pleased to see that the terracing designed to prevent mudslides in the rainy season had held up. He didn't see any sections that had collapsed.

He looked at each house as he went by them. Somebody seemed to have organized a more thorough rescue operation than he and his neighbors up the hill. They had come through with a can of spray paint and marked each house. Some had big Xs on the front, and some had an S. There were other letters also. He tentatively decided that the S stood for "searched." He assumed somebody could explain the other letters to him, probably at the meeting.

Once he passed a burned-out home. He could see where the fire had continued on up the hill, moving from dry tree to dry tree, until it reached the top of the ridge. At least two more houses that he could see had burned, too. Maybe more.

Several times he came to trees that had fallen across the road. At the first one he had to get off his bike and carry it up into a yard. It was a big deciduous tree, branching off in all directions. He could see where someone had made a start at cutting off branches, but it was going to be quite a job. He had to go behind the big ball of dirt and twisted wood that was the root structure.

There were a few palm trees that had fallen, but considering how many palms lined Doheny Drive, it was a surprisingly small number. They were supple, evolved to bend before high winds, but they were not deeply rooted.

The next blockage, about halfway down the hill, was a landslide. Tons of earth had come crashing down, taking a house with it. The house now stood partly in the road and it was leaning at a thirty-degree angle. Half a dozen men were at work shoveling away dirt on the west side of the street, and would soon have a path cleared that might be just wide enough for a car, assuming the house didn't move any more with the aftershocks. Dave had no trouble getting around it on his bike. He talked with the men for a while, and learned they were from some of the side streets he hadn't explored: Oriole, Thrasher, and Skylark. There were larger obstructions up there, they said, but they were beginning at the bottom and working their way up. Many of them intended to leave, as soon as they could get their cars out.

After that it was almost a straight, unimpeded shot to the meeting place.

There was a high wall with a gate that was standing open. Just inside the gate a few dozen bicycles, two motor scooters, and one full-sized off-road motorcycle were parked. He chained his bike to an iron fence and started up the long, asphalt driveway. There was a wide crack in it.

Around a bend he saw the house, which easily qualified as a mansion. It was two stories high, and vaguely resembled the White House, though the extravagant tropical plantings of queen palm, coconut palm, date palm, and giant bird-of-paradise trees instantly gave away that this wasn't Washington. There was a broad porch with a roof held up by pillars in the Greek style. One of them on a corner had cracked and toppled. He could see a lot of broken windows, and someone had carried a lot of debris out of the house and piled it off to one side. The pile looked very much like his own pile of new junk, with lots of glass, ceramics, and plaster. The driveway ran in front of the house and then around the side to a separate building in the back.

There was a tennis court on the other side of the building, where people were congregating. A few dozen stackable plastic chairs had been set up but few people were in them. Most were standing around two folding tables where a large coffee machine had been set up.

It was an odd crowd. There were clumps of people, three and four and five, but very little mixing. Dave thought it was probably like his own neighborhood, where people knew some of their immediate neighbors but few people more than three or four houses beyond their own. The men outnumbered the women three to one, and there were only a few children. The kids were very quiet, clinging closely to adults. Dave imagined they had rebelled at the idea of being left behind with one parent. It would be a long time before they felt secure again.

The meeting—rally, planning session, war council, whatever it was supposed to be—was supposed to start at noon, but few things had ever started on time in Hollywood except the Oscars, and an earthquake wasn't going to change that. At last a man hurried out of the house to the tennis court. He was a small man, partially bald, in his late fifties or early sixties, and he had the look and manner and walk of a man who was used to getting things done. He was carrying a battery-powered bullhorn, which Dave thought was a little excessive. Apparently the man did, too, as he raised it to his mouth, then thought better of it, and handed it to another man, Indian or Pakistani. This second man had unfolded a card table and set up a laptop computer and some speakers. He powered up the laptop and plugged in the speakers.

"I'd like to thank you all for coming today," the first man said. "For those who don't know me, my name is Richard Ferguson. This is my house. Or what's left of it."

There were a few polite, rueful chuckles.

"Before all this happened, I was the president of the Lower Doheny Neighborhood Watch. Just to let you know where I'm coming from, and let you know I have some organizational experience. I have also founded and run a medium-sized aeronautical manufacturing company, at least until recently, when demand for my product fell to zero because of the oil shortage and economic dislocation. I had been approaching retirement, had planned to play a lot of golf, and now I'm involuntarily retired, the same as a lot of you. Like you, I've seen my investments become worthless and thought I'd seen the worst that could happen. Now we all know that the loss of our money turns out to be the least of our concerns. Now we know that our very physical survival is at stake."

He probably wouldn't have been too good running for office, Dave thought—he was too straight, he didn't exhibit any of the ease at dispensing comforting bullshit so vital to that undertaking—but a candidate wasn't what they needed at the moment. Dave knew they needed a leader. Maybe this guy was it. Dave knew he wasn't. He could run a five-person writing team, and that was about the extent of his organizational skills.

"Many of you have lost neighbors, some have lost family members. There is no coroner to take the bodies of our loved ones away, no undertaker to prepare them, no funeral director to handle all the arrangements, but they are going to have to be put into the ground soon. What's the best way to do that? That is just one of the many things we will have to relearn. We will be facing challenges of the sort few in America have had to face since our great-great-grandparents' generation, or even earlier.

"But I wonder if we might not be the fortunate ones? A hard thing to say to a man whose house has just collapsed or burned down, I know, a hard thing to say to a family that has lost a loved one, or is reduced to relying on the kindness of neighbors for their shelter.

"Still, I think it may be worse elsewhere. One of the things I've most wanted to know since the quake is simply this: Just how bad is it? We know how bad it is here, in our small neighborhood. What about outside? Things were at a terrible point even before the quake. I don't think we can count on any outside help. The rest of the state, the country, the world will be grappling with their own problems and will have precious little time for ours.

"What I'm saying, in the simplest terms, is that I think we're on our own. Has anyone had any contact with people farther afield than a mile or two? Has anyone had any news of rescue operations? Shelters being set up? Firemen responding to emergencies? Police patrolling? Any signs of government at all? What I'm desperate for, what I think we all need, is information. What is the world like down there? Down below Sunset Boulevard, just half a mile from here."

He looked over his audience. No one seemed eager to be the

first, or possibly no one had anything useful to say. Dave decided he had better speak up.

"I got a cell phone call through," he said, and everyone turned to him. "I was as surprised as anyone. I haven't tried it again. My friend was down in Holmby Hills, and his house had been flooded."

That got everyone's attention. No one else was aware of the flood.

"My friend said the Stone Canyon dam broke. Lots of houses washed down the canyon. He had water on his first floor, and he is several miles away from the dam."

It took a while for the excited and frightened babble to die down. Ferguson waited it out, and then put up his hands again.

"I'd heard rumors," he said. "I'm sorry to hear them confirmed. Thanks for telling us, Mister . . ."

"Marshall. Dave Marshall. I live up on Mockingbird Lane."

"Thanks, Dave. Okay, does anyone else have any news to share?"

"I've heard gunshots," a woman said. "They sounded like they were coming from south of Sunset. I live on Wetherly, about a quarter of a mile from here."

"My friend has heard gunfire in his neighborhood, too," Dave said.

"I think all of us who live down below the hills have heard them," Ferguson said. "Friends, let me introduce Patel Govinder, a friend of mine from way back. He lives up the hill, on Blue Jay Way. He's a ham-radio operator. Patel's rig is run on solar power, so that hasn't been a problem. He probably knows more about what's going on around the world than any of us. Would you fill us in, Patel?"

"Surely. The simplest thing is to say that everywhere there is chaos. I have contacted relatives in Mumbai, and they say there is starvation, rioting, many thousands, perhaps hundreds of thousands, dead."

He went on about the world situation for a while, confirming things that Dave had suspected. The Third World was faring worst, to no one's surprise

"Okay, my friend," Ferguson said, "but I think most of us are a bit more concerned about what's happening just down the street than around the world."

"Of course. I am sorry to hear of the dam collapse. That probably explains the silence of an operator I used to contact frequently, who lived in Stone Canyon." He briefly hung his head.

"To sum up my almost thirty-six hours of communications with people in this area and around California . . . it is clear that Los Angeles is a special case, with the earthquake. But Richard is correct in thinking that we should expect no outside help. I recorded this message from the mayor of Los Angeles early this morning," Patel went on. "I found it . . . disturbing. I don't know how to—"

"Just play it, Patel."

The small man nodded, and turned to his laptop. He called up an audio file.

A female operator who sounded like a police dispatcher announced that the mayor would be addressing the city from the emergency center in City Hall. She said the message was going to go out on all available frequencies, but that most commercial radio and television stations had been silenced, so she requested that anyone capable of tuning in record it and rebroadcast it as widely as possible. The operator sounded exhausted.

There was a pause, then a man's voice, sounding even more tired than the operator.

"This is the mayor speaking. First I want to issue an appeal to any authority outside the Los Angeles area." There was a long pause.

"We need help. Please come quickly, and help us."

The man's voice broke. There was dead silence on the tennis court. The mayor took a deep breath and went on.

"Los Angeles has been struck by a catastrophic earthquake. The devastation is . . . unimaginable. The earthquake has started fires which the fire department was . . . well, there were too many to respond to . . . We need firefighters, and quickly! We need air tankers, smoke jumpers, we need rescue crews and dogs, we need any help that anyone can send us."

Another long pause.

"The city is without power. None of the generating stations are operating and a great many power lines are down as well, so even if we get generators back online—and I don't know what they're going to burn if we do . . . there will be no electrical power for the foreseeable future. None. Residents, you must take that into account in your plans.

"Water mains are broken in so many places that it will take some time to restore water service. The Stone Canyon dam has failed, and we don't know how many people may have been killed or rendered homeless by that. There is water in Lake Hollywood, apparently that reservoir is intact, and we are attempting to run temporary pipes downhill to a dispensing facility. Keep listening to . . . to whatever source you are hearing this message on for further . . . for further developments."

The man sounded on the edge of a nervous collapse. He rambled, he lost his train of thought, he paused so long that it seemed he might not go on. He couldn't seem to make up his mind about what he should he talking about. He alternated between assurances that everything possible was being done, to ever more pitiful pleas for help.

It was the exact opposite of the leadership that someone needed to show at such a time, and indicated to Dave that there really *was* no meaningful leadership in this town on this day.

But there was worse to come.

"My police chief," the mayor began, and then laughed. It was a chilling sound.

"My new police chief," he amended, "my *acting* police chief . . . she tells me she is hardly able to communicate with her remaining officers. We don't know how many officers that is, but if you are a sworn member of the LAPD, or an auxiliary, or even if you're retired, for God's sake, and you can hear my voice, we are pleading with you to muster at City Hall this evening at six o'clock for assignments. Please, don't desert your posts in the hour of your city's greatest need. I know your impulse is to stay home and protect and provide for your families, but remember that you took an oath, and we must hold you to it. You are all we have now."

There was another long pause.

"We have been in contact with a seismologist at UCLA, and he tells us this quake registered an estimated 9.5 on the scale. That is equal to the most powerful one ever recorded. There have only been five quakes over 9.0 in the last 150 years. There is a possibility that it was caused by the same thing that caused the Doheny explosion. This man is theorizing that the expanding oil and sludge has worked its way down to the Santa Monica Fault or the Newport-Inglewood Fault, possibly both. It increased pressure and at the same time lubricated the rock faces so they slipped all at once, instead of in smaller increments. Or so they tell me. Who knows if it's true?"

Again there was silence, both on the radio and at the tennis court.

"Patty, take over, okay? I can't go on here."

The new police chief was heard next. She introduced herself as Patricia Noori.

"Until this morning I held the rank of captain in the LAPD. I have been asked to take over command. I intend to do so to the best of my ability.

"The mayor has approved some emergency measures. I am announcing a dusk-to-dawn curfew for all residents of Los Angeles. Rioters and looters will be shot on sight.

"I believe that we will pull through this. Recovery will take a long time, certainly many years, but I don't believe in giving up, and neither should you. May God see us through these coming, difficult days of trial. Thank you."

The laptop was shut off, and everyone looked at each other.

"Nobody likes to hear that the police will shoot on sight," Ferguson said. "Nobody likes it that we've come to this point. But we're not going to get through it by being polite, and the police aren't going to have time for Miranda warnings. They're going to be too busy trying to survive. I've had the advantage of hearing this twice before, and having a little time to think about it.

"I think this Chief Noori is a much better leader than our mayor. But I also think it's clear that the LAPD is completely inadequate to deal with the situation we have on the ground. Do you agree?"

No one said otherwise.

"As for the National Guard . . . well, their strength and deployment is something I hope we can find out in the days to come. But I, myself, don't feel any more inclined to rely on them than I do on the LAPD.

"I think we are *on our own*. Our neighborhood. We must band together as strongly as we can, with as much organization as we can muster, because in unity there is strength. I weep for Los Angeles, for California, for the nation, and for the world.

But right now what I am most concerned about are these blocks around us, in the general area of Doheny Drive, this little valley, from the flats to the crest of the hills. I think it is a defensible area, and I think we should start thinking about defending it. And I propose that we start in on that right now."

Within an hour, with very few dissenting voices, the Doheny Militia was formed, with Richard Ferguson, former CEO of an aeronautics firm, as acting chief.

CHAPTER FOURTEEN

Dave's first turn at manning the ramparts of Doheny Drive came on the night after the neighborhood meeting, the third night after the quake.

It had been decided that intelligence would be gathered at first by monitoring what electronic media were still in operation. Then, if they decided they needed to know more, small parties might venture beyond Sunset to get the lay of the land.

Ferguson had not been elected, and so far no one had called for elections. Everybody seemed content to let him take over, since he seemed to have the best information, had been thinking about it longer than anyone but Dave, and was willing to take the job.

Dave had not revealed his own prior knowledge. He didn't intend to enlighten anyone, either. He felt nervous about his stockpiles of food and other supplies, and not only against a perceived threat from outsiders. He worried that his own neighbors might be just as big a threat to his family, when they got hungry enough.

That first day groups had been organized by street, and those groups had caucused briefly to select one person to be in charge of each group. Those group leaders were to receive new information from Ferguson and three other men who had volunteered to be his lieutenants. Bulletins would be issued as Patel found out more from the radio networks being established, and relayed verbally up the hill. Printed notices were to be kept to a minimum, to save paper.

So already a small bureaucracy had been established. Mankind was the political animal, no doubt about it.

The last order of business had been for volunteers to draw numbers from a silver punch bowl. A duty roster was to be drawn, and when one's number came up he or she was to report to the bottom of the hill—armed, if possible—to stand a watch. Dave had volunteered, along with more than half the attendees. Later that day a messenger came to his gate with the news that he was to present himself between midnight and 6 A.M. the following evening.

When he arrived on his bicycle, carrying his shotgun, he was surprised at how much had been done.

A barricade had been built right across Doheny by rolling useless cars with empty gas tanks down the hill. Some of them had been turned on their sides, providing good cover for the militia to hide behind. Dave could see a Hummer with a chain attached to it that had been used to upend the cars, and a block and tackle.

The reason he could see any of it on that night without streetlights or light coming from any of the houses was two battery-powered security spots on metal poles, facing down the street.

He was greeted by a man he recognized from the meeting two days before, who introduced himself as Art Bertelstein. He was tall and thin, in his forties, with a shock of curly yellow hair held down by a yarmulke. He was carrying a rifle, and had a revolver tucked into his waistband.

"What's my job here?"

"We're still feeling our way. Personally, I think this is all overreaction."

"Is that why you're carrying two guns?"

Art laughed.

"Better safe than sorry. I think that if we get attacked, it's most likely to be under cover of darkness. What do you think?"

"I don't know whether to expect organized attacks, or just desperate individuals. I'll tell you one thing, though. I won't shoot unless somebody is shooting at me."

"I'm with you there. What do you think about this Ferguson?"

"What do you mean?"

Art looked down at the ground, then back at Dave.

"He's sort of taken over. I don't know much about him."

"I'm willing to follow his lead for now."

Art nodded, but he didn't seem happy.

"Okay. I was never in the army. How about you?"

Dave shook his head.

There were four of them on the graveyard shift. The other two were Sam Crowley, a seventy-two-year-old retired cinematographer who lived on Kinglet Drive, and Marie O'Brien, who had run a real-estate agency in Beverly Hills. She appeared to be in her late forties, and was attractive even in rumpled clothing that wasn't too clean. Crowley was athletic-looking and completely bald. Both of them carried shotguns.

"There's another guy out there about a hundred yards down the street," Art said. "He's hiding behind a wall, beyond the range of the lights, and he's got a walkie-talkie. He's supposed to warn us if he sees anybody coming up the road."

"If he sees somebody and talks, would the people coming up the road be able to hear him?" Dave asked.

"Good question. Damn, I wish we had a soldier here."

"I have a suggestion. I saw it in a movie. You can just click the button on those radios and it will make a click on your unit. We could work out a code."

"Good idea."

"Is he armed? Yes? Then if we get into a firefight, he could surprise them by firing from behind."

"Unless he runs away. Damn. Firefights, ambushes . . . I hate this."

"Don't we all."

Art called the man at the forward post and they decided if he saw anyone coming, he would click twice, pause, and then click the number of people he saw. He was dubious about opening fire from behind, unless there was only one or two guys. Dave didn't blame him. He had been thinking like a scriptwriter. Out in the field, where the bullets would be real, it felt very different.

They stood around and talked quietly, though their eyes kept being drawn out to the street, where the lights faded into a darkness that now looked threatening. Twice they were silenced by the rattle of a distant automatic weapon, and once by a single shotgun blast. Other than that, the first night passed without incident.

Dave had spent the previous day and a half working on the guesthouse with Karen and Addison. They had cleaned out all the things no longer needed to make the guesthouse livable, and when it got dark they moved much of their food from the basement to a locked closet on the first floor.

He had mostly worked on boarding up the first-floor windows. Not just the ones that had broken in the quake, but all of them, sealing off his million-dollar view. Luckily, there weren't too many of them. On the first floor, the north and west sides were windowless, as their only views would have been of the wall and the gate. On the east side, there were three picture windows facing the patio and pool. That left the south side, which had been all glass. He used the sheets of plywood he had laid in during his shopping spree. He felt sure he could have gotten the job done in a few hours if he had unlimited electricity, and from time to time he would look longingly at his power saw. He could have run it for a short time from his solar batteries, but that would have meant turning off the small refrigerator, and that was one luxury he wasn't ready to part with. By cooling their leftovers they were able to make sure nothing went to waste.

Best of all, they had ice. The weather continued hot, and a glass of iced tea or lemonade made from powdered mix kept him going when he thought he might collapse.

Using a handsaw instead of a power saw wasn't exactly a retreat to Stone Age technology, but it felt like it. He would work for five minutes, then rest. Karen gamely offered to spell him while he rested, but she had even less success. Addison gave it a try, but could barely get the saw to move at all. Dave squirted a little oil on the blade and that seemed to help, but he was soon plastered in sawdust and feeling more than a little grumpy. At the end of the first day, he wasn't halfway through the project. He was getting a blister on his hand, despite the work gloves.

Then Karen and Addison would help hold the finished piece of plywood in place and he would nail it in. When he had the first section in place he felt a sense of accomplishment, as if he had built an entire house, but looking at how much he had left to do was depressing.

He was enormously glad when the sun went down. No question of working after dark anymore.

The three of them gathered around the dinner table for a

macaroni and cheese hot dish that was only burned a little bit on the bottom, with canned pears and string beans, and tiny cups of chocolate pudding for dessert. Karen set out a plate of biscuits made from powdered mix, but they were soggy when they bit into them.

"I'm still getting the hang of baking on the camp stove," she said.

"This isn't so bad," Dave said, bravely eating a second bite. And in fact, he was so hungry he could have eaten almost anything, including raw biscuit batter. "But I think we maybe should cut back on portions. I hate to say that, because I could eat everything on this table and still want more, but we have to make it last."

"I wish we knew how long," Karen said. "How much do you think? Fifteen hundred calories? Twelve hundred?"

"We can figure it out later. Tonight, let's eat our fill. I know there must be a lot of hungry people out there, who are getting less than twelve hundred calories."

Addison pushed her plate away.

"I've had enough," she announced. Karen pushed it back at her.

"Clean your plate, dear. My mother used to say, 'there are people starving in Africa.' Now there are people starving in Los Angeles, so count your blessings."

"I wish I could give it to them."

"And I wished I could feed the starving children in Africa, but we can't. You've just got a few bites there, and I know you're still hungry. If you want to make a sacrifice, don't open your pudding."

Dave mopped his plate with the soggy biscuit, then cleaned out the empty cans and plastic pudding containers in the tub of bathwater they had used earlier in the day and buried them under the pile of debris they had moved out of the guesthouse.

After Karen finished washing their dinnerware in a bucket of clean water, they lit a lantern and sat around the picnic table.

They had one surviving television set, a small one from Addison's room that had been knocked down but still showed a blue screen when they turned it on. But that was all they got. There was no cable service, and they didn't have a satellite dish.

Dave thumbed through all the channels, and the screen still stayed blue.

"Well, it's a better light," Karen said, turning off the lantern, "and it runs off our batteries." It was true. The flat screen made them look like they were underwater, but it was enough light to see by.

The radio was part of the home theater system. He slowly turned the big black knob, looking for stations, as the three of them clustered together in the blue light.

There wasn't a lot to hear.

He found a dozen stations, about half of them in Spanish. Many of the stations were broadcasting just music or simple tape loops advising listeners to return on the hour for news updates. Dave thought they probably didn't have the personnel to keep up the twenty-four/seven yakking everyone was accustomed to. That was confirmed when one station switched to live reports at ten o'clock. The man in the studio gave the call letters and the frequency, then identified himself.

"As we told you at nine, we will keep broadcasting as long as our emergency generator holds out. The engineer tells me he has enough gas for about a week. Write down this frequency, as we have decided to give updates on the hour.

"We are sending out our reporters as often as we can, but not many have shown up since the quake. Most of our news is coming from City Hall. Here's what they say:

"Exercise caution when leaving your homes. We are hearing a lot about people joining together for neighborhood protection, and that sounds like a good idea to me. Work with your neighbors, my friends. Get to know them."

Dave was reminded of old movies set during World War II, of London families during the Blitz, gathered around a big console radio to hear the news of the bombings. The darkness pressed in around them.

The silence was almost total between radio broadcasts. Each time a station signed off they would be directed to another frequency. The remaining stations had worked out a schedule of quarter-hour time slots. Karen jotted down the information, so they could listen again on following nights.

None of the news was good. Mostly it consisted of reports of violence, much of it of dubious reliability, as the first radio station had warned. A gun battle had broken out between police and unidentified gangs in the area of the Disney Center and continued on up Bunker Hill. Snipers were known to be in the lower floors of the Library Tower, and higher up in several other skyscrapers. More snipers had been reported from some buildings near the beach in Santa Monica.

Koreatown seemed to have the strongest organization, with armed men guarding all major intersections in the big square between about Olympic and Third, Hoover and Rossmore. Bodies were reported to be hanging from lampposts all along Wilshire Boulevard, and at the major streets entering the area. Some had signs hanging around their necks, identifying them as looters, killers, and "invaders." The Korean militia had fought several pitched battles with either Mexican and Salvadoran gangs or hordes of hungry Hispanic families, depending on what reporter you believed. Everyone agreed that the Koreans had won. It was said that food and water were still being delivered and distributed to residents of Koreatown, but that could not be confirmed, as no one from that neighborhood was talking about it.

Farther south, established black and Hispanic gangs were reported to be rampaging, though some said that was much exaggerated. The one hopeful thing Dave heard was that the elders in both the African-American and Latino communities on the flatlands were trying to work together to battle the lawless youth of both races. But once again, that was not easy to confirm. In the San Fernando Valley the story was similar. They got no news at all from the San Gabriel Valley, or from farther south in Orange County.

And once more, Dave thought, our world contracts. Orange County might as well be on the farside of the Moon. At ten o'clock they turned the radio off, then the television, and sat silently for a while.

"I wish I could call some of my friends," Addison finally said.

Dave didn't know what to tell her. Only two of her friends had lived in their canyon, and both had left with their families a week earlier. The others had lived either in neighboring canyons or down on the flats. Both places were impossibly distant at the moment.

"I'll bet you miss your cell phone," Karen said. "I know I do."

Addison said, "I try it a few times a day. No bars."

Strange as all this seemed to Dave, he knew it must be even more of a wrench for his daughter, who had never known life without her cell. No Facebook page to update, no Twitter messages to post, no texting, none of the social media that Dave had never used but which were so big a part of the young generation's lives.

"Tomorrow night you have to stand guard duty," Karen said.

"That's what I agreed to."

"I don't like it. I don't like the family to be separated, even for a few hours."

"I don't like it, either, but I think Ferguson is right, we have to stand together. You heard the reports on the radio. Some very nasty people might figure that there's more food and loot up here than down there."

"What's to prevent them from coming over the hill, behind us?"

"For one thing, they'd have to fight their way uphill from the Valley. We can hope that the people on the north side of the hills are organizing just like we are."

"But if they do make it, we're pretty close to the top. Last night I had bad dreams about people coming down the hill, not up."

Dave took her hand and squeezed it, while at the same time Addison reached for his other hand. He knew even more strongly that he would do anything, absolutely anything, to keep this family safe.

"I'll bring it up the next time I see Ferguson."

"I think we should reach out to those people on the Valley side," Addison said. "Wouldn't it be better if we all had some idea of what everyone else is doing?"

"I agree." And so now would the Doheny Militia be formulating a foreign policy, and alliances with its neighbors? It was like medieval city-states banding together, and that had to be a good thing, didn't it?

"For now, let's go to bed," he said. And they once more retreated to their cots in the tent. Before he could get to sleep, Dave felt another aftershock, and heard Karen cry out. It wasn't a big one, but probably meant they would be spending at least another night without a roof over their heads.

* * *

They spent the next day as they had the day before, putting the finishing touches on their new and smaller residence. They managed to complete the plywood work, walling off the entire first floor. There was a single door hung on heavy hinges that swung outwards. Not that it swung well, or fit perfectly, but it was stout, made from two pieces of plywood screwed together. Inside, a two-by-four could be set into brackets on either side of the door. It would take a lot of battering to bring it down.

They had made openings in several places from which they could watch the patio and the gate. From the second-floor north wall they knocked out one of the small slit windows, which now gave a view over the northern wall and into the street beyond.

Dave didn't want them to have only one way in or out of the house if they had to hole up in it, but he didn't want two doors to defend, either. So in the very southwest corner of the first floor, down at floor level, they made a three-foot-square escape hatch that could be kicked out. It would be used only in desperation, because it opened on the very lip of the cliff, and if they used it they would have to walk—or more likely, roll—down the steep hillside to the street below.

They concealed the escape hatch from the outside by arranging some empty ceramic pots against the wall and putting dead plants in them. They could be easily shoved aside and, with any luck, the family could be on their way down the hillside before anyone breaking in the front door was any the wiser.

The next-to-last task of the day was to go back into the main house and clear a path to the northwest corner, which was in Addison's room. There were two floor-to-ceiling windows there, one facing west and the other north. They were wider than the arrow slits in a medieval castle, but narrow enough that Dave could have just squeezed through them. They knocked out the glass, then cut two sheets of plywood into four pieces. They screwed one piece over the west window at floor level, and another higher up, flush with the ceiling. They left a foot-high gap between them, at shoulder height.

Getting one of the shotguns, Dave climbed the stairs again and stood at the window. He brought the gun up and poked the barrel through the gap, swinging it back and forth. He could cover a lot of the street from there, about five feet above the level of the security wall. It looked good to him, so they did the same with the north window, and then they could cover almost all the rest of the street.

The last thing they did that day was go to the room in the northeast, which was smaller than Addison's but had the same corner arrangement of windows. Both of them had broken, and they knocked out the rest of the glass.

Karen had talked him into the house, even though he thought it was ugly. Too modern, too boxy, he felt. "Very L.A.," she had said, and so they bought it.

Now he was grateful to the unknown architect for building a home that might have been designed with self-defense in mind. It had proved easier to seal away from the outside than most houses, because it was already sealed off except for the open south face. When they had prepared the two windows in the storage room in the same way they had done in Addison's room, it commanded a view of all the street. They could move quickly from one gun port to another, one room to another, or Dave could station himself in one room and have Karen look out from the other.

They ate a dinner that left Dave still hungry, but he said nothing about that. He probably ought to lose a few pounds, anyway.

Dave fell into his cot ten minutes after eating, setting the alarm for eleven thirty. At least battery-powered clocks still worked.

He slept right through it, but Addison woke him and he downed a glass of orange juice, stumbled out onto the street, and painfully lifted his leg over the bicycle. It seemed that every muscle in his body was stiff and sore as he coasted down the hill for his shift on guard duty.

Dave surprised himself by pedaling almost halfway up the hill before his legs gave out. He had made it from the bottom to the top before, but that was not after a day and a half of hard physical labor that had left him drained and hurting.

Walking the bike uphill was a little easier, but not much. About the only thing he could console himself with was knowing that there was not a great deal left to do in getting moved into the guesthouse and fortifying his land.

He was almost to the intersection of Doheny and Mockingbird when he looked up the steep hillside to his right and saw a woman stepping over the metal guardrail.

That was Sunset Plaza Drive, and even though the person up there was only about four hundred feet from where Dave stood with his bicycle, the only way to get there on streets was a torturous route that would take her almost all the way down to Sunset before doubling back on Rising Glen Road.

The woman seemed to have other ideas. She was in a big hurry. She hesitated only a moment before stepping over, her heel hitting loose dirt and skidding several feet before her other foot hit the ground. She fell back on her behind and spread her arms out, trying to hug the ground, splayed out like a starfish, looking terrified. It was only then that Dave realized it was Jenna.

She was dressed in jeans, one red tennis shoe, and a torn and filthy T-shirt. She had a backpack over one arm, but that quickly slipped off and rolled down the hill ahead of her.

Her shoe and one bare foot dug into the soil, but it was too loose. She was skidding, a shower of dry dirt going down before her.

Suddenly, at the rail a few feet above her, two men appeared. Both of them wore what looked like black leather pants. One of them had a matching leather vest, the other was shirtless. Both were large men, heavily tattooed, and they looked angry. One of them shouted something Dave didn't get.

Jenna didn't hesitate. She pulled up her feet and started to slide. She quickly lost what little stability she had, and did a somersault. Once, then twice she rolled over, scrabbling, finally getting herself turned sideways.

Dave heard a gunshot, looked back up at the railing, and was shocked to see that the shirtless one had a gun in his hand and was shooting at Jenna. She was only thirty yards away from him. The other man whooped, and the shooter slapped his friend on the shoulder. Dave knew handguns were not very accurate—this guy was holding his sideways, like he must have seen in the movies. But any idiot can get lucky.

He didn't think about it. He jumped off the bike, racked a round into the shotgun, put it to his shoulder, and fired. He knew there was no chance of doing any damage from this far away, but he wanted to get their attention.

He did. The shooter had been about to squeeze off another round, but he jerked and then ducked with his partner standing there, staring at Dave, who was already running up the street as fast as he could. Dave saw the man in the leather vest point a gun in his direction. He heard the gunshot. There was no telling where the round went. He had never been shot at in his life, and he was amazed at how much energy just the sound of the gunshot had injected into his tired leg muscles. He was almost sprinting before he stopped and put a tree between himself and the gunmen.

It had been only seconds since the first shot was fired. Jenna was still rolling down the hillside, trying to slow herself by grabbing at scrub as she hurtled by. Dave wasn't sure that was a good idea, but maybe she felt it was better to break an arm or a leg than to be shot. He raised the shotgun again and fired at the men. The one who had crouched behind the iron railing was tugging at his friend's vest, trying to get him to take cover. The vest shrugged him off and aimed again at Dave.

Dave left the tree in time to see Jenna slide from sight behind one of the houses on Doheny. He looked up and saw the shirtless one aim in her general direction.

There was the sharp crack of a rifle and then a clank as a bullet hit the guardrail a few feet from where the men were crouching. Dave could see the dust fly off the rail, but he couldn't be sure where the shot came from.

The men on the hill apparently saw the shooter, and they didn't stick around for him to take a second shot. They vanished quickly. Dave stopped, jacked another round into his gun, and aimed at the guardrail, but no one appeared. He heard the sound of two motorcycle engines start up, and dwindle away. He thought he heard at least two more rifle shots, but they didn't come from where the first one had. It sounded like someone up on Sunset Plaza was shooting at the bikers. At least he hoped so.

He sat down on the curb and breathed heavily for a while, then forced himself to his feet and hurried as quickly as he could up the street.

He reached the place where he thought Jenna would have come to rest. It was behind a series of three gated homes. A warning had been spray-painted on the wall: TRESPASSERS WILL BE SHOT.

He put his shotgun on the pavement and shouted.

"Hello in there! This is Dave Marshall. I'm a member of the Doheny Militia. I need to talk to you."

A woman peeked through a trapdoor in the solid steel driveway gate.

"I saw a woman falling down the hill. She's a friend of mine. I fired at those guys up on the hill."

"With that shotgun?"

"It was all I had. I wanted to distract them. How is my friend?"

"I don't know. My husband is back there taking care of her." She sighed, and pushed her hair back out of her eyes. "Go over to the gate and I'll let you in."

The door in the gate opened, and he stepped through.

The front yard had been extensively landscaped with things like banana trees, elephant ears, and other tropical plants. All that had now been cut back away from the house, much of it heaped into a big pile against the concrete block wall. It was drying and turning brown. The woman looked to be in her forties, with blonde hair, a little overweight, though her face was gaunt.

"Around here," she said. Dave followed her into a narrow space between the house, which seemed not badly damaged by the quake, and a privacy hedge separating the house from its neighbor downhill.

There was a patio in back, with a kidney-shaped pool. He saw a man kneeling beside Jenna, who was sitting up. He hurried over to them. Jenna's clothes were torn. She was covered in dirt, dripping with sweat. Her hair was a tangled mess, full of twigs and dead leaves. There was dried blood all down the front of her shirt, and fresh blood flowing from her nose. One eye was swollen shut, surrounded by dark purple skin. She was cradling her left hand against her body.

"I'm okay, I'm okay," she was saying. "I think I sprained my wrist and broke my nose again. I don't want to stay here, those guys might come back. There are more of them . . ." She looked up. "Dave! It's you. God, am I glad to see you."

She was trying to get to her feet and the man was trying to calm her down.

"It's okay," Dave said, taking her good hand and pulling her up. "I know her. She's a friend of mine."

The man stepped back and picked up a rifle, looking up the hill. There was no one up there that they could see. The property was protected at its boundary, maybe ten feet up the hillside, by a high chain-link fence with a gate that was standing open.

Dave felt vulnerable. He put Jenna's good arm over his shoulder and his own arm around her waist and half carried her toward the house. The woman was holding a back door open and she and her husband followed Dave inside.

Inside were cracked walls and shelves that had once held what might have been a nice china collection, now shattered and swept into a heap. Books had been restacked at random. He took Jenna to a French provincial sofa and lowered her gently onto it.

"I'm Herman Patterson," the man said. "My wife's name is Matilda, Mattie for short." The woman appeared beside Jenna with a bowl of water and some washcloths. She started dabbing at Jenna's face. Jenna winced, thanked her, and took over the job of cleaning herself. The basin was soon brown with dirt and blood. Jenna probed in her mouth with a finger.

"I think I loosened a tooth," she said.

"It was quite a fall," Dave told her.

"Yeah, if I can't get a job as a writer, maybe I can start a second career as a stuntwoman. You remember Dudley Moore rolling down the hill in *10*? Believe it or not, that scene kept playing in my mind as I was sliding. I didn't want to roll head over heels, so I turned sideways. I'm lucky I didn't break my neck."

"How's your arm?"

"It's just the wrist. It'll probably swell up pretty soon. You didn't think I got all this damage from rolling down the hill, did you?"

"That's pretty clear."

"It's a goddam jungle out there, Dave."

They thanked the Pattersons for their help, and Dave helped Jenna through the gate and onto Doheny Drive.

"Dave, I don't want to alarm your daughter. Could we just say that I slipped coming down the hill?"

"We could do that, but she's not stupid."

"No, I guess not. Do you want to know what happened, before we get to your house?"

"Only whatever you want to tell."

"I guess I had some bad luck. Ran into that gang, it was five guys and three of their girlfriends, and there wasn't a damn thing I could do about it."

Jenna had planned to set out early in the morning the day after Dave had offered her the use of his house after his family left. The quake made that impossible.

"Two buildings in my complex collapsed completely. My building, the west end fell in, and part of my apartment. The wall around my front door was so screwed up I couldn't get the damn door open, even battering at it with a hammer. So I hollered for help. Some guys came and knocked down the door.

"I joined the search parties trying to find survivors. I heard . . . oh, Dave, I heard children in there, crying out for their mothers, most of them in Spanish. And we couldn't see them, and couldn't get to them. Some of them are probably still crying. After a while, I couldn't take it anymore, and I bugged out. I'm not proud of it, but I left."

"Jenna, there's only so much—"

"—one person can do. I know that. I wasn't doing anyone any good, anyway. We needed heavy equipment, and none showed up. They were trying to move bricks and lumber by hand, and you could see it would take weeks to get to the trapped people, if you could get to them at all. I couldn't even cry anymore.

"Which was a good thing, later . . ." She stopped walking, which almost pulled Dave off balance. She looked up at him.

"I can see this story is going to take a long time, and I want to tell you . . . there were five of them, and their *women*." She spit out the last word. "I told myself it would go easier if I just . . . went with it . . . but I couldn't do it. So they beat me up some. And then they did me anyway, taking turns or two at a time. And their girls not only watched, they egged them on. I thought I knew evil, Dave, but I didn't even have a clue. You know what? I hated the women even more than I hated the men, and I hated the men more than I've ever hated anything. If only I'd had a gun. They probably would have killed me, but I might have taken a few of them with me."

She stopped. Dave waited for her to go on, but it seemed she had no more to say. Dave was just as glad. He was willing to listen to anything at all if it would help, but he had a feeling it was something she might talk to Karen about more easily. Then he remembered that Jenna and Karen were not the best of friends.

"Addison is going to know, Jenna."

"Yeah, I'm sure she will. But she doesn't need to know any details. If she asks, I'll just say yes, it happened, and that's the end of it. Is that okay? Dave, I don't want to bring all this into your house. All this ugliness."

"Don't give it another thought. We're all going to have to get used to it, and that includes my daughter. Who is tougher than you might know."

CHAPTER FIFTEEN

"So I grabbed two bottles of water and split."

Jenna was trying to heed Karen's warnings not to put too much food on an empty stomach too quickly. Dave could tell she wanted to tilt the pot up to her mouth and shovel the Chef Boyardee spaghetti and meatballs directly into her mouth, but she forced herself to take it a spoonful at a time, talking compulsively about her recent odyssey through the depths of hell, formerly known as the San Fernando Valley.

"That was the next day, not too long after sunrise, so it was maybe thirty, thirty-two hours after the quake. Next thing you know, I got lost."

She blew on another spoonful, chewed it slowly.

"I know, how do you get lost in the Valley? It's nothing but a grid between the Ronald Reagan and the Ventura. But I did. I don't think I was completely in my right mind. I wasn't processing information right.

"But it was changed, too. There were places where the streets had buckled, the pavement had been shoved up five or six feet high. There were power lines down all over the place and I was afraid to touch them until it finally sunk in that there wasn't any power, anywhere. Trees were down everywhere, and some of them had knocked down street signs. Nothing looked all that familiar."

She took another bite.

"Dave, Karen . . . Addison, I'd say most of the buildings in the Valley are ones that would be red-tagged in the sort of earthquakes we've had before. Unsafe to enter, total losses. Just bulldoze them and start over. Maybe 10 percent of the buildings I saw had collapsed completely. Piles of rubble, and some of them were fairly new, probably up to code. And still they fell down."

Karen had taken Jenna under her arm and hustled her off to the private corner behind the blanket where they kept the tub, and shouted for Addison to heat some water. Lots of water. Later she had called for clothes, and Addison had brought some of her own, because she was closer in size to little Jenna than her mother was. Then Addison got the big box of bandages and disinfectants. She took with her a glass of Gatorade over ice.

The women stayed behind the curtain for over an hour, and two tubs of gray, soapy, and bloody water were dumped by Addison. When they finally drew the curtain back Jenna looked much improved: clean and neatly dressed, with a pair of black running shoes, her hair freshly washed and combed out. In other ways, she looked awful. Washing off the dirt had exposed dozens of cuts and scrapes. There was a big bandage over her swollen eye, and lots of Band-Aids and splotches of iodine. There was a splint on her left little finger.

Dave had been ready with a pan of spaghetti he had heated up over the small propane stove. And Jenna began to eat and talk.

"Anyway, there are whole blocks that are burned-out, and blocks that are mostly rubble. People are sitting out on the street with what they've salvaged. It's a pitiful sight, they have almost nothing. Well, all I had was what was in my backpack, and now I don't even have that. But I don't give a damn. I got out alive.

"I saw a city water truck come by and it was almost mobbed. There were two cops on it, and they had to fire in the air to get people to line up for water. I got lucky, I was there when a Salvation Army truck pulled up. I think that might have been in Toluca Lake, but I'm not sure. I did walk close to the lake at some point, but I got turned back by guys carrying rifles. Protecting their water, I guess. Anyway, I was near the head of the line when the Salvation Army started passing out sandwiches. Bless 'em. That bologna and cheese sandwich tasted better than a pastrami on rye at Canter's. I don't know where they're getting their food or gas, but they still seem to have some.

"Then I stumbled on Laurel Canyon Drive and realized it was probably the easiest way over to your place. But it was getting dark, and I only made it up to Mulholland. I couldn't see very well after that. I spent the night hiding in some bushes around the parking lot of the dog park up there."

Jenna took another bite, and for the first time didn't look like a starving animal. She chewed it slowly, then looked down at her plate for a while.

"I got careless," she said. "I'd heard the motorcycles in the distance. In that maze of streets, I never could tell if they were close, or in what direction. I didn't want to meet them, so whenever they sounded close I'd find somewhere to hide. Twice I came to barricades with men standing behind them. They let me through when I told them where I was going. As long as I was moving along it was okay, I guess. A couple people tried to give me directions, but I still got lost again. I thought Wonderland Avenue would get me to that hill I rolled down, but I ended up at a dead end."

"Probably Wonderland Park," Dave said.

"That sounds familiar. Anyway, I wandered some more. The sun was going down when I heard the motorcycles again, and that's when my luck ran out. I was on a stretch of road with precious little to hide behind. Walls on both sides, not much plantings. I crouched down behind a car but they'd seen me. They dragged me out . . . and the rest is right out of a bad episode of *Law and Order*. Let's just skip right over the next eight hours, okay?"

Karen reached out and took Jenna's hand. Addison did, too. Dave thought it best to keep his own hands on his side of the table.

"Not only did they have gas, they had booze and drugs. They took me to a house they'd taken over, the eight of them. The place was already trashed. I mean a garbage pit, not just damage from the quake, it held up pretty well. Already there were filthy dishes piled up and empty cans everywhere. They had a couple of big pit bulls, and there was dog shit all over the place. They were feeding the dogs from cans of corned beef hash, chipped beef, stuff like that, but they never gave me any food at all. One of the women brought me a glass of water at one point. That was it.

"They got drunker and drunker. I mean, they'd been drunk when they grabbed me, and they kept on drinking. They tied me to a drainpipe in the kitchen, but they were so stoned they forgot to check for knives in the drawers, and there was one there. A table knife, dull as a plastic emery board. But I sawed at it for an hour and got free.

"One of the guys, a fat slob who smelled like stale piss, was passed out in the living room. I guess the others were in the bedrooms. The idiot had left a shotgun propped up in the corner. I walked over to him and aimed it at his head."

Addison's eyes were wide.

"Don't worry. I didn't do it. I don't claim any great moral qualms about it, it was a practical thing. I don't know much about guns. I wasn't even sure how to reload it. I knew they'd come running if they heard a shotgun, and how was I going to fight off seven people and two dogs?"

She paused, with a faraway look in her eyes.

"I won't lie to you. I *wanted* to kill them. I wanted to kill them all. If I'd had one of those machine guns, a MAC-10 or whatever, I think I might have tried it. Just blown them away in their sleep, or better yet, wake them up and let them see what's about to happen to them. I know some people say that killing somebody stains your soul, they say that it will haunt you, even cops, even soldiers. I don't know. I do know that, as far as feeling stained goes . . . as far as feeling stained . . ."

She finally lost it, crying silently with her head down. Karen was up instantly, then sitting beside her and cradling Jenna's head on her shoulder. Addison leaned in closer. There were tears in her eyes.

Karen caught Dave's eye and gestured with her head: *Get lost*.

Dave did that.

When Jenna calmed down again there wasn't much to tell. She found her way to the cliff overlooking Doheny Drive and holed up again for the night. She figured she would walk the long way around, but then she heard the gang coming again—you can't sneak up on anybody on a Harley—and decided her only chance was to get down the hill as fast as she could.

"Dave, I left that shotgun up there in the bushes. I just had enough time to hide it. Do you figure it's worth it to go up there and get it?"

Dave went to Ferguson's house the next day and told him about Jenna's arrival, and Karen's worries about being vulnerable from above.

Getting Jenna's shotgun turned out to be the first move in opening relations with neighbors surrounding the Doheny Drive community. And so was born the Doheny neighborhood's foreign policy. Two couples who had friends over there were sent on a diplomatic mission to Rising Glen and Sunset Plaza, the two streets that ran up the nearest valleys to the east. They reported back that the two valleys were united in one self-defense organization similar to the Doheny group. Barricades had been erected on lower Sunset Plaza and on Londonderry Place, and were being guarded around the clock. So far there had been no trouble.

Joe Crawford was sent over the hill to Trousdale Estates in Beverly Hills. He reported back that he had spoken to people up and down both Hillcrest Road and Loma Vista Drive and had seen no signs of organization there. Everyone seemed to be hunkering down in their own houses, those that were still standing. Joe was sent back with instructions to try to drum up support for a community meeting to elect a leader or leaders, to tell the people over there how they had done it on Doheny and Sunset Plaza.

Dave volunteered to scale the hillside and try to make contact with whatever people might be organizing in the hills above him. That suited him fine, as it would give him a chance to recover the shotgun Jenna had taken from the biker gang. But he wasn't thrilled about the "scaling" part.

It turned out not to be a big problem. Herman Patterson, whose backyard Jenna had fallen into, had already established relations, of a sort.

"I went up and talked with them for a while," Patterson said.

"You climbed that?" Dave had been eyeing the slope without any great enthusiasm. It was steep, and the dirt looked loose in places.

"They dropped a rope. Wait a minute. We arranged some signals." He dug in his pocket and took out a referee's whistle. He blew two shrill blasts. They waited awhile, and then a man appeared behind the guardrail.

"My friend wants to come up and talk to you!" Patterson shouted. The man on the hill made a sign with his hand, and disappeared. He returned in a moment with a coiled rope slung over his shoulder. He tied the rope to the rail and flung it out over the hillside. It might have made it to the bottom but it got tangled and landed two-thirds of the way down. He looked disgusted, and hauled it back up.

The next time he untangled it and laid it out carefully, then tied a broken branch to it. When he hurled it out, the branch landed about twenty feet upslope from Dave and Patterson.

"You said you climbed up that?"

"It's not as bad as it looks. I've made it to the top without a rope at all, when I was ten years younger. Try it, you'll see."

Patterson was right. It would be possible to climb the hill without the rope, but Dave wouldn't have wanted to try it. With the rope, it was fairly easy. Twice the ground slipped away beneath his feet but he held on to the rope until he got his footing again, and then resumed his climb.

In a few minutes he was at the top. He shook hands with the men up there. They were Gene Chao, about forty years old, and Oscar Wilson, who looked to be in his mid-thirties. They were soon joined by Gene's wife, Lisa, a tiny woman who somehow communicated that she wasn't somebody to fool with.

He quickly determined that no one up there had really gotten serious about community defense, though there had been some talk. His instructions were to give a simple outline of the steps that had been taken on Doheny, and to suggest that they call a community meeting. Dave suspected that a person with the temperament suited to leadership would step forward soon enough.

But it really wasn't any of his business. If the Wonderland people organized, so be it, the Doheny group would work with them on mutual defense, covering each other's backs. If they didn't, then they were on their own.

The four of them spoke for a little over half an hour, then they worked it out that at noon every day someone would appear at the guardrail and someone else down on Doheny, and they would alternate climbing up or down.

Before coming back down the hill that day, Dave followed the directions Jenna had given him and, with a little rooting around in the shrubbery, found the shotgun she had abandoned. It was a Winchester pump, in a canvas case with a sling. Dave wished he had bought two pump guns rather than a pump and a double-barrel, but he had taken what he was offered. It would be good to have three shotguns.

* * *

Jenna spent most of the next day sleeping in the spare bedroom in the guesthouse. When she did get up he saw from the way she was hobbling around that she was in a great deal of pain. She kept insisting that she wanted to help out, and Dave and Karen kept assuring her that pretty much all the work that needed to be done had been done. Still, it was obvious that she was deeply disturbed to be invading their home with nothing to contribute. Dave pointed out that the shotgun she had taken from the biker would be a big help, which seemed to make her feel better.

"Can you tell me what to do?"

"I don't know much more than you do," Dave admitted. "But you want to be the one who shoots first. You might miss, but you're sure to rattle him."

"I don't want to miss," Jenna said. "I don't want to be a wuss here, Dave. All my life I've been against guns, in favor of gun control. If things were the way they were, I'd still be antigun. But I can see they're needed now."

"They're great equalizers," Dave said. "But only if you know how to use them. And only if you're *willing* to use them."

"I'm willing. Will you teach me?"

So they went out in the street and up the hill, knocking on doors as they went, warning the jittery occupants there was about to be gunfire. Several people joined them with their own weapons.

The collapsed house at the top of the street served well as a target and a backdrop. No one had figured out a way to remove the body of the man who had died inside, and his wife had left for parts unknown the day after the quake.

Jenna flinched as she fired her first round, as Dave had known she would. But her hand was steady when she fired again, and the third time. She even hit what she was aiming at, though they were not at any great distance from their targets.

Both Karen and Addison wanted to try their hands, too. They ended up firing a dozen of his precious shells, but he felt they were well used. It wasn't exactly Marine Corps basic training, but at least it got all three women used to the noise and the recoil. There was a good chance they would do what had to be done if the need arose.

The sound of gunfire brought other neighbors, and the word spread that a shooting range had been established. They brought their weapons and soon were blasting away at the collapsed house.

Some people up the hill, in the Wonderland area, were drawn by the gunfire, too, and stood behind the guardrail up there and observed the action. Later in the day, Dave heard shooting coming from up there. He hoped it meant they were forming their own militia, protecting the backside of Doheny.

The two cops on bicycles looked like they had been through a war. One of them looked past retirement age. He wore a sergeant's stripes on his dirty yellow short-sleeved shirt, beneath his Kevlar vest. The other was a young woman, husky, with a blonde ponytail tied up in back, her hair black at the roots. They both wore shorts and knee-length socks, also dirty. Sunglasses completed the ensemble. They had pulled up to within fifty feet of the barricade across Doheny. Not too close, but near enough that they didn't have to yell.

"Would you put down your weapons, please?" the older one asked.

Dave looked at Art Bertelstein and Maria O'Brien, his companions on the evening shift. Art shrugged, and set his shotgun on the ground. Dave and Maria did the same.

The woman cop gestured behind her with a jerk of her head.

"And tell the guy in the bushes to come out, too, okay? We're not here to cause anybody any trouble, and he makes me nervous."

Art thought about it, then picked up the radio and made the series of clicks they had arranged. Down the street, Sam Crowley's son, Max, stepped out onto the pavement, looking sheepish. He left his gun in the bushes where he had been hiding—though not well enough, it seemed—and walked up the street to join the others as they came out from behind the barrier and faced the cops.

"Don't worry, you're not in any trouble," the older man said. "I'm Sergeant Daniels and this is Officer Gomez."

"We weren't sure there were any LAPD left," Art said.

"There's more of us left than you might think. But you're right, there's far from enough of us to handle this situation."

That's why the mayor and the chief have decided, reluctantly, to enlist the help of the various posses that are forming around town."

"What, you want us on patrol, or something?" Marie asked.

"Nothing like that," Gomez said. "We're not asking you to enlist. Mostly, we're trying to find out how many of you there are, and how well prepared."

"Intelligence has been one of our biggest problems," Daniels said. "We're getting a lot of our information from the same place you're probably getting it. Radio reports that may or may not be reliable. We're trying to pull it all together here on the ground, eyeballing it. We need to know where everybody is, and what they're doing."

Bertelstein had called Ferguson when the cops first appeared at the end of the street. Now he came hurrying up, looking winded and dripping sweat from the short walk from his house. It was another hot, muggy day, but the sweat seemed excessive.

"What's the situation, Officers?" Ferguson asked.

"Are you in charge here, sir?"

"As much as anyone is, I guess. We're a loose organization, banded together for self-protection."

"I understand. It's happening all over, and that's the biggest reason we're here. We're making a list and a map. What we'd like to do is get your name, the names of any of your lieutenants, if any, and the amount of territory you are taking responsibility for." Daniels opened a fiberglass pannier on the side of his bike and took out a clipboard. Ferguson got busy filling out the form. Officer Gomez had taken more papers from her own bike and now laid some of them out on the hood of one of the cars.

The first showed the whole Los Angeles area, from Malibu down to Long Beach, and east as far as the beginning of the San Gabriel Valley. Different areas had been outlined and lightly crosshatched in different colors with fine-tipped markers. Everyone crowded around as Gomez pointed out the important facts.

"These green zones are where the LAPD and the military are in control." She paused. "Mostly. The fact is, there is nowhere in this city where I would want to go out at night. We don't patrol at night; we've lost too many officers. And when I say we control it, what I'm really saying is that we've contacted the posses, the militias, the self-defense cadres, whatever they call themselves, and determined that they are sufficiently organized to defend themselves."

Dave saw that the green areas were patchy. There were some in the Valley, in the Sherman Oaks and North Hollywood areas, and Studio City, and much of Burbank. There were some green patches north of that, but also a lot of yellow and red.

"Yellow is places where we think there are people in control, but we haven't actually determined that on the ground. Red is just what you think it is. Don't go there. Some of it is burned-out. Some of it is ruled by gangs. The National Guard has made some efforts at cleaning them up, but they're hampered by the same constraints we are. Lack of transportation, lack of communication, and . . . defections."

She looked away from them when she said that. Even the mayor had admitted that the force had been decimated, for many different reasons. It was no surprise to anyone there that evening.

"These areas to the north, the ones in gray, we just don't know. Northridge, Chatsworth, Reseda, Panorama City, Canoga Park, east of Glendale, anything south of the 105, we just don't know.

Here be monsters, Dave thought. It was what old mapmakers had often written in areas unexplored by humans. And some of those gray areas were half an hour's drive away, in what he was coming to think of as "the old days."

"We're trying to find out which roads are passable and which ones aren't. These little Xs are places where there's a gap too big to cross, or pavement too buckled, or a collapsed bridge or overpass. Most of the freeway overpasses held up, but enough of them didn't that there isn't a single freeway that doesn't involve a detour," Gomez said.

"What would you say is the best way out of town?" Marie O'Brien asked.

"We get asked that a lot. And we're advising anyone who has fuel, or is up to a long trip on a bicycle, to leave. Everything is running short. So basically, you have the choice of hunkering down until help arrives, or trying to get out.

"You don't want to go east at all. Even if you make your way along the 10, or the 210, or the 60, you're gonna end up in the desert. People have come back from that way, and they said they were not welcomed.

"South . . . there's quake damage down as far as Camp Pendleton. There are refugee camps in Oceanside and Escondido, but I don't know if they're getting food. The whole Southland is running short on food. Hell, the whole country for all I know.

"To the west, forget about the Coast Highway. Half the houses in Malibu fell into the sea, and most of the highway with them. The 101 is a mess, at least as far out as Camarillo. You have to take surface streets to get anywhere.

"North on the 5, some of the officers have gone as far as Santa Clarita. The CHP says there's major landslides on the grapevine, from Magic Mountain on north. You could bike it or hike it, and maybe a Hummer could drive over some of it, but I can't guarantee that."

She sighed, and straightened up. Dave had known some of what she had just told them, and some of it was new. He had been thinking of taking Interstate 5 north, but had wondered about the grapevine, the twisting, rising, and falling forty or fifty miles before you came down the last long slope and into the Central Valley. If food was being grown and harvested anywhere in California, he felt it would be there. But though the Escalade was called an off-road vehicle, he doubted its ability to traverse a serious landslide.

"Bottom line, I can't recommend any of the routes out of here. But I can't recommend staying, either. They say they're working on the rail lines, but it might be a month or two before they get them straightened out enough to carry a big load of food. And I don't even know if anyone will be sending big loads of food."

There it was again. The bleak assessment. Los Angeles was on its own, the rest of America had its own problems. Angelenos weren't likely to be welcomed anywhere else, and they weren't going to be able to hold out on their own indefinitely with no power, no gas, little water, and no food coming in.

Ferguson had finished filling out the forms for Daniels and joined the others looking at the maps. Daniels took over with the second one. It was on a much smaller scale, also mimeographed, traced from a terrain map downloaded from Google before Google ceased to exist, along with the Internet. The map showed the hills north of Sunset, between Laurel Canyon and Coldwater Canyon, and as far north as Mulholland. They had marked it into seven distinct areas, each more or less cut off from the other by ridges.

"The boundaries are clear-cut here in the hills," Daniels said. "They're also more defensible than the areas down on the flatlands. Our beat is west of the 101. This is what we know. There's the Hollywood Bowl area, then Runyon Canyon and Nichols Canyon. Three different areas on Laurel Canyon, at least as far up as we've gone. Lower Mount Olympus and Upper Mount Olympus, then Willow Glen and Laurel Pass."

He filled them in on the state of organization and readiness the two of them had been able to determine by talking to the residents and doing a cursory examination of their preparations for defense and survival.

"These areas marked in orange are largely burned-out. The areas in red are major landslides."

There was a lot of orange on the map, and quite a bit of red.

"We're asking residents to make a more complete survey. What we'd like you to do is make a map and show where there were fires, what houses slid down the hill, and where roads are broken."

The officers asked them more questions about Doheny. Dave told them what he knew about the Wonderland Drive area, which the officers hadn't visited yet.

Dave watched them cycle down to Sunset. He realized they represented the first signs of authority any of them had seen since the quake, six days ago. It wasn't much, but it was good to know that at least a remnant of the city's political infrastructure still existed, and that it was trying to pull itself together.

Over the next week Doheny Drive had a few visitors, but none that came to stay.

A thick yellow line had been painted on the pavement, and a sign had been painted on a big piece of plywood and nailed to a tree near the bottom of the hill, about a hundred yards north of Sunset, positioned so that when someone reached it the barricade and armed guard were visible:

THIS IS A DEFENDED COMMUNITY

NO ACCESS TO THE VALLEY FROM HERE

LAY DOWN YOUR ARMS AND APPROACH WITH YOUR HANDS IN THE AIR. STOP AT THE YELLOW LINE. STATE YOUR BUSINESS. UNLESS YOU HAVE FRIENDS HERE WHO WILL VOUCH FOR YOU, YOU WILL NOT BE ADMITTED. WE HAVE NO FOOD OR WATER TO OFFER YOU. PLEASE MOVE ALONG. WE WILL FIRE ONLY ONE WARNING SHOT.

Dave thought the warning shot business was a bit overboard, but then he learned that some had suggested much more forceful wording, the least of which was to not bother with the "please." One hothead wanted the sign to read simply intruders will be shot. He was overruled when others pointed out that many people on Doheny had friends or relatives they still hoped to see. Since the only real threat they had faced so far had been the bikers high above them, who had been unlikely to come down in any case, even if Dave had not fired on them, it was agreed that the Doheny Militia should not be trigger-happy.

One of the sets of visitors at the end of the road had been bikers, too, seven of them on noisy Harleys, four men and three women on back. They wore some sort of club colors in a script too baroque for anyone who saw them to decipher. Dave hadn't been there that day. As it was told to him later, they were filthy, bearded, in sleeveless denim, leather pants, and thick buttkicking boots, with lengths of chain wrapped around their waists, large handguns stuck into belts and holsters, and shotguns and rifles attached to their bikes. One of them had a bloody bandage around his head.

They pulled up right on the yellow line and sat there, gunning their engines contemptuously, flaunting the fact that they seemed to have all the gasoline they needed. One of them started to draw a rifle from an improvised scabbard over his handlebars. One of the defenders fired a shot into the air.

"Well, it was in the air," he later told Dave. "At least a foot over their heads. I think they would have heard the bullet go by."

They didn't flee like scared rabbits—they were far too macho for that—but after letting his rifle slip back into place and gunning his engine a few more times and flipping the bird, the leader made a wide turn back down Doheny.

"We'll be back," one of them shouted, trying to sound like the Terminator. That prompted a volley of shots *not* aimed in the air, none of which hit anything but a palm tree.

Later, at the postmortem, there was good news and bad news. Everyone was pleased that their radio alarm system seemed to have worked well. Armed reinforcements on bicycles had arrived at the barricade only a moment after the gang had fled, which was pretty good time.

On the other hand . . .

"If you guys were aiming," Ferguson said when he heard about it later, "we are badly in need of some target practice. But we can't waste the ammo."

Luckily, it turned out there was a solution. A canvass of the neighborhood turned up quite a few air rifles, pellet guns, and even a couple paintball guns. There were plenty of projectiles for all these toys, some of them recoverable and reusable. So a practice range was established on a straight stretch of street with targets at fixed distances. Soon just about everybody was banging away every chance they got.

No one with any sense thought that firing BBs was going to turn them into stone killers, but it did improve their aim. Everyone also got to fire a certain number of real rounds from real rifles and shotguns as well, to show them what difference in noise and recoil to expect if it came to using serious weapons.

For the next few nights the number of guards at the barricade was increased, and extra patrols were assigned to walk the streets to guard against any sneak attack. But the biker boss's boast was an empty one. They never saw them again.

CHAPTER SIXTEEN

All during that week, Dave saw others at the barricades, but no one who posed any threat. They were refugees in their own city, people with no place to go, but going anyway because they couldn't think of anything else to do. Most often it was a single man, on a bicycle, or pushing a shopping cart, or on foot with a backpack or shopping bags. Some of them were armed, and some weren't. Since the grocery stores had emptied out early in the crisis, they were probably breaking into unoccupied homes for the meager leavings of those who had gone elsewhere or never made it back to their homes because of the previous catastrophe of eruption and fire, or had been stranded elsewhere due to the vagaries of the earthquake, or had simply died.

No one's backpack bulged. The shopping carts might contain a few battered cans or bottles of water or soda. One man had a shopping cart that was half-full of oranges. Dave knew that most of the citrus trees that grew in Los Angeles yielded fruit that was dry and all but tasteless, but he supposed sucking on one would be better than nothing.

Some of the people just paused and looked forlornly up the street at what they probably presumed was plenty. After all, the people up in the hills were rich, weren't they? Probably still had servants, and gardeners coming in to trim the plants. Probably had gasoline and generators and Internet service and cable TV.

Others ventured as far as the yellow line. Dave wasn't sure why. None of them looked as if they expected charity any longer. The resentment showed in some faces; others seemed simply resigned, all but defeated.

"Do you know anyplace where a man and his family can get something to eat?" one man asked. "My kids haven't eaten in two days."

"I'm sorry," Dave said. "I saw a large soup kitchen at the Staples Center. You might try there."

The man's face brightened for a moment.

"When was this?"

"A while ago," Dave admitted.

"Well, I was by there right after the earthquake, and there was nobody handing out food. Part of the Convention Center collapsed and a lot of people were killed. They were hauling out bodies. Everybody else was leaving."

"I'm sorry. I don't know what to tell you."

"You wouldn't have . . ."

"I have my own family to provide for. No matter what you might think, we don't have a lot of food here, either. I'm . . ." He realized he could only say he was sorry so many times, and it was already starting to sound hollow. The man nodded and turned away, having expected no other answer.

And what he said was true, mostly. Dave himself still had quite a bit of food stored away, and he assumed some others did, too. But it was becoming apparent that many people were running out. You could see it in the looks on people's faces. Neighbors were beginning to eye each other with looks of speculation, or even of suspicion. You could practically read their thoughts by the way they regarded you.

He doesn't look like he's missing any meals. I wonder how much he has stored away, when all we have is a few miserable cans?

Karen had taken stock, done some calculations, and cut everyone's rations down to what was needed to keep them healthy. It was never as much as they wanted. Dave was hungry most of the time and he knew everyone else was, too.

He could see it was tearing Jenna up, having brought nothing at all to the table, to be eating their food. But Karen had tried to make it clear to her that they regarded her as family, and it was share and share alike.

No one had thus far approached Dave about food. So far as he knew, no one was discussing the issue at all, but he didn't think that would last. Sooner or later, as hunger, weakness, and malnutrition began to bite, the people of Doheny Drive would have to face what it meant that some people had food, and some didn't. He was expecting someone to propose pooling all their food, and he expected that person would be a man or woman whose family had nothing left.

He was dreading that moment, and he felt sure many of his neighbors were, too.

Hard as it was to see the desperate men approach and look up the street, it was much harder when a whole family came by.

Dave missed that experience for a while, but everyone on guard duty who had been there and had to turn a family away could talk of little else for days afterward. A few affected a hard-nosed attitude.

"I'm looking out for my family. He should have looked out for his."

Most of them stopped talking that way when they saw the looks on the faces of the others who had confronted families with children. These people had haunted eyes, and some of them were prone to burst into tears without warning. The strain on everyone had been immense for a long time, and emotions were raw and on the surface.

Finally, at the end of the week, Dave found out what it was like. They came an hour or so before sunset.

There were five of them. A father, a mother, and three young children, two boys around eight and ten, and a girl of five or six. They were small people, Hispanic, of Mexican heritage but speaking English without accents. They could have been illegals who had been in the U.S. for a long time, or they could have been fifth-generation American . . . and at this point, who cared? Nobody was going to ask for a passport or a green card. To Dave, the only important thing about them was that they were hungry.

The mother was dark and pretty, but there were circles under her eyes. The father was broad-shouldered, like so many Hispanic Angelenos, and probably had some Indian blood. The family had three grocery carts that looked as if they contained all their worldly possessions. There were sleeping bags and tarps that Dave could see, clothes, a box of laundry detergent, several plastic storage containers.

The man spoke with his wife, then came slowly up the street

and stopped at the yellow line. He took off the straw hat he was wearing and held it at his side.

"I would like to speak to Mr. Alfred Charbonneau, please," he said.

Dave was on duty with Herman Patterson and Marie O'Brien. He looked at Herman, who shrugged and shook his head.

"You know Mr. Charbonneau?" Dave called out.

"I work for him. My name is Richard Vega and I have a landscaping business. Mr. Charbonneau lives on Oriole Way. He has a wife, Gretchen, and two teenage sons, Marty and Al. Could you see if they are home?"

"I don't know them," Marie said. She lived on Doheny, not very far from where they were standing.

"I'll go check at Ferguson's," Herman said. He was referring to the neighborhood roster that had been compiled.

"We're sending for him," Dave told Mr. Vega. The man nodded, then wiped his brow with a cloth that had once been white. He gestured to his family, who slowly pushed their carts up the gentle slope to the curb beyond the yellow line. They all sat down to wait. After a few minutes Vega spoke up.

"I hate to ask you for anything," he said, "but can you spare some water? We drank the last of ours a few hours ago."

Marie and Dave looked at each other. Their instructions had been clear: No one was to be allowed to approach the barricade unless someone on the other side vouched for them, and no one on the inside was to cross in the other direction.

"The hell with it," Dave said. He opened a cooler that held three one-gallon milk jugs of water taken from someone's pool that morning. There were also two cans of strawberry soda. Dave didn't know where they had come from. He picked up one of the milk jugs and started toward the small gap in the barricade, then turned around and took one of the soft drinks, too. If the owner griped later, he would replace them.

Mr. Vega rose to accept the water, but couldn't take his eyes off the soda can.

"I'm afraid none of it is cold," Dave said.

"It's been a while since we've seen ice . . . Thank you, sir. We are much obliged." He cracked the top of the can, and gestured to his children. They rose solemnly, staring at the can of pop.

"One sip at a time," their father said. "We share, remember?"

"Yes, Father," the oldest boy said, and handed the drink to his little sister. Dave had to turn away. He was choked up. He didn't like himself very much at that moment, and he hated what had happened to him. What had happened to them all. What was still happening, with no end in sight.

They waited in the shade for a while, nobody saying anything. The children made the soda last, but all too soon it was gone. They drank some water.

When Herman returned he was shaking his head.

"The Charbonneaus are gone. There's no contact information by their names, so they must have pulled out before the quake."

Vega was on his feet, and now he looked down at his shoes. He took a deep breath, and nodded. It seemed to take an effort to lift his eyes again.

"I'm not surprised," he said. "We would have got out, too, if we had a place to go. I was just hoping . . . Well. I guess we'll move on."

"I wish we could help you," Dave said. "You understand, we can't take people in. Do you have a place—"

"It's the same everywhere," Vega said. "People are protecting themselves. In the hills here, they can block off streets. Nobody has any food they can spare. That's why we had to leave home. We ran out of food. We're hoping to find someplace where they're taking care of refugees. Do you know anything about that?"

"No more than you do. There is a rumor of a soup kitchen in the Valley, maybe somewhere around Panorama City, but I can't vouch for that."

"It's a long way to walk."

"That it is. Where . . . where do you stay at night?"

Vega gave a wry grin.

"That's the least of our problems. Most of these groups don't care if you stop off in a park. They're getting crowded, though. Good thing it's not winter."

Dave couldn't think of another thing to say.

"Well, thanks for the water." Vega held out his hand, and Dave shook it. He and his family started back down the hill.

"Well, screw this," Marie said, from behind the barrier. "Mr.

Vega! Wait a minute, don't go yet. I'll be back in a minute." She took off, jogging away from them, toward her home.

It was more like five minutes, but she was back soon. She was carrying a plastic grocery bag as she slipped through the narrow barricade entrance.

"It's not much," she said, as she handed the bag to Vega. "There's a can of pineapple, a can of corn, and a jar of spaghetti sauce. Also a box of spaghetti. Do you have anything you can cook this—".

Mrs. Vega moved to stand beside her husband and reached out to take Marie's hand in both of hers.

"I am Anna. God bless you, ma'am. My children will eat tonight."

"It's not much, I wish I—"

"It is a feast to us. Bless you."

Mr. Vega was looking at the ground again.

"I've never begged for anything in my life, I—"

Anna cuffed him with the back of her hand.

"Be quiet, Richard. If we have to crawl on our knees until they bleed, then we will do so. But this wonderful lady has spared your pride and filled our stomachs. Can't you find anything to say?"

Chastened, Vega looked Marie in the eyes and nodded.

"I can't thank you enough."

"Bless you," Marie said. "It was little enough. I think you will find food and shelter soon. I know you will."

Dave watched as they walked down the street. One of the shopping carts had a squeaky wheel. It was almost the only sound on this quiet, deceptively peaceful day. He watched them out of sight, then followed Marie back to his post.

There was silence among the three for a while. Then Herman spoke.

"Don't take this the wrong way," he said. "But I wonder—"

"Don't say it, Herman. I've got a loaded gun." She sighed. "I know what you want to say. I was in India twenty years ago, I saw what happens when you give a street kid a few rupees. Next thing you know, you're surrounded."

"If those people talk about where they got the food . . ."

"He's got more sense than that. But you know what? I don't

care what the committee says. I'm single, I've got nobody I'm responsible for, and it's my food to do with what I want to."

Neither Dave nor Herman was inclined to argue with her.

"And you know what else? I'm through with this shit. I can't take it anymore. You better get someone else to take my place, because I'm out of here."

She turned and walked back up the street to her house, with her back straight and her rifle resting on her shoulder.

A few hours later, with only a little light left in the western sky, she drove up to the barricade in a white Lexus. The backseat was full, the contents covered with blankets and clothing heaped almost to the ceiling. Dave figured her trunk was full, too. There was a man he didn't know sitting in the passenger seat. He was glad to see that. He didn't think venturing out alone after dark was a good idea for a woman.

Dave and Herman had been joined by Lucas Petrelli, who neither of them knew all that well. The three of them removed the blocks from under the wheels of a Cadillac and pushed it out of the way. Marie drove until the hood of her car was through.

"Where will you go?" Dave asked them.

"Toward San Diego. I have friends there. But there's not enough gas in this overpriced heap to get me there. So if you drive south on the I-5 and see two people pushing a shopping cart, it'll probably be us."

With that, she waved good-bye and pulled all the way through. Before she reached Sunset she turned off her headlights.

Far in the distance he heard several gunshots.

"They should have waited until daylight," Herman said.

"I don't know," Lucas said. "Sometimes it's best to just do it before you chicken out. Sometimes you just have to go."

Dave wondered if he'd ever see them again.

That night he lay sleepless in bed with Karen in the guesthouse.

He had brooded about the scene at the barricade for a little over a day. He felt he had a lot to talk over with his wife.

"I can always tell when you're not sleeping," she said. "What time is it?"

"I don't know. Late. Maybe even early." He no longer looked at his watch as often as he used to. The only appointments he had to keep these days were his stints at the barricades. They went to bed not long after the sun set, and got up when it rose. Another lifestyle change, another reversion to the practices of an earlier era.

"I'm getting the feeling you want to talk about something."

"I guess I do. But to tell you the truth, I'm still not exactly sure what it is."

"Are you unhappy with me about something?"

"No, nothing like that." He sought out her hand and squeezed it there in the dark.

"You want me to light a candle?"

"That might be a good idea."

A lighter flared and Karen lit the candle. Their shadows moved as she set the candle on the nightstand. It was so much warmer, homier than electric light, Dave reflected. Not all things about losing electricity were bad.

He turned to her.

"I guess the simplest way of saying it is that I've begun to think that what we're doing is wrong."

Karen was silent for a while.

"Do you mean wrong morally, or wrong, as in not the smart thing to do?"

"Maybe a little of both. I want to do the smart thing, the right thing for our family, even though it's not always possible to determine what that is."

"You wanted us to get out," Karen reminded him. "I stood in your way."

"This is not about that. Not about anything you did, or didn't do. Karen, I'm concerned that we don't lose our humanity, trying to survive."

"Dave, what happened?"

So he told her about the encounter with the Vega family, how Herman had felt about it, and what Marie had done. He felt his own reaction had been sort of in the middle of those two, and it didn't satisfy him either way. What was the solution? Either toughen up, like Herman, turn away hungry children, or become a pushover for any needy people who came along?

"I can't imagine how awful that must have been," Karen said.

"Then let me ask you something. Would you have done what Marie did?"

There was a long pause.

"I honestly don't know, my dear. You know I was always a sucker for any needy cause that came along."

"I wouldn't call it being a sucker. You did a lot of good."

"Maybe. Lately I've come to feel I was always playing at it. The way I kept jumping from one thing to another. But I *can* say that my concern was always genuine. When I saw poor kids, abused kids . . . I wanted more than anything to help them. As for hungry kids? When I see pictures from those countries in Africa, children who are literally starving to death because of some government or warlord's ambition . . . I can hardly bear to look, because I want to go out and kill somebody."

"So what do you think? Would you have given them some of our food?"

"That gets to the heart of it, doesn't it? 'Our' food. We have it because you got an early warning, and you laid it in for us, you were a good provider, and we don't know how long it will have to last. Maybe a long, long time. I've thought about that a lot. That's why we're on such short rations. I think I could stretch it for a year, with the four of us. We'd lose a lot of weight, but we'd be alive."

"You didn't answer my question."

"I was deliberately avoiding it. What you're asking is, would I take food out of my daughter's mouth to feed the children of a stranger."

"Food which Addison may never need, if help arrives."

"I don't know where that help would come from, but okay. Say we keep it all to ourselves, and three, four months from now food shipments start arriving. How many children would starve in the meantime? We might have saved some of them."

Dave didn't answer, and for a while they were both silent again. Then Karen spoke.

"When I was a little girl my parents got into a discussion about fallout shelters."

"You know, I read that some of those are still around. I wonder how many people kept replenishing their supplies over all those years?"

"I don't remember what brought it up," she said, ignoring his question. "But they remembered my grandparents talking about it. My father's dad even drew up some plans and started digging a hole during the Cold War. He never finished it, but he made lists of what he would need. Right at the top was guns."

"I remember," Dave said. "The big question was, say you've made a shelter just big enough for your family. The alarm goes off, the bombs are on their way. You seal up your shelter . . . and the neighbors come knocking. Do you let them in?"

"The simple answer is no," Karen whispered. "They should have built their own shelter, and letting them in isn't an option. There's not enough room, there's not enough food. It's an easy answer when it's theoretical. I can't imagine the agony of listening to them, to your friends, shouting out in desperation. Pleading to just take the children, for instance. But that's not even the worst of it. The other scenario is, would you actually shoot your neighbors, kill them, to keep them out of your shelter."

"Answers to questions like that are never 'simple,' though, are they?"

"No. So what do you suggest we do?"

There was another long silence. Dave wasn't sure himself what he was proposing. He had some ideas, and a general goal, but he was still feeling it out as he went along.

"Okay, here's where I am, so far. We won't . . . we *can't* just set up a Marshall Family Soup Kitchen, feeding hungry families who drop by down on Sunset. Our pantry would be bare in a week."

"More like a day."

"Right. Is the only alternative to . . . to just seal up the bunker? Guard our gate twenty-four/seven, and stretch our food as long as it will go? Because before long it's not going to be just strangers who are getting hungry. It's going to be some of our neighbors."

"I had already thought of that. It's dangerous to have plenty when people around you have nothing."

"Have you thought of what to do about it?"

"I don't like the hunkering down and shooting it out scenario. But I don't like any of the others much better. Dave, are you talking about leaving again?"

"I guess that's pretty much it. We don't know much about what it's like in the rest of the country, but I think we can be pretty sure that things are at their absolute worst here in Los Angeles. On top of all the problems with lack of power and transportation, half the city is burned down, and the other half is collapsed. I'm not sure a city can ever recover from all those things. I think Los Angeles may be doomed."

"Then we'd better get out, don't you think?"

"Is that what you want to do?"

"No. The biggest part of me wants to do just what I said I don't like. Just stay here where I feel safe."

"The question is, is it safe, and for how long."

"I know. I'm just telling you what my gut is saying to me. But what I keep coming back to is, if I had listened to you from the beginning, or even quite a bit later than the beginning, we could be in Oregon by now. Oregon, where there's rain, and they grow food, and where we have family that will take us in. No, Dave, I'm terrified of going on the road now, with things the way they are, I'm terrified of exposing Addison to the dangers out there. But I don't trust my judgement. I was so wrong before. What I decided not long ago is pretty simple. I'm ready to do whatever you think is best. I want you to be the head of this family. Not because I want to be an obedient wife, but because I've been a bad mother."

"I don't agree with that," Dave said. "You've always been a good mother to Addison. She loves you. I love you."

"You can say what you want, but the fact remains that because I wouldn't listen to you, and because, frankly, I'd been angry with you for well over a year for various reasons, I made the worst decision of my life. And it has affected Addison's chances. Not something like her chances of getting on the soccer team, or getting good grades, or getting into a good college, but her very chances of survival. Her *life* is at stake here.

"The only way I can ever forgive myself for that is to do everything in my power to get her to a safe place. Nothing else matters to me. And right now, I just don't trust myself to make the right choices. You were right before. I hope you're right now. Because I'm going to do whatever you think we should do, and I'm going to do it with all my heart."

Though her voice had been level and calm throughout, Dave was not at all surprised that her face was wet when he put his arms around her and kissed her. They stayed that way for a long time, and eventually fell asleep in each other's arms.

Dave slept more soundly than he had in weeks.

CHAPTER SEVENTEEN

"That's just not fair!"

Sometimes Addison seemed like a young woman of twenty-something, mature beyond her years. But like most teenage girls, she could also revert to being a spoiled eight-year-old when she wasn't getting her way. Not often—she was basically a good and obedient daughter. But they had all been under too much stress, and Dave wasn't surprised at this rebellion.

"It's *my* scooter, and I want to go along with you guys. I'll ride on the back. Daddy, you have to let me go."

"Addie, that's not the way it works anymore. It has to be share and share alike, and we all own things together. And we all have to do what we do best, and not complain about it. And, bottom line, we're your parents, and we're responsible for you, and you will just have to do what we tell you to do, even when you don't like it."

"Well, *she* didn't do much to get us through this, did she? Where was she when you were buying all our food and trying to get us safe and up to Oregon? Shopping, that's where. While I was helping out."

It was the first time Addison had lashed out at her mother. Maybe it was long overdue, maybe she needed to express some of the frustration she had felt and had kept silent about as the rift developed between her parents. She seemed to have concluded that the best way to keep them together was to be a good daughter. Dave had been thankful for that—it made his life a lot easier—but now wished he had talked to her more about it, and maybe even that Addison had opened up more about the resentment she was feeling, mostly toward her mother, but to some degree toward both of them. Dave knew the feeling. His own parents had gone through a bitter divorce when he was a bit younger than Addison was now, and he remembered his anger at them.

Karen was keeping silent. He didn't know if it was from her feelings of guilt or because of her resolution to let Dave make the hard decisions and do the hard things. Speaking harshly to Addison definitely came under the heading of hard things.

Still, he couldn't let that remark pass.

"Addison, you can't speak that way about your mother."

The girl thrust out her lower lip.

"Well, she didn't help out, and I did. And besides, she doesn't even know how to ride a scooter."

Still Karen kept silent.

"You'd be surprised what all your mother knows how to do. But I'll tell you something now, Addison. Things have changed. You trusted me when I told you what was going to happen, didn't you?"

She looked away from him, took a deep breath, and gave him a grudging nod.

"Well, from now on you're just going to have to trust me on a lot of other things. And something else you're going to have to do is obey me. Without any lip."

She looked up at him again, a little astonished.

"That doesn't mean you have no say around here. We can discuss things, when we have the time for it, and you can put in your opinions. And then I will make up my mind, and you will do as you're told. Do you understand?"

He thought she was going to cry. But she didn't. After a long pause, she looked him in the eye again.

"Yes, I understand." And she turned and walked stiffly back into the house.

The argument had happened early in the morning. Dave and Karen were wearing helmets and leather jackets. Karen's jacket was from a shop on Rodeo Drive and built more for style than for protection. He was wishing they had leather pants, too, but jeans would have to do.

They had been standing beside the two scooters, facing off with Addison. Jenna was standing to one side, wondering if she should get out of earshot. She was happy to have something useful to do, someone to be responsible for.

The idea of being babysat had not gone down well. Addison wanted to go. For one thing, it was going to be an adventure, a chance to see what was happening beyond their small world.

But much more important was the fear that something might happen to her parents.

"Jenna," Dave said. She hurried over to them.

"If we don't come back, I'm trusting you to take care of Addison."

"With my life."

"That's what I had in mind."

He turned the key in the ignition, sat on his scooter, and puttered down the drive with Karen close behind him, thinking that, for once, he'd delivered a pretty good exit line in real life instead of on the pages of a script. It wasn't up there with "I'll be back," but it would do.

The reason for the argument with his daughter was this expedition out of the safe zone of Doheny. That it was dangerous Dave did not doubt. But one of the reasons he felt that he had to do it was to get some idea of *how* dangerous.

He had no kind of military experience, but he had bought some books about military strategy and tactics. He had learned some things, many of which seemed obvious, but not things he was used to thinking about and applying to his daily life.

One rule was to occupy the high ground. In most situations it was better to be up high firing down than down low, firing up. Exception: when you were surrounded by enemies and could be starved out. Of course castles had fallen, many times, but Doheny now had allies to the north, east, and west.

Another rule was that before you committed everything to a move, you had to know what you were walking into. You needed intelligence. They had a little of that from the police officers and the Vega family, but not nearly enough. You needed to reconnoiter, you needed someone to actually go there and scout out the situation.

Karen had argued against his going alone. Two were safer than one, each could watch the other's back. In the end, Dave had relented.

Another of the military principles Dave had pondered was that the map is not the terrain. Among the little bit of luggage he and

Karen were carrying in the small panniers strapped to the back were both a Thomas Guide to Los Angeles and Orange Counties, and a Garwin detachable GPS unit. He knew it was ironic that in the midst of a complete power blackout, with landline telephone, cell phone, cable, and Internet service all nonexistent, this little gadget still worked perfectly. All the Global Positioning System satellites were still in place, still sending out their signals. But neither the book nor the GPS was going to warn him of collapsed bridges, buckled pavement, or washed-out roads. That was the purpose of the trip, to find out just how much had changed, and if there were in fact any routes out of Los Angeles.

Two people Dave didn't know rolled the dead Cadillac out of the way at the barricade. There had been a brief discussion between them as to whether they should do it. One of them seemed to think that Ferguson should be notified that someone was leaving. Dave had to point out that no one had ever said a thing about people leaving, only about letting people in. And besides, they intended to return and would share information about all they saw. Still one of them resisted, saying that maybe Ferguson would want to ask them to look for specific things at specific places.

Dave didn't want to lose his temper, and was about to continue the argument in a controlled tone, when Karen spoke up.

"This isn't a prison, damn it. We can come and go as we please. Now roll that damn car out of the way so we can go about our business."

The two men looked at each other, and one of them shrugged. There was something in Karen's voice, when she wanted it to be there, that was just hard to argue with. They did as she told them.

"Nice one, babe," Dave said, as they puttered down the last yards of Doheny.

"I won't tolerate that kind of treatment," she said.

They turned east on Sunset, intending to check out the Cahuenga Pass into the San Fernando Valley.

There was no automobile or truck traffic going by on Sunset. They cautiously pulled out onto the street and looked around.

The liquor store on the corner had all its windows broken out. Dave didn't think it was earthquake damage, it had the look of looting. All the shelves inside were empty, but they hadn't been knocked over. On the other side of the street the Citibank had a crack in one wall. There were several safe-deposit boxes on the sidewalk that had been hammered open. Two men squatted out front with safe-deposit boxes stacked beside them. They were smashing a hunk of concrete on one of the boxes. They were putting valuables into canvas bags. Papers fluttered away from them on the slight breeze. Deeds, insurance policies, worthless bearer bonds, and other papers that used to be important. What they were obviously going for was gold and jewelry. They didn't seem in the least worried. One of them glanced up as Dave and Karen rode by. There was a rifle on the sidewalk beside him. The man looked back down and resumed his work.

"I don't like this," Karen said, when they were past.

"If somebody starts shooting at us, we'll fire back, but we'll turn around, okay?"

"Okay."

They each had a shotgun tied to improvised scabbards on the handlebars. Dave was wondering if they should actually be holding them in one hand and steering with the other. He decided he would rather not appear that hostile unless someone showed hostility toward them.

Most of the buildings they passed were still standing, though most had cracked walls and all of them had lost glass. But one in maybe twenty or thirty had suffered much more damage. Where the old Whisky a Go Go had been there was now only a pile of brick. Where the Red Rock Bar had been there was just a big hole now. It had slid down to Holloway Drive.

As they approached Sunset Plaza they came upon brightly colored clothing scattered on the street. Much of it was still on hangers. It had clearly come from the expensive boutiques that lined that part of the Strip. Outfits that had gone for thousands of dollars lay abandoned in the gutters, some of them run over by large truck tires.

"This doesn't make any sense," Karen said. "What good is this stuff to anybody now?"

"Maybe some women just wanted for once in their lives to wear things they never could have afforded."

"So maybe this stuff is just the excess. Pick it all over, don't waste your energy carrying it all away."

"Your guess is as good as mine."

The little white building with the Greek columns on Sunset Plaza had been turned into a guardhouse. Extending from its southern wall was a barricade garrisoned by four men and two women, all armed. They watched as Dave and Karen went by without stopping. They waved, and two of the guards waved back.

Not quite a mile along Sunset they came around a gentle curve and Dave looked up the hill for the Chateau Marmont. It was gone.

They pulled up short of a gigantic pile of rubble. It was all that was left.

Dave had never seen anything like it. All the tall buildings along Sunset that they had passed had survived. That is, they had stood up, though all of them had shed glass and sometimes stone and other ornamentation. But none had collapsed. Yet in an earthquake the size of the monster they had experienced, all bets were off. The Chateau had weathered many a quake, but something must have given out.

In normal times the place would have been swarming with news crews and state engineers looking for the cause of the failure. Now there was just an eerie quiet, as if this might have happened years ago. In normal times the hotel would have been full of guests. Dave doubted very many people had been staying there on that terrible night.

"You know," Karen said, "ever since that night I've sort of felt like we're living in a disaster movie. But never quite as powerfully as now."

This was an alteration of the very skyline of their city. This was a removal of a major historic landmark, where Led Zeppelin had ridden their motorcycles through the lobby, where John Belushi and Helmut Newton had died. It was where Greta Garbo had holed up when she wanted to be alone.

He consulted his GPS.

"We can go down Harper then across on Fountain."

Karen nodded, and they turned their scooters around, and set off down the hill.

Harper Avenue was a mix of private houses and apartment buildings, most of them only two stories high. But many of them were older buildings, and quite a few had come down. Twice they passed groups of people moving rubble with their hands, searching for valuables and sentimental items, Dave assumed. There didn't seem to be any sense of urgency, and the people looked exhausted. Then the wind shifted and a gust blew their way and he got a whiff of something awful.

"Oh my God," Karen said. "Is that . . ."

"I don't think it's dead pets."

On Doheny they had recovered and buried all their dead, except from the house at the end of the road that was so covered in the landslide that there was no point. And he knew the people working here were trying to locate something more precious than a photograph album.

They all looked up as Dave and Karen passed, paused in their work for a moment, but none of them waved. They showed no hostility; it was as if they couldn't spare the energy for anything but their grim task. Dave was glad to turn the corner on Fountain and get away from them.

They continued on Fountain to Fairfax and turned north. They had seen few people walking or bicycling up to that point, but as they approached Sunset again they began to see more. The west side of the street was mostly apartment buildings, and on the east it was a mix of apartments, small homes, and offices. They saw several people sitting in lawn furniture in the shade, and passed three cyclists going down the hill. On Sunset itself they saw three men pushing shopping carts, which it seemed had become possessions as desirable as cars used to be.

They turned east on Hollywood Boulevard. At Nichols Canyon there was a checkpoint with two armed men but no real barricade. It seemed this canyon, at least, was still connected to the community on the flats between Hollywood and Sunset. They saw many more people than they had been seeing, and it gave them a sense of security they hadn't had since leaving their own little enclave.

As they approached the corner of Hollywood and La Brea, the western edge of tourist Hollywood, there was a line of people along the sidewalk. There looked to be more than a hundred of them. There were several in wheelchairs, and one elderly woman lying on a cot. Parked at the corner were two vehicles. One was a red LAFD ambulance, its back doors open, stuffed to the ceiling with medical supplies. The other was a large white semi with the WARNER BROS. logo on the side: a grip truck. In normal times these long trailers could be seen parked at curbs all over Los Angeles. It meant a location film shoot was in progress. This trailer had a hastily painted red cross on its side, and had been converted into a mobile hospital. On the now brown and battered lawn of the Fifth Church of Christ, Scientist, folding tables had been set up and men and women in blue surgical scrubs were talking to and treating people.

Dave and Karen slowed down, then stopped.

"This is about the most encouraging thing I've seen yet," Karen said.

"No kidding."

Dave felt they had been lucky on Doheny. There were cuts, scrapes, and bruises, but they were handled either at home or with the help of Millie the nurse.

Dave had been busy up the hill, and had only heard later about the more serious cases, broken bones and bad lacerations. An SUV that still had some fuel in it had taken them down the hill to Cedars-Sinai, but it had returned with all but one of the injured untreated. The returnees reported that the place was a madhouse, with limbs being amputated in the parking lot. Only the most dire cases were being treated.

An older man had been watching them from his place in line across the street. He ambled over with a friendly smile. He was short, a bit overweight, dressed in khaki slacks and a torn Hawaiian shirt. His white hair was shaved close to the skin.

"Hi, folks. My name's Nathan. Where you from?"

"Doheny Drive," Karen said. "Up the hill."

"Nice neighborhood. I'm from up Nichols Canyon. And the next question people ask these days is, how did your house hold up? Mine got crushed on the south end by a big eucalyptus, but the rest is okay, we can live in it, and my wife and worthless son are all right, thank God."

"We had only a little damage," Dave said.

"Many dead up your way?"

"A few. More than I like, less than it could have been."

"Amen to that. I lost a neighbor right across the street, known him for thirty years, lived through Vietnam, got crushed by a goddam grand piano came crashing down on him and his wife both while they were running for the door. Just came sliding right over the goddam balcony. Broke her femur. Bone sticking right out." He paused. "She died three days later, right on my living-room couch."

"I'm so sorry," Karen said. Dave gestured to the line.

"How long has this been here?"

"A few hours. I'm almost embarrassed to be here, lots of folks have a lot more troubles than I do, but I figured I might as well try. I'm diabetic, but that's not a problem. I'm eating so little, and so carefully, my sugar's better than it's been in years. Thank God I don't need insulin. But I had a heart attack, and I was about to run out of my pills when this whole crazy oil-shortage mess started and the drugstore ran out. Anyway, this portable clinic was through here four or five days ago, and I came down and they gave me five pills. Five pills, can you imagine? Not that I'm complaining, mind you, but did you ever think you'd see it come to this, in America?"

"I'm still finding it hard to believe," Karen said, with a glance at Dave.

"Like the kids say, it's 'surreal.' Anyway, the doctor said he didn't know when we'd see any more of my medicine, but I heard that some emergency supplies came in from down in San Diego, so here I am, hoping heart medication was in that shipment."

"Do you have any idea how it got here? Train, truck, boat?"

"It might have been by mule train for all I know. Or it might not have happened at all. You hear all sorts of things, most of them turn out to be damn lies." He jerked his head toward the nurses interviewing people at the tables. "I guess I could just go up there and ask them do they have any of my meds instead of stand in line, but it's not like I've got a lot of better things to do. The Dodgers seem to be out of town, and they don't make any movies for the likes of me anymore, anyway."

He grinned, and Dave couldn't help smiling back. There was really nothing to joke about, but that had never stopped people from joking in bad situations in the past. It might even help you pull through.

Madame Tussauds was still standing, though the sign had fallen into the street. Grauman's Chinese had suffered some damage: Part of the pagoda entrance had fallen down on the courtyard with the famous footprints and handprints of the stars. Usually that block was thronged with tourists and costumed street performers posing for tips. No one was there now except one man in a Superman suit sitting disconsolately on an overturned plastic bucket. Dave wondered if he had gone insane.

At the Hollywood & Highland Center one of the big rearing elephants from D. W. Griffith's silent classic *Intolerance* had disintegrated. Karen stopped.

"Look at that," she said.

Dave looked where she was pointing, and at first didn't understand what had caught her attention. Then he saw it. The Center had been laid out so that you could see the HOLLY-WOOD sign in the hills when you were standing in the right spot on Hollywood Boulevard. It now read:

 H LLY O D

The D and one of the Ls were leaning crazily, one forward and the other back, looking like they could go at any minute.

"Well," Karen said with a sigh, "I always thought it was sort of tacky." She sighed, and pointed east.

"Onward."

They continued up Highland, dodging a fallen tree or strewn rubble here and there, past the Hollywood Bowl. As they entered the darkness beneath the 101 freeway Dave saw motion on the ground. Karen swerved to her left, almost hitting him. There was a man walking in their direction. Behind him were several dozen more, and about as many shopping carts. The man was filthy, wearing a trench coat with so many rips in it that it almost fell off of his thin frame.

"Dave!" Karen called out.

He reached for his pistol and drew it. He aimed it at the man, who stopped.

"I need a drink!" he bellowed.

"Sorry, man," Dave called out.

The others back there in the dark were sitting down, apparently just beating the heat, which was already up in the high eighties. It was impossible to tell how many had been homeless before the quake and how many were new on the street. In a few seconds Dave and Karen were back in the sunshine.

"I hadn't thought about how tough this all would be on alcoholics," Karen said.

"I guess most of them have dried out by now."

"That doesn't mean they aren't still cranky about it."

The deserted freeway was ghostly, uncanny, disturbing. He had never seen a Los Angeles freeway with no traffic at all. There was not so much as a bicycle, which struck Dave as odd. They soon saw why. The overpass connecting West Cahuenga and East Cahuenga Boulevards had collapsed onto the freeway. All lanes were blocked, side to side, by huge slabs of concrete, and on the west side tons of dirt had slipped down the hillside and covered the remains of the bridge.

"I didn't really think we could make it to Oregon, anyway," Dave said.

"You're not giving up, are you?"

"No, of course not. But I'm thinking harder about plan B."

Plan B was a lot simpler. They would go to San Diego. The Doheny group had picked up some broadcasts from the San Diego area. The city had suffered only minor damage from the tremendous earthquake, and one speaker on the radio had even claimed that the residents were actually encouraging Angelenos to come south . . . to hold off the starving hordes of Mexicans.

Dave had no idea if this was really the case, or if it was the ranting of someone with a racist agenda. But it was the only positive news they had.

"It looks like Cahuenga East is still passable," Karen said.

Dave looked up there, just in time to see half a dozen armed men in uniform appear at the guardrail at the top of the hill. They looked down through a stand of palm trees. All wore desert camouflage fatigues and body armor.

"Excuse me, sir," Karen called out. "Can we get through to the Valley on that street up there?"

"No, ma'am," one of them said. "This is a restricted area. I'll have to ask you to turn around and leave at once."

"Got it," Dave said, and put his helmet back on. Karen looked ready to ask another question but he gave her a nudge and started his engine. They headed back down the freeway.

"That's Lake Hollywood up there," he explained, when the soldiers were out of sight. "They wouldn't let me and Addison up there when we went by earlier. I guess they're protecting the water supply."

"So where do we go now? Let's don't go back where that crazy man was."

Back on the surface streets, suddenly there was traffic. A fleet of a dozen tanker trucks rumbled by, with soldiers in trucks before, in the middle of, and behind the convoy. All the tankers had been converted to wood burners and belched smoke. The troop carriers were open in back. Each held six soldiers, all with their weapons pointed outward, looking alert and ready for anything. Some of them waved at Dave and whistled at Karen as they went by, but most of them kept their eyes on the buildings, plantings, and hillsides all around them. They had the look of men who had been in combat.

"At least somebody's delivering water around here," Dave said after they had all passed by. Karen sighed.

"Okay. Where now?"

"You want to take a look at the I-5?"

"Why not? If we can't go north on it, I guess that's the way we'll go south."

* * *

The circular Capitol Records Building was still standing.

At the corner of Canyon Drive, a big tree had fallen and completely blocked Franklin.

They turned south. They saw a few people looking out windows of undamaged homes. They came out on Van Ness and went south again to Hollywood Boulevard. The next two streets to the east, Taft and Wilton, were both blocked, one by fallen trees and the next by a huge gap in the pavement that had brought down buildings on both sides of the street. But the next street, Gramercy Place, was open. They turned left and into welcome shade. Ahead of them they heard the sound of a very loud motorcycle. Karen looked at Dave, and he motioned with his head that they should turn onto one of the driveways between two buildings.

They faced the street and listened to the incredible racket. It built and built, but when it passed it was nothing like Dave had expected. He just got a quick glimpse, and it was plain that it wasn't that big a motorcycle. It was more like a mountain bike, and it was being ridden by a short man in a black suit.

He must have seen something from the corner of his eye, because as soon as he was out of sight the sound of his engine died away abruptly to a sputtering series of backfires, then died altogether.

Dave removed his shotgun from its scabbard and jacked a round into the chamber. He saw Karen had her Ithaca in her hands, too.

The man came around the corner, saw them, and stopped. He smiled and put up his hands. He was wearing a clerical collar.

"I'm unarmed, my children."

Dave cautiously lowered his weapon. It could be a disguise. The man's hair was long and straight and dark black, streaked with gray, and his face was covered with stubble. His skin was brown and he had a round face and the features of a Hispanic.

"I'm Father Michael," he said, still not approaching any closer. "I don't think I've seen you in the neighborhood."

"We're from west of here," Karen said.

"How far west?

"Just this side of Beverly Hills," Dave told him.

"Ah, yes. I've been through there. Why are you out and about? It's dangerous."

"Well, we didn't lose too many people. We're hoping to leave the area entirely. We need to see what we're up against. What about you?"

"Yes, I can't argue that leaving this place is a not good idea. As to myself, so far I believe my clerical collar has saved me from any trouble."

"Can you tell us anything that might be useful to us?" Karen asked. "Anything about conditions to the north? We're trying to get to Oregon."

"I admire your ambition. As to useful information . . . I haven't been far into the Valley. I've been commuting back and forth among the various hospitals that are still operating, from East Los Angeles to your neighborhood, Cedars-Sinai. I just came from Glendale Memorial, on my way to Children's Hospital by a rather indirect route that will allow me to stop off at a church where I'm needed. I'm afraid I will have to offer last rites again when I get there. I have given last rites so often in the last weeks . . ."

He looked haunted for a moment, then shook his head violently.

"The I-5 is completely blocked just north of Los Feliz, which I assume is where you were going. A landslide in Griffith Park, about where the pony rides were, has covered it completely. San Fernando Road is open. I have seen many pilgrims headed south, a few to the north."   •

"Pilgrims?"

"Did I say pilgrims? I suppose that's how I've been thinking of them. Of course, they are refugees. Most of them are on foot, but from time to time someone goes by in a vehicle they still have the gas to run. But I think most people who had access to gasoline have already left."

"Do you have any news from San Diego?"

"None at all, I'm afraid. And I wouldn't rely on it much if I did. I try to report just what I've seen with my own eyes. Do you intend to go to I-5?"

"I think so."

"Then watch out for lions."

Dave wondered if he had misheard. Then he wondered if the

pressure had been too much, if it had driven the priest crazy. Father Michael saw it.

"This is something I've seen with my own eyes. One rumor has it that the earthquake opened the cages at the zoo. Another says that a zoo employee, from an impulse of kindness, released all the animals. I have seen a kangaroo, or perhaps it was a wallaby. And three days ago I drove around a corner, and down the street was a lioness tearing at the body of what looked to be a German shepherd."

He shivered slightly.

"The cat showed no fear, not even the racket of my motorcycle with a broken muffler seemed to faze him. I turned around and hurried away. It's all the talk of Glendale. I know many people have been hunting for the more dangerous predators. But I suggest you keep your eyes open."

"We will," Karen said. She stared at Dave, her eyes wide.

"However, the most fearful predator of all is, of course, mankind. Lions don't have submachine guns."

"We'll keep that in mind, too," Dave assured him.

"Well, it's been nice chatting, but I must return to God's work. Be safe, my children." He put out his hand, and they both shook it. They started their engines and pulled out onto the street.

There were a lot of trees on many of the streets in this neighborhood, which was known as Little Armenia or Thai Town, and many of those were big old spreading deciduous trees that had fallen. They ended up taking many detours, and at one point, somewhere around Normandie and Sunset, they could look north and see the recently refurbished Griffith Park Observatory perched out at the end of its promontory, three domes set on a low white building. It was still standing, and looked intact.

Sunset was clear, and they were able to head east again through the medical complex of Kaiser, Children's, and Hollywood Presbyterian Hospitals. There were some LAPD on bikes, taking a lunch break. It looked like canned soft drinks and tacos.

They drove out onto the bridge over the I-5 freeway and looked over the edge. It was as empty as the 101 had been. Just to the north they could see a huge landslide that had shaken down and covered all lanes, as the priest had said.

They backtracked, then turned south on Riverside Drive. Passing under Hyperion Avenue, they entered the freeway and started south. They saw almost no one until they passed underneath the Glendale Freeway, then they began to see travelers here and there. Most of them were headed south.

Once they had passed over the dry river and the Pasadena Freeway they began to see more people. It never developed into a throng, or even a crowd—there were times when they were all alone—but it felt good to see people again, particularly when none of them seemed threatening.

They entered the East Los Angeles Interchange, the busiest interchange in the world, where four major highways intersected and tangled with each other like a bowl of concrete spaghetti. The I-5, the I-10, the 101, and the 60 entered and exited the area at different points, and the proper route for getting from one to another was not always obvious. It was a place that had defeated millions of people not familiar with the area, and had even confounded Dave a time or two.

At motor-scooter speeds and with no traffic to merge with, it was not a problem. As they passed each of the other highways, keeping to the I-5, they saw more people entering. For the first time they saw a few on scooters, one on a motorcycle, and several official vehicles belching smoke from their jury-rigged wood burners. At one point three LAPD motorcycles screamed by. The officers were riding two to a cycle, something he had never seen. The man or woman in back carried a military rifle in the ready position.

But most of the people were on foot, pushing grocery carts. Some pulled big wood-sided children's wagons, piled high with the possessions they thought they would need on the trek south.

They went under a dozen overpasses, none of which had fallen down, though some showed large cracks. A lot of overhead freeway signs had fallen, but they had been pushed to the side of the road.

They came to Hollenbeck Park, a long and narrow strip of grass with a lake running down the center, much like Echo Park. It had been turned into a refugee camp. It was a sea of people. There were many real tents, but the predominant color was blue, from the hundreds of plastic tarps that were serving as makeshift shelters.

This was East L.A. and Boyle Heights, the overwhelmingly Hispanic neighborhoods where incomes were low, unemployment was high, and there had historically been a lot of gang activity. In the best of times many of these people lived on the edge, commuting to minimum-wage menial jobs in construction, gardening, and food service.

In their earlier days Dave and Karen had liked to come here. Cesar Chavez Avenue (formerly Brooklyn Avenue) and Whittier Boulevard bustled with small private enterprise, from the taco trucks parked at the curb to the fruit carts with their colorful wares peeled, sliced, and sitting on ice, ready to be bagged with a squeeze of lime and maybe a dash of chili powder, to the tiny storefronts jammed to the ceiling with cheap imported merchandise from China and Southeast Asia. Some of the best Mexican, Guatemalan, and Salvadoran food in the city could be had cheaply in the many tiny restaurants.

There was an orange plastic fence standing between the tent city and the lake itself, going all the way around the lake at a distance of about ten yards. National Guard troops stood guard. Dave realized they were using the lake for drinking water. Across from them, on St. Louis Street, there was a large tank with a wood fire under it and pipes attached to it. That fed into a big aboveground plastic swimming pool. They were boiling the water and letting it cool in the pool. A long line of mostly women were waiting to get plastic milk jugs filled.

On the north side of the park, out on Fourth Street, dozens of blue plastic portable toilets had been lined up. The wind was blowing from that direction and the stench was pretty bad.

"I wonder how often they can empty those things?" Karen asked.

"Not often enough."

On the southeast side of the park were even more tents and tarps, completely surrounding the lake. At the corner of St. Louis and Fourth were several trucks, one of them another grip truck that had been converted to a hospital, and another that was serving as a soup kitchen. A long line stretched away from that, too. He could see other trucks in the side streets. All of them looked to be wood-powered, with the telltale burner looking like a big water heater. Somewhere, there was a factory turning them out.

"This is terrible," Karen said. "Understatement of the year."

"And we thought we had it bad."

"No, we've known for a long time that there were a lot of people worse off than we are. We've still got food, and a secure place to go to." She looked up at Dave. "Are you sure that leaving is a good idea?"

"No, I'm not sure at all. But we still need to do more exploring before we can make an intelligent decision about that."

"Not we. You. Like I said, we're going to do what you decide."

"I wish that made me happier to hear that. I mean—"

"I know what you mean. It's a lot of pressure, and I'd hate to have it all on me. We should be working as a team, but Dave, I just don't feel up to that yet."

"Let me know when you do. It would be welcome."

"Maybe soon." She sighed. "Onward."

CHAPTER EIGHTEEN

They continued on the freeway. There were still people here and there, almost all of them going south. Most of the noise-reduction cinder-block walls had fallen down. For the first time driving down this stretch of road Dave was able to see what was on the other side of them. At first it was houses, then a mix of houses on one side and warehouses on the other. A monster fire had ravaged the warehouse district. After half a mile he realized he was seeing the burned hulks of houses, too.

A pedestrian overpass had fallen and entirely blocked the road. Someone had used wire cutters on the cyclone fence running on each side, and a hacksaw on the metal supports. Dave could see tire tracks where trucks had crossed it. They had to lift their scooters onto the shattered concrete.

Then there was the interchange with the I-710 Long Beach Freeway. From a distance it didn't seem possible that they might get through. Great sections of the curving overhead ramps were missing. In some places nothing was left standing but the massive concrete supports.

Once again what was left of CalTrans, the highway department, had pushed a path through. It involved taking the ramp for the 710 and then crossing over many lanes of freeway, then onto a street called Triggs and down onto the I-5 again. It was so rough they had to get off and walk the scooters, but in five minutes they went down a bulldozed ramp and onto the freeway again.

They were well into the City of Commerce, in the heart of the industrial zone in southeast Los Angeles.

As its name implied, the City of Commerce existed to provide warehouses and light industry in a neighborhood where they could pay low property taxes. There was a small residential area squeezed between the 5 and the 710, but elsewhere it was deserted after dark except for night watchmen. It was surrounded by little towns like Bell and Bell Gardens, Downey, Vernon, Maywood, and Montebello.

Over the muted noise of their engines Dave thought he heard gunshots. He eased off on the gas, and saw that Karen had already done so. They both braked and stood side by side, turning their heads for the source of the sound.

"Up there a little bit, I think," Dave said.

"Shouldn't we turn around?"

"It sounds pretty distant. I think we could venture forward a little bit."

"If you say so."

They went another three blocks, not hearing any more gunfire. Then at the fourth street they saw and heard a crowd of people. Off to their right was the big empty parking lot of a Home Depot. The crowd of people was almost directly in front of them. Many of them had the big flat orange carts shoppers used to wheel lumber to the checkout stand. There was an alertness to their posture, and they were all looking away from Dave and Karen toward something the two of them couldn't see because too many people were in the street, blocking their view. But voices were being raised in that direction.

Some of the shopping carts were stacked with goods, cardboard boxes and big burlap sacks that might hold fifty or a hundred pounds of coffee or rice. Some of the sacks were paper, and imprinted with the Purina checkerboard.

"Are people eating dry dog food now?" Karen wondered.

"Could be. Or maybe they're just feeding their dogs."

There was a rattle of automatic weapons fire, and the crowd of people ducked as one. So did Dave and Karen. More shots, single ones this time, and many of the people in front of them turned and began to run. Some of them abandoned their carts, but more pushed or dragged them. The contents of the carts were clearly as important as life itself.

"Let's get out of here!" Karen shouted.

Dave looked around and saw a warehouse off to their right. It was made of corrugated steel, and its big door was open.

"Over there," he said. Karen saw the warehouse and took off

for it, with Dave following close behind. He glanced to his side as the gunfire quickly turned into a full-fledged firefight. As he watched there was an explosion, then another. He couldn't tell just what it was, but he thought it might be hand grenades. Was the National Guard down that street, or was it just the legendary heavily armed Los Angeles street gangs?

It didn't really matter. His last glimpse of the action before the edge of the warehouse cut off his view was of two running men falling down, shot in the back.

When they came to the open warehouse door Karen was going a little too fast. She leaned too far into the turn and the edge of the scooter's foot platform scraped the ground. Then the scooter was on its side and Karen was sprawled on the concrete. Dave jumped off his scooter and knelt beside her.

"Are you hurt?

"Just a scrape," she said. "What do they call it? Road rash."

He helped her up and followed her along the inside wall of the warehouse, behind some crates stacked just inside the door. They turned off their engines and propped their scooters on the kickstands.

"Let me see that," Dave said, bending toward her leg.

"It's all right, I tell you. I wonder if we can shut that big door?"

It was a roll-up door, wide and high enough to accommodate two big trucks side by side. And they were in luck, because if it had been electrically operated, there would have been no way to roll it down. But this was an old building, and no one had bothered to upgrade something that had worked well for years. They started toward the manual chain mechanism and were halfway there when they heard running footsteps outside.

They froze, bringing their shotguns up into firing position.

Two men came hurrying around the corner and into the warehouse. Both were black, one in his mid-forties and the other a teenager. They stopped when they saw Karen and Dave, and the older man put his hands in the air.

"We ain't armed," he said.

"Don't shoot," said the younger one. He looked on the edge of tears.

"Keep your hands up," Dave said. The younger one quickly raised his hands.

"I surely will," said the older one, "but staying here ain't a good idea. There's some bad dudes coming down the street."

As if to punctuate his words, there was another burst of automatic weapons fire and then single rifle shots in return. A bullet hit the outside of the warehouse and whined off into the distance. The steel wall rang.

"We need to take cover," the man said.

"Get back behind those crates," Dave said, gesturing with his gun.

"You got it."

The two hurried to the crates, followed closely by Dave and Karen. They made their way back behind them, into a narrow aisle.

"Stop there," Dave said. "I'm going first. Karen, you cover them. I want you guys to stop in the middle of the aisle here and sit down. I'm going to the other end, and Karen will be on the other side of you. She'll stay twenty feet away from you, and she *will* shoot if you try anything funny."

"Funny is the furthest thing from my mind. Come on, son, do what the man says." The man and boy sat with their backs against the crates. The boy was shivering, obviously scared to death. Dave hurried to the end of the aisle and peered around the corner. From there he could see the street.

"What are your names?" he heard Karen say.

"I'm Justin, and this is my son Kareem."

"Justin, I'm sorry about this, we don't mean to—"

"Don't worry about it, ma'am. I was in your position, I'd do the same."

"What were you doing out there without a weapon?"

"What I was doing was looting."

"Dad!"

"No point prettying it up. We've been hungry, my family and me. Heard there was food in some of these warehouses, being guarded by the companies that own it. That didn't seem right to me. So we come down here to see what's what. As to coming without a weapon, I had me a pistol until ten minutes ago. Lost it running away from all that shooting. I'm afraid I'm gonna miss that pistol."

"Where do you live?"

"Live in Downey, work in Vernon."

"Quiet, everybody!" Dave said in a loud whisper. "I think I hear someone coming."

It sounded like a large group. Dave peeked around the wooden boxes. He saw four men, then six come running down the street. They all paused and looked into the warehouse. All the men were young, and looked Hispanic. They were all armed, with a variety of weapons, mostly handguns but two rifles that looked military.

One of the men said something in Spanish, and four of them took off. Both the assault rifles went with them. The two who were left behind looked like the youngest, and all they had was pistols. Dave now liked the odds better, but was hoping not to have to shoot. It was not only that he was loath to take a life, but the probability that the sound would bring the others back.

"You think they in there?" one of them said. He was wearing a red bandanna tied around his forehead. His skin glistened with sweat.

"How the fuck I know that?"

"Dude, I don't wanna go in there. There a thousand places to set up on you, and those dudes could be in any of 'em. We walk in there, we sitting ducks."

"But Cuchie say we should—"

"Yeah, and Cuchie, he down the street looking for them others. I say we cool it here ten minutes, then we catch up, say ain't nobody here."

"Sound like a plan. You got a smoke?"

"What I look like, a cigarette machine? I got three, maybe four I been saving. Ain't no food coming into town, *damn* sure ain't no smokes coming in."

"Aw, c'mon, share one with me."

"All right. But don't just stand there, fool. Let's get outta the doorway. Goddam shooting gallery, this is."

Dave watched them hurry to hide themselves on the other side of the open door. He glanced back at Karen, who wasn't pointing the shotgun at Justin and Kareem anymore. The two men still sat, heads down, trying not to breathe too loudly. Dave realized he had been holding his breath, too.

Neither of the bangers could have been much older than fourteen.

Dave could hear them talking on the other side of the steel wall. He realized he had very little idea what was going on, who was involved in the fighting out there. He thought it over, and then pointed at Justin. The man looked, raising his eyebrows. Dave gestured for him to come over.

Justin got carefully to his feet, making no noise. His son watched him fearfully. The older man walked carefully, his hands in the air. Dave signaled that he could put them down. Justin stopped five feet away, and Dave motioned him closer.

"Justin, I'm going to trust you," he whispered.

"I can get behind that."

"I like it that you didn't try to bullshit me about the looting business. In my book, there's no shame in going out to get food when your family's hungry, even if you have to break into a warehouse. I'm sorry we had to meet like this, the guns and the threats."

"I've already forgot about it."

"Listen, I don't have any idea what's going on out there. This isn't my area. Anything you could tell me would help us out a lot."

Justin shrugged.

"I don't know a whole lot more than you do, probably. At first it was . . ." He stopped, and they both listened as the kids outside raised their voices. Dave didn't get the first part of it. Then one of them spoke again.

"Fuck this," the kid said. "I ain't waiting around all day. How long it take to search a goddam warehouse like this, anyway? Let's catch up with the others."

"I hear that."

Justin and Dave waited. Dave thought he heard footsteps moving away. He started to go around the corner of the crates, and Justin put a hand on his shoulder.

"Might be a trick," he whispered.

"I don't think they're cunning enough for that."

"I don't either, nor smart enough. But give it a few minutes, just in case."

Dave nodded, and gestured to Karen and Kareem. They joined the men, and Dave whispered to them.

"Very quietly, make your way toward the back and see if there's a door back there that can be opened."

Karen nodded. Kareem raised his eyebrows and pointed his

thumb at his chest. Dave nodded, and the young man headed off with Karen.

"She ain't trigger-happy, is she?" Justin said.

"She'll do what she has to do, I think. If the situation arises. But your son has nothing to fear from her. She's a good shot. Better than me."

"I ain't no kind of shot at all. Hardly ever fired that pistol, but you feel like you gotta have one down here." He gave a bitter laugh. "All my life I kept my nose clean, didn't run with no gangs, worked hard. And now look at me."

"Everybody's in a bad spot."

"Some worse than others. Those your little bikes back there?"

"Yes."

"So you got some gas."

"I put some away." Dave didn't know why he was telling this man about his business; his instincts told him to shut up, but he didn't. "I had a little advance warning things were going to go bad."

"Wish you'd have told me."

"I wish I could have shouted it from the rooftops. But who would have believed me?"

"You got a point there."

Karen and Kareem came back and reported that the back door was locked, and they hadn't heard anybody out there. They all sat down and waited, speaking softly. Dave kept an eye on the open door.

"There was already some bad shit going down before the quake," Justin told them. "About what you'd expect. Black folks against the Latinos. When the gangs realized the cops and even the Guard was pretty busy, the gloves came off. Shooting every night, bodies in the street in the morning. But before long everybody was on foot or on bicycles, even the bangers. Nobody had any gas.

"Worse than that, the food was running out. When it was clear that no food was coming in, I finally saw the light and went to the grocery, spent all the money I had left 'cause the banks didn't open, not down here, at least. This Korean family, known them most of my life, had the only grocery store still open when I went shopping. By the end of the day, it was pretty much a riot. I'd paid for my stuff, some sacks of flour, as much canned goods as they had left. But pretty soon people was just taking stuff. That Korean couple got roughed up. That was . . . how many weeks ago, son?"

"I've lost track. One day seems pretty much like another, with no TV and no Internet. All I know is I been real hungry for at least a week."

"We all been. We ain't got much left. Couple cans of soup, a little flour. Anyways, we heard a rumor about these warehouses around here, how the owners were guarding all the food the people needed. We came down here looking. Came upon some folks had a pickup truck, one of those they converted to burn wood. They had chains, and they was pulling the doors off warehouses.

"They done a dozen of 'em, and there was nothing in them worth taking. Not nowadays, anyway. Who needs a goddam flat-screen television, or a tranny for a Lexus?

"Then they opened that one around the corner from here, and it was full of stuff, sacks and crates with Chinese letters on 'em. Lots of rice in big old sacks, lots of pallets full of those ramen noodles, cans full of I don't know what. And a bunch of Chinese guys with guns. Maybe a dozen of 'em, I couldn't see for sure.

"They was outnumbered, but they stood their ground. Then the firing started, and it went on for a while, in that warehouse. We ducked around a corner. But then the firing stopped, and people started going inside. So we did, too."

He stopped for a moment, and rubbed his hand over his face.

"I ain't proud of what we did. There was dead Chinese guys all over the place, all of 'em, I guess, unless some of 'em run, and black folks and Mexicans. And people wounded, some of 'em crying out."

"God, Dad," Kareem said, with a catch in his throat.

"I know, son. And people was loading up their carts with the Chinese food. And that's what we did, too. God help us, we took all we could handle, and then the shooting started again.

"This time I couldn't tell what the hell was going on. It seemed like everybody was shooting at everybody else. It wasn't a black against brown thing, least it didn't look like it. There was some Chinese in there, and some white guys, some of 'em in uniforms.

Not cops and I'm pretty sure they weren't the Guard. Some of 'em looked like private security, but they had some serious weapons.

"We started to run, and I dropped my pistol, and we had to leave the cart behind. And the next thing I know, you two was pointing your shotguns at us."

Everyone was silent for a while. Dave looked around the crates again, just for something to do. He took a deep breath.

"It's been about half an hour and I don't hear anything. We can't stay here all day. I'm going to see what's happening out there."

"Be careful, honey."

Dave nodded. He crept to the open door. He looked back and saw that everyone was following him. Well, why not?

He reached the door and carefully looked around it.

There was a dead man lying in the street, facedown. About a hundred yards to the north was what looked like another dead body. Far away, probably to the north, they heard isolated gunshots. Nothing was moving, not even on the freeway in front of them. Any travelers were still lying low, it seemed.

Dave walked to the dead man. A stream of blood had flowed down the slight slope of the street to pool at the curb. He didn't want to do it, but he crouched down and put his hand at the man's neck and confirmed what he had already been sure of when he saw the gaping hole in the man's back. It looked like an exit wound, and it was right around the heart.

There was a pistol, a .45 caliber, maybe a Glock, not far from the dead man's hand. Dave picked it up and stood. Kareem was pointing at something on the ground.

"That's a clip for that weapon," he said.

Dave saw it and picked it up. It was empty. He clicked the release and another clip fell into his hand. It was full.

"Looks like he was reloading," he said. He pushed the clip back into the butt. He looked at Kareem, and hesitated only a moment.

"Do you know how to use this thing?"

"I could figure it out." He shrugged. "I seen it in the movies."

Dave tossed the weapon to Kareem, who caught it, looked at it, and tucked it into the waist of his jeans.

"Thanks, man."

Dave had a feeling the kid had handled a Glock before.

* * *

The pistol was back in Kareem's hand as they cautiously moved along the street until they could see the parking lot where the battle had raged. There were more bodies, and this time there were some living people. They were scuttling among the carts, some of them overturned, quickly gathering what they could. Down the street they could see more people entering and leaving the warehouse where the food had been. There were sacks of rice spilled on the pavement. Some of them had burst open, and people were scooping up handfuls and putting it in plastic grocery bags.

"I guess here's where we leave you," Justin said. "We'd better get some of this grub before the fighting starts again. And you folks, you only got a little more daylight. You'd probably better head back to the hills."

"That's what we plan to do," Karen said.

"Thanks for the gun," Kareem said. "Y'all didn't have to do that."

"I didn't want to see you unarmed."

Justin held out his hand, and Dave and Karen shook it, then Kareem's. The man and his son hurried off across the parking lot, Justin grabbing a cart with a bent wheel that made a racket as he pushed it. Dave and Karen watched them load a sack of rice onto it and move on.

"I wish them luck," Karen said.

"They're going to need it."

They returned to the freeway and as they made their way north, they began to see more people heading south again. They also saw people cautiously watching from the side streets, hiding behind houses or industrial buildings.

The scooters were not noisy, but Dave was wishing they were as silent as bicycles. After what they had seen, the last thing they wanted to do was attract attention. He worried that they presented a tempting target to anyone hungry for transportation, which could be just about anyone they encountered.

They agreed that since the main purpose of the trip had been to take the measure of the situation on the ground between them and San Diego, they should take a different route home. But the neighborhood they were in was not familiar to either of them, and was full of rail yards. So after crossing the 710 Interchange they got off on Olympic Boulevard and headed west.

They saw very few people for several miles. No one moved to approach them. Dave wondered if things might have been different if they hadn't been carrying shotguns displayed so prominently.

They came to the Olympic Street bridge over the river, which didn't seem to have suffered any damage. But just to the north the freeway bridge that carried the I-10 over the river was in ruins. Great slabs of roadway had fallen down into the concrete channel.

The freeway had fallen onto the railroad tracks on both sides of the river, and there they saw the first constructive activity they had seen in a long while. A crane mounted on a railcar had been moved into place from the north, and fitted for wood burning. People were attaching cables to the large chunks of concrete and trying to move them off the tracks. Several had already been dumped to the side, and one track was clear, though badly damaged. Other men were working to repair the tracks.

"Maybe they've got some trains running again," Dave said.

"Do you think that means we might be seeing some relief supplies soon?"

"I wish I knew."

When they reached the intersection of Olympic with the I-10, they discovered that there no longer was an I-10. From the river to the 110 the freeway had been elevated on concrete pillars. They had all collapsed.

They discussed going back over the river and thus back up the I-5, but decided to continue on awhile to see if there was a way to get past the wreckage. In particular, Dave wanted to see the Convention Center again to see if there were still refugees there.

Fifteenth Street was blocked by the ruins of the freeway, as was Sixteenth. They got onto Eighteenth and headed west. At the corner of Naomi Street there was a small church with flat stucco sides and a modest steeple. A few people were sitting in the open door and organ music was coming from within. Dave was not a religious man, but the hymn grabbed at him on some deep level, and for one wild moment he wanted to go inside, join with his fellow men and women in song. But it was getting late and they still had a long way to go though uncertain territory if they were to get home before dark, as they had promised Addison and Jenna.

There was a big open barbecue pit made of black iron set up on the sidewalk. Smoke was pouring from it. As they passed, a woman turned something lying on the grill. She watched them without expression as they passed.

"Tell me that wasn't a dog," Karen said.

"I'm going to say goat."

"From your lips to God's ear."

The fact that the dog population of Doheny Drive had fallen drastically in the last weeks was something Dave had kept from Karen and Addison. It was one of the things people had talked about during the long watches at the barricades. If anyone had eaten their pet Dave wasn't aware of it, and he doubted it. But the simple fact was that food was running low for humans in most households. There just wasn't anything to spare for a dog, particularly a large one. One man had broken down and wept as he told of putting down his dog.

Many cats, of course, could fend for themselves, finding small rodents when they had to.

"Look on the bright side," he said. "It definitely wasn't human."

They continued on Washington Boulevard, looking to the northeast every time they crossed a street, seeing each street blocked by the remains of the I-10. They got to Figueroa and could see from there that the 110 Harbor Freeway was blocked, too, from a collapsed overpass. The 110 was not elevated on pillars like the I-10, it traveled on an earthen berm except for when it crossed streets, but the berm was too steep to climb safely and they didn't know what was on the other side.

"I wonder how far south we'd have to go to get past that?" Dave said.

"Or would you prefer to go back to the 5?"

"I hate to go back . . . but we may have no choice." He studied his GPS. As soon as he had identified Georgia Street as the last one before the 110, the unit gave a little beep and shut itself off. Dead battery.

On Hill Street the city had parked a lot of buses under the freeway. The freeway had fallen on them . . . but not crushed them completely. They went down the lines, and at one point Dave could see all the way through between two lines of crushed buses.

"It wouldn't be too hard for somebody on foot to climb over what's left of the freeway," he said, "but with the scooters, I don't want to chance it."

"So you want to go through there?"

"It's that or go all the way back. Look at the sky. It'll be dark in a few hours."

"You know I don't like . . ." She didn't finish, but he knew his wife was a little claustrophobic. For that matter, he wasn't thrilled by close spaces, either. There was at least ten feet between the lines of buses, but at some points the concrete slabs didn't look much more than five feet high.

"There's no telling what might be in there," Karen said.

"Would you want to stay in there, with a thousand tons of broken concrete hanging over you?"

"I don't even want to *run* through it."

"It'll take two minutes."

"How about south, and find a way across the 110?"

"We could do that, but we don't know how far it'll be. Going back is a known quantity. We know it's clear, and pretty much how long it will take."

"Which could be too long. I don't want to be out after dark, and we promised Addison." She sighed. "Let's do it."

They got off the scooters and pushed them.

It got very dark. There were chunks of concrete they had to go around, but they found no impassable spots. Halfway in, the bad odor they had been smelling got more intense.

"Oh, God, that's awful," Karen whispered.

Dave saw them first, three bodies piled up between buses, almost invisible in the darkness. He heard a sound he didn't like, and shined his flashlight into the crack.

There was a large dog, a pit bull mix, tearing at one of the corpses. Dave felt his gorge rise, but kept it down.

The dog looked at them, then back at his meal, and seemed to decide they might take it from him. He snarled, and crouched down. Dave reached for his shotgun.

"I think we better—"

The sound of Karen's shotgun going off was beyond deafening. It sounded like the whole world had exploded.

"Jesus, Karen!"

He found he had dropped his flashlight. He picked it up and shined it into the gap where the bodies were. The thing in there no longer looked like a dog.

Dave gestured toward the far end of the tunnel. Karen nodded, and they quickly pushed their scooters into the light. Dave put down his kickstand and sat on a piece of concrete. Karen seemed a lot calmer than he would have expected. His own hands were shaking.

"Suddenly I have to pee, *real* bad," Karen said.

"I think I already did."

She laughed, and he laughed, and it relieved the tension a little.

"I'm not going back in there," she said, firmly. "I want you to watch out here, see if any people come. And don't look."

"I promise. I hope you'll warn me next time. Like, 'I'm going to shoot.' Something like that."

"I thought he started toward us."

"I'm not complaining. Not too much. You did the right thing. I'm sort of surprised it hasn't affected you more."

"It's not much different from shooting a deer. Well, except for the head exploding. I shot a few deer with my dad when I was growing up. I didn't even have to think about it. Now shut up, I'm having a hard time getting started here."

Dave did that, and finally she joined him again.

"My turn," he said.

He baptized the rear end of a squashed Metro bus, zipped up, and joined her.

They found themselves blocked in many places by fallen buildings, massive piles of brick that had completely blocked streets. There were also a large number of cracks, some of them running right through buildings that had not collapsed, but now looked as if someone had sliced into them with a giant cleaver.

They made their way to Figueroa again, and motored past the Convention Center and the Staples Center. The Convention Center looked like a squashed tin can, and the smell coming from it was intense. It would be easy to believe that thousands had died there as the refugee center turned into a death trap.

As they got farther downtown they saw more and more rubble on the streets. Entire brick walls had peeled away from the older buildings. But most of all they saw glass. The shards were piled three and four feet high in some places, and reached outward to meet another pile in the middle of the street. They had to go very slowly. Most of the north–south streets were impassable except to a tank with steel treads.

"I can't imagine what this must have been like, coming down," Karen said.

"Anybody on the street would have been sliced to pieces," Dave agreed. "The only good thing about this whole business is that it was just after midnight."

They saw no one on the streets.

"I guess the people in the condos and lofts have left," Karen said. She was referring to the people with money, the ones who had in recent years moved into the pricey accommodations of the "new downtown," mostly older buildings renovated and equipped with the sort of luxuries up-and-coming young professionals demanded.

"Not much for them here now."

Blocked at turn after turn, they eventually did intersect with Broadway, and found that a reasonably clear lane had been bull-dozed down the center. They followed it from Olympic to Fourth, and on toward Third. To their amazement, the Grand Central Market was open. They slowed down. Around a hundred people were sitting or standing on the street, eating fruits and vegetables.

"Let's stop here a minute," Karen said.

Dave raised his eyebrows at her, but turned off his motor. She put hers on the kickstand, then entered the open building. An elderly man approached Dave.

"You wouldn't have a smoke, would you?"

"Sorry, man. Gave it up years ago."

"Looks like I'm doing that, too, whether I want to or not."

"You'll be happy when you get through it."

"Right now I'm a fucking wreck."

"So what's happening in there?"

"Salvation Army," the man said. "They set up here and there in the city. It's the new game in town: figure out where the Army's going to be tomorrow. They're a lot better than the real fucking army, which has done fuck all, seems to me."

"Any idea where they're getting their food?"

"They aren't saying. People found out where, they'd probably swamp the place. So far it's been enough to keep me alive, because other than that, I ain't got *nothing*. And I want a hamburger, and most of all I want a *smoke*!"

After ten minutes Karen left the market. She was carrying a white plastic bag and looking a little guilty. She straddled her scooter and started it up.

"What you got there?"

"A head of lettuce and two soft tomatoes."

"What did you use for money?"

"They're not taking money. And I didn't want to take this but they pressed it on me. All they asked was 'How many in your family?' and the next thing I knew I was holding a bag of veggies. I tried to hand it back but they hurried me along."

"I'm not going to say you shouldn't have taken it."

"I know I shouldn't. But the idea of a salad . . . well, I gave up."

"It sounds good to me, too." And it did. His mouth was watering, and he had never been a big salad eater. It was funny how if you hadn't had anything for a long time, it sounded better than it had ever actually been.

"They had apples and oranges, other greens, turnips, stuff like that. All of it was stuff I'd have complained to the manager about at Whole Foods a few months ago. It sure did look good now, though."

"I could go for a fresh apple."

"Me, too. But these people here don't have what we have. I think I ought to give this bag to somebody else."

"You probably should."

They were both silent for a moment, then Karen shrugged, opened the hard-case pannier on the back of her scooter, and put the bag inside.

"And you know what? You're going to laugh, but it felt good to be doing a little shopping again. Sort of."

Dave didn't laugh, but he grinned at her.

"Why would I laugh? You were always an Olympic-class shopper, whether it was looking for bargains when we were poor, or big-time when you had a purseful of platinum cards. You don't want to lose your edge."

She stuck her tongue out at him, and this time he did laugh.

The Bradbury Building looked basically intact.

A few of the stone trimmings high up had broken off, and many of the windows were broken, but it was still standing tall. Well, fairly tall for 1893, which was when it had been built. It was a Los Angeles landmark whose marble, tile, and cast-iron interior atrium could be seen in movies as varied as *Blade-runner*, *Wolf*, and *Good Neighbor Sam*. It would have been awful to lose it. Dave reminded himself again that buildings just didn't matter when compared to the human loss; nevertheless, he was happy to see it.

Karen had suggested they go to the police department downtown to see if they had any advice both for the trip back to Doheny and the trip out of Los Angeles.

They rounded the corner two blocks away, drove another block, and soon they could see the new police headquarters. It was a skeletal, burned-out ruin. Like so many other buildings they had seen, there was no evidence of any attempt to fight the fire. Every window was blown out and the flames had worked their way up. The white façade facing First Street, directly across from City Hall Park, was cracked and blackened, with large parts fallen into the plaza below.

Across the street the old Parker Center had been heavily fortified, encircled with empty city buses. Police were coming and going. They were on foot, on bikes, and in a motley collection of trucks that had been modified to burn wood, then painted black. Some had light bars on the roofs, but most had nothing but LAPD stenciled on the doors.

There were half a dozen officers standing around the entrance in body armor. Some of the clothes were torn here and there. One female officer had bandages on her arms, and a man had a bandage around his head. They all looked tired, and they all had some indefinable thing in their eyes that said "Fuck with me, even a little bit, and you are dead meat." Dave was careful to keep his hands well away from his own guns.

They pulled up, not too close, and cut their engines. Dave

was about to speak, but Karen got there before him, asking if there was a way over the 110. One of the officers said there was, but it was pretty much all the way to Echo Park. The bridges near downtown were all either fallen or too damaged for vehicles.

"You might make it over them on foot, or on those scooters," he said, "but I wouldn't want to try it. Where are you headed?"

"West Hollywood," Dave said.

"Your best bet is to cross the 110 at Wilshire," the man said. "Some of the roads have been plowed free of debris. Go back the way you came and take Broadway down to Fourth, turn west, go all the way to Lucas, turn south. All the bridges are either intact or cleared away."

"A little less gang activity there, going through Koreatown," the woman officer said.

"She's right. The Koreans are keeping it relatively safe."

"Thanks so much, guys," Karen said. "And thank you for the job you're doing."

"I second that," Dave said.

"Thank you, ma'am. But you'd better get moving. After dark we don't even patrol anymore except around the hospitals and refugee centers. You do not want to get caught out after dark."

They asked about routes out of the city, but none of the cops there knew anything useful. They thanked them again, and moved on.

CHAPTER NINETEEN

Dave knew the Koreatown neighborhood reasonably well, but the quake had picked everything up, shaken it around, and dropped it all back in such a jumbled manner that it was often difficult to keep track of exactly where they were. Many street signs had been buried in rubble. At times they were forced to rely on the position of the sun to orient themselves, moving steadily west and north.

"I feel like a rat in a maze," Karen finally said.

"I'd give anything I own for a cell phone," Dave said. He was imagining Addison, remembering the promise he had made to her. And there was nothing he could do to speed their progress.

Halfway down one block two young men who looked Korean stepped out into the street. They had already passed two neighborhood checkpoints and been waved on by some older Korean men. The street was lined on both sides with high-density housing, apartment blocks four or five stories high, most of them with a tiny balcony, most of them with large cracks in their walls.

The young men—just kids, really, looking to be in their late teens—wore sleeveless T-shirts and had prison tattoos on their arms and fingers, and one had some on his neck. Their hair was cut short and spiked with gel. They wore jeans and expensive running shoes that looked brand-new. One had a revolver stuck in the waistband of his jeans, and the other was carrying a shotgun resting easily on his shoulder.

"Hey, dude, I like your bikes," one of them said, as Dave and Karen stopped about twenty yards from them.

"Thanks," Dave said. "We like them, too."

"Nice day for a bike ride," the kid went on. "How much you take for them?"

"I'm afraid they're not for sale." Dave had his shotgun in his hands, and he could see from the corner of his eye that Karen did, too. It was pointing forward, but not directly at the boys. He was hoping they could get by these punks without any violence, but he was ready for anything.

"Ah, c'mon, dude. We got money. Our money ain't good enough for you?"

"I told you, they're not for sale."

"How about you let me take a ride? I always wanted to ride one of them things, till I can afford me a Harley. Just around the block. What do you say?"

"We're really in a hurry," Dave said.

"Don't look around," Karen said, from the corner of her mouth. "Behind us."

Dave glanced in his mirror and saw the head of a third boy looking out from between two parked vehicles. The very end of a rifle barrel was sticking out, too.

"If he comes out," Dave whispered back, "shoot him."

"Hey, what you guys talking about?" the first kid said.

"Listen, we don't want any trouble," Dave told him. "These guns are loaded."

"I'll bet they are." This was the second guy, the one with the handgun, who hadn't had anything to say up to then. "And you know what? Nice white folks like you? I bet you won't shoot. Shooting gets messy, you'd lose your lunch." He pulled the gun from his belt and was raising it, holding it sideways like he'd seen guys do it in the movies, three of his fingers sticking up in the air. "So why don't you—"

Dave shot. The load went off a bit to one side of where he had been aiming, and ripped out a large part of the guy's chest on his right side, perforating his gun arm as well. The pistol went flying as the guy fell. Dave racked in another load and saw Karen twisting and bringing her own gun up. There was another shot. Dave didn't look behind him. The first kid was trying to get his shotgun aimed at Dave, but he had been badly spooked by the first shot, and he missed his grab for the barrel. He fumbled so badly, in fact, that the shotgun went clattering to the street.

Dave heard screaming behind him, but kept his own gun centered on the kid who was still standing. The kid held his hands out in front of him as if to stop the next shot he knew was coming. A dark stain spread in the crotch of his jeans. Behind him, the screaming got worse.

"Does he still have his gun?" Dave asked, without looking around.

"No, he . . ." Karen's voice was shaky. "He's not in any shape to shoot."

"Okay. Look around at the apartments. See anybody at the windows?"

The unhurt kid dropped to his knees and was trying to say something, but it came out incoherent, or possibly he was speaking Korean.

"To your right, third floor," Karen said. Dave looked that way quickly, keeping his shotgun on the kid, wishing he had eyes in the back of his head. He saw the face of a black woman peering over the top rail of a balcony.

She moved out a little and showed her hands.

"I ain't armed!"

"Keep your hands in sight, then."

She pointed at the kid on his knees.

"Kill that motherfucker!"

This brought a fresh burst of sobbing from the kid.

"We have to get out of here," Karen said, urgently.

"I know. But do you think we should leave these weapons lying around?"

"I don't know. What do you want to do?"

"Kill him!" the woman screamed again.

Dave didn't know what issues she had with him, and he didn't want to know.

"He's not our problem anymore," he shouted to her, and then to the kid, "Get on your face and spread your arms out."

"You'll shoot me!" the kid cried.

"Not if you do what I tell you." He spoke to Karen. "Can you grab that shotgun from the guy behind us?"

"It's a rifle. And I'm not sure I can."

"Do it if you can." The screaming from behind him had stopped, and as soon as the guy in front of him had stretched out on the pavement, spread-eagled, he risked a quick glance back there. Karen was off her scooter and slowly approaching the man she had shot, keeping her gun aimed at him. Karen's blast had hit him around the hips. Blood was pumping from an artery, and he was moving feebly, trying to get up and crawl away.

Dave hurried over to the uninjured kid, who twisted his head in panic, trying to see Dave, but he kept his hands pressed flat to the ground.

"Don't look at me," Dave told him, and as soon as the kid turned to face the ground again, Dave hit him on the back of the head with his shotgun butt. He hit him harder than he had ever hit anyone in his life, thinking, *You didn't think this nice white couple would shoot, did you, you cocksucker.* The kid stopped moving. Dave picked up the shotgun the kid had been too shocked to fire.

"Kill him!" the woman shouted again. "That bastard—"

"He's not my problem, ma'am." He moved to the man he had shot. He was dead. Dave picked up his pistol. He looked up at the woman on the balcony, then threw the pistol toward the door to her apartment building.

"Do what you want, but wait till we're gone, or I'll shoot you, too."

The woman said nothing, and Dave hurried back to the scooters. Karen had the rifle. She was looking pale and sick.

"Let's get the fuck out of here," she said.

They hurried down the street and around the corner, looking up at all the balconies around them. It was dusk now, and what Dave feared the most was that the three Koreans had friends in the area who might have heard the shotgun blasts.

They were in luck this time with the streets. They were able to make five blocks to the west without hindrance, then turned north and went another three blocks before a destroyed apartment building blocked their path.

"I need to pull over," Karen said.

They drove to the curb and stopped their engines. Karen staggered a few steps to the sidewalk, and threw up.

"His leg, his hip . . . just sort of exploded."

They were motoring along in the gathering dusk, seldom going more than fifteen miles per hour.

They had run into two more guard posts. Each time they had held their breaths, putting their shotguns in nonthreatening positions and slowing down to let the men see how harmless they were. Each time Dave had worried that someone had called ahead on a radio. *Be on the lookout for a man and a woman on white and pink Vespas.* It was possible they had just killed the son of one of these men. It was also possible the men would be as happy to see the end of the gangbangers as the woman in the apartment building had been, but you couldn't count on that. At each checkpoint they had been waved on.

"Dave, we have to talk."

"It's getting late, hon."

"I know, but we have to take a minute."

They were getting close to Sunset Boulevard and he wanted nothing more than to be putt-putting up Doheny, but he pulled over and shut off his engine.

"Addison doesn't need to hear about this," she said. "Ever."

"I'd already figured that out."

"I know. But what about this shotgun, and the rifle? How do we explain them? She's not stupid, she'll know *something* happened."

"You're right. I hadn't thought of that."

"I say we get rid of the rifle. We don't have any bullets for it anyway."

"I hate to. It's worth a lot now. We might need to barter it for something. And I *really* hate to part with the extra shotgun, which we *do* have ammunition for."

"I don't feel good about taking things off dead men."

"I don't either. But they were threatening us."

"Threatening to rob us."

"You point a gun at me, as far as I'm concerned, you're trying to kill me."

"You're right. I'm just still trying to get my mind around the idea that we just killed two people."

Two *kids*, Dave was thinking. Did it matter that they might have been anywhere from sixteen to twenty? Before all this, sure it did, in a court of law. If any courts of law were still functioning, he hadn't heard of them.

"Dave, do you think we might be in trouble here?" Karen asked, reading his mind.

"Well, we just committed two felonies, and then we drove

away, and that's probably a half dozen other felonies right there."

"We'd be pretty easy to identify. Pink Vespa?"

"Let's think about that later. My gut feeling is that girl would never identify us."

"If she was the only one who saw us."

"There's that." He knew there were people up there in those apartments, hunkering down for another night without electricity. He thought most of them wouldn't go to the windows when they heard gunfire, but you never knew. And one of those observers might have been the mother of one of the boys.

It was all too much to consider at the moment. He shook off his worries and came back to the issue of the guns.

"How about this? We leave the rifle with somebody at the barricade, somebody who can keep his mouth shut, somebody who wouldn't let it get to Addison. I know at least two people I'd trust with that."

"The rifle and the shotgun."

"All right. For now. Later, I can take some stuff down the hill and 'trade' for it. Come back with a plausible story, and another shotgun. I *want* that shotgun, Karen, for Addison. I've been kicking myself that I didn't buy three when I had the chance."

She thought about it for a moment. Seeing Addison in trouble *with* a shotgun, and *without* a shotgun. A no-brainer.

"Sounds like a plan."

"Then let's get going."

Addison was inconsolable.

She was also angrier than Dave had seen her since she was two.

She was a remarkably mature young girl, sensitive and smart and well behaved, having dealt with her parents' growing estrangement a lot better than he felt he would have at her age. But she was also at that age where it was possible to shed that new, uncomfortable adult skin at a moment's notice and revert to a child's view of the world, and a child's reactions.

"You said you'd be back before dark!"

"There's still a little bit of light," Karen pointed out. Dave thought that was the wrong tack to take, and he was right.

"Oh, so now I need to get out my damn *almanac*? *You promised!*"

"Addie, using bad language won't—"

"Oh, screw you!"

Her eyes were red, her cheeks were wet, her nose was running. It was a full-scale tantrum, and she had been crying for hours. Jenna was standing off to the side, knowing better than to get involved in this, but she caught Dave's eye for a moment and there was a lot of things in that look. Anger, relief, accusation. Of course she had been terrified that she would be left to raise the child on her own. Which she had vowed she would do to the best of her ability.

"Addie," Dave said quietly. His daughter wouldn't look at him. "Addie, I'm sorry. Please forgive us. We never should have left you here."

"Daddy, you promised . . ." Then she collapsed into his arms. He held her tightly, vowing once more that no matter what it took, nothing was going to happen to this girl. He held his arm out and Karen joined them. After a brief hesitation, Addison put her arm around her mother, too. Dave gestured to Jenna, who looked as if she was thinking about making herself scarce.

"What I said was true, Jenna," Dave told her. "You're family, too." Which broke her up, and she stumbled over and joined the group hug.

"Addie, I'm going to make you another promise. This one will be easy to keep. From now on, this family sticks together. Always. We won't go anywhere without you. If it's too dangerous for you, it's too dangerous for us. How is that?"

"Okay, if you promise."

"We both promise," Karen said.

"Daddy, all my friends, I don't know where they are, I don't know if they're safe or dead, or what. I miss them so much."

Dave felt stupid. Of course she worried about her friends. He had been so concentrated on family, nothing but family, and those few close friends in the posse that he had warned and thus felt a certain responsibility for. He had many other friends, but they were just people he knew, mostly professionally. None so close that he had spent a lot of time worrying about them. His parents were dead, Karen's parents were far away and emotionally remote; they spoke to them by phone on Christmas and birthdays, and it was always a relief to get it over with. He had no siblings, no aunts or uncles he was close to. To Dave, family had always meant the two women in his life, and now Jenna.

It all descended on him now. How were Bob and his family? How were Dennis and Roger? He was appalled by how small his world had become. It made him weak in the knees, thinking about how much now depended on him. Addison was just a child, Karen had abdicated to him, Jenna was uncertain of her role. It was too damn much.

Nothing in his life had prepared him for this. He was a storyteller, that was all he had ever wanted to be. He was a man who had tried to be a good father but now saw he had spent too much of his time chasing after things that didn't matter. He had a huge, all-but-worthless home, he was surrounded by former millionaires whose homes were now all but worthless, too. He had almost been a millionaire himself. When all the material things had been stripped away, he saw how useless his life had been, all his striving, all his sacrifices of the things that really mattered.

It was too much. He needed help.

That night Dave and Karen lay in each other's arms in the darkness. Dave wondered if he would ever get to sleep. He kept seeing that kid knocked over by the blast from his shotgun.

Karen seemed to read his thoughts.

"Do you think we're going to be in trouble?" she asked.

"You mean for killing two people?"

"It was self-defense. They were threatening us."

"They never got off a shot," Dave pointed out.

"But that guy I shot, he was coming up behind us. It was a trap."

"Maybe all they wanted to do was rob us. Take our scooters and our guns."

"Which could have been a death sentence, leaving us alone, miles from home, with night coming on."

"I'm not arguing with you, Karen. I'm just thinking how a prosecutor might argue the case before a jury."

"Do you think there are any juries operating out there? Or prosecutors, for that matter."

"Your guess is as good as mine. The police are still functioning, some of them, anyway, and the National Guard. I'll bet there's a jail, or some kind of compound."

"But you don't think anybody will be coming after us?"

"I guess I doubt it. Everybody wants law and order, but I wouldn't be surprised if the police have their hands full just trying to maintain order. In a near anarchy, the only law *is* to maintain order. My guess is that they're concentrating only on the most violent crime, committed by violent people, people who were bad guys before all this.

"You know, the people who did things during the Rodney King riots, I don't think they ever did anything about most of them. Not just looters, there were way too many of those, but people who killed other people. When conditions are like that, most people who commit crimes get away with them. And this situation is ten thousand times worse than the King riots. A million times worse."

"So that's the good news? For us, I mean? They're too busy trying to keep things calm, so they probably don't have time to look very hard at killings? And probably don't have the legal staff to deal with it, anyway?"

"Well, we could use some good news, couldn't we? It's also the bad news, too, of course. If things have reached the point where there's no law, it's people like us who will suffer for it. We're not used to violence. The whole population of the state prison system might be out there, roaming around, as hungry as everybody else but maybe more prepared to do something about it. What I'm thinking is, we got lucky. If they had been just a little bit smarter, it might have gone badly for us."

They thought that over for a while.

"I just don't understand those boys." Her voice caught in her throat, and he felt her tears on his shoulder. He hugged her tighter. "We had our guns in our hands! We weren't exactly pointing them at them, not *right* at them, but any idiot could see it wouldn't take us a second to fire."

"That's what I said. That was our luck. We were dealing with idiots."

"Do you think so?"

"Only in a certain sense. They might have been bright

enough in some ways, but they were slaves to their macho image of themselves. Did you notice the way that guy with the pistol was pointing it? Holding it sideways like they do in the movies? The stupidest way to aim a pistol? That's *cool*. It's so cool that gangbangers picked it up from the movies, like the Mafia picked up stuff from *The Godfather*."

"That's so awful. If they'd had any sense . . ."

"They'd still be alive. But they couldn't let us go. They had this image of themselves as the big bad gangsters, and their image of us as weak, people who would barf at the idea of shooting somebody."

"I did barf."

"Afterward, and that's the important thing."

There was another brief silence.

"What do you feel about it?" she asked.

"Feel? Not good. But I'll tell you the truth, if I had it to do over again, I can't think of what I'd do differently. We gave them every chance."

"Maybe a warning shot?"

"I don't think you even believe that yourself. *He pointed a gun at us,* Karen! What was I supposed to do? Ask him to put it down? I had to assume he was about to shoot, that was the *only* way to deal with it. And that other guy, the one coming up behind you. You think he was going to shout *boo*? They were playing for keeps, honey, and the only way to deal with that is to play harder and faster and meaner than them." He paused, and heard her sigh.

"So how do *you* feel about it?"

"I killed someone. I'll deal with it."

He thought she might be done, but there was one more subject to bring up, and it was an important one.

"Dave, I'm sticking to what I said. The decision is yours. But I told you I'd give you my opinion, and I have to say I'm not sure that leaving here is the right idea."

"Big surprise," he said, and instantly regretted the way that sounded. "No, I mean, of course you have doubts. After what happened? I do, too."

"So what are we going to do?"

"I'll tell you what we aren't going to do. We aren't leaving tomorrow. I need some time to think about it some more. And I want to see what Addison and Jenna think. Do you think we should tell Jenna?"

Karen thought about it.

"Maybe we should think about that a little longer, too."

"Fair enough. Honey, this is probably the hardest decision I've ever had to make. Getting it wrong scares me more than anything I've ever faced. Getting it wrong is just not an option. And I'm not sure I'm up to it."

Karen embraced him.

"You've guided us well so far. I'm willing to rely on you again."

"I appreciate that, and at the same time I have to say I kind of resent it. I hope that isn't too harsh."

"I think I deserve worse than that, so I take no offense."

"What I want most of all is for us to be a team again. I know you're strong enough; you were so strong when we had nothing."

"I may be ready to be part of the team again soon. But not yet." She sighed. "That was my downfall, wasn't it? Going from having nothing, struggling, counting the money, and suddenly we had it all. I couldn't handle it."

"Don't be so hard on yourself. It was my downfall, too. We both misplaced our values. The miracle, to me, is that Addison has turned out so levelheaded. With precious little help from me. She doesn't even remember the hard times, she was too young."

"She remembers."

"You think so?"

"She's told me she had more fun 'back when we were poor.' Isn't that sad?"

"If I'd known that, maybe . . . no, by then, by the time we moved into this monster of a house, I was blind to everything but getting ahead, being a big success."

"I loved you for it. The thing I did wrong was to stop loving you when times got hard again. What was I thinking?"

They were silent for a while.

"If you love me again, then everything's all right."

"I do. I always did. I just got angry and couldn't show it."

They both jumped when they heard a noise from the doorway. Dave was groping in the dark for his pistol when Addison spoke.

"Mommy, can I come in?"

Dave quickly found the electric lantern and switched it on. He had forgotten to recharge it and the light it cast was dim, but enough to see Addison standing in the doorway to their bedroom, her pillow and a blanket in her arms.

Karen got out of bed and went to her daughter. She hugged her. "I can't get to sleep. I feel like a baby, but I'm scared."

"We're all scared, Addie."

"Can I sleep in here? I can curl up on the floor."

"Don't be ridiculous."

"She's right. My daughter's not sleeping on the floor. You get in bed with your mom, and I'll go downstairs and sleep on the couch."

"I wish you'd stay, too, Daddy."

In the end Dave set up a cot a few feet from the bed. It wasn't the most comfortable thing in the world, but he felt immensely comforted to have both his wife and his daughter sleeping so close. To his surprise, he fell asleep almost at once, and slept soundly through the night.

CHAPTER TWENTY

When Dave got up at sunrise the next morning he looked at the little battery-powered weather station that had survived the quake undamaged. It was reading 85 degrees. The wind gauge was no longer working, but when he stepped outside he could feel the hot, dry breath of a Santa Ana blowing down the canyon to swirl the dead leaves around on his patio. He wouldn't be surprised if the mercury topped a hundred later in the day.

He spent half an hour painting the scooters.

He had a choice of red or black, from some spray cans left over from a project he didn't even remember. He went with black, wanting to decrease their visibility as much as possible. When he was done they looked awful, full of drips and smears, but at least neither one of them looked pink. He kept worrying about that possible APB: *Be on the lookout for a blonde on a pink Vespa and a man on a white one.*

"Great job, Dad," Addison said, when she saw the results. "You just turned two nice rides into eyesores. No self-respecting thief would dare steal those. He'd die of shame, driving around."

"That was the idea." Dave wasn't so sure. Any ride at all with gas in it might be desirable now, a clapped-out Ford with a full tank better than a Rolls with no gas.

That she was speaking to him at all he regarded as better than he might have hoped. But she had never been one to bear a grudge for long.

He had often found that doing things that didn't require a lot of thought were the times when he came up with his best ideas for new stories on the TV series. What he usually ended up doing was the quintessential Los Angeles activity: driving. He had driven as far south as San Diego, west to Santa Barbara, east to Palm Springs, always on the freeways so he didn't have to give any thought to where he was going. Inching along or tooling down the highway at eighty-five, it was all the same to him. He would plug his iPod into the stereo system and let it shuffle at random through the hundreds of selections he had stored there, from Bach to Beyoncé. About half the time he would arrive back home with at least the seed of an idea and would summon his posse to his office in the guesthouse, where they would gorge on deli takeout he had brought up the hill from Canter's on Fairfax and toss out ideas for plot developments and jokes.

But when he was done with the painting, he was no closer to a decision than when he started. He left the house for his shift at the barricade, and suddenly everything changed.

Dave arrived at the barricade on his bicycle a little after eight. Art Bertelstein and a woman he didn't know were already on duty, hot and out of sorts. The woman was introduced as Peggy Wysocki. She looked to be around forty, and was dressed in Iraq War desert camo gear. Ferguson was there, too, looking bad. He was drenched in sweat, his skin was grayish, and his hand shook as he mopped his face with a towel. His eyes were hollow and haunted.

"Marshall, where have you been? You're ten minutes late."

Dave didn't feel he owed anyone an explanation, though an apology was in order. Where had he been? Taking care of his own business. He hoped Ferguson wasn't forgetting that guard duty down there was voluntary. He hoped the man wasn't letting himself turn into a petty general. He wondered if the man's deterioration was the result of the heavy strains of leadership—which Dave could easily understand, feeling overwhelmed to be responsible just for his own family—or the fact that he, like many others, had run out of a medication he needed.

"Sorry I'm late," he said.

"You've got a visitor," Ferguson said, jerking his head toward the other side of the barricade. Dave looked there and at first didn't see anybody, then spotted a young man sitting on a curb in the shade of a tree, drinking from a plastic water bottle. He wore spandex cycling clothes, a yellow jersey with a Nike swoosh and black shorts with blue racing stripes and bold letters that said PINERALLO. A bicycle that looked very high-tech was resting on the grass beside him. He was in his mid-twenties, with buzz-cut blond hair and a pleasant face that women would find irresistible. He had the lanky, wiry build of the long-distance racer. He looked up, smiled, and sprang to his feet, walking easily to stand a few feet away from the barricade.

"You're Dave Marshall," the man said. "I recognize you from pictures my dad sent me over the years."

Dave suddenly grinned.

"You're Teddy Winston!"

"Guilty. Dad sent me over here to talk to you. But . . ." He extended a hand to indicate the barrier and the armed people on the other side.

"Let him through," Dave said. "I know him."

"Doesn't sound like it to me," Ferguson said. He was frowning. "How about we see some identification?"

Teddy didn't miss a beat, his smile didn't falter.

"Sure. It's back in my saddlebag. Can I bring my bike up closer?"

Ferguson grudgingly nodded, and Teddy hurried back to his bike and walked it back to the barricade.

"I've got a pistol in here," he said, as he opened the flap of a canvas pannier.

"Reach in and take your hand out very slowly," Peggy said.

"Sure thing." He did as he was told, and brought out a wallet. He thumbed a California driver's license from it. He passed it over to Peggy, who studied it and seemed satisfied.

"Says Ted Winston, all right."

"He's the son of one of my best friends," Dave explained. "I've never met him. He lives in San Diego."

That got everyone's attention, almost as much as if he had said Teddy had just arrived from the moon. Peggy handed Teddy's ID back to him and gestured for him to come around the barrier.

"Sorry about that. Can't be too careful these days."

"Believe me, I know where you're coming from."

Then they all wanted to know what things were like in far-off San Diego, but Dave took him aside.

"We're going up to my house and talk it over. I'll tell you all about it later."

Ferguson was frowning.

"I don't think you should desert your post."

"Desert my post? I'm sorry, Richard, but if you remember, this is volunteer duty. I'll take someone else's shift, but you'll have to find a replacement for me now."

Things felt a little tense for a moment, and Dave wasn't sure which way things would go, but he felt he had to establish some boundaries.

"Sure," Art said. "Richard, you stay here for a few minutes, and I'll go find somebody to take his place."

Ferguson didn't like it. He stalked off toward his home.

"I'm worried about him," Peggy said.

"For more reasons than one," Art agreed.

Dave got on his bike and pedaled off up the gradual slope of the hill, with Ted Winston at his side.

Dave made it halfway up the hill before Ted diplomatically suggested that they get off and walk the rest of the way.

"This bike isn't geared for hills, anyway," he said. Dave had no doubt that Ted could make it up the hill in any gear and hardly break a sweat, but was grateful the younger man had offered the old fart a face-saving way of avoiding a heart attack.

Nevertheless, he was still exhausted and dripping sweat when they finally made it to the gates of his home.

Ted's arrival triggered Karen's hostess gene. Ted politely refused the offered food, and Dave wondered if that was going to be the new paradigm, not accepting such offers for fear the host really couldn't spare it. But he did accept a glass of iced lemonade.

But there was no stopping Karen. While everyone else sat around the table in Dave's office, she bustled around her makeshift kitchen preparing a tray of snacks. She arranged saltine crackers around the edge of the tray and opened a pot of cheese spread and a can of smoked mussels and another of pineapple chunks. When it was all out there everyone at first tried to resist, but such modest treats had already become such a novelty that soon someone would reach for a cracker with a dollop of sharp cheese, thinking they would have just one. Before long everyone was noshing, including Ted.

"My father says you want to get out of Los Angeles," he said.

"We were intending to. I had decided we would leave today or tomorrow. But I've been wrestling with that decision all night. We took a trip yesterday, reconnoitering. I'm no longer sure it's a good idea."

"Where did you go?"

"South. We were thinking of San Diego."

Dave was itching to hear about Ted's journey north, but the younger man wanted to hear their story first. Dave told him, with help from Karen, leaving out the part they had agreed no one else should hear. They had talked it over and decided there was no point in shielding Addison from hearing about the violence around the warehouse. She couldn't be protected from everything. She needed to have a more realistic picture of what was out there. She would be fearful, but also more alert. They would keep from her only the fact that her parents had killed.

Addison was hearing that story for the first time, and her eyes were wide but she seemed steady again. No doubt she was reflecting on just how much danger her parents had been in. He didn't mention the dead bodies, but he was sure her imagination could fill them in.

"So, aside from that food riot, you didn't run into any other trouble?"

"We saw some . . . signs of gang activity in Koreatown. We saw some kids who might have been thinking about robbing us, but we—"

"I'm sure they were going to rob us," Karen said, with a straight face.

"But we got away from them."

"You were lucky," Ted said, flatly. "Things like that can happen anywhere. Some places are worse than others, but there are roving bands, too."

"You know this for sure."

Ted nodded. "I've been out almost every day, and some nights, scouting around. I've seen some roving gangs, mostly on motorcycles, some on foot. Every once in a while there's a car full of them. I've been shot at."

"What did you do?" Addison asked.

"I ran like hell," Ted said, with a smile. But the smile didn't last long. "Three times I've had to shoot back. I won't lie to you.

At least twice I hit somebody. No telling what happened to them. I didn't stick around to find out."

"You do what you have to do," Karen said, not looking at Dave. "Yes. You do."

Dave wanted to get off the subject of things you had to do. Addison's eyes had gotten even wider while listening to Ted.

"At any rate," Ted went on, "there aren't nearly enough cops around. I'm sure some were killed in the quake, and transportation from their homes has been a problem. Some have been killed in the line of duty. And I'm sure some simply resigned, informally, when they saw how dangerous things were getting out there. They have to think of their families, just like everybody else. For whatever reasons, you're largely on your own out there. Does that fit in with your experience?"

"I'd say so. We saw cops around the police station, and some around the hospitals. It's not complete anarchy, but it's not good."

"Yes. My dad, my brothers . . . we've all agreed on several things.

"Number one, *anywhere* else is better than Los Angeles now. Sure, we know there are other places, like the Texas oil patch, that are completely uninhabitable, but they're out of our range, anyway. But elsewhere, in California or Nevada or Arizona or Oregon, no matter how hard the lack of fuel, food and water shortages, they don't have the worst natural disaster in American history on top of that. Nobody has said anything officially, so far as we know, about casualties from the quake, but I think tens of thousands have died. Los Angeles is a dying city. Do you agree with that?"

"From what we've seen, I'd have to," Dave said. "Somebody has been plowing routes through the wreckage, but we didn't see anything like rescue activity going on, except for neighbors helping neighbors."

"Okay. With a lesser disaster, I'd say it would make sense for you to stay holed up here in the hills. It's easier to defend than our house is. But we feel that no place in Los Angeles is going to be really habitable in the long run. People are planting gardens, but it's going to be hard or impossible to find the water to grow the crops, and it takes more time than we're likely to have before you *get* a crop.

"You can't grow rice here. I don't see wheat fields happening anytime soon. People are planting corn, but it takes months to get a crop. The important thing to remember is that Los Angeles was built in a desert. It's going to become one again. The aqueduct is not flowing anymore."

"I didn't know that."

"We don't know why. Probably the quake, though there are rumors that the people up north have turned off the faucet." He looked at Dave. "I guess I'm telling you some things you already know. After all, you're the one who laid it all out for Dad, just how bad it could get . . ."

"I want to know everything you know, and everything you've figured out."

"Bottom line, we feel we have to leave."

"We saw some people on the 5 freeway," Karen said. "Not a lot of them."

"That could be because of the rumor that the San Onofre nuclear plant has suffered a meltdown."

That remark was met with a brief silence.

"By meltdown, do you . . ." Dave stopped himself. "Wait a minute. If you came from San Diego . . ."

"I had to pass by it, right. Only I didn't."

"How'd you manage that?"

"I had no choice. The interstate is closed at the southern end of Camp Pendleton, and I presume at the north, too. And San Onofre is—"

"—right on the north end of Camp Pendleton," Dave finished for him.

He had driven that road many times. Bounded by the exclusive communities of San Clemente to the north and Oceanside to the south, Camp Pendleton was 125,000 acres of barren land and twenty miles of unspoiled coastline, virtually empty except for scattered Marine Corps structures. It extended almost twenty miles inland, into the hills. One had only to look at the suburban sprawl to the south and to the north, to imagine the many hundreds of billions of dollars those miles of shoreline would be worth if the Marines ever decided to abandon it.

About five miles of the northern stretch was the San Onofre State Beach, and smack in the middle of that were the twin containment domes of the Southern California Edison nuclear plant.

"It's kind of far from here, isn't it?" he asked.

"That was our thought, too. But the Marines who turned me back said the area was unsafe. I knew how to ride around Pendleton; I've done it before many times. I also knew how to stay off the highways as much as possible. There are bike paths, and some trails that you can manage with an off-roader, which is what I was riding. So I passed about fifteen miles to the east of the plant."

"Which way was the wind blowing?" Karen asked.

"Well, that has me a little worried. It was coming from the west, and blowing pretty hard. If those plants did crack open, I might have been exposed to some serious radiation."

Karen reached across the table and squeezed his hand. He smiled back at her.

"I'm not worrying too much about it. If I had it real bad, I figure my hair would be falling out by now, diarrhea, vomiting, the whole nine yards. Maybe I got just a little dose, won't show up for years, if ever. Or maybe I got no dose at all."

Dave saw that Addison was crying. He took her hand. She wiped her tears away with the other hand.

"It seems like it never ends," she said, sounding very young again. "The bad things just keep on coming."

"And we'll just keep on fighting them, Addie," he said.

Ted disposed of the rest of his epic journey north in a few terse sentences. He encountered problems along the way, he said, both natural and quake-induced barriers and encounters with people who didn't wish him well, didn't want him passing through their territory, or wanted to take what he had. The natural impediments were dealt with fairly easily in most cases by altering his route. The human problems were more complex and worrisome, but he claimed he hadn't had any major problems. Dave suspected there was a lot more that he could say.

"So," he said, and took a deep breath. "My family has decided that a trip north is our best bet. Mostly because of the water situation. We're still months away from the rainy season, and you know how short that can be, even in a good year. Dad wants you to come down and meet with us, see what we've done, see if you agree that traveling together is a better idea than traveling alone."

"I already agree about that," Dave said.

"We'd like you to come down today, if possible. We plan to leave either tomorrow or the next day."

"So soon?" Karen asked.

"Look, I can go outside and leave you guys alone to talk it over if—"

"I don't think we need to do that," Dave said, glancing at Karen. Ted watched the interchange, and said nothing. "When do you want to get started?"

"As soon as possible."

A problem soon became apparent. Dave didn't feel good about leaving the house and all their resources unguarded, and he didn't feel good about leaving someone behind to look after things. In that regard there was only one option open to him, considering the promise he had made to Addison.

"Don't worry about it," Jenna said, before Dave even broached the subject. "I'll be happy to stay behind and look after the place."

"Jenna . . ."

"Honest, Dave, I'm happy to do it. Look, man, I came here to sleep in your house and eat your food and drink your water with nothing but a shotgun, and you had to climb a mountain to get the damn shotgun." She looked down for a moment. "Actually, what I want is a seat on Bob's bus when he pulls out of this nightmare town, with you guys following along. Do you think he'll be interested?"

"If he's not, we won't be going with him. Like I said, you're with us now."

Ted had overheard part of the conversation, and now broke in.

"Listen, Jenna," he said, "if I hadn't found you here, my next stop was supposed to be your apartment. Now I'll be heading over to Glendale to Dennis and Ellen Rossi's house, then I'll try to find Roger Weinburger. One thing Dad made clear to me is that he regards you all as family. You're all invited."

Jenna had to turn away. She walked to the edge of the drop-off and stood gazing out over the ruined city.

"Dad has tried to convince a few other friends to come, too," Ted went on, in a lower voice. "So far, no takers. So believe me, Dave, you're not only welcome to come, we really need you. You and Jenna and Dennis and Roger are people he trusts absolutely to watch his back while he's watching yours."

"Teddy, you'll never know what a load you've taken off my back."

"Not all of it, surely."

Dave laughed.

"No, I've got a feeling we're all going to be carrying a big load for a long time. But it just got lighter."

"I don't know you, Dave, but Dad has always spoken highly of you. I know you understand that we're all going to have to expect a lot from each other. We're all going to have to do things we never expected we would have to do. You have a child and a wife. My brothers and sisters have children. I don't think I need to say a lot more than that."

"You don't," Dave agreed. He and the younger man shook hands. Then Ted put on his helmet and was off down the street, headed for the wilds of Glendale.

It didn't take them long to get on the road. They loaded the Escalade since it would make sense to use the trip to transfer some of their things to the Winston house. If it turned out they wouldn't be going with the Winstons, they could always bring it all back.

They told Jenna to use a bicycle to join them if things got hairy. She insisted she wouldn't have to. They left her on the street, holding her shotgun, and Dave watched in the rearview as she hand-cranked the metal gate back in place over the driveway.

"Are you sure we should leave her behind?" Addison asked. She clearly still had separation anxiety.

"Addie, I don't like leaving her, but I don't think she's in much danger up here."

"Okay." She was clearly still unhappy about it.

He drove cautiously over the slope where he and others had filled in the crack in the road. It was steep and rough, but the big SUV was up to it. He took it slow down the hill, never getting over fifteen miles per hour.

They pulled up to the barricade. Luke Petrelli and Sam Crowley and his son, Max, were on duty, and they didn't look happy to see the Marshall family. They made no move to roll the gate car out of the way. Dave turned off the engine and got out of the car, noticing that Karen had her shotgun where she could fire through the windshield if she had to. Her other gun was on her lap.

"What's the matter, guys?"

"It's Dick Ferguson," Petrelli said. "He had a heart attack not long after you went back to your house with that guy. We just sent him over to Cedars to see what they can do for him."

Not much, Dave thought, but kept it to himself.

"I'm sorry to hear that. So, can you move that car and let us through?"

"What's that you have in the vehicle?"

"My family, and stuff that belongs to us."

Petrelli didn't like that, but he didn't pursue it. At that moment Dave didn't give a damn whether he liked it or not. He didn't like the whole situation. From the corner of his eye he saw Karen shift slightly in her seat.

"We're talking about tightening things up around here," Petrelli said. "Some people weren't too happy about that friend of yours who just left."

"What are you saying? That we can't have visitors?"

Petrelli looked even more sour.

"Never mind. So, are you leaving us?"

"I don't see how that's your business."

"Because some people have been saying we should all pool our food and fuel, share and share alike."

Dave really didn't like the way the conversation was going.

"Like I said, it's nobody's business but our own, but we aren't leaving. Not yet anyway. We expect to be back tonight. Do I need a hall pass for that?"

Petrelli clearly didn't like Dave, but apparently he didn't think he had enough support to institute new rules on his own. He made a face, and gestured to Sam Crowley.

"Roll that thing back, would you?"

Sam got in the car and released the brake, and his son shoved it out of the way. Behind him Dave could see the car being moved back into place.

"Gee," he said. "I thought that went well, don't you?"

"I'm not sure you should have told him we're coming back," Karen said.

"I was thinking the same thing. Sorry."

"Well, who expected that we'd get that kind of problem from our neighbors?"

I did, Dave thought. Maybe not so soon. But adding it up he realized it had been two weeks since the quake, and months since the stores ran out of food. Maybe things were worse than he had expected, sooner than he had expected.

"What about Jenna?" Addison asked from the backseat.

"I hadn't thought of that," Dave admitted. He looked at Karen. "Do you think we should go back and get her? Do you think someone will think our stuff is unguarded?"

"We might just have the same problem getting back through the barricade. Then getting out again. I think we should see Bob, unload, and come back up the hill."

"I hate to leave her up there."

"Let's go back," Addison said.

"Addison, that's your father's decision to make."

"I don't get a vote?"

"Sure you do. But he gets a veto, which overrides everything. Until we get somewhere safe, anyway."

"Mom, we're never going to be safe again," Addison muttered.

Dave hoped that wasn't so, but in the short run he couldn't deny it, so he said nothing. Keeping the lies to a minimum.

Ted had given them directions for the easiest route to Holmby Hills, avoiding the biggest obstacles. Dave took them down Doheny, then west on Sunset into Beverly Hills. Sunset was blocked at Hillcrest by a shift in the earth that had elevated one side seven feet above the other. No bulldozers had come along to make a ramp, so they turned south on Arden, then west again on Carmelita. All along the way the massive trees that lined most residential streets in Beverly Hills had been uprooted, falling every which way, some of them onto the very expensive mansions.

Addison gawked at it all, and stayed silent. She knew these

wide, peaceful streets, which never carried a lot of traffic. She had cycled over them with her friends, some of whom lived there. When they passed one such house, seemingly undamaged, she broke her silence and pleaded with her parents to go check on her friend Brionny. Dave parked the Escalade and led the way up the path to the two-story faux-Tudor house. The front door stood wide open. Dave waved at Addison to stay back and held his shotgun at the ready as he approached the house. He knocked on the doorjamb.

"Hello inside. This is Dave Marshall and Addison Marshall. Anyone home?"

Addison looked up at the second floor.

"That's where her bedroom is," she said. She cupped her hands and yelled. "Brionny, it's me, Addison. Are you there?"

There was nothing but silence.

"Can we go inside and look?"

"I don't think that's wise, Addie. Let's go around back."

They followed the concrete drive. Dave kept his eyes on the upstairs windows, looking for any movement. He saw nothing.

There was a four-car garage in back, off to the side of the big, empty pool that was already coated with dirt and leaves at the bottom. All the garage doors stood open, and there were no vehicles inside. But as they got closer to the pool they saw that someone had driven or pushed a black Rolls-Royce into the deep end. It sat down there with a smashed grill and broken springs. No one was in it.

"Why did they do that?" Addison wondered.

"Maybe it was somebody having fun. I think this place has been looted."

"I guess we better get out."

"Addie, we'll assume they got out and have moved to someplace safer, okay?"

"I will if you will."

Their path took them past the home of another friend. This one was long and low and modern, mostly concrete, and everything but the walls had burned.

Addison didn't ask to get out and look as they drove slowly

by. And she didn't suggest they visit the addresses of any of her other friends.

They turned south again on Rodeo Drive. The first block was residential and had suffered about the same amount of damage as the other streets they had driven. That took them to the long, linear park bordering Santa Monica Boulevard. It was covered with ragged tents and shacks built from wreckage probably salvaged from the ruined homes to the north. Many of the shacks were empty, already collapsing. The reason seemed to be the exodus of people walking down Santa Monica.

None of them looked violent. Most looked too exhausted to be any trouble to anyone. They were of all races and probably from all walks of life. On the north side of the street National Guard troops were stationed every hundred yards or so.

"What do you think?" Karen asked.

"I don't know. They're going west, so maybe some rescue efforts are going on in Santa Monica. Refugee camps, something like that. What do you want to do?"

"I'd like to find out where they're going, but I'd really like to drive down Rodeo Drive, too."

"Down Rodeo?"

"I know it sounds silly. But I spent a lot of time there before . . . before all this. You know I've been regretting that. I know those days aren't coming back again, and I don't want them to. I was just hoping that we could come this way so I could . . . I don't know, lay all that to rest. Does that make any sense?"

Dave wasn't sure it did, but he was willing to try anything that would bolster Karen's retreat from "those days." What would it cost him? A drive across the street and down two blocks out of their way. A few minutes. And he was a little curious to see the legendary street himself.

The center of the shopping mecca of downtown Beverly Hills was only two and a quarter blocks long. There were many other serious contenders in Los Angeles for its prized role of most expensive street, but Rodeo Drive was where the tourists wanted to come and walk. If you were on a tourist bus the odds were that there was nothing, not even a scarf or a pair of sunglasses, on those two blocks that you could afford.

The street was devastated. The entire west side of the first block had burned. On the east side there was not one pane of plate glass intact. There had been a fire there, too, but it had spread to only a few of the buildings. The streets had been strewn with rubble and merchandise, but something had come through and pushed it all onto the sidewalks.

It was colorful rubble. In there were the remains of dresses that would have cost the entire yearly income of the average American family. Karen watched in silence as they passed some designer shops whose logos had survived, though nothing else had. Galerie Michael, Cartier, Valentino, Tiffany, Bulgari, Celine, Ermenegildo Zegna, Van Cleef and Arpels, Chopard . . . most of them names Dave had no real knowledge of, except that some of them had appeared on his credit-card bills in years past.

All of it gone now. Broken, looted, burned, crushed, the bright, useless guts tossed out into the street by nature and by looters who had no use for a ten-thousand-dollar gown unless there were diamonds to tear off it.

They came to the end of the street, where Wilshire angled by them and the Beverly Wilshire Hotel stood on the other side. At least some of it stood. The entire east wing of the building had fallen down, crushing the ornate stone façade that stretched the length of the block, spilling rubble to block the south lanes of Wilshire, knocking down the trees in the median. The trees had been cut and shoved aside to clear the north lanes, where another straggling line of pilgrims were trudging toward the west. Like the ones on Santa Monica, many of them were pushing carts or pulling wagons. Most of the stuff was wrapped in tarps, but Dave could see some of it. There were bottles of water, but most of what he could see would fall under the category of family heirlooms. There were framed photos and albums, some of them damaged. He spotted a few small porcelain figurines in one wagon. There were boxes of paper, marked with legends like "2002-2008 TAX INFORMATION" and "MORTGAGES AND DEEDS." He took it as a sign of optimism, that these people hoped such things would someday be valuable again.

"Let's get out of here," Karen said, flatly.

"Did it help at all?"

"No. It just made me feel stupid. Maybe that's a good idea."

Dave made a careful right turn and crept along with people walking on either side of him. They passed a watering station. There was a tank mounted on a flatbed truck and two folding tables set up on the sidewalk. It reminded him of the stations they set up for the Los Angeles Marathon, but there was no Gatorade and the paper cups were not being discarded onto the street but reused until they were falling apart.

"Let's pull over there," Karen suggested. "I'll just be a minute." She left her shotgun pointing down toward the floor and got out of the Escalade. Her Smith & Wesson was still tucked into the waistband of her jeans. Dave twisted around to watch her, but couldn't see much with all the cargo in the back. He opened his door and stepped out, looking back over the roof. He saw Addison trying to look back, but unable to do so.

"Dad, can I—"

"You stay where you are." His tone of voice brooked no argument, and she obeyed him, although with a deep sigh and crossed arms.

Karen had struck up a conversation with a woman in torn jeans with a Red Cross badge pinned to her dirty white shirt. No one seemed too concerned that Karen was armed, including the National Guardswoman who stood not far away. The woman talked as she filled paper cups with water and passed out some scruffy-looking oranges and apples. There was a pot of soup simmering on a grill with a few hundred people waiting in line, most of them sitting on the curb.

Karen was back in a few minutes.

"Drive," she said. Dave eased back into the flow of pedestrians and cyclists.

"She says people who want to leave are being evacuated. She hasn't seen it for herself, but they say there's an aircraft carrier parked just off the coast."

"Those things are nuclear powered, they're supposed to be able to run for ten years or more without refueling. Did she say where they're being taken?"

"She didn't know. Most people think it's to the Bay Area."

They talked it over for a while as Dave inched along, and

once more came to the stark realization of how little they knew, and how easily what they thought they knew could be nothing more than wild rumor.

"Maybe we can get on that aircraft carrier," Addison suggested.

"I wonder if Bob and his family know about it?" Karen said.

"We'll soon find out. Hell, maybe it's the smartest thing to do, but I doubt we'll be able to take this car, and I *know* we wouldn't be able to keep all this food. If we get on that ship, we become part of this mass of refugees, totally dependent on others for everything in life. I don't like that idea much."

Karen scowled.

"Neither do I. But we might be safer than striking out on our own."

"Daddy, I can hardly stand to see these people. They have nothing but what they're pushing in their carts." Tears were running down her cheeks. "But I don't want to get out and walk, either, unless we have to. I'm so ashamed."

"Addie, we'll get to Bob's and talk it all out. This breaks my heart, too, but I don't want my family walking into a refugee camp unless there's no other option. I'm sorry, but I'm not ashamed, and you shouldn't be, either."

"Amen to that, Addison."

They were coming to the intersection of Santa Monica and Wilshire. The street would have been impassable had bulldozers not come through at some point and heaped up the glass and stone and brick that had shaken off the tall buildings on both sides. They were one of the few private vehicles on the road, and he caught several people casting covetous or even angry looks at them. He very much wanted to get out of this crowd.

"Mister. Mister! Can you please help me?"

Dave was startled, and reflexively reached for his pistol. Then he saw it was a young woman walking along beside the Escalade a few feet away from him.

"I've been asking everybody, and nobody can help me."

She was small, thin, with bedraggled blonde hair and a light summer dress. It was impossible to tell what she had been before the quake, but now she was homeless, dirty, and desperate. She was holding a tiny baby in a pink blanket.

"I have to have some formula," she said. Her eyes were dry

but desperate. Dave suspected she was all cried out, too tired for tears. "She can't tolerate my milk, she keeps throwing it up. I have got to find some formula."

"I'm so sorry. There's nothing we can do for you."

"Dad, maybe some condensed milk?"

Dave gritted his teeth. He didn't want anyone there to know they had food. If he thought condensed milk would help the baby, he would have pulled over and found some, but he suspected that was no good, and the girl proved him right.

"No, I tried that, she spits it up, too. Do you know anyone who has any formula?"

"I'm afraid I don't. Really, I'd help you if I could but . . ."

He realized she was swaying, starting to stumble. He stopped quickly, at the same time reaching out with both hands to grab the baby's blanket. He had her, but then she began to slip. He managed to get a grip on the baby's arm as her mother's legs went out from under her and she collapsed to the pavement. The baby was naked, and weighed almost nothing.

Addison and Karen were out of the car before it stopped rocking from the sudden stop. Another woman from the crowd reached the fallen mother before Addison and Karen could get around the car, and a third gently took the baby from Dave. He sat for just a moment, his heart hammering at how close it had been, then carefully eased out of the driver's seat, careful not to step on the fallen woman.

"Get her in the shade!" someone said. Dave got her under one arm and one of the other women got the other. They lifted her and carried her to the meager shade of one of the ornamental trees that had not been buried under rubble. Addison had the baby, and was following right behind him. They set the mother down on the ground. Dave wasn't sure she had ever completely passed out, but she was woozy.

"Where's my baby?"

Addison handed the child to her mother.

Dave caught Karen's eye and gestured to her. He leaned close to her ear and whispered.

"Get back to the car and close the doors."

She nodded, and took Addison's arm.

Dave watched the two women tending to the mother. From the corner of his eye he watched his wife and daughter.

Dave had thought it was a sweatbox inside the Escalade, but somehow it was even worse outside. The thermometer in the car had been reading 98 when he got out.

He walked slowly back to his family.

"Is there any water we can get to easily?" he said, quietly.

Karen opened the back door, took two bottles of water, and grabbed a washcloth. She twisted the cap off one bottle and soaked the cloth. She handed the wet cloth to one of the attending women, who began dabbing it on the flushed and sweaty face of the mother. Dave was desperate to move on, but he knew he couldn't at the moment. And it didn't surprise him when Addison had an idea.

"Daddy, I want to let them ride in my place. I can walk along beside the car. We're going in the same direction, aren't we?"

"Not very far, Addie."

"Well, every little bit helps."

He knew that she was right. What would it cost them to take her a mile down the road? He consulted his mental map of the area and knew he could get the mother and child to Century City, where he hoped there might be an aid station, possibly even one with some baby formula. Then he could head north for Bob's house.

When he turned onto Santa Monica a few minutes later, he had finally found a use for the steel rails that jutted out on each side of the Escalade beneath the doors.

They had always struck him as purely ornamental, features added to this theoretically "off-road" vehicle to make it look brawnier, more heavy-duty. In reality, just one more chrome-plated decoration for an auto detailer to polish. But in a pinch—and was there ever more of a pinch than this?—they could function like an old-fashioned running board, though they weren't nearly as broad.

So now Addison and Karen were walking along beside the SUV. In the front seat was the young woman and her baby. Their names were Melanie and Missy. Dave wasn't clear which was which, and it hardly mattered.

In the backseat was an elderly gentleman who had been sitting by the side of the road with his crutches. The man's wife had her feet on the running bar on Dave's left, along with another young mother whose three-year-old boy was sleeping in the lap of the old man. On the other side were two more people who, for whatever reason, had been unable to go on but were able to cling to the side of the Escalade. Another elderly couple were sitting on the hood, on a blanket Karen had provided because the metal was too hot to touch. Dave was proceeding at just about a walking pace. Other people kept looking at him as he passed, obviously badly in need of a ride, and he had to ignore them. This was as far as he was willing to go in the passenger department.

So he puttered along, knowing he must look like a San Francisco cable car.

He hadn't been sure how long he would have to drive like that, but it turned out to be a little less than a mile, as he had hoped.

As they approached the Avenue of the Stars, which cut through the heart of Century City, it was clear that it was a center of activity. There were National Guard and LAPD and Los Angeles Sheriff's Department vehicles parked on the street, as well as trucks from the Red Cross. A large tent had been set up and was functioning as a hospital.

Some of his passengers had told him they hadn't seen any signs of authority in weeks, other than a few bicycle cops who were usually too busy to do much other than answer a few questions. That was how many of them had learned of this exodus.

There was no soup line in Century City, but police were urging people on, telling them the next feeding station was two miles down the road, under the 405 freeway.

As soon as he stopped, Addison was out and pulling Melanie and Missy toward a Red Cross station. Dave had no choice but to wait, as Karen hurried after her.

"Don't let her out of your sight!" Dave yelled. "And don't get out of my sight!"

"I won't. I'll get her back. Damn her!"

Dave saw Addison find a man in green surgical scrubs who at least looked like a doctor. He relaxed a little and took the chance to look around him.

The first thing he noticed was a line of four big bright red double-decker buses, painted with American and British flags, reproductions of the famous Hollywood sign, and come-ons like SEE THE HOMES OF THE STARS. You used to see these buses parked at the curb in front of Grauman's Chinese and the Hollywood & Highland Center as sweaty, sunburned tourists got on and off and gawked and took millions of pictures in the vain hope of seeing somebody famous. The buses had been altered with the now-familiar stacks of wood-burning generators, and they emitted clouds of thick smoke.

He turned to one of the men who had been clinging to the side of his car, but had now stepped off and was sitting in the street.

"Why don't you go over there and see what's happening?" he said. "I suspect they're giving rides to seniors and disabled."

The man looked suspicious, and Dave realized he thought he was being ditched.

"I'm not going any farther down this road anyway," he told the guy. "So you have nothing to lose."

After one more sideways look, the old gentleman heaved himself to his feet and stumped toward the buses on his crutches.

Addison caught his eye and held up a can of baby formula. The mother was holding another. Addison hugged the mother, then Karen did, too, and they helped her board the bus, then came hurrying back and took their seats.

"She was lactose intolerant," Addison said. "They have a special formula for that, but not much of it. The doctor said their best bet was to get her down to the boat at Santa Monica, where they had a better hospital. I . . . Daddy, I—"

"It's okay, Addison."

"I'm sorry, Daddy. I know we're not supposed to split up. I wasn't thinking. But it's the only thing I've done in a long time that's made me feel good."

"I feel good, too. Just don't do it again, okay?"

Before they could get going again Karen had to get out and explain to their passengers that this was the end of the line for the Marshall Transit System. Response wasn't instantaneous. Two of the people Dave had begun to think of as barnacles seemed to think they had signed on for a ride to the beach. Karen explained that the red tour buses would take them there, in much more comfort. Dave was about to get out and physically remove them, if he had to, but they finally gave up.

Feeling virtuous about what help they had rendered, but most of all feeling relief at no longer being surrounded by tired, hungry, sweltering, and possibly angry people, he made the first right turn he could, and drove down the silent Club View Drive.

They made it to Wilshire easily enough. Twice they passed neighborhood militia posts, told them they were heading to Holmby Hills, and were waved on through.

The Los Angeles Country Club was off to their right, and for the first few blocks they could see the golf course through some cuts the residents had made in the big hedge that surrounded it. The hedge itself was dry and brittle, and the grass on the course was dead or dying.

At the junction with Ashton they were confronted with the worst damage they had seen yet. They were by then almost inured to seeing collapsed buildings. There were literally thousands of them. But here Dave had to stop and they all got out to take a look.

They had seen too many cracks in the earth to count, starting with the big one that had opened just east of their house. This one dwarfed the others. It ran north to south, and was thirty to forty feet wide. The far side of it was twenty feet lower than the edge they stood on. It went down until it was too dark to see well, and it looked like it had swallowed a dozen houses. It was just a jumble of wood, brick, and vehicles, all crushed.

They looked at it for a while, then silently climbed back into the Escalade.

A few side-street detours finally brought them out onto Wilshire, where the chasm had crossed the road directly beneath a skyscraper.

No earthquake code ever written could create a building that would stand when the ground opens beneath it. There was little left of the twenty-some stories but unidentifiable wreckage that lay in a heap across Wilshire Boulevard. It had crushed the Department of Water and Power Building on the far side of the street and badly damaged the tall condo building across Comstock.

"That crack is pointed right at Bob's house," Dave said.

"Teddy didn't mention it," Karen pointed out. "It must not have reached them."

"You have to figure they had quite a shake."

"We all did, Daddy."

Dave drove to Beverly Glen and turned north.

CHAPTER TWENTY-ONE

Bob Winston's part of Holmby Hills was on the edge of the informal line that marked the boundary between midrange mansions and truly huge estates. He was quite close to the sprawling grounds of the Playboy Mansion and the mansion built by Aaron Spelling in 1988. People who had once lived in the neighborhood were Jayne Mansfield, the Bloomingdales, Bogart and Bacall, and Gary Cooper.

This was the lifestyle that Karen had recently aspired to, and that Dave had come close to being able to afford. If he had had one more hit show, they might have made it, though part of Bob's good fortune had been to come into serious Hollywood money at a time when buying a medium-sized mansion in Los Angeles was still within the reach of the medium-sized wealthy. He had also invested well. Holmby Hills had been about as exclusive as it got in Los Angeles. Now it was a disaster area.

Judging from the filth on the houses he could see, the wave of water coming from the broken Stone Canyon dam had averaged five or six feet high when it came churning down the streets. The terrain was hilly, but not excessively so. It was enough that buildings on high ground had escaped damage, while ones in hollows had been submerged up to the rooflines. When the waters receded they left behind a foot-thick layer of muck, mixed in with a great many uprooted plants and trees, half-buried vehicles, debris freshly shaken off homes by the quake, household furnishings, and even pieces of houses.

And bodies, of course. They passed several lumps where bodies, already half-buried, had been covered over with earth and marked with crosses.

The streets gave the Escalade its first real test as an off-road vehicle. In places it was fairly smooth, running over mud that had long since hardened in the summer sun. In other places a bulldozer had shoved up an earthen berm. It was clear that the berm was a palisade that could be used to defend the houses that lay hidden behind it.

In places the dirt of the road was deeply rutted, right down to the cracked asphalt, which was broken into chunks. The big SUV squeaked and bounced as Dave slowly drove along, trying not to get stuck high-centered on a hump in the middle of the street.

"There's somebody behind that wall over there," Karen said.

"I see it. Try to look harmless."

They bounced on until they were close to where he thought Bob's house was. Somebody stepped into the road. Dave recognized Mark, one of Bob and Emily's sons. Mark was on the tall side, like all of the Winston family, with a receding hairline, blue eyes, and a strong chin. He looked to be nearing forty. He was dressed in khaki work clothes and thick boots and he wore wire-rimmed glasses. He gestured to them, waving his free hand toward a break in the otherwise impenetrable high hedge, his other hand holding a firearm that looked like an M-16. Dave turned right and bumped over the ruts in the road. He ended up on what must have been Bob's driveway, though it was now covered with a layer of dried mud. In fact, the whole yard was now a dusty desert with a few half-buried, dead shrubs surrounding the four tall palm trees still standing. He could no longer see the cobbles that had made up the circular driveway and small parking area.

The house was in a shocking state.

It was a sprawling two-story brick structure, almost eight thousand square feet not counting the detached four-car garage and separate workshop. Bob had told him it had nine bedrooms and seven baths, all but a few of them closed up as his children had moved away to their own lives. Dave could see the dozens of diamond-shaped steel plates with bolts protruding, all painted to match the color of the brickwork. You could see plates like that all over Los Angeles. The bolts were screwed onto long metal rods that went all through the structure and tied it together much more tightly than the original builders. It was earthquake retro-fitting, and the work on Bob's house dated back to shortly after the Northridge quake of 1994, when suddenly engineers had more jobs than they could handle reinforcing older structures.

In spite of that, there had been damage. There were two cracks in the outer wall, one of them fairly minor, the other reaching from the ground to the eaves, a foot wide in some places where bricks had fallen out. The house had a high, peaked roof that had been covered in terra-cotta barrel tiles. A great many of them were now lying on the ground, baring the wood and tar paper beneath. The house was L-shaped, with the long leg parallel to the street. The northwest corner had caved in, the roof falling to the second floor, the big timbers cracked, and the smaller planks sprung free. All the windows in front had been boarded up. There were slits for guns to shoot from.

Shortly after the quake the water from the broken dam must have arrived. It would have come from the north. They would have to get the story of that from Bob and Emily. Dave suspected it was a harrowing one. The high-water mark of mud on the house was about three feet.

Mark came up to Dave and stuck his hand out.

"We met once, Dave. I'm Mark."

"This is my wife, Karen, and my daughter, Addison."

"Addison. Nice name. Pleased to meet you, ladies. Dave, drive around the house to the back." He made a waving gesture toward the house, and Dave saw a hand come through one of the second-floor gun slits and wave back.

Mark trotted on ahead of them, and rounded the corner into the backyard. Dave drove over what had been the side driveway and was now a dirt lane, and pulled up beside the garage, which looked undamaged. They all got out of the car and stretched. It had been a long, slow drive.

The first thing they noticed was that the thick trees and shrubs that had completely shielded the grounds from the country club in back had all been cut down. So had the high chain-link fence. The same thing had been done with the houses on both sides of Bob's place. The view of the golf course was unobstructed.

Dave was not a golfer, but he had visited the Los Angeles Country Club a few times as a guest for lunch. From the dining room and the grounds out front he remembered the two courses had a lot of tall trees lining the fairways, and naturally the grass was always perfectly cut and a sparkling emerald green.

That was all gone. Most of the trees had been cut down, and the fairways were brown. Where there had been sand traps and low places, filthy-looking brown water now stood.

"We're boiling and distilling it," said a voice from behind him. He turned and saw Bob coming toward him. He didn't look good. He was wearing an improvised eye patch and walking with a cane, favoring one foot that was tightly wrapped in bandages. One side of his face was a big, yellowish bruise and his cheeks seemed sunken.

"Fell down the stairs in the dark right after the quake," he said, shaking Dave's hand. "Sprained an ankle, cracked a couple of ribs, and something poked me in the eye when I smacked my head on the floor. Lisa says I'll probably still be able to see out of it. Quite a face, huh? I don't heal as fast as I used to."

He turned to Karen and embraced her, then shook hands with Addison. Dave saw Bob's wife, Emily, coming up behind him. She smiled at them, and set a pitcher of water on a picnic table beneath the only tree remaining in their backyard.

"We're so glad you made it safely," she said. "I hope you didn't have any trouble along the way."

"Not really," Karen said.

Other people were coming out of the house and the workshop. Dave noticed that most of the adults had handguns in holsters, and some carried rifles or shotguns. Bob started making the introductions.

"This is my oldest son, Mark. He's an engineer, and the man who is going to get us out of here."

"We already met."

"Mark's wife, Rachel." Rachel was Jewish, and though not Orthodox, was faithful enough that she had insisted Mark convert before she would marry him. She was barely five feet tall, a foot less than her husband, and a little chunky. Her hair was thick and blonde, but black at the roots. The grip of her small hand was almost as firm as her husband's. She was followed by Sandra and Olivia, identical twins of fifteen with red hair and freckles. They each held one hand of their younger brother, Solomon, nine. He had the close-set features and friendly smile of Down Syndrome.

They had all been gravitating toward the picnic table. Beyond it was a deep, kidney-shaped hole where the pool had been. The bottom of the pool had cracked, and it was filled with the same dried muck that had covered everything in the flood. The fiberglass waterslide had been knocked over by the wave. Dave gratefully took a glass of instant iced tea from Emily and swallowed half of it at once.

Next in the parade of Winstons was Marian, the younger daughter, in her early thirties, average height with an athletic body and hair cut short. She was carrying her four-year-old son, Taylor, on her hip. Dave remembered Bob's worry when she had joined the army and been deployed to Afghanistan. Her parents didn't approve but they weren't the sort to stand in the way of their children. She had returned unharmed, physically. If she had other issues, Bob had never talked about them, but after leaving the military she had separated from her husband, Gordon, and moved back in with her parents, where she had been living for at least the last two years. Dave's impression was that she hadn't decided what to do with her life yet, though there had been talk of the Police Academy.

"Her husband's the one you probably noticed upstairs," Bob said. "We're standing twenty-four-hour watches these days. There's been some trouble."

Dave didn't ask about the state of their marriage. He assumed that things might look a lot different to a couple in light of recent events, that previous troubles might seem a lot less significant. It had certainly been that way between Karen and himself.

"So. You've met Teddy, I assume."

"Yes, he's the one who told us to come over here."

Bob looked pained.

"His lover, Manuel, is among the missing. It's so easy to lose contact now. They were both planning to come up here, but Manuel had to go check on his own family in Tijuana. Even though they've disowned him. He had to sneak back into Mexico, how's that for irony? So we don't know where Manny is, but we hope he's safe.

"Peter is in England. It's been months since we talked to him. He said it was just as bad over there as it was here. That was before the quake, naturally. He was looking into finding a sailing ship that might take other Americans across the Atlantic, but even if he made it, there would still be the whole continent to cross. And George is still in New York, as far as we know. At least he was the last time we talked to him. He and his family had no plans to join us out here."

"Except when winter arrives," Emily said, darkly.

"Yes, there's that. Last time we spoke he said he had some friends upstate, around Woodstock. They might be up there."

Dave had been doing a head count. Peter and George were impossibly far away, and of the others he had seen two of Bob and Emily's six children, and one spouse, Rachel. Gordon was upstairs, and there were four grandchildren, ages fifteen to four. Teddy was accounted for, somewhere in the area searching for Dennis and Roger and their families. That made eleven, counting Bob and Emily, and fifteen people counting Dave, his wife and daughter, and Jenna. That left the oldest child, Lisa, and her husband, Charles, both doctors, and their two children of high-school age . . . Elyse and Nigel, if he was remembering correctly. He was about to ask about them when they were interrupted by a sound he hadn't heard in a while: a police siren coming up the street.

A white Hummer with a red cross on the door turned the corner and stopped twenty feet away. Two uniformed LAPD officers, a man and a woman, got out of the front doors and held the rear doors open. A tall woman with graying hair tied up in back got out, followed by two teenagers. All three were dressed in green surgical scrubs.

"Here they are, Mr. Winston," the female officer said, with a hint of pride in her voice. "Safe and sound, like we promised you."

"Thank you, Janet. We appreciate it." Bob glanced at Dave. His eyes were full of anguish. "No questions just yet, my friend," he whispered, and got up. He walked toward Lisa, his daughter, holding out his arms. She collapsed and fell into his arms, sobbing aloud. Bob embraced her. The two children stood a little apart from them.

"Charlie was killed in the quake," Emily said, quietly. Karen gasped, and Addison looked agonized.

"Lisa was working at the UCLA hospital, where she'd been putting in sixteen, eighteen hours a day for weeks. Now everything's been moved to Cedars-Sinai. The patient load was overwhelming, with a lot of gunshot wounds and medical emergencies that they were running out of medicine to treat. On top of that, they were understaffed. By and large, everybody who could report to work did report to work." Her face darkened. "Though there were a few who simply stopped coming in. I'd never seen Lisa so angry as when she told me about those people, a few doctors and nurses who lived within a reasonable distance and just never showed up when things started getting really bad. A lot of high-tech doctors found themselves practicing medicine on the level of poor, third-world nations."

Dave remembered that Lisa's husband had been an orthopedic surgeon with a large sports-medicine practice of his own. Charlie had treated several Lakers and Dodgers for knee injuries.

Across the way, as the police escort turned around and headed out, Lisa and her children were still talking to Bob. Emily filled them in on some of the rest of the story.

The only thing that saved Lisa was that she had stayed late at the hospital. She had been due home before dark that evening—as a doctor, she still was able to get gas for her car, and the commute to Sherman Oaks that sometimes could take two hours on the nightmare 405 freeway now could be done in ten minutes at any time of the day. Charlie had been working at a hospital in Reseda, a little closer to their home, and was in their bedroom, sleeping the four hours he was allowing himself before heading out at sunrise to face the new day and the new patient load. The quake had destroyed the bedroom and pinned him beneath a roof beam.

Their children had worked for two hours to get him out. Fighting through a daze and in terrible pain, he self-diagnosed a punctured lung, two broken legs, and a probable concussion before he became irrational, then unresponsive.

They got him into the car and Elyse headed toward Valley Presbyterian Hospital through a city changed in an instant to a place they hardly recognized. Everywhere it was pitch-dark, except where buildings were burning. There were people in all the streets. Dodging around them, she didn't see the three-foot gap in Van Nuys Boulevard until too late. She slammed on the brakes, but her front wheels dropped into it. The car was just hanging there, in no danger of falling in but unable to back up.

Eventually they persuaded a few people to help rock the car until the front wheels could gain traction. They set off again, one wheel so far out of alignment it threatened to shake the car apart.

As the sun was rising they checked their father again, and could find no pulse.

The journey took them all day, and could have been an epic story in itself. The left-front wheel fell off somewhere on Sunset Boulevard. They continued driving. The cooling system failed shortly after that.

They covered their father with a blanket and set out on foot.

They found their mother in the parking lot beside a hospital, up to her elbows in blood. They drove together back to the abandoned car, loaded Charlie's body into her car, and took him to her father's house.

"That's his grave over there," Emily said, quietly. Dave saw a mound of earth with a wooden plaque stuck into the ground. The name Charles Tomasino, and the dates of his birth and death had been carved on it. Wilting flowers stood in some of the vases that had survived the quake.

Bob, Lisa, Elyse, and Nigel were walking slowly toward the rest of them sitting around the table under the tree. Lisa was leaning her head on her father's shoulder. She was six feet tall, just an inch less than Bob. Tears were streaming down her cheeks.

"Lisa, my darling, you've done all you possibly can," Bob said. "They're saying the evacuation is really picking up steam now. Soon your patients will all be headed north, where there's sure to be a lot more doctors and intact hospitals."

"But we don't know that. How do we know they're going to a better place?"

"I'm pretty confident of it for a simple reason," Bob said. "I can't imagine there's anyplace on the Pacific Coast that's worse than this."

"I feel strongly that my place is with my family," Lisa moaned. "I failed my children when the quake hit, and I—"

"Mom, there was nothing you could have done by coming home," Elyse said, with a touch of anger. "We've been all through this. We agreed that nothing could have saved Dad but a medevac helicopter."

"I know that, but . . ."

"But you feel guilty. So do I. If I hadn't driven into that hole . . ."

"It was already too late, Elle."

"I'll second that," Nigel said. "Why don't you both just shut up about it? It's so over. You got a decision to make, Mother. What are you going to do with us?"

Nigel was sixteen, a year younger than his sister, a beanpole even taller than his mother and grandfather. His hair was jet-black and straight and hung to his shoulders, and he had multiple piercings of his ears and nose. He wore black jeans and heavy boots, but on top he wore the same surgical scrubs as his sister and mother.

Dave and Karen had nothing to contribute to the Winston family discussion about what Lisa and her children should do when everyone pulled out, headed for Oregon. It was a terrible situation for her, already saddled with guilt over the death of her husband, to have to decide to abandon the sick and injured of Los Angeles.

"You don't have to decide until tomorrow," Emily finally told her. "We need you, but you know that. But I have to put it to you in the strongest possible terms, Lisa. Whatever you decide to do yourself, letting your children stay here is wrong. They have to go with us, it's the only right thing to do."

"I won't leave without Mother," Elyse said, firmly. Nigel said nothing.

"We'll decide tomorrow," Bob finally said.

Most of Bob's workshop was filled by a big school bus that looked like it had been worked over by the production designers from *The Road Warrior*.

After a long talk with Bob, Mark had concluded the same thing that his father had. Maybe Dave's story of a crude-eating bacteria was wrong, but what if it was right? What was the harm in stocking up on survival supplies, and boning up on alternative sources of energy?

In fact, as a problem-solver by nature, he had spent more hours than Dave had researching and speculating about what the situation would soon be like if Dave's story was true. He hadn't liked the results he got any more than Dave had.

Even before gas rationing began, he had built one of the first wood-burning vehicles in the area, converting an old junker he bought for a few hundred dollars just to see how it worked. To his surprise, it didn't perform all that badly. The chief problem was the bulk of the fuel.

"The other problem with burning wood to power your vehicle," Mark said, "is that you can't just feed logs into a stove. It has to be chopped finely. So I bought the biggest wood chipper I could afford."

He was showing them around the workshop and garage, where he had stowed everything they planned to take with them on the journey north. The chipper looked hard-used. It had wheels and a trailer hitch.

"I rebuilt the engine, sharpened the blades, and bought replacements. It will take twelve-inch logs. Better to split them into smaller chunks; got axes for that. But you toss branches in there, it will eat them and spit out chips in a second. Got a couple of chain saws over here. Palm trees will be the easiest, I think. Up in Oregon, there should be plenty of pine, if they haven't cut all of it down already."

They moved on to the school bus.

All the glass had been removed from the side windows and replaced with metal plates, which also covered the body of the bus. There were two gun ports on each side. The armoring was quick and sloppy. A parapet had been built on top of the bus, made of wood, about four feet high. It ran all around the top of the bus. The whole thing looked quite heavy, and Mark confirmed he had beefed up the springs and shocks.

Inside, there were fold-up bunks along each side and the back was packed with supplies and luggage. A hole had been cut in the roof near the front, and a wooden ladder was bolted to the roof and the floor. Mark climbed up and Dave followed him.

He had thought the platform on top would be a defensive position, but he was wrong. The back end was half-full of wood chips. There was a blue tarp that could be fastened over the top. Mark showed them how one could gain access to the burner from up there, open it up, and shovel chips into it.

After that there was just the other truck. It still had the orange-and-white colors of U-Haul on the cab. The box in back had been painted black.

"I bought this one," Mark said. "Cheap. This was long after the rationing started, and the guy was amazed to get a buyer at all."

Dave stood with Karen and Addison and they all looked at what the Winston family had accomplished. Dave closed his eyes for a moment. Then he turned to Karen.

"We're going with them," he said.

"I know."

She put her arm around his waist and hugged him.

They spent the next hour discussing which route they should take. There were only a few options, but each had its advantages and drawbacks, and each had its proponents. The arguments got heated at times, but never angry. Dave got the feeling that this large family was used to hashing things out vigorously without coming to blows or harboring resentments.

In the middle of the discussion Sandra and Olivia left them and went upstairs to relieve Gordon from guard duty. The twins had at first been deemed too young, at fifteen, to stand a watch, but had eventually prevailed. They stayed together not just because they were very close, but so they could watch the street and still take care of little brother Solomon. They had been his willing and loving caregivers for a long time.

Gordon came down to join them. He was dark-skinned, originally from Jamaica but a naturalized citizen for half of his forty years. He had met his wife, seven years younger than him, in Afghanistan, where he had worked for the United Nations and she had been a sergeant in the army. He had a wide smile and a face weathered prematurely, was of average height, but looked very strong. He introduced himself as an associate professor of governmental studies at Cal State, Long Beach.

The family eventually agreed on first trying the I-5 through the Grapevine into the Central Valley, as the most likely choice. If that was impassable, they would consider other options. Mark, who Dave was seeing could be a pain in the ass sometimes, continued to lobby for the 101, nearer the coast, as more likely to provide wood for his hungry burners, but he conceded defeat.

But that was not quite the end of it. There was one more option they had to discuss, and it was first voiced by Elyse, with some backup from her brother, Nigel, and her aunt Rachel, Mark's wife.

"Why not go on the ship?" she said.

The opposition to that idea was immediate and strong, coming mostly from her mother and her uncle Mark, who glared at his wife. Rachel seemed unmoved by it.

"I just don't trust them," Lisa said. "I've asked and asked around the hospital, where are these people going? Nobody knows, or if they do, they're not telling."

"Mom, what do you figure? They're being dumped in the ocean?"

"That's silly," Mark began, but was cut off by Lisa.

"Of course not. But you ask the National Guard where the ship is going, and all they'll say is 'North.' To a refugee camp in the north. San Francisco? Oregon? If it's Oregon, maybe we *should* go. But there's just something wrong with getting on a ship whose destination you don't know."

"I'd like to know where we'd be going, too," Mark said. "But one thing I can guarantee you. When we got there we'd have *nothing*. The clothes on our backs, maybe a suitcase. But no vehicles, no tools, no food of our own. They will *not* be loading a school bus onto an aircraft carrier."

They tossed it around a little more, but soon gave it up, because one of the things Teddy had promised to do before returning—that afternoon with any luck—was to cycle to Santa Monica and see what he could find out on the scene of the evacuation itself.

They unloaded the Escalade. Now that they would be traveling with a school bus and a U-Haul truck, they would be able to take all the food remaining in his basement.

"Bring all the water you have," Bob said. They were standing at the back of his property, looking out over the golf course. He pointed out to the muddy remains of the floodwater that had inundated the neighborhood.

"See that puddle out there? Used to be a sand trap. Mark has put a water tank in the back of the U-Haul. We drove the truck over there and filled the tank. It's clean; we treated it with bleach. I worry about water most of all. Whichever route we take, it's a long ways to a river that flows year-round. We'll top off the tank whenever we can, but I want all the bottled water we can carry."

"You got it," Dave said. Then he saw something that surprised him. A slightly ragged-looking horse was approaching the little pool. It walked through the mud, lowered its head, and began to drink.

"Look, Daddy!" Addison had appeared at his elbow, apparently drawn by some special sense horse lovers possessed.

"There are three horses out there," Bob told her.

Addison walked out onto the golf course.

"The whole golf course is surrounded, so they've been allowed to wander."

"Daddy, we have to go get Ranger," she shouted. "He needs to stretch his legs. He needs to eat some grass. It's not good for him to be cooped up in the garage all the time."

Ranger had not been cooped up all the time—Addison had taken him out for a trot every day, going up the hill to the top and then halfway down and back—but Dave knew what she meant. It wasn't a good life for a horse.

"We'll bring him here tomorrow," he promised her. "And if we're going to do that, we need to head home."

Dave and Karen thanked everyone for everything, and vowed to be back the next day as early as possible. They all knew better than to set a time. There were just too many things that might cause a delay.

They made it to the Beverly Hills Hotel and a few blocks beyond before they came on a crack in the ground that couldn't be driven over. They went south on Rexford and then east again on Elevado, and were about to turn north to regain Sunset when they heard gunshots.

All their windows were down, and it sounded as if the shots were coming from the south, down a street that might have been Hillcrest and might have been Arden; the street sign had been knocked down.

Karen immediately stuck the barrel of her shotgun out the window. In his rearview, Dave could see Addison looking around in all directions. He wanted to find some cover. There were many houses, many driveways, some of which led to garages in back, but he didn't think he dared drive around behind any of them, as there was no way of telling which were occupied. If he had been in one of them, and had heard the guns, he knew he would have shot at the intruder. So he waited, putting his own shotgun across his lap but ready to throw the car into reverse and back away as fast as he dared.

It sounded like a major battle. There were no automatic weapons, but the shots kept coming. Whatever was happening was coming at them from the right, from the south. He started to back up.

"Dave, look!" Karen shouted.

Three large dogs had rounded the corner ahead of them. One was a Rottweiler, another a black Lab, and the third some large exotic breed he couldn't identify.

"Roll up your windows, everybody," Karen ordered. Dave hit the switch for his window, and saw that Addison was doing the same.

The Rottweiler looked as savage and scary as that breed always did, and he looked well fed. Not so the Lab. The black dog's ribs were showing, and he didn't move with the easy self-confidence of the Rottweiler.

Suddenly the Rottweiler turned and snapped savagely at the black Lab, which whined and cringed away. Dave realized the Rottweiler was the pack leader, and that he enforced his position ruthlessly, by dealing out fright and pain to anyone anywhere near his size. He felt sure that Rottweiler had not always been a stray. He could very well have been a pampered and gentle pet. That was all gone now. Dave had only to look at the dog's eyes to know he was a killer. The veneer of socialization had worn off quickly when the pangs of hunger began to gnaw inside. Beneath the training, under the calm exterior, the heart of a predator still beat, and when push came to shove the Rottweiler knew how to behave, how to hunt, how to assert leadership.

The pack was larger than they had realized. A dozen other canines came tearing around the corner, like some crazily effete, Beverly Hills version of the Hounds of Hell. It was all happening very quickly, but he had time to spot a Labradoodle and a Goldendoodle and a Schnoodle. There was an Afghan hound and a German shepherd, more traditional large dogs.

There was even a big standard poodle whose pom-pom clip was looking very ragged. And yapping on the edges of the pack were a few small to medium-sized dogs—a miniature pinscher, a cavalier King Charles spaniel. All of them were dirty, with matted coats and what was probably dried blood around their muzzles. And in the eyes of all of them was something he had never seen in domesticated dogs: a wild, relentless gleam that was a combination of unfamiliar physical hunger and the bloodlust excitement of running with the pack.

He could even see how it would work within the pack. Surely the very tiniest, the most overbred of these animals had been unable to keep up, and had probably become prey themselves. The other small dogs must have learned to keep to the edges of the pack, tolerated as long as they kept out of the way while the big dogs were feeding. They would be surviving on the scraps left behind by the alpha male and his lieutenants. Surviving, that is, until the moment the pack became hungry enough and there was no other prey around.

The three big dogs in the lead slowed down and approached the Escalade, cautiously, but showing no fear. The Rottweiler stopped by Dave's door and regarded him as a shopper might look at a lamb chop in a butcher's case. This animal was smart enough to know Dave and his family were safe inside the steel beast. *But just open that door, just a little,* the dog seemed to be saying to him.

Only wide enough to put the barrel of a gun through, Dave thought back at him.

"Dad, let's get out of here. This is scary."

"David, look! Ahead of us!"

Dave jerked his attention away from the bottomless black eyes of the Rottweiler and was in time to see two people come zipping around the corner on bicycles. The barking was even louder now, loud enough for a hundred hounds, though there weren't nearly that many. One was a man and the other a woman, both were dressed in shorts and boots and helmets and wore yellow T-shirts with POLICE on the back, and they were trying to get away from half a dozen dogs in the medium-to-large category. The woman was in the lead, desperately trying to guide her bike with one hand while with the other she worked at ejecting an empty magazine from her Glock.

The man's pistol must also have been empty, because he was using it as a club to beat at the face of a dog who had him by the leg. His screams chilled Dave to the bone.

"Somebody help us!" the female cop was shouting.

Dave put his shotgun across his lap with the muzzle pointed toward the door. He was glad he had sawed off the barrel; it made it easier to handle the weapon in the close confines of the car. He grabbed the gun by the stock and then opened his door a crack. As he had expected, the Rottweiler had to explore this, and soon his own muzzle was there, dripping a long rope of drool. The dog scratched at the narrow opening with a bloody paw. Dave shoved the barrel into the dog's face and pulled the trigger. The shotgun roared and jumped in his hand, and the dog was gone.

"We've got to help them," he shouted, and pushed the door wider. He saw that all the dogs had been startled and were racing away from him. All but the pit bull that was attacking the officer. That one seemed determined to hang on, no matter what.

He jacked another round into the shotgun. The barking of the dogs was louder than ever.

"Addison, stay in the car!"

"Daddy!"

He stepped on the dead dog and out of the car. A German shepherd began to approach him. Dave took aim and fired, and the dog tumbled backwards. He was amazed at just how much damage a shotgun could do when taken directly in the face.

The female officer was off her bike and had managed to get her gun reloaded. She quickly killed three of the dogs closest to her, then kicked a small one high into the air, not wasting a bullet on it. The dog howled all the way to impact with the ground, and howled even louder when it landed and seemed unable to get up.

Another shotgun blast startled him, and he looked to his right and saw Karen was out of the car. She had dispatched another large dog that had been coming up on him from behind. Her eyes were sweeping the terrain, the shotgun at her shoulder.

The woman had reached the man and dog and pressed the barrel of her Glock to the pit bull's eye. She fired, and the dog's forepaws stopped scrabbling at his prey.

But he didn't let go.

As Dave reached them, the woman had taken her baton from

its ring on her waist and was flailing away at the dead dog's head. Her partner kept crying out to get the goddam dog off of him.

"I think you'll have to pry his jaws apart," Dave told her.

She looked at him with dazed eyes.

"Son of a bitch won't let go. Fucker is *dead*, and he won't let *go*!" She seemed to be at least partly in shock. Her hands were shaking, and she was covered with small bites and scratches, including a bad one on her left leg. She didn't seem aware of any of them.

"Try sticking the baton down between his jaws."

"Don't touch his teeth," Karen cautioned as she came up beside them.

"We haven't had any reports of rabies. But I don't want my hand in his mouth, anyway. Just thinking about what he's been eating lately."

The woman was doing as Dave had suggested, but was having a hard time getting the baton between the massive jaws. Karen had broken her gun open and was inserting new shells as they watched.

"I'm going to shoot again," Karen said. Immediately the shotgun fired, and Dave looked around. Another large dog was lying on the ground, spurting blood.

"Mom, another one!"

Karen turned as Addison shouted, and killed another dog.

"Cover us," Karen said, as she opened the smoking shotgun again. She got her gun loaded and snapped it shut. She handed it to Dave. She lifted the tail of her shirt and reached for a sheath knife in a leather scabbard. He recognized it as a piece of equipment they had taken on their long-ago camping trip.

From the corner of his eye he saw Karen sawing at the knot of muscle on the side of the pit bull's mouth. The male officer cried out again, but made no move to stop her. Dave stood, gaping, as the dog's lower jaw came free.

A large part of the officer's thigh looked like raw hamburger. A large chunk of his flesh hung loose. Blood oozed from the open wound. Dave turned away.

"Oh, God, I am so fucked," the man moaned. He was trying to get to his feet, but didn't seem to have the strength for it.

Karen and the woman got on each side of him and tried to lift him, but they weren't able to at first. Dave moved forward to help.

"Don't, Dave," Karen said. "You keep watch. Officer, reach under him and grab my hands. We'll lift him that way."

Dave turned to the Escalade. "Addison, crawl to the back and unlock the hatch. *Don't* lift it. You got that?"

"I got it, Daddy." Dave could see her hurrying to the back. He turned, and saw that Karen and the officer had managed to lift the injured policeman and were staggering along behind him. He hurried around to the back of the Escalade, made sure that Addison was safely out of the way, and lifted the hatch. He moved a few feet away so he could see if anything was approaching them from the sides of the vehicle. Karen and the woman got the man seated on the deck. Both of them were dripping with sweat. They paused for a moment, then heaved.

"Karen, take the gun and I'll help with that."

She moved out of his way. He saw Addison coming around the backseat, where she knelt and caught the man as he leaned back. She pulled on his shoulders, her eyes wide when she saw the horrible extent of his injuries. They got him inside and the woman officer crawled in beside him. Dave closed the back and he and Karen hurried around to get back into the car.

"The bleeding's getting worse," the woman said.

"What's the best route to a hospital?"

With the female officer—whose name turned out to be Melissa—giving directions, the trip to Cedars-Sinai didn't take long. Dave drove as fast as he dared while Karen and Melissa tried to stop the bleeding.

"At first there were just some smaller packs," Melissa was saying. Dave wasn't sure she knew she was talking, the words just came pouring out of her. "They were starving, mostly. There were some do-gooders, PETA, the animal shelters, folks like that, tried to feed them. Kibble, I guess, people weren't eating that. Not yet, anyway.

"At first we just ignored the dogs. Hell, I like dogs. I mean, I liked them. I don't think I'll ever be happy to see a dog again, though. Now, I'd shoot them on sight, every damn one of them, if we didn't have orders not to waste bullets."

They reached the stream of refugees. Dave turned against the tide and crawled along. Most of them moved aside. But a few were slow, and some looked hostile. One man right in Dave's way stopped pushing his shopping cart and stood defiantly.

"Honk your horn, Mister," Melissa said.

Dave honked, which just seemed to make the man angrier.

"Fuck this," Melissa said. She opened the door behind Dave, leaned out, and shouted.

"Get out of the way! Police emergency! Move to the side of the road!"

The man with the cart wasn't impressed. He started to reach into his cart.

"You don't scare me, bitch, I need that—"

She fired a round into the goods piled into the shopping cart.

"If your hand comes out of that cart with a weapon, you're dead," she said. "The next round goes into your leg, and you can fucking *crawl* to the hospital. Police emergency!"

The man got the message, and quickly shoved his cart aside.

"Get moving," she said to Dave. He passed the man, and could see in his mirror that Melissa kept the gun trained on him until they were safely past.

It went more smoothly after that. Most of the people who had heard the gunshot were already at the side of the road. He eventually got up to twenty miles per hour. He soon reached San Vicente, and turned south.

"How's he doing back there?" he asked.

"He's passed out," Karen said.

"He still has a strong pulse, though," Addison added. She had taken a first-aid course, and was proud of it. Dave could see her holding her fingers to the man's neck. She looked pale, but steady. He felt proud of her.

They passed the Pacific Design Center, those three giant, oddly shaped buildings in primary colors with all-glass exteriors. Much of the glass was broken, leaving jagged teeth of red, blue, and green.

He crossed Melrose, which had a few people on foot, all headed relentlessly west, and within a few blocks arrived at the hospital.

The place was still in business, but there didn't seem to be a lot of people left in the outdoor infirmary. There were two of the

Hollywood tour buses and one city bus, all running on wood chips, and stretcher cases were being loaded onto them. Hospital beds sat right out on the street, protected from the sunlight by the long shadow of the main hospital building, but the heat coming off the pavement was still stunning. Big tents flapped loudly in the hot, dry Santa Ana wind.

"Officer down! Officer down!" Melissa was shouting, still hanging out the door. Two cops looked up and hurried over. They lifted the hatchback and shouted for a stretcher. In a very short time the unconscious man was on the stretcher and being rushed toward one of the tents.

"Lord, I hope they have enough stuff to treat him with," Dave said.

The three of them sat in silence for a moment. Melissa had hurried off with the medical team, too busy to say thank you. Dave didn't blame her.

"Well," Dave said. "I think that's enough excitement for one day, don't you?"

Karen let out a little guffaw. She looked down at her hands, covered with dog blood, and began to shake. Dave leaned over and put his arm around her and pulled her as close as he could. He watched Addison in the rearview mirror. She was still wide-eyed, but seemed calm.

"Addison . . ."

"You don't need to say anything, Daddy."

"We did what we had to do."

"You think I'm going to be mad at you for killing the nice little doggies? If I'd had a gun, I'd have shot the fuckers, too."

"Addison," Karen said, wearily.

"Mom, *please* don't get pissed over my language."

"I'm sorry. Reflex, I guess. But still . . ."

Addison moved up and put her arms around her mother from behind.

"Okay, I'll watch my mouth. But I'm so proud of you, Mom."

"Proud?" The concept seemed to baffle her.

"The way you . . . the way you cut . . ." Suddenly she was crying.

"I just did what I had to do," Karen said.

"We all did," Dave said softly.

"Things are different now, Mom." Addison was getting her sobbing under control, with just a slight hitch in her breathing. "I know that. I don't know what happened to you two when you went out yesterday, what you did, but I know you're not telling me something. And that's okay, I don't want to know. Maybe someday you'll tell me, and that's okay, too. But I know school's out, and not just for the summer."

Dave didn't think he could sum up the situation any more eloquently. School was definitely out, and when it would be back in session was anybody's guess. Addison was already a long ways toward being grown-up, but she would have to make it the rest of the way in a hurry, because the only classes being held now were going to be in the famous school of hard knocks, the cauldron of bitter experience.

They drove now like a NATO patrol through the mean streets of Kandahar. Karen kept her shotgun across her lap, the muzzle pointed out the window. In the back, behind Dave, Addison held the other shotgun pointed in the other direction. Simply rolling up the windows would be protection against any dog attack, unless Stephen King's Cujo made an appearance. Dave didn't worry about them. They wouldn't come sneaking up; they would come baying and barking. It was humans who were good at surprises, and at attacking from a distance.

It was a clear shot back up San Vicente. They crossed Santa Monica without incident. A road blockage forced a diversion on Cynthia Street and they all stayed alert, looking for an ambush, but they made it to Doheny and across Sunset.

"Home sweet home," Dave muttered, as they pulled up to the barricade. There was none of the warm feeling he usually associated with getting home to his family after work—at least until his marriage started to go really bad—but the feeling of relief was awesome. Although the people behind the barricade didn't look all that welcoming.

"I think something's happened," Karen said.

Dave felt it, too. There were three men behind the dead cars: Lucas Petrelli; Max Crowley, the son of the old cinematographer; and Alfred Charbonneau. Dave had never taken to Petrelli, the times they had stood watch together. Petrelli had assumed the position of Richard Ferguson's right-hand man.

Petrelli and Crowley rolled the gate car out of the way. Dave drove through, and Petrelli positioned himself in front of the Escalade with his hand out. With his other arm he cradled a rifle. From the corner of his eye Dave saw Karen shift her shotgun slightly, so that the barrel was back inside the vehicle.

"Is there a problem?" Dave asked as Petrelli and Crowley came around to his side of the car.

"Ferguson's dead," Petrelli said. "Heart attack last night." He walked around to the driver's side and looked in the window.

"I'm sorry to hear that."

Dave could see the man was genuinely shaken, and he thought a little bit better of him. The feeling didn't last for long.

"We're having a meeting tomorrow morning," he went on. "Some of us feel like we need to make some changes."

"Oh? What sort of changes?"

Petrelli didn't say anything for a few moments. The blistering Santa Ana winds blew his unruly hair around his face. He was about Dave's age, but looked a lot older. When he did speak it was without any warmth.

"Where have you folks been?"

"Visiting friends."

"When you left you had a whole bunch of stuff in back, under a tarp."

Dave still held his tongue.

"Some of us would like to know what it was, and what you did with it?"

And do you have any more? Dave said to himself.

"Well, I'll tell you, Lucas," he said. "It was a whole shitload of none-of-your-business, with a little bit of go-fuck-yourself on top."

He heard Karen shift in her seat. He glanced over at her, and saw that her shotgun was pointed at Petrelli. Petrelli's rifle was still cradled in his arm, pointing at the ground. There was a sour look on his face as he also glanced at Karen. The man shifted slightly on his feet, and Karen moved again.

"I'd stay real still if I were you, Mr. Petrelli," Karen said. Dave didn't look over at her, but he moved his hands off the steering wheel and leaned back against the seat. He didn't relish the idea of a load of shot passing a few inches in front of his face, but he knew Karen would fire if she had to.

Petrelli stood very still. Dave wondered if he was thinking about making a move. He looked beyond Petrelli at the other two. Crowley seemed angry, but he didn't have a weapon in his hands. Charbonneau looked ashamed. After a moment, he turned and walked slowly away from the car.

"Dad, you might want to cover your ear," Addison said from the backseat. "This shotgun is near your ear, and it will be real loud when I fire it."

Petrelli looked in the back, and scowled.

"Well," he said. "Go on then." He gestured with his head, and Dave started to take his foot off the brake.

"Sleep well tonight," Petrelli added.

Dave had a momentary wild urge to take the pistol out of his waistband and shove it into the man's face and pull the trigger, and pull it again, and again, and again. He felt the savage anger rise in him, and his hand actually started to move.

No, some part of him said. *Have we come to that? Former neighbors killing each other over a few scraps of food?* And he knew he hadn't.

Not yet, anyway.

"I like that," Karen said. "'A whole shitload of none-of-your-business.'"

"Good one, Dad."

"Well, I am a comedy writer."

He looked over at Karen as he drove up the hill, and saw she was stifling a laugh. His glance was enough; she burst out, helplessly. From the backseat, he heard Addison joining in. He found himself smiling. It felt like the first time he had smiled in months.

"You women can certainly be cruel." That got them laughing harder.

"'A little bit of go-fuck-yourself,'" Addison snorted. "That one needs a little work, Dad."

"Yeah, it was the best I could do on a moment's notice. But it'll do for television."

* * *

Dave could see Jenna's face in the upstairs window, one that he had partially boarded over for defensive purposes, as they came up the street. He was surprised to see her there. From that vantage point she could cover almost all the street. She waved at them, and he could see her shotgun in her other hand. Then she disappeared.

He parked the car on the short approach to the gate, got out, and tugged on it before remembering that he had instructed Jenna to keep it padlocked. They all waited a moment and then heard Jenna working the key. The gate started to roll, and Dave grabbed it and helped her push it open.

"Hurry, hurry, get inside," Jenna said in an urgent whisper. Dave looked quickly all around him. The street was deserted, but that didn't mean much. A man with a rifle could be hidden in a dozen places quite close by.

He drove through the gates and the women pushed the gate shut behind him. Jenna snapped the lock back in place, and finally seemed to relax a bit.

"What happened, Jenna?"

"Well . . . a few hours after you left I heard some people talking outside the gate. I went down there, quietly. One of them said he didn't like the way those windows had been boarded up, with the openings for rifle fire. He said they'd be sitting ducks if anybody was up there. The other one said there was nobody up there, he'd seen you guys leave, and would he for chrissake hold on to the fucking ladder, so he could get over the gate and unlatch it. They didn't know I was here, and they didn't know it was padlocked. But I heard their ladder clang against the gate and I shouted out at them not to come over.

"They talked some more, too low for me to hear, and then one of them shouted out, asked me who I was. I told them I was a friend of yours.

"'You're lying,' one of them said back. 'You're there to get the food.' Then he said he was coming over, and we could split it. I fired the shotgun into the air, and I heard the ladder fall. 'We've got guns, too,' one of them said. And he stuck a pistol barrel through that little gap there, where the gate meets the post. He fired a shot—you can see where it hit the house, over there—and I about wet . . . Well, I sure didn't want to get into a shoot-out with them, so I backed up and got behind the corner of the house and I told them that if either one of them stuck his head over that gate, I'd blow it off. They talked some more, and then I heard them moving off. I went up to that room at the corner and I didn't see anybody. And I've been up there ever since. And now, I really, really need to pee. Can you hold this?" She handed the shotgun to Dave and hurried away to the latrine.

Dave, Karen, and Addison watched her go, then looked at each other and for a while they said nothing. Dave was regretting leaving her behind. So what if looters had found his stash, down in the basement? Was it worth putting Jenna through that? Tiny little Jenna, already suffering from the horrors she had been through.

Karen put her hand on his arm.

"She volunteered, David," she said.

"Still."

They walked over to the pool and stared at all that water.

"Too bad we can't take it with us," Addison said.

"I was sort of hoping to take a last dip in there," Karen said. "Sort of like old times. Couldn't do that before, because we were using it for drinking."

"You can," Dave said. "We can sit in it and cool off a little. What do you say?"

"I say, where's my bathing suit?" Addison said, and grinned.

They did that as the evening waned. It was glorious, the first time any of them had had a real bath in a long time. The water was clean, though no longer potable, since the chlorinating had long gone out of it. They took turns swimming, two at a time, since Dave wanted someone always on watch at the corner on the second floor.

When darkness had fallen completely, they used the faint light of kerosene lamps to load the Escalade with more food and bottled water. Dave attached the horse trailer and they put in all the hay and oats they had left. Dave tied the scooters on the sides and the bicycles on the roof. They would look like twenty-first-century Okies.

Then they all spent an hour going through every part of the house and guesthouse and basement, looking for things that might be useful, anything they might have forgotten. They would not be coming back, and it was all too easy to see themselves by the side of the road wishing for that one little item they had forgotten.

Then they ate a meal of beans and Spam on tortillas, which was surprisingly good. Dave decided he was getting used to Spam.

They agreed that someone should be on watch all night. Thieves were likely to be more bold under cover of darkness. Karen took the first watch. It had been a long, long day, but Dave didn't expect to have an easy time falling asleep. With any luck, this would be their last night on their own as a family, the last night in their old home, and his last night as the sole protector and decision maker.

He was asleep almost as soon as his head hit the pillow.

Outside, the wind that had been blowing all day was whipping itself into a frenzy.

"Wake up, dear. Wake up."

Dave struggled into a state of semiconsciousness from a particularly bad dream. There had been dogs in it, and that was all he remembered, and he was grateful for that. He wondered if he would ever feel the same about dogs again.

"I've made some coffee," Karen said. It would be that instant stuff, but it would do. Right then, chewing on coffee grounds out of yesterday's filter would probably do. Spooning Taster's Choice granules right into his mouth would probably do.

"I know how exhausted you are. I drank so much coffee I'm worried about getting to sleep. But it's twelve midnight, sweetness, and I am officially off duty."

"I'll wake up, don't worry."

He gulped the warm coffee from the cup she handed him, felt a little jolt from it, took a deep breath, and watched her kick off her shoes and lie down on the slightly sweaty place on the bed he had just vacated.

"Not even a sheet tonight," she said. "Just my clothes. God, when will that damn wind stop blowing? It drives me crazy, not to mention the heat."

"I know. I feel edgy, too. Even more than usual."

Woolgathering again, he thought, and leaned over to kiss his wife.

"Sleep tight," he whispered, and left her there on the bed.

CHAPTER TWENTY-TWO

For the first two hours he was okay. It was best if he kept moving. He prowled restlessly from one vantage to the next, looking out over the dark street, seeing the same two lanterns in the same two windows in the same two houses. He knew he could do this, he knew he could stay awake his entire shift. No problem.

He was jerked back awake by the sound of his gun hitting the floor.

His heart hammered as he groped around in the dark, found the steel barrel, and carefully picked it up.

He was dripping sweat. He used the bottom of his T-shirt to wipe his face, and then looked blearily out the window. It was getting light out there. An orange glow was starting to creep over the horizon.

What he needed was more coffee. He got up from his lawn chair and was halfway across the room before it struck him.

Something was wrong with this picture.

He went back to the window. The wind was blowing straight into his face, as it had been all day, from the north. He thought it might be thirty miles per hour, gusting even higher. It was loaded with grit, which made him squint, but the problem was clear even if the view wasn't. Since when did the sun come up at the northern horizon?

As he watched, a tiny tongue of orange-white flame licked over the top of the most distant hill. Dave was instantly wide-awake. He stood there a moment longer and, sure enough, there was another flame. This one writhed into the air, and it didn't go away. He realized he had been smelling smoke from the moment he woke up. He hurried down the stairs, then out of the ruined main house and onto the patio.

"Karen! Addison! Jenna! Wake up!"

In a moment Jenna's face appeared at the window of her room upstairs in the guesthouse, just a pale shape in the darkness.

"What is it?" She sounded scared, and who wouldn't be after her experience the day before?

"Get Karen and Addison up and have them come outside. Take it slow and easy, stay calm, don't panic."

"I'm already panicked. What's wrong?"

"Tell you when you get here." Her face vanished, and he immediately thought of something else.

"And Jenna!" When she stuck her head out again, he spoke in a normal voice. "I'm going to be shooting the gun a few times. Don't worry, nobody's coming after us. Tell Karen there's no need to lock and load, okay?"

"What the hell, Dave?"

"Just do it."

He turned away and hurried to the gate. He was shouldering it aside when he heard a gunshot from far away, then another. Somebody had the same idea he did.

He went out into the street, pumped his shotgun once, and fired it into the air. Then he did it again, and a third time for good measure. He listened for a moment, and heard two more shots—sounding more like a pistol than a shotgun—from the same direction the first ones had come. Somebody else was awake, and trying to rouse the neighborhood.

No 911 to call. No telephones to alert one's neighbors. The neighborhood watch had some walkie-talkies, but he didn't have one. He hoped someone who did was calling around. He wondered if the fire was even visible from the barricade far down the street. Even if it was, their attention would most likely be turned the other way, to the south, where they all expected any human threat to appear.

He heard a noise coming from the garage and at first he had no idea what it was. Then he realized it was Ranger, banging around in there. He heard a high-pitched whinny. Even if the human watchmen hadn't smelled the fire yet, the horse had, and he didn't like it one bit, being tied down in the dark.

Good Lord, what am I going to do about that? he wondered.

Jenna exited the guesthouse first, followed by Karen and Addison. All three had been sleeping in their clothes.

"There's a fire over the hill," he said, making an effort to keep his voice calm and cool, to show none of the alarm he was feeling. All three of them looked to the north, where the orange light was already a lot brighter. The first writhing spire of flame had now been joined by three more.

"Ranger!" Addison cried. She started toward the garage, but Dave snagged her.

"Not yet, you don't," he said. "Listen, everyone. We should have time if we stay calm and don't panic. We don't know if that fire will be coming down this canyon, it might go down to the east, but if it does, the wind will blow it faster than we can run."

"I've got to get Ranger down the hill, then!"

"No, first you've got to calm him down, and you're not going in there until I can go with you. I don't care what you say about being able to control him, you've never had to handle him when he's got his wind up over a fire."

She looked defiant, but said nothing.

"Jenna, Karen, gather up everything we need that we haven't already packed."

"Dad, we *have* to take care of Ranger. He'll hurt himself."

"We're going to do that right now."

He followed her toward the door leading into the garage. She was waiting there, hopping from one foot to the other. He was about to open the door when he heard another sound from far down the hill. It started as a low growl, then rapidly rose in pitch until it was a scream. He realized it was an old-fashioned hand-cranked siren. He thought he remembered something about someone's finding one in their attic or basement, probably some shiny brass antique salvaged from a fire department.

"Dad-*dee*!" Addison cried, tugging at his arm. "We *have* to get my horse. *Now!*"

"Yes. Come on, and be careful."

He turned the doorknob and entered the garage, Addison close behind him.

Ranger was rearing, but the rope holding him was short enough that he wasn't able to rise very high. But he was pulling hard, and to Dave it looked as if he might just break free with a few more sharp tugs.

"Would he feel better if I opened the garage door?" he asked.

"I don't *know*, Daddy. Let me just talk to him."

Dave was reluctant, but he finally said okay.

"But you've got about five minutes to calm him down. No more."

She nodded, and slowly approached her horse. She was talking to him. Dave caught the word "steady," and that was about all. It was all in a low, soothing voice, like a mother cooing to her child. Baby talk, or maybe horse talk.

Still the steel horseshoes clattered on the concrete floor. Addison took a few careful steps toward Ranger, and Dave slowly eased his shotgun so the barrel was pointing a little higher, and moved to one side so he could get a clear shot at the animal if it came to that.

Ranger's hind legs suddenly slipped out from under him and he sat down hard on his rump. For a moment he was almost still, stunned or surprised. Addison hurried forward before Dave could say anything, and the next thing he knew she was holding his halter with one hand and had her arm around his neck.

"Addison, get away from him!"

"It's okay, Daddy, I've got him."

Then she was lifted almost off her feet as the horse got his back legs under him, tossing his head as he did so. She held on, and the horse dropped his head again, only to toss it once more. Addison's weight seemed nothing at all to the powerful creature. She was up on tiptoe, the rubber soles of her shoes squeaking on the floor.

"Steady, Ranger, steady, boy. You calm down now."

"Addison, you're going to have to let him go."

"I won't, I won't. Open the garage door, Daddy. He's really got the wind up, I'll have to walk him for a few minutes."

"You've got three minutes left, honey. Then we cut him loose."

He moved toward the garage door and lifted it.

"Hurry, Daddy!"

She had untied Ranger before he had the door entirely up. Now Dave was almost knocked off his feet as the horse charged past him. Addison was being dragged along. She was shouting at him now, and Dave turned to see that she finally got him turned. He was still breathing hard—Dave could hear the powerful snorting, as if he had just finished a race—but he began to trot in a circle. Maybe that familiar activity would calm him down. He couldn't tell if it was working or not. But

Addison continued to hold on, and the horse was no longer try-ing to buck.

That was the good news. The bad news was visible behind them, and it was very bad news indeed.

The entire ridge at the top of Doheny Drive was on fire. The flames were twisting in the wind, spiraling like hellish white-orange tornadoes. A million sparks and a thousand larger chunks of burning debris were being lifted into the air, where some of them burned out, but many were coming south, falling into the houses and streets and very dry trees below. He could actually hear the roar of the flames now.

Karen was pushing the gate back on its tracks. Jenna was throwing things into the back of the Escalade. Dave glanced again at his daughter and her horse, and the animal seemed calmer. He couldn't say the same for himself.

"Never mind packing anything else!" Dave shouted at Jenna. "Help Karen get the gate open." Jenna hurried to do as she was told.

"Dad, the trailer isn't hooked up."

Cursing his failure to have everything ready the night before, Dave took one more look at the approaching flames and then got into his vehicle. He started it up and began backing toward the hitch on the front of the trailer, shouting for Karen or Jenna or somebody to guide him. Karen hurried over.

"We don't have time for this, Dave," she said.

"I'll give it one try," he said. "That trailer's half-full of things we'll need. If we can get the horse in, that's good. If we can't . . ." He didn't need to go on.

Karen said nothing, either. She went to the back of the Escalade.

His taillights illuminated Karen first in white, and then red when he pressed on the brakes. She motioned with her hands. *Back. Back, back, back.*

"Cut it to the left," she called out. He saw her looking at the trailer, then glancing at Addison and Ranger, still involved in a battle for dominance.

"Too much. Back to the right. Back . . . back . . . a little more . . ."

He eased his foot off the brake pedal, just a tad, letting the idling engine move the car toward the trailer. He fought the urge to get out and take a look himself. Karen knew what she was doing. He would just have to trust her.

She held her hand out suddenly, palm toward him.

"I don't know if that's good enough," she called out. "Maybe you should pull forward a little bit and cut back."

It'll have to be good enough, he thought, throwing it into PARK and getting out of the open door and hurrying around back.

The tongue of the trailer hitch was a good three inches away from the ball on his back bumper.

"Help me out here," he told Karen. They both shoved on the trailer tongue. It moved an inch. They shoved again and it didn't move at all.

"One more time," he said.

"On three," Karen said. Her face was red in the taillights, and covered with beads of sweat.

"One . . . two . . ."

On three Jenna appeared on the other side and pulled. The tongue touched the ball and slipped over it, but only partly.

"Hold on, ladies!" Dave shouted, and cranked the wheel quickly until the support post was off the ground.

"I'm losing it," Karen grunted.

"Hang on one more second . . ."

He kicked the trailer tongue and it slipped down over the ball.

"Got it! See how Addie's doing." He didn't look up as he locked the tongue over the ball. He got the tailgate of the trailer unlatched, and it crashed to the ground, which startled both Ranger and Addison.

Maybe the trailer was too crowded with all their other supplies and bales of hay. Maybe Ranger just didn't want to be in an enclosed space with the world smelling of smoke, with the orange of the flames reflecting in his wild eyes. When Addison led him toward the rear he shied away from it like a racehorse refusing to enter the starting gate. Addison got him back under control, walked him in a circle with the horse shaking his head so violently she could barely hold on.

Once more she led him to the rear of the trailer, and this time he reared up, lifting his front legs two or three feet off the ground.

"One more try, Addison," Dave said, solemnly.

"Daddy, I can get him in."

"One more try," he repeated. "Sorry, sweetie, that's all you get."

As his daughter brought the big horse around once more, patting his neck and speaking to him in a soothing tone, Dave looked to the east, toward the two stories of what used to be his house. There was orange light coming from behind it. From *behind* it, from the *east*, the direction of the only road out of here. In the brief time they had used hitching up the trailer, the fire had come down the hill.

He turned back in time to see Ranger once more refuse to enter the trailer. At the same time, a small burning branch fell from the sky and landed near the garage door in a shower of sparks and glowing coals.

"A firebrand!" Jenna shouted. That was a term Southern Californians knew better than most Americans, and when they used it they weren't referring to a political agitator. When a firestorm got going, like the one currently charging over the hill above them, high winds blew burning debris up into the air. Some of it could be of considerable size.

Ranger shied away from it, momentarily jerking Addison off her feet as he spun wildly. She was dragged a few yards, but managed to get one foot under her, then the other, and continued to plead with the horse.

"That's all the time we have," Dave called to her. "You're going to have to let the horse go."

"Daddy, I know I can—"

"Addison, let go of the horse and get in the car," Karen said.

"Mom . . ."

"Get in the goddam car, now!"

The girl held on for a moment longer, then let go of the rope. Ranger seemed confused for a moment, then bolted toward the open gate.

"Ranger!" Addison screamed. Karen grabbed her daughter and held her firmly, because she was trying to follow her horse into the orange-tinted night.

"Mom, he's going the wrong way!"

"He'll figure it out," Dave said. "He knows the way down, away from the fire. You rode him down and back just about every day, remember?"

Dave hoped it was true, but it was a fact that the stupid animal had raced to the west, where the street quickly curved and went up the hill.

"Now get in the car with no more argument."

She didn't say anything, but she didn't move, and Karen had to pull her toward the open back door. Dave slammed the trailer ramp closed.

Karen happened to be on the driver's side. She didn't bother to go around and take her customary place in front. She shoved Addison in onto a pile of supplies they had heaped haphazardly in back, and Jenna slipped into the front seat.

"Go, go, go!" Karen called out as she slammed the door.

Dave moved the transmission into DRIVE and cautiously pressed on the accelerator. The trailer resisted him with a rusty squeak, and then the unwieldy combination began to roll toward the street. There was a loud scrape as the trailer tongue hit the asphalt and dug out a deep gouge. The scooters banged alarmingly against the side of the car, but the knots held. Then they were moving down the steep hill.

The first thing Dave noticed was that the orange light he had seen in the east was coming from two houses on the far side of Doheny, right in his path.

It was barely two hundred yards to the intersection. The houses themselves were not completely involved yet, but the foliage around them was going up like Roman candles, spouting sparks into the air.

"Hurry, Dave," Karen called from the backseat. "Can we get by that?"

"It may blister the paint, but I think we'll be okay. Roll up your windows."

As he said that, a series of larger firebrands landed in the street in front of him. He drove around the nearest one and was approaching the dirt ramp they had made over the deep gap in the pavement when he heard the clatter of hooves behind him. He glanced in the rearview mirror and saw Addison, who had never stopped looking out the back window, rise so quickly her head bumped the ceiling.

"Ranger! He's coming! He's coming down!"

Dave put on the brakes for a second and the horse dashed

past him and was up and over the ramp in seconds. His tail was flying as he galloped straight toward the burning houses. Something uphill must have scared him even more than the fire.

Dave soon found out what that was. A low, brightly colored vehicle appeared behind him with a screech of tires as it came around the corner, and then he heard the high-pitched whine of an engine more suited to the racetrack than to urban-neighborhood streets. It went past him in a flash, a yellow Ferrari that was barely higher than the Escalade's big tires.

The Italian plaything hit the ramp badly, and far too fast. For a moment it was airborne, then it hit the ground at an angle and roared up onto the curb on the north side of the street. There was a shower of sparks as the car, which had a ground clearance of only a few inches, scraped up onto the sidewalk. The driver somehow got it straightened out and back on the road. The engine was even louder, and Dave could see that most of the exhaust system had been left on the sidewalk.

"Who was that?" Karen asked.

"I have no idea. Hold on, everybody."

Dave got the front wheels of the Escalade onto the ramp and started up. Behind him, the trailer moaned in protest. If the hitch were to come loose, this would probably be the place for it, he knew. And if it did, so be it. They would abandon it, and he wouldn't spare it a backward glance.

It protested even louder as he got the back wheels on the ramp, then was silent for a moment as the big vehicle climbed, then cried out in pain again as the front wheels went over the top and the hitch was strained to its limit, at a very bad angle to the car. Dave juiced the accelerator and for a moment all four wheels smoked, and then the trailer lurched over the hump and was once more pushing him down the hill. They were gathering speed.

"Dave, should you—"

"Karen, don't distract me now. The last thing I need is . . ." *a backseat driver*, he thought, but bit the words off before he could say them. The last thing *she* probably needed was an angry word from him.

"Sorry," she said. "My bad."

He was almost at the T-junction with two burning houses ahead of him. He glanced to his left and saw one of the most terrifying things he had ever seen. It looked like a solid wall of fire rolling down the hillside. No wonder Karen had been nervous; she had probably seen it before he did, with his attention focused forward.

When he quelled his moment of panic he saw that his imagination had contributed a lot to his first impression. The fire was moving, and it was coming down the hill, and it was coming toward them and it would be there very soon, but he had a few minutes. He managed to make himself apply the brakes as he approached the intersection, though his every instinct urged him to take the turn at the highest speed he could manage, even if it meant going up on the two left wheels.

The tires squealed as he made the turn, and he felt terrific heat on the left side of his face. He let the Escalade find its own line through the curve, a line that took it perilously close to the curb on his left but with what looked like enough room to get by.

One wheel of the trailer hit the curb and it bounced high and came down hard. Dave winced, then saw the trunk of a palm tree almost dead ahead. The Escalade missed the tree by inches.

None of the women said a word. Probably too terrified.

"Is everybody all right back there?"

"I got bumped around a little, but we're okay. Right, Addison?"

"I'm okay, Mom."

"Jenna?"

"No problems, boss. That was some great driving."

He realized, incredulously, that she was serious. Well, maybe it was great driving, and maybe he'd just been taking the curve too damn fast.

He calmed himself down with a deep breath, straightened the car out, and steered down the middle of the road. He hardly needed his headlights, the bright light of the following blaze cast a long, black shadow ahead of him but illuminated the sides of the road with a hellish light. He only had to stay in the middle.

At the intersection with the street just below his, only a short distance on a map but a long way down the hill, the guardrail on his right had been smashed. A twisted piece of metal poked into the night sky. Twin streaks of burned rubber led directly into the hole. How could an idiot manage to go off the road there, Dave wondered, when the street went perfectly straight for another hundred yards? Dave was sure this was the launching pad for the yellow Ferrari that had passed them seconds ago. Maybe something had broken in the steering when he jolted up over the curb.

He had to slow to a crawl as he reached the 180-degree turn on Heartbreak Hill—there was simply no way to take it at any speed. Behind him the trailer weaved back and forth as he braked. He was alert for any wreckage below, but he didn't see anything at first. Now he was a good ways below the fire, and the darkness enfolded them again. He moved as quickly as he dared, going due north now, toward the second 180-degree switchback. He looked up the terraced slope above him, but all he could see were the flames that were cresting on the drive above.

Suddenly, Ranger appeared in front of him, standing sideways on the road, breathing heavily.

"Daddy, let me get out and get him!"

"No, Addie, I can't do that."

It was academic, anyway, as the horse neighed loudly and bolted again, downhill. Dave heard a frustrated cry from the back. Now that the horse had moved he could see what had stopped it. The yellow car must have flown for a while, but it wasn't an airplane, no matter how streamlined the designers had made it. He could see the groove it had plowed in the terraces above them.

Flames were growing higher up there. Now the remains of a six-hundred-thousand-dollar car lay half on the street and half-off, upside down, its shattered nose on the asphalt, its rear end on the dirt, its back broken.

"Nobody could have survived that," Karen said.

"I don't think so, either, but we have to look."

"I guess you're right. Yes, you're right." He felt something tapping on his shoulder, and realized she was handing him one of their Maglites. He took it, stepped out of the car, and hurried over to the wreck. As he approached it, he thought about the gun in his waistband, and had the awful realization that if anyone was alive in there, the only help he might be able to offer would be a bullet to escape death by fire.

He crouched and shined the flashlight into the small gap left between the crushed roof and the edge of the sprung door, which hung open a few feet. If someone was alive, he realized, he just *might* be able to pull him out.

He needn't have worried. There was only one man inside, and his skull was clearly crushed. He took in the ruined side of the man's face, saw the way his jaw had been almost ripped off, and looked quickly away. He stood up, and smelled gas. He hurried back to the car.

"Dead," he snapped, and put the Escalade in gear again.

He eased around the Ferrari and continued down the hill. Soon they were passing Kingfisher Drive, then Meadowlark Terrace, both streets that angled off to the right. He could see that Addison had moved across the back to stare hopelessly up each street.

"Daddy, he could have gone up any of those streets. They're all dead ends."

"I know, honey, but that will leave him no place to go, right? He'd turn around."

"Maybe not until the fire blocked off this end. Can't we—"

"Hush, Addison," her mother said. "Your father has to concentrate. And he's right. Ranger knows the way down, he wouldn't go up any of those streets."

There were taillights ahead of him. More of them appeared as he continued down the hill. As he approached Oriole two cars came speeding onto Doheny, forcing him to put on the brakes again.

"You had the right of way!" Jenna shouted, indignantly.

"I don't think that counts for a lot tonight."

On down the hill more cars were appearing. Three people on bicycles zipped past him as he once more slowed to a crawl behind a Mercedes SUV. It was developing into a traffic jam. He had had no idea there were still so many people living on these streets.

"The fire's gaining on us," Karen said.

Dave could see it in his rearview mirror. He was down to ten miles per hour, and he knew the fire could travel a lot faster than that. Sparks had begun to rain down all around them. He could see fires starting in the brush beside the road.

"Karen, keep an eye on it. If we get totally jammed up here, we might have to get out and run for it."

"I'll dig out some blankets," Addison said. "We could put them over us, maybe it would keep the sparks off."

"Good idea," Dave said. He didn't know if it would help much, but it would give her something to do.

"We could pour some water on the blankets," Jenna suggested.

"I like it," Karen said. "We have a lot of bottles back here."

Dave heard Karen and Addison scrambling around, but concentrated on the cars ahead of him. One car had just stopped, right in the middle of the road, three cars ahead of the Escalade. The driver of the car behind the blocking car stepped out, one foot still in the car, and started yelling. Dave rolled his window down and he could hear them.

"Get that piece of shit out of the way!"

"I'm out of gas! We need a ride!"

"If you don't move it, I'm going to push you out of the way! Move it, damn it, we don't have much time!"

The driver of the stalled car got out, waving a pistol around. The second driver hastily got back into his car.

"Everybody get down," Dave said. He slid down as far as he could, still looking out the windshield. He heard one of the doors opening and saw Jenna step out on her side, crouching behind her door like the cops did on the television, her shotgun resting on the edge of her open window.

Ahead, the stalled driver had gone back to the second car and was pointing his gun at the man who had yelled at him. Two women got out of the stalled car, looking terrified, going to each side of the second car.

"I'm sorry, I'm so, so sorry," one of the women was saying, over and over, sobbing as she got into the backseat of the car. The other woman couldn't tear her eyes away from the sight of the fire bearing down on all of them.

"Get in the fucking car!" the driver yelled at her. Then he turned his attention to the man with the gun. "Push that piece of shit out of my way, or I'll do it for you."

The man with the gun got into his car and released the foot brake and it began to roll down the hill, the man's left leg still outside the open door. As soon as the right front tire hit the curb the second driver gunned his engine. His front tires smoked as he screeched around the first car, catching the rear bumper and tearing it off, then smashing into the open door. If the man with the gun hadn't quickly rolled to his right and gotten his leg inside, it would have been crushed. As it was, the door was severed and tossed twenty feet into the shrubs on the right side of the road.

"Hey, stop, damn it!" the man with the gun yelled, tumbling out of his car and falling into the street. The next car in line almost ran over him, but managed to brake in time. He stood up and aimed at the first car, and then a remnant of sanity seemed to return. He must have realized he had a better chance of hitting the women in the backseat—one about his own age and an elderly one, possibly his wife and mother?—than the angry man who had hit his car. He began to run down the hill after them, still holding the pistol in his hand.

The man in the next car didn't take the time to get out and move the bumper out of his way but simply rolled over it. Dave knew he would do the same when it came to his turn. But the car in front of him rolled over the piece of metal and it snagged on the undercarriage. The car's driver ignored it, speeding up with the bumper leaving a bright trail of sparks as it dragged along the pavement.

Off to his left Dave could see something happening that was what he had most feared. He could only get glimpses of it between houses and the thick plantings, the tall trees, the privacy walls, but when he could see the eastern slope of the canyon it was clear that the fire was leaping from treetop to treetop. It was windy enough down on the street, and he knew it would be blowing even harder up there. And for the first time he felt a backdraft, air being sucked in from the west as the fire consumed the oxygen and shot a great plume of heat and flame and sparks and whole burning branches high into the air. The fire was speeding along up there like a runaway train from hell, consuming the streets up the hill, Oriole Way, Skylark Lane, Thrasher Avenue, Tanager Way, Blue Jay Way, and on across the ridge to the streets over there, the ones that led down to Rising Glen Road. His whole neighborhood, and the one to the east, was going to burn.

The firebrands were falling thick and fast now, and something crashed down on the roof of the Escalade. It was burning, that was clear.

"Honey, we need to get that off the roof," Karen shouted at him.

"I don't think we have time, Karen."

"The bicycles are up there, Daddy."

"Maybe the tires will burn off them," he said. "We have a few spares in the trailer, don't we?"

"Yes, I put them there," Jenna said.

"Then I won't stop until we cross Sunset. I don't want to lose my place in line here, we might never get back in."

The backdraft was blowing harder now, fanning everything, including the burning branch on the roof. He could see sparks flying off to his left, and a few of them swirled in through his open window. It was bringing searing heat with it. He saw Jenna reach up carefully to touch the roof, and quickly draw her hand back.

"That ceiling liner might catch fire," she said.

"Throw some water on it."

Somebody in the back started to do that, but it was hard to throw water upwards from a bottle. A lot of it splashed on Dave and Jenna.

"That's enough of this shit," Jenna said. Dave heard her unbuckle her seat belt. She grabbed a bottle of water from Karen. "I don't like having a fire over my head." And with that she hoisted her small body up onto the windowsill, hanging on to her seat with one hand while with the other she reached over the roof and poured water onto the burning object up there.

"It's a branch," she shouted. "Not as big as it sounded, but it's a hell of a thing to be blown into the air by the wind."

"Get back in!" Dave told her.

"Just a minute. Anybody got a cloth they can hand me?"

Addison quickly pushed the edge of a blanket into Jenna's free hand. A moment later Jenna had pulled the burning branch off to one side and tossed it into the road. When she slithered back inside she was slapping at her hair.

"Ouch! An ember fell on me."

"Put it out with the blanket," Karen told her. Jenna did that.

"Are you hurt?"

"No. Just a little singe."

"Thanks, Jenna, but please don't do that again."

No one said anything as Dave continued down the hill at

about fifteen miles per hour. He was nearing Sunset now, and wondering what he would find when he got there.

When they reached the choke point between the flatlands and the hills where the car barricade had been, where Dave had spent nights and days sitting in a lawn chair with his shotgun across his lap, he saw that some of the cars had been shoved aside.

But the area two blocks north of Sunset, where all the streets that branched off Doheny had poured all their traffic, was jammed. Once more Dave was amazed at just how many people still remained holed up in the canyon, in their houses without electricity or running water, behind their privacy walls, hoping to sit it out.

It hadn't done them any good. It was all going up in flames now. His decision to move his family had been the correct one, but taken and implemented about twenty-four hours late.

Horns were honking, fenders were crunching, and voices were being raised as all the vehicles jostled for position toward a gap that, even though part of the barricade had been shoved back, was not quite wide enough for two cars to pass simultaneously.

"If somebody would just shove that damn Cadillac another three feet to the side, twice as many cars could get through," Jenna grated.

"You think I should try that when we get up there?"

"Can you do it without punching our fender into a tire?" Karen asked.

"I don't know. Probably."

"If you don't know, then don't do it," Karen said, with finality.

"That's probably what all the others who already went through were thinking."

"Then that's the way we should be thinking, too."

"Mom, what about those people behind us? Shouldn't we try to make it easier for them?"

"They'll get through," Karen said, but her voice lacked conviction. Dave could see Addison looking at her mother with a bit of shock, but she said nothing.

Dave wasn't sure the people behind him would have enough time, either. Hell, he wasn't yet sure *he* would be able to get through before the fire consumed them and everything around them. He saw that his thermometer was reading 130 degrees, and realized that was as high as it went. It felt hotter than that. It was going to be a close thing. He would have felt better on a bicycle. Several times, while he was stuck there barely moving, cyclists had whizzed by him, weaving in and out of the stalled traffic. In his rearview he saw some people getting into cars, apparently with the consent of the people inside. It was a sight that warmed his heart. It showed that things had not *completely* degenerated.

He moved a car length forward, then another, as burning debris continued to shower down all around him.

What would he do when he got there? Zoom on through, or take a chance on blowing a tire?

He was still wondering about that when there was the sound of gunfire. The shots sounded like they were coming from behind him. There were four of them, and they sounded like handguns. There were other shots, but they sounded more distant,

"Get down, Addison!" Karen shouted.

"Everybody down!" Dave told them.

The shots galvanized the people in the cars ahead in a way not even the approaching fire had done. Most people had no idea just how fast the fire could move, *was* moving, but they had a pretty good idea how fast a bullet traveled.

With the roar of half a dozen engines, the cars ahead of him began to surge forward, pressing into the gap in the barricade. At the same time Dave felt something shoving at the trailer behind him. He heard the trailer hitch adding its protesting squeal to the cacophony of sounds that was partly the start of a drag race and partly a demolition derby. Ahead of him fenders were crunching together, cars were scraping sides.

"That's enough of this shit," Dave muttered, and stepped on the accelerator. The big vehicle lurched as he steered toward the gap which the car ahead of him—a black Infiniti with Virginia plates, of all things—had not completely passed through. He slammed into it but the impact was lessened because the car was not standing still, it was moving forward, pushing the car ahead just like Dave was pushing the Infiniti. For a moment Dave thought he was going to climb right up onto the Infiniti's trunk. But instead he ended up smashing both the taillights and popping the trunk open.

And suddenly he was through, the cars ahead of him were separating, some of them weaving erratically but at least *moving*, at least *getting out of his way*.

He sped down Doheny, mildly surprised to find that the trailer was still behind him, though it was swaying alarmingly. He jounced over Sunset with half a dozen cars in front of him in his headlights. Doheny broadened as he crossed Sunset.

He heard more gunfire, and brake lights flared red ahead of him. One car quickly showed its white backup lights and began to move in reverse. It got about twenty feet before plowing into the black Infiniti. The tires smoked and shrieked, but it was clear the two cars were now hopelessly tangled.

The shots seemed to be coming from the single high-rise apartment building on that block, off to the west, his right. Dave could see that a fire had started on the second floor and burned its way up, blackening all the balconies he could see. He spotted two shooters crouching behind the balcony grills on the third floor. They had rifles, and were shooting into the cars that had stopped on the road. So far their fire was concentrated on the cars in front of him.

Then he saw an extremely odd sight. A city bus had been parked at the curb to his left, on the east side of the street. Now it was moving, but not in a way he had ever seen any bus move before. Its front was swinging out, toward the middle of the road, but its rear end didn't move away from the curb. Something on the other side was shoving the bus, which sat on six flat tires, out into the street. He could hear an engine laboring on the other side of the bus. A bulldozer or a big truck, he realized.

And he knew something else. Somebody had set a trap for the people fleeing the fire. They had established a killing zone, with shooters on both sides of the street. He spotted one in the window of a three-story apartment building on the east side, and he felt sure there would be more.

"It's a trap, Dave!" Jenna shouted.

"I know."

"We've got to get out of here, right now!"

He didn't know how many shooters there might be behind him, but he thought it made sense that there wouldn't be any more beyond the bus, which was resisting whatever was pushing it as its wheel rims plowed into the surface of the street with a terrible racket. The ambushers meant to corral all the cars right here and leave them nowhere to go.

He turned and looked behind him—noticing that Karen had spread herself over Addison, who was struggling to get her head high enough to look out—and saw men entering the street from both sides. They were ragged, some of them shirtless, all of them dirty. There were six or seven of them, and they all carried rifles or handguns. Biker gangs? Criminals? Hoodlums, former drug dealers or addicts? Or merely hungry, desperate people? Whatever they were, they were survivors, so far, and they expected to extend their survival by taking what belonged to him, and possibly taking his life and those of his family. Dave assumed these guys wouldn't hesitate to kill them if they resisted, and if they surrendered, who knew what they might do?

Still looking back, he saw some of the men approach the cars backed up behind him and point weapons. One man smashed a window with his handgun and reached inside, trying to pull someone out. People were getting out of another car with their hands up. They had nowhere to go, not really, and could only hope they would just be robbed, not killed.

He looked forward again and saw that some of the people ahead of him had stuck rifle or shotgun barrels out their windows. One man was partially out of his car, one foot on the ground, and he was firing up at the men on the high-rise.

He looked to the side and saw Jenna crouched in her seat, half out the window, aiming up at the high-rise. Her shotgun boomed, and boomed again.

"Get moving, Dave!" she shouted.

He gunned the engine, steered around the car in front of him, which chose that time to start forward. The car hit the driver's side of the Escalade as he passed it, rocking it, but the big SUV shouldered it aside, and then both vehicles were headed for the narrowing gap as the city bus was shoved still farther into the street.

"I got one!" Jenna shouted, as she slid back in and searched her pockets for more shotgun shells. Several spilled out into the seat and she groped for them.

There would be room for them both, Dave thought, the Escalade and the Infiniti.

Then there was gunfire to his left, where the other car was.

It suddenly veered off and went up over the curb over there. Dave couldn't see what happened, but assumed the driver had been shot. He kept steering toward the gap.

There was another shot and his window shattered and his lap was full of tiny shards of safety glass. His left cheek and forehead stung, and he felt blood leaking into his left eye. *How bad am I hit?* he wondered. No time for that, worry about that later.

While he was still fifty feet from the moving bus, a man stepped out from behind it. He looked determined, and he had a large weapon in his hands. He was fat and shirtless, and his arms were covered with tattoos. The gun was military, and Dave knew it could rip sizeable chunks out of the Escalade and his family.

The man fired a shot into the air, then pointed the gun directly at Dave. He was shouting something Dave couldn't hear.

Suddenly Dave knew why the man wanted him to stop, alive. He wanted prisoners. What the man would do with male prisoners Dave didn't know, but he knew what the fat fuck would do with women.

All right, screw it, he thought, and steered directly at the man. Once more the big fellow shouted, and then started to step behind the bus, his weapon still leveled. His chances of blowing Dave's head off as he passed were excellent. He braced himself for the shot. So he was not entirely surprised when a gun went off practically beside his ear. The windshield shattered, letting in the hot breath of the night, and he was driving almost blind, trying to see through the cracked glass, wondering why he was still alive. Then he realized the shot had come from inside the car, and he saw Karen's shotgun barrel beside his shoulder. He was almost deaf in that ear, but he could still hear out of his left.

"*Step on it, David,* get out of here!"

The gun barrel pulled back and as he passed the bus he got a quick glimpse of the big man, limping, bleeding from one arm and one leg, struggling to bring his weapon up again. The man saw Karen's gun barrel poking out of the broken driver's side window and he hit the ground. Dave winced, waiting for Karen to blow out the eardrum of his other ear, but she apparently couldn't get a good shot, and Dave swept by. In his rearview he saw a man leap off the tow truck—MIKE'S TOW, AAA APROVED— and scurry for cover. The big man was sitting up, aiming the military rifle again.

"Karen, get down!"

He heard the stutter of the rifle and the impact of the slugs. His side mirror was torn off, but most of the bullets were hitting the back of the trailer. The firing stopped, and he was moving into darkness. He stuck his head out the side and saw nothing ahead of him, noting that he had only one headlight left, on the right side of the car.

"Is anyone hurt?" he called out.

"We're okay back here," Karen said.

"I think I got some glass from your window," Jenna said, breathlessly. Dave looked over, and saw her clutching a bloody patch on her leg.

"We need to get a little farther away from the action," Dave said.

"Sure. No problem."

"Daddy, you're bleeding."

Dave wanted to touch the side of his head to see how bad the damage was, but didn't dare let go of the steering wheel.

"My God." Karen sighed. "I think we survived it."

Gradually the light from the fire behind them diminished, and soon they reached a point where the remaining headlight outshone the firelight.

He was passing the corner of Elevado when Addison cried out.

"There's Ranger! Daddy, it's Ranger! Please stop, we need to get him!"

Dave would never know if he would have stopped just for the horse, but he had already been planning to pull over, intending to assess the damage to the Escalade and the trailer. He turned to the right and drove fifty feet or so, and there the horse was, standing in the middle of the road, picked out in the headlight beam. He was breathing heavily, and showed no inclination to run. Perhaps he had heard Addison's voice, perhaps he was relishing the security of being a good distance from the fire. Maybe he was simply too exhausted to run much farther. He just stood there as Dave pulled over to the curb.

"Maybe we should turn off the lights, too," Karen suggested, as she got out of the car and hurried after her daughter.

"Light."

"What's that?"

"Light. We only have one headlight."

"Whatever. Addison, don't you dare approach that animal until I get there!" She switched on her flashlight and caught up with Addison, who was standing a few feet away from the horse and speaking to him.

Dave eased out of the Escalade. He went to the back of the trailer and played his flashlight beam on it. Three rounds had hit it, but the shooter had missed the tires. If Dave had been shooting that's what he would have aimed for, but he supposed the guy's aim had been thrown off a bit by soaking up part of Karen's shotgun blast. He hadn't been able to see how badly the man had been hit, but he knew it hadn't been the full force of the shot, or he would have been dead.

He looked over the tailgate and saw something of a mess in there. There had been cases of canned goods stacked near the front, and two of the bullets had plowed into them. He saw condensed milk leaking onto the floor, and some other cans had been blown open. There were bales of hay on the right side of the trailer. The third bullet had gone harmlessly into the hay.

Heading forward, he saw that his remaining scooters were intact, no bullet holes. Above, the bicycles looked okay.

He saw in front of him that Addison, helped by Karen, had captured and calmed Ranger. Addison had his halter and reins in hand and was patting his big head.

Wait a minute. Why was Jenna not out of the car?

". . . Dave . . ."

It was little more than a whisper. Dave shined his flashlight into the car and Jenna winced as the light hit her face.

"Jenna, are you all right?"

"I thought I was . . . I . . . think I may have been hit worse than . . . I realized." She looked down, and Dave followed her gaze with his light. Her jeans were soaked in blood.

"Karen!" he called out. "I need you over here."

"Just a minute, we—"

"Now, Karen."

She caught the urgency in his voice. He was pulling on the door handle but the door was jammed, bent out of shape by the recent fender bender.

"Maybe you'll have to get in on the other side," he told Karen, as she joined him. He tugged again, with no result, then put his foot against the rear door and pulled as hard as he could.

The door popped open and he almost went down in the street, still hanging on to the handle.

"See how badly Jenna is hurt, and if you can do anything for her."

"Jenna , . . is she . . ." Karen turned her light on Jenna.

"I think I got shot," Jenna gasped.

"Daddy, what's—"

"Addison, the ramp is down, get that animal into the trailer. Right now, first time, no hesitation, no misbehaving on his part, or we leave him here on the street."

Addison looked shocked, but obeyed without question. That job would keep her out of the way while they determined how badly Jenna was hurt.

Karen got out her big knife and explored Jenna's right pant leg, where most of the blood seemed to be coming from, for a place to begin cutting. She was about to go all the way down and begin at the bottom hem when Dave spotted a small hole on the inside of Jenna's right thigh, about midway between her crotch and her knee. Karen gingerly inserted the point of the blade into the hole.

"This will probably hurt."

"I don't feel a lot of pain," Jenna whispered. "Feel . . . really weak . . ."

Karen continued cutting on the fabric, and Dave felt his stomach heave as he saw more and more blood. He controlled it, at least for the moment, and held the flashlight as the work went on. Dave could feel the car shift as Addison loaded Ranger into the trailer.

Soon the leg was bared.

"What do you think?" Jenna asked. She was looking up at the ceiling.

"You should be okay," Karen said, but she was looking at Dave, and slowly shaking her head. Since Karen didn't know any more medicine than basic first aid, Dave was at first puzzled by the gesture, until she added a shrug, which clearly meant *How the hell should I know?* He felt the same way, and agreed that reassuring words were what Jenna needed to hear, no matter how bad the actual situation was.

"It doesn't look all that bad," he said. One thing was clear, and a hopeful sign. The wound was not pumping blood. It was steadily oozing, but if an artery had been severed, surely the blood would be gushing out. At least that's what he told himself. He was fairly sure of something else, and passed the information on.

"It looks like a small-caliber bullet wound to me, not that heavy weapon the leader of the group was carrying. Maybe a .22 rifle."

"Ranger's in the trailer," Addison said. Dave had heard the tailgate clang into place while they were cutting away Jenna's jeans, and she had hurried to them a moment after that. "Mom, shouldn't we bandage her up? That's what they said in first aid, the most important things to do are stopping the bleeding and establishing an airway."

"That's what I was about to do," Karen said. "I'd like a sterile bandage to put against the bullet hole, Addison. Do you know where they are?"

"I can find them."

"How bad is the bleeding?" Jenna wanted to know.

"I'd say it's not too bad," Karen said.

"What about a tourniquet?"

"I don't know," Dave said. "Didn't I hear that you weren't supposed to do that unless the bleeding was really bad?"

"I think so. Let's get it bandaged and then let's get her to a doctor."

Addison found the first-aid supplies, and Dave got out of the way as Karen opened packages and pressed them to the wounds. They quickly became soaked. In the first-aid kit was a book he had skimmed over some weeks ago. Addison took it and quickly thumbed through it while Dave held the flashlight.

"It says first try to stop the bleeding with pressure," Addison told her mother.

"Okay. Jenna, the bleeding's slowed down a lot."

Jenna said nothing, just nodding. She was sweating profusely, Karen shined her flashlight on her face, and she reacted sluggishly.

"Dave, her skin is pale, and her hands feel cold."

"Sounds like she's going into shock," Addison said. She flipped to the right page and scanned it rapidly. "I think you're right. Are her fingernails turning blue?"

"Yes."

"Is she having trouble breathing?"

"No," Jenna said. "But it's starting to hurt, and I'm feeling sick."

"Can you take her pulse, Mom? Find out if it's fast but weak?"

"I don't think we have enough experience to know what fast or weak are. I think we should get her to the hospital. Isn't Cedars close around here?"

"It's just a few blocks away."

"It says here no fluids except intravenously," Addison sad. "Give her oxygen, some other things we can't do. We need to keep her warm. Can we find a way to lay her flat and elevate her feet? That's supposed to bring her blood pressure back up."

They managed to get the seatback to a forty-five-degree angle, but then it was blocked by all the cargo in the back. They shifted enough of it so they had the seat almost level, and Jenna supine. Karen elevated her legs by placing her feet on the dashboard.

CHAPTER TWENTY-THREE

Cedars-Sinai was only half a mile away, but no trip was as easy and obvious as it had been before the quake. They had to wind through some back streets, but eventually they came out onto San Vicente a few blocks north of Beverly and headed south along the long, gradual curve, having to dodge around only one fallen tree, and then the huge, hulking mass of the Beverly Center was looming before them, lit a pale orange by the fire to the north. In his rearview mirror Dave could see the fire covering the hillside. He assumed it wouldn't spread quite as rapidly in the urbanized setting south of Sunset, but beyond that there was simply no telling how far it might reach.

The northern end of the Beverly Center was mostly intact, the Macy's sign still on the slab side of the building above the parking levels. But there was something wrong down Beverly to the east. That part of the building seemed to have collapsed.

Straight ahead of them the road was reasonably clear, with the first of the high-rise buildings that made up the Cedars complex throwing back crazy reflections of the fire from hundreds of broken windows. There were no signs of life that Dave could see, not a single lighted window.

"Straight ahead, or right?" Dave asked.

"Didn't Lisa say they were treating people in the parking lot? There's a big one just past that street that goes under the building."

"Gracie Allen Drive," Dave said. Dave had always liked the name of that little, two-block street that tunneled under one of the hospital buildings, just across from the entrance to the Beverly Center parking levels. "Let's try to go around, first."

Dave put the car in gear and headed south. But not for long. His headlight picked out a massive pile of rubble completely blocking San Vicente. Just before it, and partially obscured by the collapse, was a six-foot wall of dirt and cracked concrete and asphalt where the earth had heaved and broken and thrust up. The crack seemed to run directly beneath the southern part of the Center, where Bloomingdale's had been.

"I don't think we should drive under that building," Addison said.

"We'll take a look. It stood up this long, it should stand up another ten minutes."

He made a wide circle and headed back north.

He hadn't noticed it in his rearview, but as soon as he was turned around he saw the headlights coming toward them. He heard Karen and Addison shifting around. Glancing back, he saw that Karen had her shotgun barrel out the window behind him, and Addison held hers at the ready.

He slowed to a crawl and they all watched as the other vehicle came on, not slowing at all until they were almost side by side. It was a red Toyota SUV, and the odd thing about it was that it was smoking. Not from the tailpipe; the body of the car was giving off wisps of smoke.

"Stop right there!" Karen shouted, and aimed her gun at the car. It kept rolling for a few more feet, until Dave could see into the driver's seat. The man sitting in there held his hands off the steering wheel, palms spread.

"We're not armed," he wheezed, tiredly. Now that Dave could get a good look at him, he saw the man was badly burned on the left side of his face. He had burns on his arms and hands, too. There was moaning coming from the backseat, where Dave could see the heads of two people. One was a man and the other a woman, and the man seemed to be unconscious. Both looked burned.

"Those people in the back," Karen said. "I need to see their hands, too."

"I don't know if they can hear you, and I'm not sure they can move."

"I said, I need to—"

"It's okay, Karen, I can see them. They're all hurt badly."

She didn't say more, but her gun never wavered.

"We live up near the top of Rising Glen," the man said. "The fire caught us flat-footed. One minute I was sleeping, the next everything was on fire. The heat! I never saw anything like it. It was on us, we got in the car, and we drove through fire all the way down the hill."

Rising Glen was the next canyon to the east of Doheny.

Now that Dave could get a better look at the Toyota, he was astonished that it was still moving. The paint was blistered. Some of the body panels were made of fiberglass, vinyl, and probably other kinds of plastic Dave wasn't familiar with. The heat had warped these panels. The windshield was intact, but partially blackened. There were streaks where the man had wiped off enough of a space to see through. The left-rear tire was flat, almost gone, just remnants of flayed rubber. It was as if the man had driven the Toyota through hell's car wash.

"We're all burned, we're looking for medical help," the man said.

"Well, there's nothing on this side of the hospital," Dave told him. "We're going back up to Beverly, try to go around and see if there's anything happening on the other side. We've got a gunshot wound here, and—"

"Gunshot? What the hell happened?"

"They were waiting for us as we came off the hill. Men with guns. Lots of them. We barely squeezed through the ambush."

"Ambush." The man sighed. "My God, my God, what have we come to?"

"David, we don't have time for this. Jenna's started to bleed again."

"Right. Sir, there's no point in going south. Bloomingdale's collapsed into the road. It's completely blocked."

"Beverly's no better. We tried that way."

There was a brief silence.

"Then I guess it's got to be the Gracie tunnel," Karen said.

"Mom, I don't want—"

"Be quiet, Addison. It'll only take a few seconds. Sir, we're going under the building, right over there. You're welcome to follow us."

"Could you possibly help me change a tire? I don't know how much farther we can go on this one."

"Sorry, we just don't have the time. I wish you well." Dave put the Escalade in gear and pulled away from the man and his burned family, feeling very low. But what could he do? They would find help on the other side, or they wouldn't, and nothing he could do was going to change that.

Addison seemed to have developed a specialized claustrophobia that Dave knew was often suffered by survivors of earthquakes. She didn't like to be indoors, but she could tolerate that. What gave her the real horrors was to have anything of great weight suspended over her head. As soon as Dave drove into the underpass beneath the medical complex she began to whimper, and she buried her face in her mother's shoulder. Karen murmured soothing words and hugged her.

Dave wasn't happy to find that he, too, didn't like being under all that concrete. Unable to help himself, he scanned the ceiling for cracks, and was horrified to find several. Each time he saw one he felt the tires crunch over cement dust and bits of rubble. He had a strong urge to floor the accelerator and get the hell out of there, but made himself maintain a cautious five miles per hour. This would he a hell of a place to have a breakdown, or get stuck.

He was glad of his caution when he came to a large chunk of concrete positioned perversely just where he would be least likely to see it. Looking up as he steered around it, he thought he could see the roof of the parking level above him.

From behind, he could hear Ranger rearing and stomping, whinnying his distress. That alarmed him, since the horse couldn't see anything of the situation, and he remembered all the stories about pets and zoo animals acting agitated just before an earthquake. This would be the worst possible time for an aftershock.

It couldn't have taken him more than thirty seconds to travel through the tunnel and out the other side, but it seemed much, much longer. Then the night sky opened out again, with the fire to the north casting faint orange light over the scene.

"We're through," he told the women. "The guy in the Toyota is right behind us, if you were worried about him, Addison."

"I was, but I forgot all about him for a while there. I'm so pissed off at myself. I never knew I could be so damn scared. I'm such a wuss."

"It's all right, honey," Karen said, "and no, you're not. I was scared, too."

He paused at the place that he always thought of as the quintessential Hollywood location: the intersection of Gracie Allen Drive and George Burns Road. Each of the streets was only two blocks long. The intersection was right at the heart of the Cedars-Sinai Medical Center, the hospital of the stars.

Looking to his left, Dave saw that a curved pedestrian elevated walkway had fallen into the street in a heap of twisted metal beams.

The corners to his left held the Thaliens Mental Health Center and the Theodore E. Cummings Family Patient Wing. Both were silent, with no lights showing through the broken glass of the windows. To his right and behind him was the Broidy Family Patient Wing. The block of George Burns Road to his right was also blocked by a partial collapse of one of the hospital towers up near Beverly. The other corner was a large open space, formerly a parking lot, now just another abandoned aid station. It smelled of human waste and sickness. Paper trash that looked like medical packaging was strewn all over, and it was swirled around them by the Santa Ana wind entering the hospital canyons and not finding an easy way out.

When Karen played her flashlight over the jumble of beds and bedpans, empty plastic blood and glucose bags, food trays, equipment racks, billowing, filthy sheets, and bloody wads of gauze, it was clear that no one was home.

"They've moved on," Dave said.

"Honk your horn, anyway."

He did, and in a moment the Toyota pulled up near him and began honking, too. The echoes were loud in this space surrounded on three sides by tall hospital buildings. They waited a moment, and tried again.

"Hey, dude, cut it out. I'm trying to get some sleep!"

Dave jumped, Addison made a stifled squeal. Hearing a voice in that place and at that time was like being tapped on the shoulder during a stroll through a haunted house at midnight.

"Flashlight, Addison!" Dave shouted. The beam clicked on and she shined it out the window on her side. Soon the beam picked out a tall, long-haired man dressed in filthy, bloodstained green surgical scrubs shambling toward them from the direction of one of the hospital buildings. He held his hands up lackadaisically, and squinted at them.

"I'm not armed, folks. You can lay down them shootin' irons."

He kept coming, and Dave tentatively decided he was harmless, since he could see no place where he could have concealed a handgun. The bottoms of his scrubs were so carelessly tied they looked as if they might fall off at any moment.

Karen quickly got out and ran around the front of the car. She held her shotgun aimed in his general direction, but pointed at the ground.

"That's far enough, sir," she said. The man shrugged, and stopped walking. He stood about ten yards from the car, loose-limbed either from exhaustion or what Dave thought might be some very good drugs.

"Are you a doctor?" Dave called out. The man laughed.

"Might as well be. I'm the closest thing to a doctor left in this spook house. I been doing things it used to take a doctor to do. No, man, I'm a nurse."

"Where is everybody?"

"Blew town, dude. Marching to the sea. Like Sherman. Like lemmings. All but yours truly. When the soldiers came, I found a place to hide. I'm not going to the ocean. Sharks in the ocean, man."

"Are you saying they were forced to leave?"

"Shit, I don't know. All's I know is the soldiers came, navy soldiers."

"Sailors."

"And Marines. Looking for a few good men." He leaned forward with comic intensity, put his hand close to his mouth as though imparting a confidence, and stage-whispered, "I have it on good authority they're taking them all on that big-ass aircraft carrier, that *nuke*-u-lar carrier, as a former president used to say, and dumping 'em. Feeding them to the sharks. No place to put 'em, no food to feed 'em. Make 'em walk the fucking plank, man. Yo-ho-ho."

". . . hurts . . ."

"What was that? What did you say, Jenna?"

"She said she hurts, Daddy."

Dave looked at Jenna, rolling her head slowly from side to side. It looked like her bandages were wet again.

"Hey, man, you got a casualty in there? Somebody hurt?" He straightened up a little and mooched over to the car, leaned in and looked at Jenna. Dave heard the burned Toyota accelerating away in a clatter and a shower of sparks, but didn't pay much attention to it. He was debating if he should let this man examine Jenna or if they'd be better off just heading to the Winston house as fast as possible. Was he really a nurse? Was he insane, or just stoned? Both?

Before he could decide the man held his hand out behind him, and called out.

"Flashlight!"

It was a sad parody of a surgeon, but after a small hesitation Karen slapped the Maglite into his hand. He leaned into the car and shined the light into Jenna's face. He reached out and, with surprising tenderness, peeled back one of her eyelids and studied her pupil. Then he put the light on Jenna's bandaged leg and poked gently at it. Jenna had no reaction.

"She's passed out. Which is probably good. That's gotta hurt like hell. And the blood keeps oozing out of there. If you don't tie it off, she could bleed out pretty soon. You have something I can use for a tourniquet?"

They opened the door and improvised a tourniquet out of a torn blanket and a wooden spoon, which the man tightened and then fastened in place with duct tape. The ooze of blood stopped.

"You can't leave that on, like, forever, dude. Loosen it a little every ten minutes or so, let blood get to the leg. See if it's still bleeding. You have to get her to a doctor who can take a look in there and see what's going down, sew her up. Otherwise, she's gonna lose the leg. Might lose it anyway. I've seen a lot who did. I've done all I can do."

"Thank you for that," Karen said.

"Hey, that's why they pay me the big bucks." He paused, swayed on his feet, caught himself before he fell. "Say, dude, have you got any weed back there?"

"I'm sorry."

He shrugged. "Half the people in California have a medical condition that feels better with weed. Just thought I'd ask."

"Here," Addison said. She hadn't gotten out of the car when Dave did, but had watched the treatment from the backseat. She had apparently been busy. Tears were running down her face as she thrust a plastic bag out the window. The bag rattled with the sound of cans.

The nurse took it and looked down into it, then reached in and pulled out a can.

"Peaches, man! Haven't had any of *those* for a long time. In heavy syrup, the best kind for when the world ends. I'm gonna have *such* a sugar rush! *Muchas gracias*, sweetheart!"

"Hasta la vista," Karen said, getting back into the car. Dave got in, too, and started it and put it in gear. As they drove off Dave saw the man scuffing through the parking lot, where he sat down on a bed facing the approaching fire. He felt guilty about not offering the man a ride, but he had shown no signs of wanting to leave. He didn't think the fire posed much of a threat to him, with all the concrete parking structures in the hospital complex to take refuge in.

He realized he had never asked the man's name.

The next morning never dawned. As they got closer to the Winston house a sick, grayish light gradually worked its way into the landscape, not much better than the night. The glow of the fire, though it was increasingly distant as they worked their way west, still overpowered what sunlight worked its way around the cloud of black smoke that obscured the horizon to the north and east and south. Dave once caught a glimpse of a band of blue to the west, but it was a pitiful thing.

The wind was still blowing powerfully, shifting from time to time, and each time it blew from the northeast they were showered with a thick fall of ash. No embers, no firebrands, just gray, powdery ash that swirled like a terrible snowstorm and came in the windows and soon coated them all.

By the time they got to the Winstons the wind had veered and was coming from the northwest, but it brought little relief, as everything was obscured by ash swirled into devils by the relentless wind. Dave honked the horn as they pulled into the driveway. Karen hit the ground running, going around the back of the house as Dave eased the SUV and trailer after her.

Bob Winston was standing near the rear border of his property, hands on his hips, looking east at the conflagration that seemed destined to eat the entire city. He turned when Karen came up to him, listened to her, and hurried back toward the house.

Dave got out at the same time as Addison.

"What can I do, Daddy?"

"There's nothing you can do for Jenna. Either Lisa is here, or she isn't. You better take care of your horse."

Addison looked dubiously at Dave, then at Jenna, unconscious in the front passenger seat. He knew she was desperate to tend to Ranger, but was glad to see she had her priorities straight.

"Go on, sweetheart. There's really nothing we can do."

With one more agonized look, she went around to the back of the trailer.

Karen joined him and they waited, impatiently. There was nothing to do but watch the fire, and from Bob's backyard they had an excellent view of it, out over the relatively clear grounds of the country club.

The hills were burning brightly, but maybe not so fiercely as they had been a few hours ago. There wasn't much left up there to burn.

"Could we see our house from here?" Karen wanted to know.

"I don't think so. I think there's a ridge or two in the way." He put his arm around her waist. "But it's all gone, Karen. You know that."

"Of course I know that. I'm wondering why it isn't affecting me more."

"It was already in pretty bad shape."

"Well, for all that, it was a roof over our heads. We're homeless now."

"So are a few million Angelenos. And we're better prepared to handle it than 99 percent of them."

Lisa and her two children came running out of the house. Dave saw Nigel pause for just a moment and stare to the east at the towering flames, then hurry on with his mother and sister.

Dave and Karen moved out of the way as the three arrived. It was quickly apparent they were used to working as a team. Many days of Elyse and Nigel helping their mother at the hospital had made them all terse and efficient. Only a few words were spoken as they shined a light into the gloom of the front seat, and carefully unwrapped the bandages.

"We need to get her into the house where I have some room to move," Lisa said. "Elyse, you start some water boiling, sterilize those scalpels, you know the drill. Did you wash those rubber gloves?"

"Yes, ma'am." She hurried off.

"Do we need to get a board or something to move her?" Karen asked.

"I don't want to take the time. Let's just lift her out of there. We need to do it carefully, I don't want to put too much strain on that wound. Nigel and I will work her out of that seat, and then I need you, Dave and Karen, to move in from either side and support her as we get her out."

They got Jenna into the house, and Lisa told them to go outside. They rejoined Bob and stood side by side for a while and watched the fire.

"I think the wind has died down a little. Has it?" Dave asked.

"Hard to tell. Maybe."

"It feels like it's blowing in from the coast now. Unless I'm turned around."

"You're right. That's west, behind us. If it stays that way, the fire might blow away from us." He stopped, and frowned. "I understand Jenna has a gunshot wound. Were people shooting at each other, trying to get out?"

"It almost came to that. But it was sort of an out-of-the-fire-and-into-the-frying-pan situation. As soon as we crossed Sunset, we ran into an ambush."

"Oh, my God."

"That's what I thought. Bob, the bullet that hit her came through *my window*, must have missed me by inches."

For a moment he couldn't go on.

"They were waiting for us. We must have been some of the last ones through the gauntlet they were building, a jackleg barricade with cars and a bus. We took some fire, and we shot back."

They were both silent for a moment, watching the fire. It was hard to tell for sure just where it was burning, since Dave was not that familiar with Bob's neighborhood, but it was clear that it was now far beyond Sunset, eating its way through the more urbanized areas of West Hollywood and the eastern part of Beverly Hills. It might be as far south now as Melrose, maybe even Beverly. He wondered if it was at Cedars, and if their helpful, stoned nurse was in a safe place.

* * *

Lisa worked on Jenna for almost an hour, and when she was done she was far from happy with the result.

"The bullet nicked the deep femoral artery," she said. "Not the main femoral. If it had been an inch to one side, it would have and you would have had no chance to save her. That was good work, by the way, putting on that tourniquet."

"We didn't do it," Dave admitted. "We weren't sure we were supposed to. I'd heard you could cause more harm than good. Like, she might lose the leg."

"She might lose it anyway. It will be touch and go. I might as well warn you, too, that there's a good chance she won't make it." She paused, and looked puzzled. "So who did put on the tourniquet?"

"Some guy at the hospital. We went there, hoping to find you or any doctor, but there was no one there but this male nurse." He told her about their experiences at Cedars. They were standing in Bob's backyard, with Karen and Addison and Elyse and Bob. Nigel was back in the kitchen tending to Jenna.

"They started moving everyone out yesterday, not long after I came back here. We went back there to work some more, but almost everyone was gone. Soldiers—Marines, I think—were herding everyone out. They wanted us all to join the march down Santa Monica that you told us about, they said Los Angeles was being evacuated, everyone was being loaded onto aircraft carriers and taken away. They wouldn't tell us where. They wanted me and Elyse and Nigel to go that way, too, and we might have been forced to—"

"Not on your life, Mother," Elyse said. "We might have started out in that direction, but I know we could have slipped away and come home, when it got dark."

"Anyway, we didn't have to. We've made friends with those members of the LAPD who are still on the job. One of their priorities is getting doctors to and from hospitals if they live close by, you saw them bringing us home the other day. Sergeant Gomez and Officer Murkowski told the Marines they'd take us a ways down the evacuation route, and as soon as we were out of sight they brought us here."

"I've become a big fan of the LAPD," Bob said, with a smile.

"So . . . I don't know the guy you met, but he probably saved Jenna's life."

She suddenly cried out. "I hate this! Hate it, hate it, *hate it*! We ran out of almost everything at the hospital. I brought some things home with me, in case we're really going to make this crazy trip—scalpels, needles, surgical thread, a lot of things that we used to use once and then discard—but I felt like a thief bringing home so much as a Band-Aid. We lost patients we could easily have saved, from infections after surgery. We amputated arms and legs that could have been saved with proper care. It's like we've been thrown back to the Stone Age."

"Actually, more like the turn of the twentieth century," Bob said, gently. "Lisa, you did the best you could, I'm sure of it."

She sighed.

"It's just so frustrating that the reason I couldn't do any better is that we just didn't have a tenth of the things we needed. We kept waiting for help to arrive. I know what you said, you and Dave and Mark, that help was never going to arrive, but in my heart I didn't believe it. I mean, this is the United States of America! We've never let anyone down like this, not even if the disaster was on the other side of the world. We're always there as soon as the dust settles."

The group stood silently for a while, watching the progress of the flames.

"I was afraid it would burn right up to the edge of the golf course," Bob said. "Then I was hoping it might act as a fire-break. Not many trees out there."

"Don't be so sure," Dave said. "If it burned those houses over there, and if the wind was blowing right, it would send a lot of firebrands into the air. There's no telling where they would come down."

"What would you suggest?"

"Post somebody up on the roof on this side of the house, if you can. If we see it come within a few blocks and it looks like it's still headed this way, I say we need to get out, even if we're not ready."

"There's still some packing to do, and Mark is still working on the vehicles, but we could go if we had to. We were waiting on you, and on Teddy to report back. You know, we still haven't made a final decision on which way to go."

"Can Teddy find you, if you have to abandon the house?"

"We set up a rendezvous point. If he comes back and sees the house is burned, we'll meet him there. If we can."

Teddy arrived on his bike and the whole house turned out to hear his report, except Jenna and those on lookout duty.

"First, I have some bad news. I was able to swing by Dennis Rossi's house in Glendale. Well, I mean where his house used to be. The whole neighborhood is gone. Burned to the ground. I found the lot; the number was painted on the curb. I was hoping for a note or something, but I couldn't find anything."

After a long pause, Bob spoke up.

"And Roger?"

"Like I told you, I probably wouldn't have time to get all that far out where he lives. It just wasn't possible."

Bob nodded, slowly.

"Then I guess he's on his own. Go on, son."

"The coast route north is definitely out. The Pacific Coast Highway is blocked by landslides. The one I saw, close to Topanga Canyon, took most of the road into the Pacific, and I could see one beyond that one where half a mountainside came down and buried the road. The 405 is impassable at the Getty Center. I tried to get around it on the west side of the freeway, but a lot of Saint Mary's College up on that hill over there looks like it's just gone, and the roads with it. There are some fire roads up there, but I didn't think it was worth my time to look at them, since they're even more fragile than the road I saw that caved in."

"No point in it," Bob agreed.

Teddy paused to take another drink from a bottle of warm Gatorade. He had run out of bottled water during his long scouting expedition. Now he was carefully rehydrating, a few sips at a time.

"I didn't bother with Roscomare Road," Teddy went on. "Beverly Glen, Benedict Canyon, Coldwater Canyon, Laurel Canyon, all impassable. That just leaves the 101 freeway through the

Cahuenga Pass, which could get us to the I-5. It's been bull-dozed clear. I made it as far as Universal City, and on to the interchange with the 170 and the 134, and I'm sure our vehicles could make it, too."

"That sounds like our path north, then," Rachel said.

"I wouldn't count on it. I talked to some other riders. There are quite a few of us out there. They've been all over the place, and by talking to them I've made a pretty good map of what's open, what's blocked, where the most dangerous neighborhoods are."

They were all gathered around or sitting at Bob's large picnic table in the backyard. Dave had seldom seen such a sweaty, dirty group. The temperature had climbed once again as the unseen sun rose and the hot wind blew from the north, and Bob's thermometer said it was ninety-eight degrees. The ash was still falling, coating everything and everyone. The group looked like coal miners just emerging from the ground. The soot found every crack and crevice in the skin and worked its way in, and the streams of sweat running down most of their faces didn't really clean it off so much as smear it around.

"So don't leave us hanging, Teddy," Bob urged his son. "What do you know?"

"What I *know*, what I've seen with my own eyes, I've already told you. And from here on, I'm reporting what other explorers have told me. I have no reason to doubt any of them, and a lot of reason to trust most of them absolutely. So the big news is that I-5 is impassable farther north."

There was a murmur of concern from the assembled group. Interstate 5 was the Main Street of the West Coast, running all the way from Tijuana to the Canadian border. Many of those present had been pinning a lot of hope on the assumption that it would not be blocked, or if it had been, then some government agency would have bulldozed obstructions out of the way.

"I met a woman coming back down the freeway. I was only as far north as the exchange between the 5 and the 118, in San Fernando. She said that from Santa Clarita on, the road was virtually destroyed."

"You trust this woman?" Gordon asked.

"She was desperate to get to Bakersfield, she said her chil-dren had been up there spending a few weeks with their grand-parents and she had planned to join them, but then the quake came. She was crying a lot, and totally exhausted. I couldn't think of a reason in the world why she would lie to me, just to screw around with me."

"I can't see it, either," Gordon said.

"Okay," Bob said. "So far you've eliminated some of our options. Do you have any good news?"

"Don't shoot me, I'm just the bearer of bad tidings, but I'm afraid the answer is no. So far I've cut down our land options to just two, as far as I can see. Everyone agrees that west toward Palm Springs and Arizona—desert, any way you look at it—is not on the table. We either go west to the I-15 and cross the mountains there, and from there up to the Central Valley and Oregon. Or, we go south, which as most of you know, is the option I've been in favor of from the start."

"You said 'land options,'" Dave said.

"Yeah. As in, should we try to go overland at all?"

He looked around at his family and Dave's family. Dave knew where he stood on joining the mass exodus—or maybe it was better to think of it as a deportation—being carried out by the nuclear navy and the Marines. He and Karen had talked about it. They didn't want to get aboard an aircraft carrier and be shipped out to parts unknown. But if the Winston family decided that was the best idea, then they would tag along.

But now, with Jenna badly wounded, the equation had changed. Maybe it would be better to turn themselves in to the navy. Wouldn't they have medics, and possibly medical supplies?

He knew that there were partisans for both the land and sea options, but he wasn't always sure who they were. He guessed Lisa and her children would opt for the carrier, because it would have at least the basics for medical care. Then she was the first to speak up, and she surprised him.

"I was leaning toward going on the boat," she said. "Until today. There was no question we were being forced out, staying behind wasn't an option. They had trucks for the stretcher cases, but they wedged them in like sardines in a can. There was a lot of shouting and tempers lost, and I saw several people who didn't want to leave clubbed to the ground and thrown in trucks with bars on the windows. If not for our police friends, me and my kids might have been on those trucks."

She paused a moment to let them all think that over.

"The vibe was very bad," her son Nigel agreed.

"Well, I'll chip in again," Teddy said. "I think it's even worse than my sister knows about."

That brought the few murmured conversations to a halt. Teddy took another deep swallow of Gatorade and went on.

"I went to the coast, of course. I could see the aircraft carrier from the hills in the Palisades, then I went down into Santa Monica. I climbed up onto the sixth floor of a building and I could see them on the highway and on the beach, thousands and thousands of them, as far as I could see. They were surrounded by barbed wire. With my binoculars I could see the Marines guarding them. I could see the boats being rowed back and forth from the Santa Monica Pier—most of it is still standing, if you can believe that—to the carrier. All kinds of boats. Most were being rowed by crews, like old whaleboats.

"I wanted to know more but I was afraid of getting roped into that situation down there, so I started back, taking the back streets. A couple of guys came out of a house and hailed me. They were in civilian clothes, but they claimed they were sailors and they had slipped away at night and jumped ship."

"Did you believe them?" Addison asked.

"I didn't know what to think, at first. Tell you the truth, I kind of liked them, they didn't seem like mental giants but they were fed up, pissed off, outraged by what they had seen and done. Something made me think they might be lovers running away together. Maybe I'm just a romantic. Anyway, they hadn't been ashore farther than a block away from the beach until today, and they wanted to know what conditions were like farther inland. Were there any communities who might take them in? Were we all really starving to death down here? Because they sure as hell were starving where the government was taking them."

Once more there was a solemn silence.

"They were off the USS *Ronald Reagan*, one of the two carriers that are being used to transport refugees from Los Angeles to the north. They've made two trips, one to somewhere in Puget Sound—they weren't very clear on just where, but it was an island—and the other to Alameda. Alameda is an island in San Francisco Bay with only half a dozen ways on and off. At the east end of the island is the old Alameda Naval Air Station. That's where they took the refugees. 'Dumped' them, according to my sailor friends.

"I have to say that these guys looked haunted. They said it was pretty bad here, on the beach in Santa Monica, but it was just as bad and maybe worse at Alameda and Puget Sound. They never got ashore in those places, but they heard stories from sailors who had, and they were horrific. There was cholera, not enough clean drinking water, not much medical care, and a severe shortage of food. Obviously no food is being brought in here to Los Angeles, but it's apparently not a whole lot better in the rest of the country."

"Why would the government move people from here to a place where things are worse?" Emily wanted to know.

"I wondered that, too. The sailors just laughed when I asked them. One of them said 'Orders is orders.' My guess is that an order came down to *do* something about the disaster in Los Angeles, and the only thing anyone could think of was to move the people somewhere else. Since shipping food and water down here for hundreds of thousands, maybe millions of people was not an option—you can't ship what you don't have—getting people out of the disaster area seemed like the next best thing. The orders came down, and the captain is determined to carry them out, whether they make sense or not. Whether or not they're doing any good or just moving the problem around. This whole evacuation thing strikes me as rearranging the deck chairs while the *Titanic* is going down. It's the military mind, I guess. I don't know much about it."

"I do, and I understand it perfectly," said Marian. She was sitting on the ground with Gordon, who had his arm draped over her shoulder. She was small, compact, but had a fierceness about her that made it easy for Dave to see her as a soldier.

"I don't know what sort of command structure still exists," she went on. "I'd expect the military to be in better shape than civilian governments, they run disaster scenarios all the time, and I'll bet they had a fuel reserve better than civilians have access to. But their conventional fuel is probably running out, which leaves them with just the power to run their nuclear ships. Those babies can go for twenty years without refueling. Anyway, bottom line, I agree with Teddy. Orders came down; orders will be carried out. Maybe they're even doing some good. Those sailors didn't see everything."

"You're right, and even their shipmates who went ashore didn't see everything. But most of it sounded plausible. They said the people who live in the Bay Area are not happy with this relocation. The navy is keeping them penned up on Alameda, but they say the locals aren't taking any chances, they dynamited the bridges and the tunnel. They're patrolling the mainland shore, and they're shooting to kill. They have enough problems as it is, just as everybody else in the country does, and they're terrified of these people. Our friends and neighbors, people from down south. Hungry and desperate people, thousands of them."

"We might get that reaction anywhere *we* go, too," Lisa said.

"We could. But . . . well, I hope the people wherever we end up can see us as an asset. We have food. We have vehicles that run. We have a wood chipper. We have you, Lisa, an M.D. We have bicycles. We even have a horse."

"All things people could take away from us."

"My hope," Bob said, "is solely that we be allowed to become a part of a community. I would be prepared to donate everything we've got to a communal pool of resources, share and share alike, privation as well as wealth." He looked at Dave, who looked at Karen. She nodded.

"We have no problem with that."

Bob looked slowly from Lisa to Mark and Rachel, then to Marian and Gordon, then to his wife. Each in turn gave some form of silent assent. So the broad goal was agreed to by acclamation.

"I don't think at this point there's any need for a show of hands," he said. "My sense of the meeting is that no one is supporting the option of going to Santa Monica and getting on the boat, if any of you ever did. If I'm wrong, speak up now, tell us your arguments, and we will throw it open to discussion."

"No way," Mark said.

"I didn't like them, even before Teddy's story," said Lisa.

There were other murmurs and headshakes, and no opposing opinion was expressed. Bob looked at his watch.

"All right. It's almost ten. If we see the sun at all today, it's probably going to be when it sets. There is still a lot to do. Marian, you've been doing such a good job of organizing things, I'm going to leave that in your hands. You have that list we made of things that still need to be done?"

"I have it. People pretty much know what they need to do, but I'll keep track of progress and pitch in when I can."

"Me and Addison and Dave are available for anything you need done," Karen said.

"That's right. What Mom said."

"Okay, family. This is going to be like a wagon train, you know. Anything we leave behind you'll never see again. Anything we desperately need and forget to take . . . well, you get the picture. So *think*! Do we need this? *Really* need it? Can we do without it? Marian has the lists we've made up, she'll check things off as we load up. If you think of something that isn't on the list, bring it to this table and we'll talk it over. Now, those of you who have assignments, get to them. Those who don't, see Marian. She'll have some work for you to do, I guarantee it."

CHAPTER TWENTY-FOUR

As the work proceeded through the late morning and early afternoon everyone kept one eye on the fire. Rest breaks were usually spent standing or sitting on the edge of the golf course, looking east.

Solomon, Rachel and Mark's Down Syndrome nine-year-old, was set the task of monitoring the weather vane and anemometer, which had been knocked over in the quake but was undamaged enough that it could be remounted on a pole over the workshop. He sat at a table facing the fire with a clock and called out the wind speed and direction every fifteen minutes. He seemed happy in this work, was totally devoted to it, to the point that he had to be coaxed into taking his afternoon nap. Every time he shouted, the people within earshot would shout back, "Good job, Solomon!"

They could see that the fire was spreading south and east, having missed Holmby Hills by no more than a mile and a half. Soon the entire eastern horizon was billowing thick black smoke. It was too far away for them to see any actual flames.

Somewhere around noon the wind veered. It became a brisk breeze from the ocean, bringing the temperature down fifteen degrees to a more tolerable eighty-two. The wind gusted to twenty-five miles per hour, which picked up the soot and ashes that had covered all the land to the west, and blew it in their faces. Everyone tied wet handkerchiefs over nose and mouth, but they couldn't keep the foul, gritty stuff out of their eyes.

The westerly winds blew the smoke that had been hovering over them toward the east. The sun came out over a landscape that had not burned, but nonetheless looked blasted, hellish, with the ashes covering everything. Eventually the air cleared and the almost unimaginable extent of the fire could be seen. There were still no visible flames—the fire front had to be ten or fifteen miles away from them by then, eating its way inexorably through the middle of the city—but the smoke rose up to the infinite sky, a boiling black wall that looked like some monstrous wave that was about to crest and crash over them. Like the famous "face of Satan" in the dust cloud raised by the fall of the World Trade Center, you could imagine all sorts of images in that black wall if you were imaginative and superstitious . . . and Dave thought that in the face of such a thing, we were all superstitious. He had seen a total eclipse once, and had experienced some of that feeling, had understood why the ancients had danced frantically and raised a great racket to scare away the dragon that was eating the sun.

Dave's job was to help Mark in the workshop. He didn't know how he had been elected to the post, but he didn't mind. He figured it would be good to get a better idea of how everything worked. The job didn't require a lot of brains, so he had plenty of time to think. He had an idea, so when they took a break he sought out Bob.

"I presume we won't be leaving tonight?" he asked.

"I would certainly be against it. But we'll talk about it this evening, if we get the needed work done. See what people think."

"And it's pretty certain that we'll be heading south. Toward San Diego."

"I don't think that's been established yet."

"No, but I don't have much faith in the I-15 route north. In fact, I don't think we could get to Oregon, not anymore."

"Maybe just Northern California?"

"Possible, I guess. Anyway, either direction, east and then north, or straight south, there's the fire to consider."

"Yes. I've been worried about that. I'm thinking we may have to wait another day. I don't want to mess with the fire."

"That's wise. But I think I can solve two of our problems at one stroke."

"You have a route around the fire?"

"No. I don't know where all it's burned. I think we should go through it."

Bob half smiled, as if he thought it was a joke. But then he saw that Dave was serious.

"Did you enjoy your last trip through fire that much?"

"Not so's you'd notice. I guess through the fire isn't what I meant. I think we should follow the fire. Head for the places where the fire has burned out. Even if we go east, we will be crossing a lot of the areas that the fire has burned out. And when you think about it, those areas should be the safest places in Los Angeles."

Bob smiled.

"I see what you mean."

"Anybody who *was* there is either dead, or they fled the area."

"But it will stay pretty hot for a while, won't it?"

"We'll have to see. If it's too hot, we stop. It will cool down, eventually." Dave looked at his watch. "I'm due back at work. I'll run all this by Mark. Okay?"

"By all means. What time is it?"

"Just after four."

"We'll all be meeting at eight. We'll talk it over."

The fire grew more distant. Every fifteen minutes Solomon called out the wind speed and direction, which stayed from the west and between ten and twenty miles per hour, but the wall of smoke scarcely seemed to diminish at all. It filled the eastern sky, mostly a roiling black. Every once in a while there were traces of other colors of smoke, yellow and red and green. The consensus among the people watching was that it was produced by burning chemicals in refineries or warehouses. Fairly often they heard distant explosions, and one around five o'clock that rattled the windows. There were many things that might blow up as the fire advanced: paint in cans, bottled gases, dynamite and other explosives, and who-knew-what sort of exotic chemicals. Dave worried about that, about entering the fire area where deadly gases might be lingering, but he supposed if the wind changed direction, they could be in danger from that even where they were working. They had a Geiger counter, but no way of detecting traces of airborne chemical poisons.

The work was essentially done around sundown, and everyone but Mark and Teddy gathered in the backyard to make final plans. Mark was still tinkering with his various constructions, and Dave suspected he could happily keep doing that for several more weeks if left to his own devices. He was the sort of person who had trouble meeting deadlines because nothing was ever quite at the level of perfection he was after. But Rachel had told Dave that when there was no more time, that he must now lay down his tools and accept that what he had was good enough, she could usually drag him away.

The sense of the meeting was that they would leave as soon as the sun came up in the morning. If there was no sunrise again, then they would leave as soon as it was light enough to see.

The proposal to follow the fire was a little more controversial.

"I'm afraid it will be too hot," someone said.

"Then we'll detour," Dave suggested. "I think we could at least go to the western edge of the fire area, which should be the coolest by now. If it's too hot, then we turn south and try to go around it."

"Or east," said Lisa.

"Or east," Dave agreed. "But I'm pretty sure we *can't* go east without crossing through the fire area."

"It would be like Moses and the Children of Israel," Sandra said. "Following a pillar of fire."

"It was a pillar of fire by night," her twin sister Olivia pointed out. At least Dave thought it was Olivia. "In the daytime they followed a pillar of smoke."

"So will we." Sandra pointed to the east, where an orange glow lit the horizon.

"I think Dave's suggestion is the right way to go," Bob said, with uncharacteristic bluntness. "We go to the edge of the burn area and see what's what. Make a decision there. Any objections?"

There were none.

Teddy had joined them, washed up and dressed in his cycling clothes. He had slept most of the day and eaten twice. Nobody begrudged it because they all knew he was expending more energy than any three of them put together, and providing the only completely reliable intelligence regarding their surroundings. And, of course, he was laying his life on the line every time he cycled away from them. Bob and Emily always knew that the sight of the bright yellow jersey on his back might be the last they ever saw of him, in life or in death.

That night he was wearing all-black clothing, and he had a proposal that didn't make anyone happy.

"I want to strongly suggest that you folks wait one more day."

That was greeted by a buzz of conversation, and a deep frown from his father. Teddy waited it out.

"I had always planned to be your advance scout," he finally said. "I could save you a lot of trouble by going ahead and seeing what the best routes were. But the little walkie-talkies we have are pretty short-range. If you're all on the move, and I get farther away from you than about half a mile, I might never find you again. The only way I can see to avoid that is that when I'm scouting, you have to stay where you are so I can be sure of getting back to you."

"Or you could not scout at all," Bob pointed out.

"Then I think you're throwing away a big advantage," Teddy said, rather forcefully.

There was a brief silence, then Marian spoke up.

"I have to agree with my little brother," she said. "Intelligence is critical in a situation like this. Teddy can range farther than any of us. We *need* to know what's ahead of us before we walk into it. After that, communication is critical, and we have to deal with the limitations we have. Our only means of talking at a distance are those pitiful little radios. When he goes farther than a few miles he has to know where he's coming back to. You can no longer say 'Meet me at such-and-such a place at noon.' If one party can't make it . . . you might never see him again."

She paused to let everyone think that over.

"I agree with Dad that after we get moving, Teddy should range ahead only a short distance, but this one time, he can save us literally days of travel if the route to the east is impossible. You can no longer drive to San Bernardino in a couple hours from here. It will take us at least a few days, I'm sure."

"And I can get there by midnight, I'm sure of it."

"What? Midnight?" That was Emily, clearly terrified at the prospect. "When would you leave?"

"In about ten minutes," Teddy said.

There was more consternation, most of it from Emily, with Bob stone-faced beside her. At last he held up his hand.

"I can see you're determined to do this, son. And I can certainly see the advantages to us all . . . if you come back."

"I have every time so far, Dad." He held up his hand, stopping his father. "No, sorry, I shouldn't kid about it. I know it's dangerous, but in some ways I don't think it's as dangerous as what we all will be doing, either tomorrow morning or the next day. If you insist on going tomorrow, I'll stay here and go with you, mostly because I believe if we split while we're both moving, there's a good chance we won't meet again."

"You really think so?"

"Yes. And think about this. You all will be traveling with a lot of stuff people will want to take from you. All I'll have is my bike and a sack lunch. I'm highly maneuverable and I'm good at hiding. You will be slow, with limited options as to where you can go, and there's no way you're going to hide a school bus on the road. Dad, we need for me to do this. Say the word, and I'll be off. And I promise to return by sundown tomorrow."

Teddy packed some high-energy food and a canteen, kissed and hugged everybody, and accepted their good wishes. He took off fifteen minutes later under the light of an almost full moon, and quickly vanished into the darkness.

The next day was bad for everyone, excruciating for Bob and Emily. Not much work got done for the simple reason that there wasn't anything significant left to do.

The sea breeze died down to nothing and no other wind came up. To the east the smoke could still be seen rising, but it no longer completely obscured the sky. Everyone hoped it was because it was dying out, but feared it was just growing more distant. With the calm, the brief respite of lower temperatures was over, and the thick, dirty air closed in around them and soon had everyone coughing. The thermometer never climbed into the hundred-degree range that they had been experiencing, but the higher humidity made it feel worse. Dave looked at it and marveled that, in the days before the fire, the air had been clearer than he had ever seen it. His family had been granted a brief glimpse of what Los Angeles air had been like around the time when the crazy nickelodeon people had arrived from the East Coast with their movie cameras. It was easy to see why people would have wanted to come there to live. The views from his backyard had been stunning, all the way to the blue Pacific.

Around noon Marian got the idea to organize what she called "fire drills." First she gathered all the weapons they had and made sure they were unloaded. In addition to the three shotguns and two revolvers the Marshalls had brought, the Winston family had an arsenal of their own. Bob had some rifles, a few shotguns, and two pistols. Lisa and her husband had been opposed to guns, but Mark had several, and Marian and Gordon had some serious firepower between them. Teddy had a Glock.

There was the problem of ammunition for the various firearms, with quite a bit available for some, very little for others. Marian had taken inventory early in the packing and made sure it would all be handy in an emergency. Now she passed around the weaponry, each to the one she felt best able to handle it.

Then she assigned duties and positions for several scenarios she had devised. There was some grumbling, if no outright opposition, at first, but as soon as they saw the chaos that resulted the first time she blew her whistle and everyone ran around like headless chickens, bumping into each other and failing to find their posts or their weapons, people buckled down and got serious about it.

She had them disperse over the area, and drilled them on returning to what she designated as their campground in a hurry. Most of them got into the bus, which she felt was the most defensible vehicle, and took up firing positions. After three or four repeats of that exercise she made some adjustments until she felt her forces were optimized.

Then she had them all board the various vehicles and, at a signal, get out and find cover to protect themselves from attacks from various directions.

"Remember, people, no plan survives first contact with the enemy. We've drilled in ideal situations here; what we encounter in the field will never be ideal. You'll have to *think*, and you'll have to *adapt*, and do so in a chaotic, frightening situation. You will probably be scared to death under fire. You'll have to deal with it."

She let them think that over for a while, and then she started all over on the drilling. By late afternoon she had them responding to every command in a reasonably coherent order. She pronounced them as ready as they would ever be.

* * *

As the afternoon wore on into evening, Bob grew pricklier than Dave had ever seen him. Usually the mildest, most fair, slowest to anger of men, he spent much of the day hobbling around on his cane, his eye patch making him look like a bad-tempered pirate, growling at anyone who got in his way. He found fault with the smallest of things, and actually shouted at some of his children.

As the sun neared the western horizon just about everybody but Solomon was worried, and even that young man clearly picked up that everyone else was on edge. He jumped at every noise, and twice he forgot to announce the time, temperature, and wind speed and direction, a job he was so proud of that he cried when he realized he had neglected it.

People spoke to each other warily, with one eye always on the driveway where Teddy would appear, when he came back. If he didn't get back by dark, there was no question in Dave's mind what the decision about leaving would be. It would take more than one day missing, and possibly more than one week, before the families would set out on the long trek without Teddy.

At one point Nigel and Mark got into a shouting match and for a terrible moment it looked like they were about to come to blows. Luckily, Gordon was nearby and stepped between them, speaking calmly and slowly. The two shook hands and apologized to each other, and even embraced. Dave saw that Mark was crying.

When the sun was almost at the horizon, the sound of Teddy's old-fashioned squeeze-bulb bicycle horn electrified everyone. A great cheer went up when he wheeled around the side of the house, waving his fist over his head as if he had just won the Tour de France. He was grinning, but Dave saw that his right leg from the knee down was streaked with blood.

"Just a fall," he shouted as he got off his bike, wincing as he put his weight on the injured leg. "Not more than a mile from here. Stupid rookie mistake, too. Looking up at some wild parakeets in a palm tree. I need some *ice water*! But I'll take just the water."

He sat down on the aluminum chair Elyse brought over for him, and gingerly poked at the bad scrape on his knee.

"Looks worse than it is," he said, as Lisa started to wash the blood away. He took a bottle of Costco water from Gordon, twisted off the top, and chugged about half of it. Solomon came up lugging a bucket, which Teddy thanked him for and then splashed over his head, which caused Solomon to laugh wildly. Teddy poured the rest of the bucket over the child's head, which made him laugh even more.

"I was looking up at the parakeets, listening to them chatter, and the next thing I knew I was skidding along the road, first on my knee, then on my shoulder." He twisted a little and showed everyone where his jersey was ripped, with another scrape there, not nearly as bad as the knee. "How about it, Sis? Will I ever walk again?"

"I'll tell you later. I probably won't have to amputate. Your head, that is."

"That's a relief. I think I pulled a hamstring, too. Damn good luck it was so close to home. That would have really slowed me down. Made me late."

Dave noticed Bob off to one side, grinning broadly and wiping away a tear. His bad mood was forgotten.

They brought Teddy food and more drink. It was almost dark before Mark finally lost patience and demanded he report what he'd seen.

"I can summarize it in three words," Teddy said. "We're going south."

"I had already been as far east as Pomona," Teddy started out. "I was able to retrace the route easily in the dark. I saw no one. I saw very few lights. It wasn't too hard to cross the trail of the fire. It burned toward the south a little west of Echo Park. That's still intact. It didn't reach downtown. After that, it was just quake damage. I suppose when we start out we'll find out just how far south it burned."

"That's good news," Mark said. "About crossing the fire zone. How hot was it?"

"Pretty damn hot. There were places where there was sticky asphalt, and some places where it must have burned away completely and there was just hot concrete that was beneath it. But it didn't hurt my tires. I didn't like walking on it, but you could touch the ground with your hand, it wouldn't burn you. You wouldn't want to hold it there long, though. I assume it's cooler by now.

"The worst thing was the air. A hundred different stinks, none of them pleasant. It felt like a sauna. I sweated a lot, and I drank a lot. I used up the gallon of water I took. Lord, I don't think I've ever been that thirsty. Not even dirty water anywhere on the ground, not that I would have drunk it."

From his previous trip, Teddy had known that the quake damage to the 10 freeway had been a bit less severe the farther west he went, though it was still substantial, with many freeway overpasses fallen onto the roadway.

He had started seeing signs of life around Covina, a little west of Pomona, getting near the San Bernardino County line. Every few miles there were checkpoints, manned around the clock. Usually they consisted of a row of cars or trucks, sometimes city buses across the highway, or they had been set up behind piles of concrete that were the remains of overpasses. They all had fifty-five-gallon drums with fires at night, burning scrap lumber. None of them gave him much trouble, just asked him a few questions and let him pass through. They weren't worried about lone men on bicycles. Like the associations in the Hollywood Hills, they were there to prevent the passage of outlaw gangs. They also intended to prevent any mass exodus into their communities, and told him they had already turned back large numbers of refugees.

"I got the impression that the people they turned back were arriving with nothing but the clothes on their backs. Starving, many of them. I don't know how they'd react to a group like us, with vehicles and all our other resources. Possibly if we could convince them of our usefulness, we would be allowed through."

"But we don't want to settle in east county," Rachel said.

"You misunderstand me. I don't think they'd want us. I'm not sure if they would even allow us to pass through. Maybe, maybe not. These are hard people now, Rachel. I feel sure that, at first, it was tough for them to turn away women and children who were in bad shape. But as time goes by, it gets easier. I didn't see a lot of sympathy in their faces. They may be sick about it, but they're doing it every day, turning away people. They're doing what they think they have to do, protecting what they have."

All the checkpoints were slowing him down, so Teddy decided to try farther north. Up there just below the foothills of the San Gabriel Mountains was the I-210, aptly named the Foothill Freeway. It joined the I-15, the route north to the Mojave Desert and Las Vegas. Teddy hoped there might be fewer roadblocks up there.

"No such luck. As soon as I headed north I ran into National Guard troops. They were allowing no one through. They were guarding the water. There's some sort of lake in the park by the freeway."

"That's Puddingstone Reservoir," Rachel said. "There's a water park up there, Raging Waters. We used to take the kids there."

"Raging Waters!" Solomon said, with excitement in his eyes.

"Probably not raging at the moment," Teddy said, ruffling Solomon's hair.

"We had the same problem a while ago, when me and Addison went exploring," Dave said. "There were troops around the Hollywood Reservoir."

"Makes sense, I guess, to guard the water supply. God knows Los Angeles doesn't have enough of it. Anyway, I tried half a dozen ways to get around it, but it was no go. They've blockaded a large area around the lake. So I kept heading west on the 10."

Progress was slow, and by noon he had made it only as far as Rancho Cucamonga, where he was finally able to head northeast on the 15. At first he was optimistic, as most of the bridges were intact, though there were many cracks. And soon he was on the fifteen-mile climb up the Ontario and Barstow Freeways.

"I was going along pretty good there for a while. I made it to the junction with the I-215, and it looked passable for a school bus. I went another three miles, to the first big turn in the freeway. And that's where I stopped. This time I saw it with my own eyes. A landslide has completely covered the freeway. I made my way around it, and when the next curve began, back to the west, you can see for several miles there. I counted two more landslides. Nobody was working on them. But not far from me, to the west of the freeway, there were people working to clear some slides over the railroad. There were men laying new track. I went over and talked to them. They claimed to be working for some government program, the state of California. They were being paid in food. They weren't interested in money.

"They said their boss told them that clearing the rails is a priority. Nobody had any plans to reopen the freeway. Trains can haul a whole lot more per ton of wood or coal burned. Or so they told me."

"They're right," Mark said. He looked like he was about to explain the differences in energy use, but Bob waved him to silence. Teddy looked at his father.

"I really don't have much more to say, Dad. My trip back was uneventful until I fell off the bike. I confirmed two things. We can't get out of here by going east, unless we go all the way to Palm Springs. And the ground the fire has burned over is passable, though it's pretty hot. It will get cooler with every day that passes."

There was a long silence. It seemed clear to Dave that their course had now been set, and that it would be to the south. At last Marian spoke.

"The only question I have," she said, "is will we have enough wood to fuel our vehicles until we get out of the burned area. I'm assuming there won't be very much wood left after the fire has passed. Mark?"

Their chief engineer and tech guy pondered it.

"Of course it depends on how far we follow it, but I'm pretty sure we'll make it. I'm assuming that we could always duck out of the burn to one side or the other and find trees or collapsed houses there. Old wood from houses is ideal, actually, because it's seasoned and very dry. We won't even have to dry it out by putting it into the jacket around the wood burners."

"What jacket are you talking about?" Lisa asked.

"The wood burners are two cylinders. The burner sits inside a larger cylinder. While the wood is burning, you shovel wet wood chips into the larger one and the heat bakes out the water. Then you feed those dry chips into the burner. I think we'll be okay."

"So speaks our science guy," Bob said, solemnly. "And to my mind all other alternatives have been closed off to us. We could skirt the edges of the fire, I suppose, but our route is south. Does anyone object, or have a new idea?"

No one spoke up.

"All right. Follow the fire? Or skirt the fire?"

"Follow," Teddy said promptly.

"Follow," Mark agreed.

"I agree," Dave said. "Follow."

"Follow," Karen said.

"Follow!" Solomon shouted, to cheers and laughter.

There were no dissenting voices raised.

"Then south it is, behind the fire. It will be like you said, Olivia, we'll be like the Children of Israel. A pillar of smoke by day, and a pillar of fire by night. Amen."

"And you're Moses," Lisa said, seriously.

"Ohmigod no. I have no idea where the promised land lies."

"You'll find it for us," Addison told him. "With my dad to help out."

"Just don't expect me to part the Red Sea for you idiots. Or even the Puddingstone Reservoir."

The level of excitement was high as the darkness closed in around them. By the light of two Coleman lanterns the two families moved about, many of them remembering last-minute chores. Even the lanterns were turned off two hours after sunset, to conserve fuel. By then everyone was supposed to be in bed, with flashlights beside them for emergencies. They were not to be used frivolously, for though they had a good stock of batteries, there was no telling how long the supply would have to last. They had to be conserved.

Conserve, conserve, conserve.

Everyone had spoken that word before the disaster, in terms of recycling, land use, preservation of resources, carbon footprint, and climate change, but Dave had come to realize none of them had had any idea what real conservation meant. They had lived in a throwaway society, where they consumed things like razor blades that could not be resharpened, plastic or paper shopping bags instead of net or canvas bags, ballpoint pens that could not be refilled . . . all the garbage of plenty. No one repaired small appliances anymore; if your toaster broke, you threw it away and got another.

Now they had finite supplies of so many things they used to take for granted. Batteries were a good example. No one had any idea when new ones would be available. But even more basic, how about candles? Both Dave and Bob had laid in a supply, but it was now obvious that it wasn't nearly enough. Candles could be made at home . . . but how? You could probably find string for the wicks, but what about the wax? How did you make wax? People used candles before they were made of wax. What did they use? Tallow? Suet? Dave didn't know, and could only hope someone in the families did, because they would eventually run out.

And soap. What did pioneer families use for soap? Dave had inventoried what they had, and knew that even if used sparingly it wouldn't last more than a few months. What then? When would stores be restocking the shelves with Irish Spring? With the transportation system in the country unable to deliver even enough food to feed the population, how long would it be before any company could have the basic ingredients shipped to their factory, much less ship the finished product to stores?

And toothpaste. The Marshalls were down to their last two tubes, and Dave didn't know how much the Winstons had. What did you use when you ran out of toothpaste? Baking soda? And where did you get that?

Those thoughts and many others swirled through his mind as he took the first watch of the night. He sat at an upstairs window, the cracked walls of a ruined room around him, and gazed out at a night where the only light came from the moon.

Just before his shift ended, two motorcycles came down the street, Harleys from the deep-throated burbling roar of their engines. He racked a round into his shotgun and got off his chair. He looked out the window. All he could see were two headlights, coming his way from the south. They paused once, a few houses down, then moved on. They paused again directly in front of the Winston house.

Two people prowling around at night, with the gasoline to run a big motorcycle, could only be one of two things: bad guys, or cops. He followed the lead headlight with his shotgun barrel.

The driver gunned his engine once and Dave thought he heard voices, though it was hard to tell over the sound of the engines. Their taillights appeared, flashed bright red for a moment, and they turned off on a side street. He listened until the sound faded away.

He hoped they were gone, but he wasn't going to count on it. If he were going to break into a house, he wouldn't pull up on a Harley and walk right in. He would park his hog and come back quietly under cover of darkness. Could they have been scouting the Winston house? Might they know which houses on this street were inhabited, and thus likely to have things worth stealing? He thought it was unlikely—he pictured guys like that as smash-and-grab types, acting on impulse rather than a grand plan carried out over several nights—but he knew he might be stereotyping. Not all brutes were stupid.

He heard Gordon calling out softly as he approached the room. This was standard procedure when relieving the guard on duty, since it wasn't wise to startle an armed person who might be asleep. Gordon knocked on the doorjamb and stuck his head around, all but invisible in the darkness.

"Come on in. I'm too nervous to fall asleep on duty."

"I heard motorcycles. I'm about fifteen minutes early, but you might as well knock off for the night."

He described the drive-by, showed Gordon where the bikers had gone, and shared his thoughts that it might be a ruse. Gordon agreed, and assured Dave that he would be alert for any possibility. He patted Dave on the shoulder and took his seat at the window, scanning the empty street.

Dave took his small flashlight out of his pocket and moved carefully down the hall and the stairs. There was a light in the dining room, and he looked in to see Lisa sitting on a chair at the long table, reading a book by candlelight. Jenna was illuminated by the flickering light, on her back, still unconscious. She looked all too much like a corpse, with a white sheet tucked up under her chin.

Looking at Lisa, Dave was struck by a pang of nostalgia. It had been a long time since he had read a book. All his life he had had one book going, which he would read in odd moments of leisure. Nothing heavy; he read mysteries for the sheer escapism, most of the time, though he enjoyed a good biography or the occasional historical work. Now the world of fiction seemed so frivolous. The stories all concerned a world that no longer existed. On every page he would encounter people talking on cell phones, texting each other, going to Web sites. People in the books would be hopping into cars and driving at will, anywhere and everywhere. They got on airplanes. They called the police. They went to movies. They had televisions, and backyard cookouts, and cocktail parties. They worried about elections, and the crisis in the Middle East. They robbed banks and made big corporate deals and chased each other in exotic locales for the secret papers. None of that had meaning anymore. It was impossible to care about it.

"You'll strain your eyes," he said.

"I'm used to it by now."

"How is she doing?"

"Her vital signs are unchanged. Blood pressure is low. Heartbeat is steady. She's running a fever, 102 last time I took it. If I had her in a hospital, I'd say her chances were excellent."

"How about her chances here?"

"Fifty-fifty. The thing that worries me the most is infection. We're watching the wound. There's still a chance she could lose the leg. We have to wait and see."

"Let me guess. She shouldn't be moved."

"I agree with your diagnosis, Dr. Dave. Bouncing around in that bus is not going to do her any good."

"What are her chances, when we move?"

"Less than fifty-fifty."

That was all she would say, but it seemed clear enough. They were going to be putting her in grave danger, but they had no other option.

He left Lisa and Jenna and found his way to the bedroom he was sharing with Karen. It was too hot for anything but a sheet. Karen was lying beneath one, sitting up with a pillow behind her. She squinted when his flashlight beam touched her, and he moved it away. He started to remove his shirt. She lifted the sheet and held it away from her body. She was naked.

"I'm sweaty, I haven't washed my hair, and I know I must smell like a pigsty," she said. "Plus, I haven't shaved my legs. But would you hold me for a while?"

"I'd be happy to, if you promise not to give me whisker burns with your legs," he said, stripping off his pants and rolling over toward her. "As for the smell, I doubt I'll be able to detect it over my own reek."

They embraced, and kissed, and then just held each other for a while. But soon she began breathing a little harder and her hand crept down his belly and tugged insistently. She was ready for him when he got on top of her and entered her.

They made slow, lazy love for a timeless stretch, and all the rest of the world seemed to go away. They were both slick with sweat and gritty with soot, and neither of them minded it at all. To Dave, the female scent of her was better than the finest perfume, the feel of her under his roaming hands was intoxicating. He licked her and massaged her and thrust into her, and she wrapped her legs around him and pressed her heels into the backs of his thighs and devoured his tongue and nibbled his neck and shoulders.

They paused near the end, and he told her he was very close.

"I ran out of pills a few weeks ago, you know. I could get pregnant."

"Would that be a bad thing?"

"Part of me doesn't want to bring a child into this awful new world."

"I know what you mean. But life goes on, doesn't it?"

She gazed up into his eyes, and for her answer she dug her heels into his buttocks and ground herself against him.

"Go for it," she said.

He came after several thrusts, almost crying out before remembering there were people all around him, and the walls were cracked. He knew she was close, too, so he kept on until she arched her back powerfully enough to raise herself off the bed, and bit down on her finger to stifle her own cry. She shuddered, over and over, and he was filled with love for her.

He collapsed on top of her and she held him tightly. He softened, feeling a sense of loss, not wanting to leave her, but it was inevitable. He kissed her sweaty brow and rolled over. They lay side by side, thighs pressing together, breathing hard. Dave became aware of a sound coming from down the hall.

"Is that someone crying?" he asked.

"It sounds like . . . Is it Rachel?"

"Could be."

"I think it is. And I don't think she's crying. At least, not the boo-hoo sort of crying. So she's the kind of girl who can't do it quietly." And she started to laugh. Dave put his hand over her mouth, but soon he was laughing, too, both of them trying to smother it as best they could. Then they lay together and listened to the sounds of lovemaking coming from the next room. As they listened she took his penis in her hand and gently squeezed and stroked it.

"You're an optimist," he said, grinning.

"Can't blame a girl for trying."

"I'm not the young man I was, you know."

"Still, this may be our last time alone for some time to come."

"Karen, I really doubt that I can."

But he was wrong.

Since the Escalade had the most forgiving suspension of their three vehicles, it was determined that Jenna would be loaded into the back of it. She was small enough that one of the rear seats could be folded down and her stretcher placed on it, with her head behind Karen's seat. The other rear seat was left in place for Addison to sit and monitor her. Lisa had taught her how to use the blood-pressure cuff, and she also took her temperature and examined the wound dressing, looking for new bleeding.

The scooters were still slung on each side of the Escalade, but they were now in better slings, tied on by Marian, who knew how to tie knots that could be easily released in an emergency. Their bicycles were still tied to the roof, and the space in back not occupied by Jenna or Addison was filled with water jugs, blankets, and mattresses made from bedsheets sewn together and stuffed with clothing they didn't plan to use.

The old U-Haul truck was more than adequate to carry most of their supplies. Mark had made the box bullet-resistant by welding sheets of steel to the sides and rear to a height of five feet, with special armoring around the cans of gasoline. He would be driving it, with his wife, Rachel, literally riding shotgun.

The top of the school bus bulged with a big blue tarp covering all the chipped wood that could fit under it. At the front of the platform was the stoker's position. When enough chips had burned, his or her job was to lift the top of the burner with a chain and shovel dry chips into the burner and wet chips into the jacket around the burner, giving the uncured fuel time to be dried out by the heat. After the chips were dried a hatch at the bottom was opened and the burner was shaken to make the chips drop into a bucket, which was then lifted by a hoist back up to the roof. It was a cumbersome process, and hard, sweaty work. All of them except Solomon and four-year-old Taylor had tried their hand at it, and they would take turns.

Fueling the U-Haul entailed driving it up to the side of the school bus with the burner close enough for a stoker on the bus roof to shovel chips into it.

There would be eleven people riding in the school bus: Bob and Emily; Lisa and her children, Elyse and Nigel; Mark and Rachel's children, Sandra, Olivia, and Solomon; and Marian and Gordon and their son Taylor. Teddy would do what he did best, ranging ahead on his bike and reporting back on conditions ahead. Choosing the route would be largely up to him.

As the first light of dawn showed to the east, the caravan was already taking shape and powering up. Mark was trying to be everywhere at once as he got the fires going in his burners and scrambled to make ever finer adjustments. Dave and Bob watched him with some amusement.

"At some point we'll have to tell him that's good enough," Bob said. "Nothing is ever quite up to Mark's specs."

"He gets the job done."

"He sure does. If only he could recognize when it's done well enough."

But Mark surprised them by announcing he was ready to start. Bob looked at him, nodded, and called his clan together.

"I'm not going to make a speech, and I don't offer prayers, but I think it's time for a moment of reflection. Just a moment. We've had a fine life in this old place. I just want to say that raising you all here has meant everything to me."

"I will offer a prayer," Emily said. "It's for those of us who couldn't be here. For Peter and his wife and children in England, and for George in New York, and for Teddy's partner Manuel, wherever he may be. May they all be safe and healthy."

"And for Roger and Dennis and their families, absent Posse members," Dave added, "wherever they may be."

"Amen," several of them said. Dave saw many tears, looked at Karen, and saw that she was crying, too.

"We never got to say good-bye to our place," she said. "And I know we'll never see it again."

Dave put his arm around her. "Let's just wish for new beginnings," he said.

"To new beginnings."

He hugged her close, and held out his hand for Addison, who joined them.

"Ranger okay?" he asked.

"He seems eager to go. He gave me no trouble at all about getting into the trailer."

"Good." He paused. "You know there's a chance we'll have to abandon him somewhere along the way?"

"Yes. I know." She tried to look brave, but he could see it was hard for her. They didn't have a lot of hay and oats. If forage couldn't be found, Ranger would have to be let loose, to survive or die on his own. The fact was that they might have left him behind to graze on the remains of the country club, except that Bob, and later Mark, had strongly argued that they needed the horse as a possible argument toward admittance to whatever community they might encounter that might otherwise be reluctant to admit outsiders. Horses were bound to be valuable in the new order of things, as transportation or to pull a plow.

The meeting broke up, and they all went to their vehicles. Bob remained outside for a moment, looking up at the faces of the drivers and passengers in the three vehicles parked side by side, and the faces of the others looking out the school-bus windows or down from the platform on top.

"I feel like I ought to say something dramatic, like 'Wagons, ho!'"

Gordon, standing on the steps of the school bus, said, "How about 'Ladies and gentlemen, start your engines.'"

"That'll do. Start 'em up, folks."

Dave turned the key in the Escalade's ignition. Next to him Mark engaged the starter on the U-Haul, and it ground to life with a burst of black smoke from the tailpipe. On the other side Marian cranked up the school bus, which coughed, stuttered . . . and died. She tried it again, and nothing happened.

Mark jumped down from the U-Haul cab and hurried over to the bus. He stood on the bumper and reached into the hoodless engine compartment. He had several tools on his belt, and he selected one and made some adjustment.

This time the engine turned over for about ten seconds, and then caught. It belched out an even bigger cloud of smoke, including some that went right into Mark's face. Coughing, sooty-faced, Mark was still grinning. He pumped his fist in the air and ran back to his truck.

The order of travel had been the subject of some debate. There were good arguments for placing any of the three vehicles in the lead, and good arguments against any of them. The lead vehicle was likely to be the first one to run into trouble, and many of the Winstons were in favor of letting the bus lead, because it was the most heavily armored and had the most firepower. But Dave and others argued that because all the children except Addison would be riding in it, the bus should be in the safest position, which most agreed was the middle.

Mark wanted to take the lead in the U-Haul, but the danger of having it hijacked with all their provisions seemed greater if it was in the lead.

In the end, no one was really sure what the best order would be, and so Dave had argued hard for taking the lead in the Escalade. He pointed out that, even with the trailer, the SUV was the smallest vehicle they had, and the easiest to turn around. They all agreed that running was always the better option than fighting, something they would do only if forced into it. Turning around rapidly would put the trailer between Dave and his family and incoming fire from a threat ahead of them.

They would try that arrangement, with Dave in the lead and the bus following him, and at the end of the day talk it over again and maybe try out a new arrangement.

Dave recalled all that, knew his arguments made sense, and believed deeply that everyone on the trip would have to shoulder equal responsibility and equal exposure to danger. But it was not quite the same to volunteer to take point and to sit in his car with his family around him and have to actually do it.

He had debated having Addison ride on the bus, but in the end he and Karen had decided to stick to their agreement and not split up the family. And he discovered that he felt a lot better with her behind him in the car than he would have if she were on the bus. She had a shotgun in her lap, as did her mother.

Karen and Dave both had loaded pistols handy. And he was as ready as he would ever be.

He started the engine, put it in gear, and slowly pulled down the Winstons' driveway just as the first rays of the sun broke over the eastern horizon, now clear of smoke. He drove into the street at about five miles per hour and saw in his improvised side mirror that the school bus had fallen in behind him.

At last, the caravan was moving. If only they knew their destination.

CHAPTER TWENTY-FIVE

They made it easily to the edge of the burn area. Teddy knew all the streets in the area, which were passable and which were blocked. He stayed out ahead about a hundred yards, sometimes turning around to ride beside Dave for a moment and update him on which direction they would be taking, then pressing on ahead.

The fire seemed to have died out around San Vicente Boulevard. Here was where the wind had shifted. To the west of San Vicente they encountered mostly earthquake damage. To the east, almost everything had burned.

There were exceptions. The old Hollywood Farmer's Market was undamaged. But just beyond it, the newer, upscale shopping center, The Grove, had been devastated. The diamond-patterned streets of the old Park La Brea housing had not burned. They moved down Third, around the bulging hill where the tar pits had been and the art museum had stood. It was just beyond this, at La Brea Avenue, that they reached the area of total devastation. Everything to the north, south, and east had been completely involved, every last building and every single tree. It was a hellish landscape, all black and shades of gray.

They paused here to test the ground. They would not stop long. The problem with a wood-burning engine was that it couldn't be shut off. The fire would continue to burn, wasting precious fuel, until it went out. Then it had to be reignited. Because of that they had agreed that all stops except for emergencies would be as brief as possible.

People tested the ground with their feet. It was bare concrete, except at the edges where what looked like melted asphalt had run toward the gutters. Marian poked at the stuff with a stick, got some of the goo on the end of it, and gingerly touched it.

"Warm, but it won't burn you," she announced.

They approached some of the brick walls, which were the only things standing. Even some of those had collapsed. They could feel heat still radiating from the bricks, and from the concrete, but nothing seemed too hot to touch.

"Looks like it's okay to go on," Teddy said.

"I agree," said Bob. "So let's do it."

Everyone hurried back to their vehicles and Dave started his engine. He pulled forward and entered the ruined city.

It made the earthquake damage seem minor. As far as they could see, nothing was intact. Whole blocks were nothing but piles of ashes. Sometimes they could see metal objects in the ash heaps, which were probably the twisted and half-melted remains of major appliances. Of the brick buildings only the shells remained. It reminded Dave of pictures of German cities after firebombing, except that few of these buildings were that tall, most only one or two stories.

It was a wasteland that stretched as far as the eye could see. Nothing was familiar. The iron posts holding the street signs had been twisted by the heat of the fire. They would soon have been lost except for something Dave thought was ironic. The network of GPS satellites in orbit was still functioning, and could pinpoint their location to within about ten yards. One was built into the Escalade, and there was a detachable unit they had installed in the bus. But it was surreal, looking at the bright network of streets on the small screen, with parks and landmarks, stores and gas stations neatly marked, and then to look up and see the reality.

Every now and then, through a caprice of the wind or some other unknown factor, they would pass a block or two that had not burned. There were mostly houses, and the paint had been scorched off them, the wood baked brown. Dave wondered if so much oxygen had been sucked from the surrounding air that they had been unable to ignite. The houses looked like they had been sitting in the desert, desiccating, for a thousand years.

Progress was very slow. Dave had thought he was moving slowly at five miles per hour, but he quickly saw that he would seldom be traveling any faster than that, and sometimes considerably slower. Teddy was clever at finding routes around the many obstacles in their path, but they had to take long detours, and sometimes stop completely to attach a chain to a tree so that the bus could pull it out of the way. Sometimes a block and tackle was needed.

By late afternoon they had only gone as far as Rosewood Cemetery at Venice and Normandie. And here was another quirk of the fire. The trees inside the fence were widely spaced. The fire seemed to have danced along the tops of the trees without ever getting down to the ground. The brown grass had not caught fire. Again, Dave figured it was something to do with lack of oxygen.

Mark decreed that they call a halt, which everyone was happy to do. It was hard work, just driving, or even sitting on the alert for trouble. The heat was almost unbearable. They were drinking water faster than they wanted to, but they had no choice. They could not risk dehydration.

The reason Mark stopped them was that he needed to replenish their supply of wood chips, and he needed to see how the chipper functioned in the field. As with so many other things they had brought along, the failure of the chipper would be disastrous, leaving them no hope of getting very far.

The gates were open. Dave pulled in, followed by the other vehicles. Addison was out quickly, lowering the tailgate of the trailer and bringing out her thirsty and hungry horse. They had brought a basin for Ranger to drink from. This worried Dave, since water was such a problem, but no one was showing any reluctance to fill it and let the animal drink his fill. He sincerely hoped that situation continued, and that they came across another source of water soon.

Mark, in charge of the engines and their fuel, was out and about immediately, trying to do everything at once. He handed out the chain saws and hurried around, picking the trees he felt were the best sizes for feeding into the wood chipper. Soon the silence was broken by the purr of the chain-saw motors and the louder screech of the chains cutting into wood. When the trees were down and being dismembered, a sort of bucket brigade was formed to carry lengths of wood to the chipper. Mark started it up and began feeding in the branches and smaller pieces while Marian and Gordon swung axes to split the larger pieces of trunk into smaller bits the chipper could handle. The chipper was very loud. All the sounds of activity were very strange to hear amid the stark, leafless trees with their burned tops, and the thousands and thousands of tombstones. Dave remembered that Hattie McDaniel, the first black American to win an Oscar, for her role in *Gone With the Wind*, had been buried here after she was refused interment at Hollywood Memorial Park. He wondered where she was.

It was hot, sweaty work, and they all had to take a break every half hour or so. When Dave took a break he joined Bob and followed Addison as she led Ranger from one promising patch of grass to the next one. She was determined to get as much free forage into him as she could before they moved on, which Mark said should be in about an hour.

Addison got ahead of him, and then he saw her stop. She turned around and came toward him, walking fast, leading the horse behind her. Her face was white. Dave hurried over to her.

"What's the matter, Addie?"

For a moment she couldn't get any words out. Tears began running down her cheeks.

"Don't . . . don't go over there, Daddy."

"Honey, what is it?"

"You shouldn't go over there."

"You go back to the group, Addison. We'll join you later." He gave her a gentle push, and she didn't resist. She was walking stiffly, like a robot.

Dave and Bob hurried in the other direction, toward a tall monument that was circled by a road. As soon as they reached the road they knew what had so horrified Addison. There were five shapes huddled together on the ground. Three were adults, the other two were children. Next to them was a dog.

"They don't look badly burned," Bob whispered.

He was right. Their clothes looked charred and browned in places, but their faces hadn't blackened. They had more of a reddish color. Dave smelled something, and realized it was cooked meat. He turned aside and vomited.

Bob didn't look good, but he managed to keep his food down.

"They were dead before they were exposed to the heat," Dave choked out. "That's why no blistering. They just started to . . . to cook a little, and the fire moved on."

"But what killed them?"

"No oxygen. They suffocated. Oh . . . my God." Dave had looked farther, and now he spotted dozens more corpses, possibly as many as a hundred, just from where he was standing. He saw that people had thought they might seek refuge here, in the open space. But the fire had stolen all their air. They had died in family groups or alone. Some were in the fetal position, some were stretched out on their backs.

"It doesn't look like they suffered too much," Bob said, hopefully.

"I think you just get short of breath, gasp for a while, and then sort of go to sleep. At least I hope so." Dave looked at the children again. "This is the most horrible thing I've ever seen."

"Please, let it remain so."

"Oh, Bob, what am I going to do about Addison?"

"All I know is to offer comfort and love."

They found Addison with her mother. They were embracing and rocking slowly back and forth. Others were watching, probably wondering what had happened to make her feel so terrible, but they all kept their distance. Karen looked up and frowned at Dave, as if she blamed him for it. Well, maybe he should have kept her closer. He shrugged, helplessly, and she relented.

"Everyone, please pause for a moment," Bob called out. The chain saws and the chipper fell silent. They gathered around.

"You have all stayed close to the vehicles. Addison went farther afield to find forage for her horse, and she has made a gruesome discovery. There are many dead people up in that direction. Dave and I saw about a hundred. I have no idea how many there might be elsewhere. People tried to ride out the fire here, and they seem to have been asphyxiated.

"Every instinct I have tells me we should give them a decent burial, but there are simply too many of them. It would take a bulldozer to dig a mass grave. We just don't have the time or the resources. I want to do something, and all I can think of is a moment of silence. Those of you who pray, please do. If you don't pray, please do whatever it is you do to honor the dead. Thank you all." He stopped speaking and bowed his head.

Dave saw Lisa get on her knees and put her hands together. Her daughter, Elyse, knelt beside her. Nigel remained standing, looking at the ground. Marian stood at attention, crying silently. Gordon crossed himself, and put his arm around her. Solomon looked confused, but got on his knees as well. He laced his fingers together and looked at his mother, who knelt beside him and embraced him. Mark looked uncomfortable, but knelt beside his wife and child.

"I must add," Bob said, after what he judged a suitable interval, "that Addison has just had a very bad emotional shock. Please, all of you, give her all the support you can. She needs us all now."

That brought a swift reaction. Everyone headed for Karen and Addison. Some of them were crying, and Addison began to sob loudly. He knew it was better if she got it out as quickly as she could. Once more he felt helpless, and knew there was nothing he could do about it. He didn't join the group. He would talk to her later.

Work had to resume quickly, and in another half hour they had taken on all the chipped wood they could. Ranger was loaded back into the trailer, presumably with a stomach that, if not full, was at least not as empty as it had been. The wood burners were stoked with new fuel, Dave started his engine and pulled out of the cemetery behind Teddy on his bike, and they headed south and east again.

They were able to get on the I-10 and follow it for a while, and they made good progress. But they soon came to a section that had formerly been elevated, and now was just a long pile of rubble. There was no place to get off, and they had to backtrack. Teddy swore that it had been possible to get as far as the 110 Harbor Freeway before the fire. They assumed that the heat had weakened the already damaged structures and they had fallen down because of it. In the end they had to go all the way back to Normandie before they could find an undamaged exit. Then it was down to Adams, and east again.

They had intended to get on the 110 from there, but they could see that the overpass a block to the south was down, blocking it. Teddy returned at that point and said that he had been to Exposition Park, and there were wide, unburned, open spaces there where it might be good to make camp. There was a hurried discussion and it was decided, though there were still some hours of daylight left, that they should stop for the night. Everyone agreed that they would need extra time to get the things done that were necessary before darkness fell, and they needed some leeway to find out just how long all those things would take. So they turned south on Figueroa.

The campus of the University of Southern California began at the corner of Jefferson Boulevard. The grounds were much more crowded than its crosstown rival, UCLA.

Everything had burned thoroughly, trees and buildings, and more than a few people. It was there that they saw their first burned corpses.

It looked to Dave like there had been a substantial population still residing on campus. It seemed that at least some of them had decided to try to weather the oncoming firestorm in the brick buildings rather than flee to the south.

The dead people they saw must have been the ones who had seen their folly too late, and tried to cross Exposition Boulevard, because there they lay, unrecognizable except for being vaguely shaped like human beings. It was a sight that firefighters must be familiar with. The corpses looked shrunken, lying on their sides, arms and legs drawn up into a not-quite-fetal position. All clothes were burned away, and the skin, too. What remained was blackened. It was impossible to tell age, race, or sex.

They saw five of these horrific remains on the street. How many might be on the campus itself was anybody's guess, and not one that anyone wanted to learn more about.

The destruction of the campus looked total. Yet across the street the fire seemed to have jumped along the treetops again, leaving the ground untouched. Teddy said the Natural History Museum farther to the west was a burned-out shell, but the Museum of Science and Industry on Figueroa was almost intact. An old airliner—Dave thought it was a DC-8—had been knocked off its supports and was nose down on the ground, but it was not burned.

When they came to the entrance to Exposition Park that led to the Memorial Coliseum they saw that the grassy area leading up to it was undamaged, so they pulled over there and parked. They formed the vehicles into a triangle and made the gaps between them as narrow as possible. They had not seen a living person all day, but they weren't going to start out being incautious.

Dinner that evening was Spam stew with canned vegetables, surprisingly good with the spices the cooks added to it. Or maybe it was just because he was ravenous, Dave thought.

There was debate as to whether or not they should have a fire. Some felt it was better just to burn enough wood to heat the food, that a larger fire might attract unwanted attention . . . which was any attention at all, whether from people seeking to do them harm or from possibly starving people who they could hardly refuse to serve with a bowl of Spam stew. A slight majority favored cutting some of the trees in the area and making a small fire to huddle around in the forbidding night. That notion carried the day.

Dave and Karen put up their tent with no trouble. Addison elected to sleep in the Escalade, where she could keep an eye on Jenna, who still had not regained consciousness, though at least her condition didn't seem any worse.

Teddy set off a little before sundown, and everyone assumed he would be ranging to the south, scouting their route. But he returned a few minutes later from the direction of the Coliseum, looking pale and sick. He beckoned to his father.

Dave watched the two talking, and saw that Mark was doing the same. He wondered if he should join them and find out what was going on, and when Mark started over there he followed. Bob was looking grim.

"Teddy says the Coliseum is full of bodies."

"By full . . ."

"Thousands, he says. Most of them on the field."

The Coliseum had been built in 1923, and had later hosted both the 1932 and the 1984 Olympics. It was a huge concrete bowl, and Dave could understand why people might have seen it as a refuge from the fire. What he couldn't understand was why they were all dead.

"Were they burned?"

"They didn't look like it." And suddenly he was crying with great, wracking sobs. Teddy had always seemed pretty stoic, but when the dam burst it let go with a torrent. Bob put his arms around his youngest son and hugged him tight. Dave turned away, not sure if his witness was welcome. The first thing he saw was most of the rest of the Winston family on their way toward Bob and Teddy.

"Teddy found something awful in the Coliseum," Bob told them.

"What?" Addison asked, fearfully.

"A lot of dead people" was all Teddy would say at first.

"I thought I understood how those people died in the cemetery," Dave said. "But this just seems like too big a space to me, I mean for all the oxygen to be sucked out. I can't see that it would have reached a killing heat in there, there's too much concrete around them, and it doesn't seem to have been scorched."

"What about chemicals?" Marian wanted to know.

"I hadn't thought of that," Dave said.

"Just beyond the Coliseum is the swim stadium. Wouldn't they have a lot of chlorine stored there?"

"I would think so. Do you think the fire burned around the pool?"

"I'm not going to go look," Teddy said.

"No, of course not," Bob agreed. "And if it wasn't chlorine from the pool, it could have been any number of things around here. Who really knows what's in all these thousands and thousands of warehouses?"

"It's mostly residential around here, but within a few miles there are plenty of industrial areas. The wind could have carried just about anything here."

"I think it's one of those things we're never going to know, unless somebody from the government comes in and does an investigation."

"That could happen. Not soon, I guess, but somebody will come back here, someday. Don't you think?"

It was Teddy asking, but no one wanted to venture an answer.

When it got dark everyone gathered around the fire in the oil drum. There was a tribal feeling to it, and Dave could easily imagine the comfort such a fire must have provided to the humans who first tamed it. Sometimes emotional comfort had to take precedence over tactical considerations. Marian had been the one who argued longest for a dark camp, a camp that wasn't as easy to spot. But once it was dark and the fire was going, she settled easily in with the rest of them and seemed to enjoy it.

She had, however, changed the arrangements for standing guard. Now there were to be two people posted at all times concealed somewhere out there in the dark, watching and listening for anyone approaching. The people standing guard would be able to send any of half a dozen coded clicks on a walkie-talkie to people inside, without revealing their position. Marian pointed out that, in the event of an attack, it would be useful to have someone behind the attackers to give them something extra to think about. She had advised all the guards that, if they had to shoot, shoot the attackers in the back if possible. There were no gentlemanly rules in combat.

Dave was allowed to choose his own position when it came time for him to stand a watch, the only conditions being that it needed to provide some concealment, be east of and at least fifty yards from the encampment. He selected a tree and shinnied up into one of the lower branches. Now all he had to do was stay quiet, and not fall asleep.

Which was why he had chosen to be in the tree. If he fell asleep, he would fall out. He felt it must have worked, because though he had been very tired, he was still awake and alert when he was relieved after two hours without incident.

The night passed quietly.

According to the GPS, the fastest route from the Winston house to the Coliseum was a bit over eleven miles. According to Dave's odometer, they had driven nineteen miles, and they had done it in about twelve hours, including the fueling stop at the cemetery. That was a bit over one and a half miles per hour. From where they were, it was about 135 miles to San Diego. That was traveling by freeway, with no obstructions. If eleven miles turned out to be more like nineteen, it would be more like 230 miles they had to cover. At eleven miles per day, that was twenty-one days on the road.

Three weeks.

He showed his figures to Bob and Mark, and they agreed that was a good rough estimate. Some days they might do better, some days worse. There was simply no way to predict what they might encounter, including obstacles so imposing that they might have to retrace their route for many miles.

The trip could take more than a month.

Dave had pitched their tent close to the Escalade and helped Addison make a comfortable bed in the back of the vehicle. Jenna had still not regained consciousness, but Lisa said her vital signs were promising, prognosis "guarded." Addison had managed to get some water into her by carefully spooning it to her lips. Lisa said they would soon try some warm chicken broth.

The next morning Addison reported that Jenna had mumbled and at one point cried out, but had never seemed aware of her surroundings.

Breakfast was corned beef wrapped in freshly baked tortillas. Dave longed for some real leavened bread, but in one more parallel to the Children of Israel who left Egypt in such a hurry they didn't have time to let the bread rise, he understood that tortillas were quick and easy to make.

But he had had so many of them by now that he would have preferred matzo.

They broke camp quickly and were on the road again by eight.

They had intended to cut over to the I-5, but street after street was blocked, and they found themselves moving due south either on the 110 Harbor Freeway or on the roads close to it. But the 110 had elevated sections most of the way down to Florence Avenue and most of those were collapsed. They stayed mostly on Figueroa all morning, a broad street that had had no buildings tall enough to block the road when they fell down. The obstructions were all in the form of cracks and gaps in the road, and those sometimes went on in both directions for a mile or more. There seemed to be something in the geology down in this part of Los Angeles that had lent itself to fractures and slippage, so that an area they had thought might be easy to traverse turned out to be harder than anything they had yet encountered.

It had been a poor neighborhood, as much of the basin between the I-10 and the I-405 had been. Small businesses, many of them dealing with auto parts and repair, including a lot of large junkyards, had lined Figueroa before the fire. Now only the junk remained, charred free of paint and rubber and anything else that would burn. It smelled bad, sometimes acrid enough to burn their noses, and everyone was worried about toxic gases, but the worst they experienced was a dry, hacking cough as a result of the smoke, ash, and soot.

When they were forced off the main street they were in neighborhoods that had mostly consisted of single-family houses on small lots, with some two-story apartment buildings here and there. Like most white middle-class Angelenos, Dave had not been down here all that often. He recalled that some of the houses had been ramshackle, poorly kept, with junk in the yards. But many others had been well maintained, painted, with flowers or vegetable gardens. They had been the pride and joy of the owners, who were usually black or Hispanic. It had been no small thing to own even a tiny home in L.A, where a two-bedroom, one-bath, one-thousand-square-foot home in a neighborhood as unglamorous as Watts could still be worth upwards of a hundred grand.

All of that was gone, all the small dream homes and the ugly stucco apartment houses. They had always been close-packed, and the fire had swept through them completely unhindered. Every block had completely burned to the ground. Very little remained but the concrete foundations. Here and there were the hulks of major appliances, and there were thousands of burned-out cars. Everything in the cars was gone except the metal. Some of the cars and houses were still smoking, and the smells were nauseating. Everyone was hoping they could somehow break out of this area before they had to make camp for the night.

Time and again they were diverted from their intended course by yawning cracks in the ground, or fifteen-foot drop-offs, or raw, new cliffs. They kept being forced farther and farther to the west, and came upon Jesse Owens Park only by accident. It was at the corner of Century Boulevard and Western Avenue, far to the west of where they had wanted to go. The park was a large L-shaped space with several baseball diamonds, a soccer field, and a nine-hole golf course. Most of the trees were along the south side, which is probably what had saved it from the worst of the fire. Those treetops had burned, but not completely. Once again there was brown grass for Ranger to eat.

They had not come nearly as far as they had hoped, and much of that had been in the wrong direction. It had taken them nearly all day. They were on the edge of the area that had been affected by the fallout of the Doheny oilfield explosion and fire. They desperately hoped they would not be forced to go farther west. That way lay LAX, and the area they knew to be very bad even before the earthquake. It could only be worse now.

Once more, it was frustrating to have no news from anywhere in the area, to be going forward essentially blind. As they made camp on the golf course and sat around the fire eating another meager meal, they debated whether or not they should continue to follow the path of the fire, or try to strike out beyond it.

"I say proceed as we have been," Bob said. "I know it's awful, but you realize that for two days now we've seen no one. That is all to the good. People we run into will likely be needy or angry or predatory, or all three."

"You're forgetting that we might run into people as well prepared as we are," Lisa said. "And those are likely to be out of the burn area. Maybe they're hunkering down, waiting to be rescued. Maybe they could be talked into joining up with us. Like you say, there's safety in numbers."

"I see your point. But after all that's gone down lately, I'd have a lot of trouble trusting anyone I don't know already."

"That's awful," Addison said, then looked chagrined to have entered the argument, where mostly adults spoke, in spite of their promise that the teenagers would be treated as adults. "Sorry," she added.

"No need to be sorry," Emily said. "It *is* awful. I don't like to think that's the sort of world we're living in now, but maybe it is."

"We should take each case as we come to it," Marian suggested.

They tossed it around a little more, and still hadn't reached a decision when Teddy spoke up.

"I want to keep following the fire for at least one more day," he said. "You people think you've been up a lot of blind alleys. Done a lot of backtracking. Let me tell you, for every mile you guys have backtracked, I've done three. There's been no point in telling you about the streets that didn't pan out, but there have been a bunch of them. I just come back and tell you there's no way through there, I don't mention I went two miles to find that out. And I take off in a new direction, and come back and tell you we have to go back again, and you think I haven't been scouting good enough."

"I don't think that," Bob said.

"Whatever. I think I'm the only one here who knows just how truly impenetrable this maze of streets has become. And from my travels outside the burn, I can also tell you that it's *much* worse out there."

"Well, if it comes to a vote, I'm voting with Teddy," Karen said.

"I don't think we really need a vote," Bob said. "Unless I hear strong objections, we'll continue to follow the fire tomorrow."

There were no voices raised.

An hour before sunrise Jenna regained consciousness for the first time. Addison was changing the dressing on her wound by the light of a small flashlight when Jenna cried out and tried to grab her hand. She shined the light into Jenna's haggard face.

"What's going on? What are you doing?" Her voice was a breathy rasp.

"Oh, Jenna, I'm so glad you're back."

"What happened? Where am I?"

"We're on the road, trying to get out of Los Angeles. You just stay still here, I have to go get Lisa. Okay?"

"Okay." Her head dropped back on the pillow. Before Addison could leave she raised her head again. "I think I wet myself," she said.

"Just be still. I'll take care of that." Addison had been changing Jenna's improvised diapers. "I'll be right back. Please don't move around. Okay?"

"'Kay."

Dave had been having trouble getting to sleep. He had just begun to doze when he heard his daughter's voice, and he was out of the tent quickly.

"She's awake," Addison whispered. "I'm going to get Lisa."

He took the flashlight from Addison and got in the car

behind the driver's seat. He took her hand and squeezed it. She returned the squeeze, feebly.

"How are you?"

"You tell me. What happened?"

"I'm not sure if—"

"My leg hurts something awful. Did I break my leg?"

He wasn't sure what she should be told and was thinking it over when she closed her eyes again. Her mouth fell open and he was pretty sure she was asleep, but they opened again when Lisa opened the door beside her.

"How were her vital signs?" Lisa asked.

"Her temperature was up a degree," Addison said. "I didn't take her blood pressure yet."

"I feel hot. Real hot. And my leg hurts."

"You were shot," Lisa said, holding Jenna's eye open and quickly shining a penlight into it. She then pulled away the sheet covering Jenna. Her pants had been cut away and she was wearing nothing but a T-shirt. Dave looked away, not from her nakedness but because the wound was ugly, pinkish around the edges, crusted with blood and something yellowish.

"I was about to clean it," Addison said.

"Jenna, it's not looking too bad, but it has to be cleaned again or it might get infected. You were asleep the last times we did it. I'm afraid I don't have any morphine or anything like that. It's going to hurt."

"Do you have to?"

"I'm afraid so."

"I wish you wouldn't. I'm not brave."

"You just holler if you have to."

Dave had to hold her arms while Addison threw herself over her legs. She kicked and she struggled, but she had no real strength. After a few minutes she passed out. Dave released her arms and wiped his brow, which was covered with sweat that had little to do with the heat.

"I wouldn't want to do that again," he said.

"We have to keep it clean. But I don't have much alcohol left."

"How do you do it?"

"You don't get used to it, believe me. You just stop showing it." She looked at Dave, and her face was grim. "Painkillers were the first thing we ran out of. Just pray I don't have to take off her leg. I've amputated a dozen legs and arms in the last week. You just work as quickly as you can. Like battlefield doctors during the Civil War."

Dave looked up and saw that almost the whole party was gathered around the Escalade. The first rays of the morning sun were bringing light to the eastern sky, which for the first time in a while didn't have much smoke in it.

Lisa faced the assembled group.

"Jenna's awake. Or she was. For the first time her condition is a little this side of critical. But there's something else. Moving her around today could put her right back in danger. I'd like to suggest that we stay here all day."

"I'd go for that," Teddy said, surprising everyone. "I really could use a rest. Maybe just a few little forays to get ready for tomorrow."

Mark didn't seem happy with the idea, but after a little resistance he admitted he could use the time to chip more wood. Others chimed in with tasks they might work at while not traveling, and still others admitted that they were exhausted, hadn't slept well last night, and would be grateful for a chance to unwind a bit.

"Then without further objection . . ." Bob said, looking around, "I declare this to be a day of rest." He looked at the chain-link backstop where the vehicles had been parked. "Anyone for baseball?"

Dave had thought Bob was kidding, and he had been, in a way, but the idea caught on when Gordon produced a couple of bats. He started batting a tennis ball around, and before long Sandra and Olivia were fielding the grounders he hit to them. Others joined in, and eventually two small teams were formed. Bob, still walking with a cane, stood behind the plate umpiring. It was slow-pitch, Gordon or Elyse serving up easy lobs to the plate.

Dave was vaguely disturbed by it all. It wasn't that he was against anyone having fun. Or maybe it was. Maybe it seemed wrong to have fun in this ruined city. Maybe it was wrong to ever have fun again.

And he knew that was ridiculous. Soldiers who faced death every day nevertheless found ways to amuse themselves and each other. Who knew when the next respite might be? Who knew if any of them would be alive tomorrow?

When he saw that Jenna was awake again and had asked to be taken outside, he cheered up considerably. Her stretcher was in the shade and Addison was cooling her brow by wiping it with a damp cloth. She was propped up on pillows and watching the ball game.

"Like I told your wonderful daughter, I don't remember a thing about getting shot. Last thing I remember is you guys coming back and how happy I was to see you. They tell me there was a big fire."

"Biggest ever. We barely got out. We might not have made it except for you and your shotgun."

"Really? Damn. I wish I could remember."

"It's not one of my most pleasant memories."

"Lisa says she might gradually get it back," Addison said.

"It would be a mixed blessing," Dave told her.

"Hey, Dave, your turn at bat!" Rachel yelled.

"My turn? I didn't even know I was on a team."

"You're giving us credit for too much organization. We just take turns batting and pitching and running after balls. Here, take it."

Dave took the bat. Three whiffs and he was out of there, and he found himself laughing. He was amazed at how much better it made him feel. *I used to make a living on my sense of humor,* he thought. He could tell a pretty good joke. He was a competent singer and a lousy but enthusiastic dancer. He had to make sure he and his family could enjoy things like that again.

CHAPTER TWENTY-SIX

In the early afternoon the baseball game was over, all the chores that needed doing had been done, and lunch had been eaten. They had a treat with their canned beef stew. Emily had made real bread with yeast and baked it in the makeshift camp oven Mark had built. It came out well, though a bit doughy in the middle. Emily promised that the next time they had a bit of leisure she would do it again and get it right, even though no one was complaining. Dave thought it tasted like pure ambrosia.

There was a little shade under the trees in the park, so after lunch most of them sat around under them. Some brought out pallets and dozed. Others talked.

Dave noticed an odd thing. There was discussion about what they would do tomorrow and on the following days. They talked a little about the events of the previous days, of their experiences in the fire. Teddy told of some of his experiences and Addison and Karen talked about what it was like fleeing for their lives, first from the fire and then from the would-be carjackers. But that subject ran out quickly, too.

What did you talk about after civilization had crumbled? Dave tried to recall what they had talked about before the oil went bad. It was already getting hard to do.

You talked about what other people you knew were up to. You could call it news or, if it was juicy, you called it gossip. Well, Dave had lost contact with all of his friends. Some of them lived at various places around the country, or in Europe or Australia. Australia might as well be on Neptune now, but you didn't need to go that far afield to be in a foreign place. Oregon might as well be on the farside of the moon. Without telephones, the only people you would know well were those who lived close to you, and the only way to keep in contact with people at a distance would be by mail. Now the mail hadn't been delivered for months. In some ways they had reverted to the nineteenth century, when most of the people you knew would be living in the same community. Walking distance, or horse-and-buggy distance. In other ways they had gone even farther back. At least people in farming communities had been able to write distant friends and put a two-cent stamp on it and know it would be delivered in days or weeks.

If you weren't talking about friends, you could always discuss the television shows or movies you had just seen. That had been popular watercooler talk for a lot longer than any of them had been alive. Now not only were there no new shows to discuss, there were probably very few watercoolers to gather around.

And what of the Internet? It had gradually taken over a large part of Dave's life, as it had so many others'. That had been how he got most of his information. He had stopped subscribing to the *Los Angeles Times*, and seldom watched TV news unless it was a breaking news story, like 9/11 or the explosion of the Doheny oil field.

In recent years television, telephones, computers, both desktop and handheld, had been merging into one cybernetic colossus that so far didn't even really have a name. Cyberspace? Maybe, since more and more of everyone's lives were being lived virtually, from social networks to online games to things Dave knew he had probably never even heard of. It was all gone, swept away in a matter of weeks.

Dave had noticed that Addison, Elyse, Nigel, Sandra, and Olivia sometimes gathered together in a teenage huddle. He had seen them get out their defunct cell phones and look at them morosely for a few seconds, as if ready to pounce with their thumbs if even one reception bar showed up. If there was even one cell tower out there still operating, they would instantly try to call or text their friends, people they hadn't seen or talked to in weeks.

He remembered that shortly after the cell phones stopped working Addison had gone through a grouchy few days, completely unlike her usual positive disposition. He realized she had been going through a withdrawal very much as if she had been taking an addictive drug. And he recalled, ruefully, that he had felt some of the effects himself when his PDA was no longer able to interact with other machines around the world. He had been addicted, too, but he thought it was nothing like what the teens were feeling. He could remember a time when there had been no cell phones, no personal computers, no social networks. A world without them was imaginable to him. To them . . . well, they had grown up in a world where all these things were taken for granted.

Dave brought this up—what do we talk about now that all our usual sources of entertainment and distraction are gone?— and that itself became a topic of conversation for a while. The younger ones especially seemed glad to bitch and moan for a while about how much they missed their phones and computers and the wide world they opened to them. But it wasn't the loss of the instruments themselves that troubled them. It was the sense of connectedness, and more importantly, those they had been connected to. None of the children had been in contact with most of their friends for weeks or months. Olivia soon broke down in tears as she recalled all the good friends she had been unable to talk to, or even find out if they were dead or alive. Nigel just stared at the ground and looked bitter, as if he blamed the adults present for what they had done to his world.

And why not? It certainly hadn't been Nigel's fault. The only consolation Dave could find was to realize that for as long as he could remember, and probably for a long time before, children had been bitching about how their parents had screwed up the world. He recalled how the Boomers were bitter at the nuclear world the previous generation had made for them, and his own frustration, as a child of Boomers, at just how screwed up those goddamn egotistic sixties hippies had made everything.

Dave's heart went out to them. He recalled how important his friends had been to him at their age, how badly he had missed some of them when, at a slightly younger age, he had been sent off to camp in the days before every child had their own pocket communicator, like in *Star Trek*. His parents had given him a phone card, but who was he going to call? Many of his friends had been out of town for the summer, too. And if he did call them, what would he say at long-distance rates? They would call him a pussy or a homo for calling up to say he missed them. These teenagers around him phoned and texted constantly, and they never seemed to have an awkward adolescent lack of words.

Why, these kids today just don't know how good they have it!

Dave smiled at himself, thinking he could have made a pretty good episode of his former sitcom out of some of that. The old man realizing he was saying the same things his father had, and his father before him. *I'm an old fogy,* he realized.

"So what did people do before electricity, Mom?" Addison asked, with a sly grin. Karen elbowed her.

"Well after we got all the chores done—like plowing the south forty; we pulled the plow ourselves, you understand, we were too poor to afford a mule—we gathered around the windup gramophone in the parlor and listened to Edison cylinders all night."

Bob had to explain what an Edison cylinder was. "Not from personal experience, you understand. We were too poor for that. No, we got out the fiddle and the washtub and the harmonica and had us a hootenanny in the hayloft. Playin' that old devil music, ragtime and Dixieland."

Mark leaped to his feet and grabbed Rachel's hand and started a wild impromptu country dance with much foot stomping and swinging his partner around. Soon the others were clapping along until they collapsed against each other, laughing and sweating. There was applause and laughter.

"Seriously, folks," Gordon said, when it had died down, "the Victorians had a thousand ways to amuse themselves. There would be a piano, most likely, or if you were poor there were other instruments. Many, many people learned to play. Before the record player really took off the main thing they sold in music stores was instruments and sheet music for the piano. People were expected to hone some talent, and it didn't have to be music. You could learn to recite some famous bit of poetry, or passages from Shakespeare or the classics. There were amateur theatricals, and tableaux, where you would dress up in costumes and pose. And, of course, card games. Anyone for whist?"

"Did we bring a Scrabble board?" Lisa said. "I'm a killer Scrabble player."

"No, but it shouldn't be hard to make one," Emily said.

"Or people told stories," Gordon went on. "I don't know if they made them up or memorized or retold old classics, probably some of both."

"Anybody know any good stories?"

"None really suitable for children," Dave said. Addison threw a stick at him.

"There's always reading, of course," Emily said.

"I'm all in favor of reading, but it's not real social," Elyse said.

"I was speaking of reading aloud."

"Oh, Mom," Mark said, suddenly enthusiastic. "I remember you reading to me when I was little. I'd love for you to do it again."

"Which would you prefer, *Green Eggs and Ham* or *Hop on Pop*?"

"C'mon, Mom, I'm all grown-up now. I was thinking of *The Little Engine That Could*. That, or *Lolita*."

It turned out there was some enthusiasm for a group reading. Even those who had been dubious at first soon gathered around when it actually began.

Much of Bob and Emily's library had been ruined by the earthquake and flood, but of those books that had remained on the shelves or out of the water Emily had insisted on selecting some of the very best and bringing them along. There were five boxes of them, and they had been arranged along one side of the school bus where Solomon and Taylor slept, as an extra layer of protection in case they encountered weapons high-powered enough to shoot through the steel plate.

Books could stop bullets. Though he hated the thought of books being destroyed, there was something in that notion that Dave liked.

Emily went into the bus and came out with half a dozen books, which she laid on the table and let people walk by and examine. Then they voted, and the majority favored *To Kill a Mockingbird*. All the adults and Addison had read it, but the other teens hadn't and no one had any problem with hearing it again.

Emily opened it and began to read.

" 'When he was nearly thirteen, my brother Jem got his arm badly broken at the elbow . . .' "

By the time night fell they were all gathered around the small fire, even those who hadn't been interested in the reading at first.

Emily read for half an hour and then went off to help prepare the evening meal. Gordon took over, and then passed the book on. They listened while they ate, and until a little past sundown. Even then, many of them wanted it to go on into the night, especially Sandra and Olivia, and even Nigel.

That night in their tent Dave and Karen made love quietly, and then lay in each other's arms.

"This is the best day I remember in a long time," she said.

"Weeks, at least," he said, and she laughed.

"I know. It's hard to remember sometimes that this has all been going on for only a few months. And the worst of it a lot less than that."

"Our days are more full. Full of things that have real meaning. That's part of it. It's getting hard to remember how worried I was about writing that screenplay."

"Everything seems unimportant now, except you and Addison and the rest of our extended family."

"How did we lose that? Not as a couple, we've talked about that. As a civilization? As a culture? Most of us spent most of our time doing things that really didn't do all that much to improve the world."

"Art is important, darling."

"Not the 'art' I created. 'Fess up. Did you like the show?"

"It was funny at first."

"Most pilots are funny. But where do you go from there? We milked the same jokes for years."

"Lots of people laughed."

"They laughed at *The Beverly Hillbillies*, too. I can see it now, on my headstone: HE WAS ALMOST AS FUNNY AS *GILLIGAN'S ISLAND*."

That got a laugh out of her.

"Well, don't forget it kept us in groceries for many years."

"Yeah, and robbed me of a lot of time seeing my daughter grow up."

"And spoiled me rotten. Would you have preferred to be an insurance agent?"

"No. But I wish I'd written something more important."

"Laughter is important. And your life isn't over. Scoff if you want, but people are still going to need art."

"But maybe not in movies or television."

"Sure they will. The world's not over. Civilization isn't over.

We'll scramble back. It's going to be a lot of hard work, but we will."

"I'm willing to work."

"And anyway, if there are no more movies or television, you can write a book."

"I can, can't I? I think I might like that."

For the next week they followed the fire, and finally came out of the burned area in Anaheim, about a mile north of Disneyland.

In that time they did not see another living human being. They did find a lot more dead ones, but nothing like there had been in the Coliseum. The corpses were scattered here and there, usually singly but sometimes in small groups. All were burned beyond recognition, and all of them were starting to smell. They announced their presence from a block away.

Once more, they did not have the time or energy—or after a few days, even the inclination—to bury them. If the dead were on the sidewalk, the caravan usually just drove on by, but they had not become so hardened that they felt good about leaving them lying in the middle of the street. So the adults took turns pulling them to the sidewalk and, sometimes, if a pile of ashes and embers was handy, shoveling a little of that over them to at least conceal their awful, incinerated nakedness.

Addison and Elyse offered to take their turns, but it was halfhearted, and neither argued when their parents gently told them no. Sandra and Olivia did not volunteer, and Sandra could not even look at the bodies without being sick. But Nigel insisted, and got his way. Dave was sure it was a macho thing, feeling his manhood was at risk if he joined the girls on the sidelines. He had no problem with that, but saw that the boy was very quiet for a long time after his turn had come and gone. Luckily, the dead were not so numerous that anyone was likely to have to take removal detail more than once a day.

Their route took them south on Western or the side streets paralleling it, then onto the Imperial Highway and east until they were blocked again, turning south until they reached the 105 freeway. The exchange was destroyed at Wilmington Avenue and there was no way to get off to the south, so they had to bump over some rubble and head north again for several blocks, and when they reached 110th Street they saw an amazing thing. The Watts Towers were not as tall as some people imagined, and finding them was not always easy. You usually didn't see them until you were almost on top of them because surrounding buildings and trees got in the way. But all that was gone now, and there were the Towers, still standing. They paused for a moment to get out of the trucks and look at them.

"They stood up to the quake." Emily laughed in delight.

"No, wait," Mark said. "There were three main ones. I only see two."

"I think the one in the middle fell down," Bob said.

"You're right. That's too bad. But the fire didn't harm them."

"I wouldn't be too sure," Mark said. "They were in bad shape. I heard they were being restored, but it was tricky. I'll bet if you got up close, a lot of that concrete and glass has fallen off. They're held up by the iron framework underneath."

"Then let's don't get up close," Karen said. "I'd like to remember them like this."

"Works for me."

On they went, through Lynwood, Paramount, Bellflower, Artesia, Cerritos, Hawaiian Gardens. Small towns that you would never know you were in except for the city-limits signs, part of the megalopolis of what used to be separate towns with orange groves between them, jostling each other, with little real identity. Towns that, if you lived somewhere else, were only exit signs on the 5, the 405, the 605, or the 91. Towns that you either barreled through at seventy-five miles per hour or inched past at five miles per hour or less, looking around and thanking your lucky stars that you didn't live there.

They began to see signs that someone had been at work trying to stop the fire, and in several places they seemed to have succeeded, but at a cost. The fire that followed the San Francisco earthquake of 1906 was finally stopped by firemen who blew up buildings in its path, and the same thing seemed to have been done here.

Yet this fire had advanced across such a large front that the dynamiting had been only sporadically effective. They crossed areas where they could see that all the buildings had been deliberately destroyed. No earthquake could have shattered brick and timber as thoroughly as what they were seeing. They found areas where seven or eight or ten blocks of buildings had been blown up, and downwind of these places the buildings hadn't burned. But the fire had swept around these barriers and, farther downwind, had come together again. Apparently no one had had enough dynamite to create a long enough firebreak to stop the conflagration entirely.

But the thing that had finally stopped the firestorm before it swept all the way to the sea seemed to have been a shift in the wind. When the relentless Santa Ana had finally stopped blowing, the fire could no longer leap over the wide main streets, and they began passing places where the north side of the street was mostly consumed, and the south side was intact, except for the quake damage they had seen everywhere.

And still they saw no people. Everyone had fled, or died. Dave remembered the wall of flames advancing in his rearview mirror, only a block behind him, chasing him down the hill. These people had probably had most of a day to see it coming, and it must have been quite a sight, as if the whole world were on fire.

Near the end of their eighth day on the road Teddy returned with bad news.

"We can't continue south," he said. "Not here, anyway. There are refugees, thousands of them, penned up behind chain-link fences all along the 91. They're being guarded by what look like Anaheim cops and armed civilians. One fence runs along the south side of the freeway, and another one to the north. There's no shelter that I could see, just bare concrete. I don't know what they're doing with those people, but it doesn't look good. I went ten blocks east and then ten blocks west, and it's all the same. Anaheim is sealed off, and they're serious about it. I tried getting close to get a better look, and a cop pointed his gun at me and ordered me to come to him. I took off. He didn't shoot, but I wonder if he would have if I got closer. It seems the fire didn't reach Anaheim, but the tide of refugees did. And they're not wanted."

"I wonder if they're getting any food?" Lisa said.

"I don't dare get close enough to ask. I don't want to end up in that enclosure."

They got out the maps and studied the situation.

"Oh, man," Mark said. "I didn't realize Anaheim was so big. It goes all along the 91 to the north, and miles to the east, all the way to Yorba Linda."

They were in Buena Park, just to the northwest of Anaheim and just north of the 91 freeway, near the intersection with the 5.

"Do you think they're guarding that whole border?"

"I don't know. But we can't keep going south here. It's either east or west if we hope to go around it."

"If only we knew where the fire went," Dave said. "I think the majority of the refugees would have headed due south, because that's the way the fire was going. If they headed east or west, they'd be able to see it was gaining on them. Don't you think?"

"That would seem the logical move. And that took them to Anaheim, where people saw them coming and decided they couldn't take them in."

"I wonder how many more communities did the same?"

"We'll have to find out, I guess."

"You know," Rachel said, "I guess you can understand something and still not like it. I don't like it at all."

"I don't imagine the citizens of Anaheim like it, either," Karen said. "But we know what it's like. We turned people away, didn't we, Dave?"

"We did, and it haunts me. And I find myself thinking, what goes around, comes around. Now we're the ones looking for a safe haven."

No one advanced a good reason why they should test the goodwill of the Anaheim city fathers, so it was decided they would stay a safe distance from the stockade and look for a way around it.

Everyone was hoping that the surrounding communities were not as organized, or as forbidding, as Anaheim. They soon found that no one was that organized, but neither were they very welcoming.

Skirting the boundaries of Anaheim to the west, they found themselves going south on Knott Avenue, and after a forced turn to the left, they were passing Knott's Berry Farm. At first all they could see of it was part of a wooden roller coaster that had suffered some damage. Just beyond it was a big, triangular parking lot with trees growing from small islands between the long rows of marked spaces. And here was a refugee camp. They were about to drive past the lot when Dave saw a flashing blue light behind them, pulling up fast.

"Uh-oh," he said. "We're busted."

A Buena Park motorcycle cop pulled in front of the caravan as Dave shut off his engine. The policeman got off, carrying a shotgun pointed at the sky, and didn't approach the caravan.

"Drivers, get out of your vehicles. If you have weapons, leave them inside."

Dave looked at Karen and Addison, then at Jenna, who was now well enough to sit up, though she was still on her stretcher. He didn't wear his pistol in his waistband when he was driving, so that wasn't a problem. He opened the door.

"Be careful, Daddy."

"I will, sweetheart." He got out, holding his hands away from his body. He heard the doors of the bus and then the U-Haul open. He heard Mark and Bob come forward to stand beside him.

The cop had them stand a good distance from the Escalade and lean forward with their hands against its sides so they could not make any quick moves, and he patted them down with one hand. He told them to move around to the front of the car, presumably to shield himself from anyone in the bus who might be aiming a weapon at him.

"Sorry about that," he said. "I don't like scaring your little girl, but we have to be cautious. We get some bad guys coming through here."

"No problem, Officer," Dave said.

"Where are you folks from, and where are you headed?"

They had talked it over and decided that they would not mention Holmby Hills or Hollywood. When questioned, they had agreed to simply say they were from Los Angeles, which wasn't a lie. Bob told the officer that.

"As for where we're going . . . the best I can say is that we're looking for a home. A place to settle down."

"My own home was destroyed in the first hours of the fire," Dave told him. "Bob's wasn't, but we all had to get out because it was just too unsafe."

"How many of you are there?"

"Eighteen," Mark said. "Dave here has his wife and daughter, and a friend who is badly wounded from a gunshot. The rest of us are Bob's children and grandkids. Five of us are minors."

The cop sighed.

"Well, it kills me to tell you this, but you can't stay in Buena Park. We don't have enough food to feed our own for very much longer. At some point we may all have to evacuate to Seal Beach, where the navy is taking people to San Diego."

"Are you sure?" Mark asked. "They were doing the same thing in Santa Monica, and what we heard was they were all going north, to Alameda and Puget Sound."

The cop kicked at the ground with his boot.

"We've heard rumors to that effect, too. Tell the truth, most of us don't know what to do. Everything's gone to shit. My little boy is hungry all the time."

"That's just what we heard, from some of the sailors on the aircraft carrier. Do you have any news you could pass on to us? Like how are the roads to San Diego?"

"I wish I could. I haven't left Buena Park since the quake. I heard you guys up north had it worse than we did."

"Yes, it was."

"Well, there's still very little news on the air. Just a few ham-radio stations, none of the big ones. The city council is operating in the dark, like almost everybody, I guess. We hear the roads to San Diego are impassable." He nodded toward the car park with the vehicles and shanties. "People in there might know more than I do. Some of them have been around, a little."

"Would it be possible for us to stay an hour or two and talk to them?"

The cop sighed.

"Here's the deal. The people in the lot are being treated as citizens. They got here quite a while ago. But they're all we can handle. The council has decided that any new refugees can stay twenty-four hours. Get a meal, some water if they need it. Then they have to be moving on. I'm real sorry, honest."

"It's a better deal than your neighbors to the east are offering," Bob said.

"Don't be too hard on Anaheim. They've had ten, twenty times the refugees we have. They let them in at first. Now, what can they do? They get some kind of soup and a little bread every day, and even that is more than Anaheim can really handle."

"We're not condemning," Dave said. "We turned people away in our neighborhood, too."

"Ain't it the shits? Did you ever think you'd see Americans . . ." He couldn't go on for a moment. "Sorry. I've been on shift twenty-four hours. I've seen things I wouldn't have believed a year ago. I get the feeling the government has abandoned us."

"They do seem to be evacuating people," Mark said. "Maybe they think they're doing the right thing."

"Not so's I can tell. Anyway, what do I know? Are you going to stay the night?

Everybody thought that was a good idea. They might be able to relax their vigilance a bit with other people around.

"Well, you can park any damn place you want. Oh, I meant to ask you, who made those wood burners for you?"

"That would be me," Mark said, and instantly looked as if he might regret it.

"No kidding? We've got a guy tried to build some, but he must be missing something, 'cause he hasn't been able to get any of them to work. Maybe if I sent him over here, you could take a look at it?"

"Sure, why not?"

They watched the cop motor away, and Mark let out his breath.

"I was real worried there for a minute," he said. "I thought they might want to requisition our vehicles."

"It could happen, I guess," said Bob. "Our best bet would probably be if you show them how to build their own, then they wouldn't need to steal ours."

"Or we could just take off now," Dave suggested. "A few miles down the road and we'd be out of Buena Park, he'd never find us again."

After a brief discussion it was decided that staying one night with people who had come from elsewhere was too valuable an opportunity to pass up. So they swung into the parking lot and moved slowly down the rows.

There were a few big RVs and a lot of vans and SUVs, but the majority of the vehicles were standard sedans. People were living in all of them, and in rope-and-canvas shelters or wooden lean-tos obviously made from quake wreckage. Some of that wreckage seemed to have come from the buildings of Knott's Berry Farm across the road. It was brightly colored, even festive, and looked wildly out of place in such depressing surroundings.

They pitched camp in their usual triangular formation, and started making tentative forays among the people already there.

They ended up staying three days.

They were not pressured to stay, but after the first day it was obvious no one would mind if they stuck around, from the city council to the police to the campers in the parking lot.

Lisa was not the only doctor remaining in Buena Park, but there were not many of them and all were overworked and perhaps a little less likely to visit the refugees than the longtime residents. One more was always welcome. She set up shop with Elyse and Nigel doing the nursing duties. This small town had not yet run out of things like morphine and sterile bandages.

While Lisa helped out with the community's medical needs, Mark attended to its mechanical ones. He was gone for most of the first day, visiting the city workshops where people were trying to convert vehicles to burning wood.

"I was incredulous at first, that no one knew how to do it," he said when he returned. "I mean, it may not be intuitive, but it's not, as they say, rocket science. Then I remembered that I downloaded the plans from the Internet, and the only reason I did was that you warned my father what was coming, Dave, and he warned me. I only looked into it because . . . well, what if? So thanks again for the heads-up, Dave."

They set up a workshop right there in the parking lot. Word got out and a lot of people showed up to see the burners built from items scrounged from hardware stores and warehouses. By the end of the third day they had equipped half a dozen city trucks with burners, and a lot of people had gone to their homes with the intent of building their own.

There was a water truck that came by every day, and they refilled their big tank and all the empty plastic jugs and bottles, which they had saved. Ranger got his fill of water every day, and had plenty of places to forage.

While Mark and Lisa were engaged in their own specialties, everyone else circulated through the impromptu trailer park and talked to people. One of the first things they learned was the reason why the camp was here in this particular parking lot and not somewhere else. It was because of the chicken dinners.

Knott's Berry Farm had originally been just what the name said: a place where boysenberries were raised and sold. In the 1930s Mrs. Knott started serving chicken dinners to travelers on the main road from Los Angeles to Orange County. It grew from there into an entertainment complex rivaling Disneyland, but they still served their signature chicken dinners, around four thousand of them every day. Naturally, they always had a lot of chickens on hand.

When the park was closed because few people were able to get to it anymore, chickens kept arriving. The Knott's management brought in freezer trucks to store the excess. When the gasoline ran out they found solar generators to keep the motors running. And when things got critical, when people began to run out of food, they opened a soup kitchen.

It was free. They didn't serve chicken dinners and what they did serve would certainly have horrified Mrs. Knott, but it was a nutritious—if rather thin—chicken soup that, on many days, was all the patrons would have to eat that day.

As the crisis dragged on many people left, and the cooks made less soup each day, and put less chicken in it, trying to stretch it out until help arrived. Now that the bleak consensus was that help might *never* arrive, it was about as thin as it could be and still be called chicken soup, but they were still serving it. No one knew how much chicken was still in the freezers or how much flour and dried vegetables were in the larder to make the noodles and other ingredients that went into it, and none of the cooks would say, but every day they were feeding around five hundred, most of them from the parking lot.

Dave and Karen and Addison went across the street to the evening meal the first day. They hadn't planned on eating since they still had their own food, but everyone insisted. So they sat at picnic tables and chowed down on what everyone was calling

"Knott's Not-So-Famous Chicken Soup" and one bread roll each, no butter. They scoured their bowls like everyone else, and helped with the washing afterward. It was a satisfying meal, and actually surprisingly tasty. There was no shortage of spices. Just a pinch or two in the vats made all the difference.

During the meal they questioned their neighbors about their experiences since the crisis began, since the quake, since the fire. There were heartbreaking stories, but these people had for the most part not been hit as hard by the quake as the people farther north. The fire had missed them.

As for intelligence in the military sense, there was not a lot of that floating around the campground. It didn't surprise Dave, because everyone was living with the same limitation: the great difficulty of traveling much farther than you could pedal on a bicycle in a day. Those who traveled farther seldom came back to report on what they had seen.

Radio was slowly coming back on the air, but the information it broadcast was highly suspect, often contradictory, and frequently political. No one trusted the government broadcasts. They had heard things they knew to be untrue, and if they'd lie about one thing, why not lie about others? The military evacuation was being promoted like a free trip to the Bahamas. Milk and honey—or at least rice and beans—were promised at the end of the journey. All the information they had to the contrary was the word of two deserting sailors . . . and Dave trusted them much more than he did the government propaganda.

The people in the parking lot felt the same way. Some of them listened to commentators with various points of view. Radio preachers were there, and they were a happy bunch, reminding listeners that all the recent travails were the result of human sin, that the apocalypse was in hand, already begun, so repent. And by the way, I told you so.

Right-wingers discovered a new conspiracy every day. Some of them might even be accurate, at least so far as the government had covered it all up until it was too late to do anything about it. As for the bacterium itself, it came from Russia, from China, from Al Qaeda, from the Jews, from the commies. Or from our own government. No one doubted that the bug had been deliberately released, and a thousand explanations for why someone thought that was a good idea were advanced, all fairly loony. The notion that it was all the prelude to an alien invasion was gaining traction, and there was much debate about where the aliens would be coming from.

The left wing wasn't much better. Plenty of loonies there, too. The dominant paradigm was that the whole thing had been planned and carried out by the oil companies. Dave hadn't understood why Big Oil should do such a thing until he heard part two of the argument. The oil companies had been secretly buying up all the world's coal for at least a decade, against the time when the oil ran out, which everyone agreed was inevitable, disagreeing only on the date. True? Bullshit? Who knew? If they had been involved, it had probably been a big bummer when the markets not only crashed but were obliterated, making all their stocks worthless.

Another story from the far left was that this was Mother Nature, the planet itself, getting revenge for all the damage humanity had inflicted on it. Dave thought he would have to smoke a lot of dope to believe that one, but it was a popular theory.

There were so many low-power radio stations coming back on the air, and so much misinformation and so many conspiracy theories that it all became essentially worthless. Word of mouth was more reliable, in that most people had no reason to lie about what they had seen with their own eyes, but the trouble was almost no one had seen anything farther away than three or four miles. They got a lot of information about towns to the north, very little from the south, where they were going.

After their meal, Dave and Karen and Addison took a walk through the park.

The last time they had been there was a little over a year ago, with several of Addison's friends. They had spent the day riding the roller coasters. Karen went with them on most of them, but Dave had stayed on the ground. He had no fear of heights, and no problem with speed, but the twists and turns did him in.

That day Knott's was a sad place to see. It was not deserted, since some of the children from the camp played there under the supervision of a volunteer, but the presence of so few children somehow made it even more spooky. Addison was on Ranger and rode him on ahead, as they had been assured the park was safe. Dave and Karen followed more slowly.

"The rides didn't do so bad in the quake," Karen said. "I thought they'd all be on the ground. Big metal pretzels that somebody stepped on."

"I think it's a great sign. The farther we get from Hollywood, the less damage we're seeing. I think if we make it to San Diego, the damage might be minor."

"I wonder how long it will be before anyone can come to a place like this again?"

"Probably about the same time there's a need for sitcom writers again."

Karen sighed, then kissed him.

"Are you planning to be a farmer?"

"Probably. I'm planning to do absolutely anything that needs doing, wherever we settle. I expect that will be stoop labor, planting and harvesting corn or wheat, picking apples. Whatever. I don't expect to be good at it at first. But I'll learn."

"And I guess I'll have to learn to be a farmer's wife."

"Wife, hell. You'll be a farmer, too. When Ranger gets tired of pulling the plow, I expect I'll just hook up you and Addison."

She punched him, then laughed and kissed him again.

"Whatever it takes," she said.

"Whatever it takes."

From the first day they arrived the people in the caravan had noticed people coughing and blowing their noses. After Lisa examined them, she told Bob it didn't take a doctor to make the diagnosis.

"Headache, sore muscles, chills, extreme tiredness, cough, runny nose . . . one girl was running a temperature of 103. It's the flu."

On the last day of their stay, four of them came down with the flu. They were Sandra and—not to be outdone by her twin—Olivia, Emily, and Teddy. As they were departing the next morning Bob was sitting with his wife in the bus. He mopped her feverish brow with a damp cloth.

"Well," he said, "look on the bright side. It isn't cholera."

"Keep your bright side to yourself, all right?" Emily came back at him, miserably. "Until you get it, anyway."

"It is a bright side, though," Lisa said. "I can guarantee you that cholera is out there. Also typhoid. Maybe a lot of other things."

Neither Bob nor Emily commented on that. Lisa was once more in a bad mood, and it was easy to understand why. She had lost a patient to the flu the previous evening, a four-year-old girl.

Everyone was shocked to hear it, and that made Lisa angry.

"People die of the flu, okay? Every year, thousands of them. Usually twenty thousand or more. More children get it, but more elderly die of it. That's even in a hospital. These children . . . they're malnourished. They're weakened. So are the adults, the oldest most of all."

"Lisa, no one is accusing you of anything," her father said.

"I know you're not. It's just . . . I've lost so many, so very many."

CHAPTER TWENTY-SEVEN

Teddy was in no shape to scout for them.

The flu hit him hard, with a high temperature and chills that left him shaking. Despite his doctor's advice he got on his bike and pedaled it around the parking lot while the others were packing. He made it about a quarter of a mile before he lurched off, stumbled over to a curb, and vomited. After that he walked the bike back and was helped into the bus with the other sick passengers.

The healthy ones gathered when they were ready to roll, and hashed out whether they should stay another day or two. Or even three.

"I'm against it," Mark said. "We know we can't settle here. We know there are other refugees on the road. Yeah, I said refugees. The only difference between us and those hordes at the Anaheim city limits is we're better equipped. I figure all those communities south of us are filling up rapidly. They're going to start shutting the gates, like Anaheim, if they haven't already. Which means we have to get wherever we're going as soon as possible."

Mark's argument carried the day. They said a few good-byes to people they had begun to see as friends. Addison in particular was devastated to leave a girl of her own age named Guadalupe, who she had grown close to in a short time. And, Dave thought, possibly to her handsome brother, Francisco. But after some tearful hugs and kisses, she boarded the Escalade without complaint.

"Do you think there's any chance we might see them again, Daddy?"

"I wish I could tell you, honey. You can see how difficult travel is now. But it won't always be that way. Things will get better, and we may not have to travel too far to find a place."

"But we don't really know, do we?"

"No, Addie, we don't."

Though Teddy was sick, they still needed someone to scout for them. There were other volunteers to take on the job on bicycles, including Dave, but he knew there was something better. It would, however, require some renegotiation with Addison.

"Daddy, you promised."

"I know I did. That's why we're having this family meeting. Karen, do you want to say anything?"

"Yes, I do. Addie, I'm very impressed with how grown-up you are, even more than you were before all this happened. You never beat me over the head with how superficial I had become, or your father with how obsessed with work he was."

"Mom, I . . ."

"It's okay. I know you had issues with both of us. The only good thing—the *only* good thing—to come out of this chaos is that it brought our family back together, and made both your parents see what was really important in life. I am so proud of you for not hating me." Suddenly Karen sounded uncertain. "You don't hate me, do you?"

"Oh, *Mom*." Dave almost had to laugh. Addison had managed to tell her mother that she was being silly, that she still loved her, while still not surrendering an ounce of her teenage sulk over what her father had proposed.

"Good. Because I never stopped loving you. I just stopped showing it. I love you so much that it's very hard for me to do what I'm about to do . . . which is to tell you to stop behaving like a little brat, and *grow up*!"

Addison jumped as if Karen had slapped her.

"You want to be treated as an adult. That means that you have to contribute on an adult level. To all of us, not just me and Dave, but the whole new family. They need scouts. We have scooters. Now, if you're going to whine and try to hold me and your father to a promise made when circumstances were different . . . well, I guess you're just going to have to learn that sometimes promises are broken, because they have to be. Not because we want to leave you, or because we don't love you, but because this is something that has to be done, whether you like it or not. I don't like your father going out there alone, and I'm not crazy about doing it myself. But an adult puts all that aside, weighs the options, and does what's right for everybody, not just for herself.

"So here's where we stand, young lady. This is going to happen, whether you approve or not. But it would be so much easier if we did it with your approval, and didn't have to come back to your resentment. Can you let go of it? Can you release us from the promise we made?"

Addison's chin was quivering, but she was managing to hold back the tears.

"I'm just so scared, Mom."

"We all are. But I know you'll be brave. You've shown us that already."

The girl was silent for a few moments, then nodded.

"Do what you have to do," she said. "It's all right with me. And I'll only get angry if one of you doesn't come back. Then I'm going to be really pissed."

It was a compromise, but it seemed to work pretty well.

Either Dave or Karen would motor ahead on one of the scooters, leaving the other parent with Addison. When they discussed it before facing their daughter, Dave had suggested they point out that, worst case, she would not be left an orphan. Karen had stepped on that at once, and Dave had quickly seen that she was right. That observation would only emphasize to the girl that every time one of her parents left her, there was a chance that she would have only one parent at the end of the day. Best not to discuss that part of it at all. She was smart enough to understand the risks. Why emphasize them?

Dave took the lead on the first day. He kept his hand on the shotgun at all times, ready to aim and fire in an instant. Or at least, he hoped, faster than whoever he was shooting at. And always, always, he kept in mind that if it were humanly possible, running was infinitely better than fighting.

The first day passed without incident. They were still trying to make their way to the I-5, but managed only to get to Garden Grove at the end of the day. They saw people but didn't interact with anyone other than to wave at those who waved at them. It was a reminder that, though there were certainly predators out there, the vast majority of people were as decent and harmless as they had ever been.

There was less quake damage down here, but that didn't mean there weren't plenty of blocked streets. Usually there were at least a few people still living on those streets, and often they were willing to talk. Dave quickly found that these people were almost always familiar with the neighborhood, which streets were passable and which were not. It saved some time.

Sometimes the residents just stared at him, hands on their weapons, sometimes with a speculative look. In his best moments Dave thought the look said "I wonder if he's got anything to eat?" In his worst moments, he wondered if their thoughts were more like "I wonder if he'd be good to eat?" He told himself he was just being overimaginative. These people were still a long way from cannibalism. Weren't they?

In any case, no one overtly threatened him, though he was clearly being told to move along, he was not welcome. One very large man even told him so. Dave just waved at him and accelerated away, his back prickling.

He quickly developed a new appreciation for the work Teddy had been doing. And a new dread of letting Karen do the scouting the next day. But he knew it wasn't a question of "letting," and that she would insist on taking her turn.

Addison was doing her best to look grown-up and unconcerned when Dave returned close to sunset with his last report of the day. Karen had told him that Addison had spent the day always looking ahead, and had sighed in relief every time they heard the putt-putt of the little Vespa.

"Your old man can handle himself," he said. "Which means, at the first sign of trouble I run like hell."

"Just keep doing that, Daddy," she said, solemnly.

"Didn't have to run once today. Saw nothing but nice people. I think all the bad guys are keeping their heads down. They've found out that solid citizens like us are ready to shoot back."

"Don't shoot back, Daddy. Shoot first."

"No, run first. Then shoot if you have to. But I don't think I'll have to."

Karen didn't have to shoot the next day, either, but Dave got his first taste of what it had been like for his girls the day before. He was on edge every time she drove away, and almost over-whelmed with relief every time she came back. She made five scouting forays that day, and his anxiety increased with every one. *At this rate,* he thought, *I'm going to see if a man can actu-ally die of worry.*

Jenna, sitting up in the back, did her best to keep Dave and Addison's spirits up.

"Karen's a fighter, and a survivor," she said. "I'd be more worried for any bad guys she comes up against than I'd worry about her."

Dave glanced in his rearview. Jenna was much improved, but she still looked ghastly. Gaunt and pale, with bags under her eyes, she was weak and slept a lot. And, of course, she was deeply frustrated by being unable to be much help.

"Cargo, that's what I've been reduced to," she said in a moment of self-pity.

"Cargo that's pretty handy with a shotgun," Addison told her.

Karen's last report was that the way was clear down Magno-lia Street to the 22 Garden Grove Freeway, which also looked pretty good. The caravan stopped for the night with the freeway in sight. Dave heaved a huge sigh of relief.

The next day Dave easily found a route onto the 22, and they headed west. There was no need to range very far ahead, as the freeway was broad and nearly straight, and the drivers could see almost a mile ahead. The smoke from the fire had blown away, and the air was as clear as it had been a hundred years ago. So Dave hung the scooter from the roof and got in the passenger side, with Karen driving.

They traveled farther than on any previous day, and yet it was not an encouraging day. The freeway was largely intact, with only two fallen overpasses to go around. But every time they left the freeway they encountered roadblocks. They were manned by police in uniforms, or hard-eyed armed men and women. The message couldn't have been clearer: Keep moving.

At first they stopped and talked with the people at the road-blocks, but they didn't get much information beyond the very basic lowdown on what they might expect at the next town down the line, and that was never good.

At the Santa Ana city limits Bob talked to the police sergeant in charge of the detachment blocking the highway.

"We're letting people through if they look nonviolent," the man said. He looked them over with a critical eye. He apparently concluded that the Marshall/Winston party didn't pose a threat to his community. But that was as far as he would go.

"By through, we mean *through*. No stopping in Santa Ana, unless you have relatives here. And we check, believe me."

"What about the town to the south?" Bob asked him. "Is it Tustin?"

"It *was* Tustin. They've incorporated with us, and we're all Santa Ana now. They don't want you folks, either. Sorry about that."

"What's south of that?" Karen asked. "Irvine, right?"

"Yep. And I don't know squat about Irvine."

"Do you know if they're letting people through down there? In Anaheim, they were turning them back."

"Is that so? Didn't know that. But I know the city council considered doing that, too. Voted down by five to eight, something like that. Come back in a week, they may have changed their minds."

"We're trying to get to San Diego."

"Good luck with that. My advice to you, go back to Los Angeles."

"There's nothing to go back to."

"I know. I'm sorry. It's just that, far as I know, there's nothing for you down south of here, either."

Santa Ana was not entirely heartless, they just didn't want to accept any new citizens, like so many other cities. But at the next gap in the freeway a small rest area had been established. There were some tents for the ragged and discouraged people there, who numbered no more than thirty or forty. None of them had motorized transportation. Some were pulling wagons or pushing shopping carts with their few possessions.

There was a soup kitchen, and a doctor seeing patients in a white trailer with a red cross on the side. But there was a hand-painted sign letting the travelers know that they were welcome for only twenty-four hours, and then they would have to move along. They would be moved by force, if necessary. No exceptions.

Lisa came back to the group after she had spoken to the doctor.

"That business about 'No exceptions' isn't written in stone, at least not to Dr. Garabedian in there. Though the city council may not know about it. He says he won't send someone on if they're desperately sick. He's kept a few, taking them to his own house. One of them died. From cholera."

"They're drinking contaminated water," Nigel said.

"People don't have much choice, after a big disaster. It's happened all over the world, in places like Haiti. I'm not sure which is a worse death, though, dehydration from no water, or from diarrhea."

"Well." Bob sighed. "Shall we move on?"

The story continued the same as the day wore on. They made good time, but continued to be unwelcome.

They made it through Tustin to the 55 Costa Mesa Freeway and decided to travel down it. They got about halfway to the 405 and came to another roadblock, this one deadly serious. Abandoned cars had been stacked up and converted into a steel fortress completely spanning the freeway. While they were still a quarter of a mile away there was a gunshot. They stopped instantly.

"I guess it was a warning shot," Bob said. "If they wanted to kill and rob us, they would have waited until we were closer, right?"

"Makes sense," Dave said. "I guess that gunshot says 'Turn around, we don't even want to talk to you.' "

They headed back to the 5. They never discovered whether the roadblock was maintained by the city of Costa Mesa or some independent band.

* * *

They reached the city of Irvine that evening. Once more they were not welcome, but were allowed to spend the night in a park the city had set aside for people passing through. They filled up on water again. The next morning they were stopped by Irvine police from cutting wood. There was nothing to do but keep heading southeast on the 5.

When they came to the 133 Laguna Freeway they turned due south and followed it. The land was barren, but after a mile they began to see isolated stands of trees, brown and dry after the long summer. There was no one around to stop them, so they cut down as many as they needed and filled the top of the bus again.

They had hoped to reach the 73 San Joaquin Hills Transportation System, which was a fancy way of saying toll road. It started at the 55 in the north and cut through a lot of unpopulated land like Crystal Cove State Park and Laguna Coast Wilderness Park. Avoiding towns had begun to seem like a good idea.

But it was not to be. There was another roadblock just before the freeway entrance. Someone behind it used a loud-hailer to tell them they had to turn around unless they had relatives in Laguna Beach.

"But we only want to get on the freeway," Bob shouted back.

"We'll let you on if you're going north. If not, Aliso Viejo doesn't want you, either. You'll have to go back to the 5 or the 405."

And that was that. Their only consolation was that the side trip had replenished their fuel, and it hadn't taken long on the open road, and took even less time on the return.

They rejoined the 405 south to the 5, and made it to Mission Viejo, yet another community with a twenty-four-hour visitor policy. They made camp on a golf course with a dozen other families.

None of their neighbors talked about food, probably because most of them didn't have any. The temporary guests were being advised to boil their water, and most of them seemed to be doing it.

The soup being doled out was thin and tasteless. The Winstons and the Marshalls ate a cold, meager supper, a few at a time, in the bus.

"We're not learning much about these towns," Dave said. "Are they growing crops? Is food coming in from somewhere? Are they eating their dogs and cats?"

"That's the sort of thing they don't want us to know," Rachel said. "If they're prosperous, they don't want to tempt the transients."

"Same as us," Lisa pointed out.

"And if they're desperate," Dave said, ". . . well, I'm guessing if they were *desperate* desperate, they'd be confiscating our stuff. I guess that's good news. Maybe not too many people are starving."

Mission Viejo was not welcoming of strangers, nor was San Juan Capistrano.

They saw more refugees on the road. There were the inevitable shopping carts, but more and more of them were simply walking, with nothing but their clothes and whatever might be in their pockets. The human tide they had seen going to Santa Monica had become a trickle here, but it was all flowing relentlessly south, toward Capistrano, Dana Point, and the sea. These people were the most destitute they had yet seen. Some of them had stopped walking. They simply sat by the side of the road.

"I can't take much more of this," Karen said, as they passed a man, woman, and child sitting in the shade of an overpass.

"I know what you mean," Dave said. Then, "Fuck this. Sorry, Addison."

"I agree, Daddy. *Fuck* this."

He pulled over and shut off the engine. The bus and truck pulled in behind him, and Mark and Bob got out and hurried to the Escalade.

"What's the problem?" Mark called out.

"We have to have a meeting," Dave said.

"Right now? What do we need to talk about?"

"Just get everybody out, would you? I'll tell it to everyone at once."

* * *

"We're at the end of our rope," Dave began.

"In what way?" Lisa asked.

"I want to cut my rations in half," Addison said.

Emily looked shocked.

"There's no need for that."

"I want to give what I don't eat to that child back there." She jerked her head toward the family under the bridge.

"Dave and I, and Addison, we just can't stomach it anymore," Karen said. "I think a little part of me dies every time we pass a child like that. A child whose parents seem to have given up. A child who is obviously starving."

"So you want us to cut our rations?" Marian said.

"I don't know what I want." Suddenly Karen was crying. Dave put his arm around her. "I want this to be over with. I want to never see another starving child."

"I can't stand it," Addison said, quietly.

For a while no one had anything to say. Then Nigel spoke up.

"I feel the same way. My food doesn't taste good anymore, even though I'm hungry all the time. I have to choke down every mouthful."

"Me, too," Elyse said.

"Okay," Bob said. "I'm sure we all feel the same way. But what do we do? Do we cut down to half of what we've been eating?"

"If we do that, we'll get weak pretty fast," Lisa said. "I'm not saying we shouldn't. I'm just saying."

"All right," Mark said. "I'll play devil's advocate here, if no one else will. We've got one proposal to go on half rations."

"I didn't propose that. I just said it for me," Addison said.

"All right, honey."

"Don't call me honey."

"I'm sorry. But others sounded like they'd do it, too. Now, you all understand that if we start feeding everybody, our food will be gone in days."

"I think that's clear," Gordon said.

"So I assume that's out."

No one disagreed with him.

"But we're all suffering from . . . what can I call it? Guilt, I guess, and a lack of self-worth. I know I feel it in my guts every time I have to pass people like those back there. It tears me up, because I want to provide for all of us, too. I think our morale has never been lower. So, is there some middle ground? Without putting ourselves in too much jeopardy, without threatening our own survival, is there anything we can do?"

"I just wanted to feed that little girl back there," Addison said, dejectedly. Dave was so proud of her he felt tears starting in his eyes.

"Then that's what we should do, Addison," Emily said.

"But what after that?" Mark insisted.

"Well, there's triage," Elyse said.

"What do you mean?" her mother asked.

"Maybe that's not the right word. In an emergency, we treat the ones we can save. We leave the strongest for later, and we don't treat the hopeless cases."

They thought about that.

"That's not quite how it goes," Lisa said. "But I see your point. Do we diagnose people, feed the ones who are failing but not hopeless?"

"I didn't mean anything so formal," Elyse came back. "What I meant . . . like that little girl back there. I don't know if she's dying. I know she's hungry. Her parents look like they've given up. How about we just do it on a case-by-case basis?"

"What basis?" Mark asked.

"I don't know. But I'm with Addison. I want to give her something to eat. I know we can't feed the world, but I hardly feel like feeding myself." Elyse began to cry, and buried her face in Lisa's shoulder.

In the end they didn't make a policy, as such. They decided to play it by ear.

First Addison put a loaf of home-baked bread, a can of corned beef, one of Campbell's cream of mushroom soup, a two-liter bottle of water, and a packet of Tang into a brown paper sack and walked back to the family beneath the overpass. She went alone.

Everyone watched as she squatted down and spoke to the

people. She handed over the sack, talked some more, then looked at Dave's watch. He had set a five-minute time limit, and she obeyed it. The woman stood and hugged her, and Addison came back, wiping away tears. At first she couldn't talk about it. But she recovered eventually.

"They haven't had any food for three days. A few passersby have given them water, but that's all. They have nothing. The father has pretty much given up. They've been sitting there all morning. They have no idea where they are. I told them they could follow this freeway to Capistrano and the sea. That's right, isn't it, Daddy?"

"Yes, you got it."

"I think the mother will get them on their feet again. I told them there are bound to be refugee centers somewhere, and told them of the evacuations we'd seen. I don't know if any of that is true."

"It doesn't matter," Karen said, hugging her daughter. "If they stay there, they're dead. They have to keep moving. At least they have a chance if they keep moving."

From then on they helped out the people who looked the most desperate. It might not have been logical—some of those people were probably going to die anyway—but it was very human.

It was the ones sitting by the side of the road with their children that they favored. They reasoned that if you were still moving, it wasn't all that far to Capistrano. They had no more idea what to expect there than the walking refugees did, but it was clearly the only possibility of finding something to eat.

They did take one precaution. They made sure that no one else saw them handing out food. Gordon and Marian had been in some of the poorest places of the world, and knew how it could be if you gave money to beggars there. You could quickly be swamped by indigent and desperate people. So when they decided on a particular family, they stopped the bus such that it blocked the view of the occasional walker, gave away the food quickly, and moved on at once. They didn't stay around for thanks.

Addison, Sandra, and Olivia became the informal rescue committee. Jenna had been moved into the bus, and the twins joined Addison in the Escalade. They had made up half a dozen

CARE packages at a time, all of them similar to the first one, and they studied each prospective recipient and talked it over. It was an emotional process, nothing with any rules. They tended toward the people with the youngest children. They didn't try to justify who they fed and who they passed. There was no way to do that, just as there was no way to feed them all.

Dave had been worried that his daughter would want to give away the whole store, in which case he would have to say something, as he was sure someone else would if he didn't.

But she was careful, and so were the twins, treading a difficult line between stinginess and largesse. Dave could see it was taking a toll on her, and was proud that she had taken the burden on herself. He would not have wanted it. He felt the burden might be just a little bit easier to bear than the one where they had been passing by everyone. By the end of the first day of their new charity, they had given away seven sacks.

That day also brought them to the end of the line.

The town of San Juan Capistrano proved to be just like all the other towns they had passed through since leaving the burn area. All the exits from the freeway were guarded. Someone had set up a soup kitchen that was actually serving more than soup, with some distressed apples and oranges and refried beans on tortillas. There was a small stretch of freeway that had been set aside for transient camping. But no one was being allowed to stay.

"You can pitch a tent for the night, or you can continue on your way," a cop told them. "Or, about a mile from here you can join the refugee camp set up by the navy at Dana Cove. There's some food. They say an aircraft carrier will pick them all up one day soon. That's all I can tell you."

When they asked, the cop reluctantly wrote them a pass for one of their party to go down Harbor Drive to check out the camp.

Since it was Dave's turn to scout, he was about to take down the scooter when Addison spoke up.

"Let me take Ranger," she said. "He needs the exercise."

"Addie . . ."

"Dad, it's time I took some adult responsibility, don't you think? It's not like I'll be heading into the unknown. This looks safe. Isn't it, Officer?"

"I'd say so, ma'am." He looked at Dave. "She was my kid, I wouldn't let her go alone at night. But I've got a daughter about her age, and she's volunteering at the camp. She'll be okay."

"Let her go, Dave," Karen said.

So he gave in. She quickly got the horse from the trailer, saddled up, and took off at a trot down the street, waving to the party as she left them.

"It's pretty grim," she said, an hour later. Ranger was grazing in a patch of grass by the freeway, and everyone had gathered to hear her report.

"The stink, well, it's awful. There's blue plastic toilets, and they're all overflowing. It's a big marina, looks like it was fancy once. It looks pretty run-down now. Most of the boats are gone. There's this road that goes out to a long island."

"Landfill," Bob said. "As I recall, there's a breakwater and a man-made island."

"Anyway, that's where the people are. Out on the island. That road is the only way off, unless you swim. There was a tank on the road, with a big gun. The gun was facing out to sea, to the island. Where the refugees are."

"Prisoners, more like it," Gordon said.

"I wouldn't argue with that," Addison said. "There were some Coast Guard boats moving around. I found one girl from the town and I talked to her for a while. She was angry at all the people who had come there. I think she thought I was from town, too. She thought . . ." Addison paused, and made a face. "She thought they all ought to be pushed into the ocean. She said her family's boat was out there, and they couldn't get to it. She said they had looked at it with a telescope and there are people living on it. She wanted to go out there and evict them. I wanted to bitch-slap her so bad."

"Best you didn't," Dave told her.

"People get insensitive," Emily said. "They are so worried about their own situation, they—"

"You're too kind, Mother," Lisa broke in. "Yes, we've hoarded our food. But to worry about a goddam boat at a time like this? That girl didn't get that way after the disaster. She's been that way for a long time."

"That's what I thought, too," Addison said. "Anyway, I didn't tell her I was from out of town. I think she might have spit on me."

"You did good, Addison," Dave said. "And I'm assuming we don't want to join the party out on the island?"

Nobody disagreed with that, and once more they were on the road.

Dave scouted ahead again on his scooter.

San Clemente was another closed community. He drove by the guarded exit ramps without speaking to anyone. He made good time through the San Onofre State Beach and then, to his surprise, crossed under intact power lines and saw, off to his right, the twin domes of the San Onofre nuclear power plant. There were a dozen tanks parked on the side road, Old Highway 101, and at least a hundred troops. They watched him go by, but made no move to stop him. Could the plant still be in operation? He wanted to ask them, but they didn't look very friendly.

There had been almost no traffic on the road since he left Capistrano. He wondered if the lack of people meant someone knew something he didn't know.

He soon found out. A little over a mile from the power plant, at what had been a truck weighing station made of glass and steel and looking a bit like a spaceship that had just landed, a solid line of tanks were spread out across the road. Twenty or so foot soldiers—probably Marines, since beyond them was Camp Pendleton—were spread out in front of the armor in attitudes of parade rest.

It seemed a bit excessive, given that Dave was almost the only person on the road. But as he got closer he saw a group of people sitting beside the road in the shade of the only tree close to the freeway. He slowed, stopped, and cut the motor.

"They're not letting anyone through?" he asked to group in general. No one answered for a while. All of them had the ragged, defeated look he had seen so much of lately. Hungry people, people without much hope left. Finally one man spoke up.

"Nobody while I been here. I tried to ask 'em for food, and they shot at me."

"Shot at you?"

"They shot in the air, Tony," one woman said.

"I wasn't paying no attention to where the bullet went. Like to pissed my pants. Would have, but I'm too dry to piss. You got any water?"

"Not enough for all of you. I'm sorry."

The man eyed the gun in Dave's belt. He looked far too weak and tired to make a play for it. And once again there was that horrible choice. What was in his canteen was barely enough for even a swallow for all the people there. Still . . .

He tossed his canteen to the man.

"Give it to the children first," Dave said.

"Naturally." There were only three small children, and their mothers held the canteen for them, careful not to spill a drop. One of them cried when the water was taken away. The other two just sat back on the ground.

It was accomplished peacefully, no fighting for the scarce water. When they were all done, Tony tossed the canteen back to Dave, obviously not wanting to alarm him by getting too close.

"Sorry about draining you dry," he said.

"That's okay. I had some an hour ago."

"You gonna go talk to those soldier boys?"

"I'm going to try. Good luck to you."

He had gone no more than half the distance to the line of soldiers and tanks before a man in uniform stepped forward with a rifle and a bullhorn. The rifle was pointed in the air, which was a good thing, because he fired it, once. Dave stopped immediately, almost falling off the scooter.

"That's far enough, sir," he said through the bullhorn. "No one is allowed into this interdiction zone."

"Listen, please," Dave shouted. He was just close enough to make out the man's face. "All I want to do is pass through the camp. I'm with a—"

"Absolutely no admittance, sir."

"I'm telling you, I'm with a group, we have our own food and water, we're not destitute. We just need to get to San Diego. There are women and children with us."

"No admittance, sir." There was no emotion in the man's voice.

"Please . . . Can I come closer and talk? We just need to get through. If I could speak to your commanding officer . . ."

"These orders come from the commanding officer, sir. No one is allowed through."

"But . . . why? We're not spies, we will only take an hour to get through the camp, we can't possibly—"

The man fired another shot into the air.

"Sir, I have been patient with you. I am instructed to fire one warning shot if someone approaches to the point where you are standing. I have just fired two. My third round will be into your body if you come any closer. Do we understand each other?"

Dave could think of nothing to say. He stared across the unbridgeable gap, a gap that was not only physical but was somehow moral, ethical, a gap between power and helplessness. The might arrayed against him was ludicrous, more appropriate for repelling an invasion than stopping a single man on a Vespa.

And it was such a short distance. Twenty miles to Oceanside. From there it was only fifty miles to San Diego.

Something inside him snapped. He raised his fist and screamed.

"Tell your fucking commanding fascist officer that David Marshall was here, why don't you, you Nazi fuck! Tell him that if I survive this, if anyone in my family *doesn't* survive this, I will find him, and I will tear off his head and shit down his fucking neck. I pay your salary, you prick. I paid for your training, I paid for your weapons, for your fucking tanks. I am a *United States citizen*, and you work for *me*, shithead. Your men work for me. They are supposed to protect me, and my daughter, and my wife, and my friends. And now you threaten to shoot me? Well fuck you and the tank you rode in on!"

Part of him knew this was possibly the stupidest thing he had ever done, and yet it was impossible for him to stop. The rage, the bile, poured out of him. It wasn't for himself, and it wasn't just for the family. It was for the people he had just shared his water with. It was for the seven families his daughter had decided to feed . . . and for the thousands they had been unable to feed. It was for every hungry person they had passed on their journey, and every person they had turned away from Doheny Drive. It was for all the sad and sick plodders on Santa Monica Boulevard, and the people in camps he had never even seen, in Santa Monica and Dana Point. It was even for the people who had turned them away from their communities, people who were basically good but had little or nothing to share . . . and for those who shared anyway.

The sane part of him noticed the men in the ranks behind the officer stirring restlessly as the curses came screaming from his mouth. Angry at him, or just possibly angry at their officers? Either way, he knew he was in danger. The man with the bullhorn had put it down and his rifle was no longer aimed into the air.

Struggling back to something approaching calm was one of the hardest things he had ever done. Finally, still boiling, still shaking with rage, he shut up, spit on the ground in the general direction of the soldiers, and turned his scooter around.

For the first quarter mile he felt a target on his back, felt it in the form of an itch he couldn't scratch even if he had reached behind him. But no shot came. When finally he dared look back he could no longer see the men and tanks.

CHAPTER TWENTY-EIGHT

"We've come all this way. For what?"

It was Rachel, voicing the thought they were all having.

It didn't seem that morale could get any lower. When Dave returned with his news the group had decided to pitch camp beside the road and consider their options. Mark, always the planner, had spread out the map and enumerated their options.

"West is out, unless we want to swim to Japan. Dave tells us that south is out. To the north, we have a string of towns that have already turned us down. Our only choice is to head east."

"How?" Bob asked.

"Backtracking is the only way I can see. All the way north to the 91 and the 71. Then east to Corona and the 15, when we can cut south again through Temecula. South of that there's a lot of agricultural land."

"How far back to the 91?"

"About forty miles. And remember, the farther north we go the worse the quake damage gets. Maybe fire damage, too. We don't know how far east the fire spread."

It didn't look promising.

Marian was peering over Mark's shoulder. She pointed to a line on the map.

"What about this?"

"Route 74. The Ortega Highway. Don't even think about it."

"It looks sort of twisty."

"Twisty doesn't even come close. It goes up into the mountains, two lanes wide, and most of it is cut into the mountainside. One landslide would be all it would take to stop us cold."

Bob was looking at the map, too.

"I've driven it, and Mark is right. But we're quite a ways from the epicenter. We've been seeing less and less damage. It's not a populated area. Isolated ranches and getaway homes. We probably wouldn't encounter much human resistance."

"I tell you, it wouldn't take much in the way of fallen rocks or collapsed roadway to stop us in our tracks."

"I think it might be at least worth taking a look," Emily said. "And as I recall, it's well forested. Finding wood would not be a problem."

"That's true," Mark conceded. "But the road . . ."

"What's this at the end of the line?" Elyse asked.

"That's Lake Elsinore," Bob said. "Largest natural lake in Southern California."

"So it's a community with water."

"Yes, it's a pretty big lake."

"How many people there?"

Bob thought it was twenty or thirty thousand, spread out over a fairly large area. To the north there wasn't much between the lake and the city of Corona, and to the south and east there was a lot of rural and semirural land. To the west there were only mountains.

For once the group seemed almost evenly divided. Mark had his allies, and Bob had his. The debate was civil, everyone being too tired and discouraged to bring real passion to the arguments. But Bob and Emily were in favor of trying the mountain road, and so were Dave and Karen, and eventually Mark gave in.

The next morning they would set out for Lake Elsinore.

The first miles were not difficult.

They passed through rolling hills with scrub brush and copses of trees. Caspers Regional Park appeared on their left, nothing to write home about. Ahead of them bare rolling hills began to rise. They saw few signs of human habitation other than dirt roads branching off to the sides, some gated, some not. There were some cattle guards, so Dave assumed the roads led to ranches down in the hollows. As the road cut through the first of the hills there were some small slides of rock and dirt, but nothing they couldn't drive around or bump cautiously across.

It was a nervous ride. Around every corner might be an

impassable barrier, a length of road collapsed into a canyon below, or a boulder the size of a house blocking their way. There were plenty of boulders that size and much larger, waiting to fall.

They started coming to hairpin turns, making a full 180 degrees, as they wound their way up the hills. Twice they had to stop for fallen trees. These were both old and dead. It seemed the jolting this far south had not been enough to topple most living trees.

They did not see another human being all day.

Then they came around one bend and found the worst obstacle yet.

It was a rockslide much bigger than any they had seen before. Most of it was dirt and rocks that looked as if they could be moved, with some heavy lifting by several people. But there were twenty or thirty that could very well be immovable. They stopped, and everyone got out to look at what might very well be the end of the road.

"Well, now we know why we haven't seen anyone coming up from the other side," Mark said. Dave thought there might be a little *I-told-you-so* in his voice.

Nigel climbed up on the rock pile, followed quickly by Sandra and Olivia. Dave followed them, kicking tentatively at some of the larger rocks. None of them budged.

"So what do you think, people?" Bob asked. "Is this the turnaround point?"

"No way," Nigel shouted. "No way. We can *move* this. Unless there's a *really* big rock under this pile, we can *move* this, guys."

Dave wasn't so sure, but he didn't feel much like turning around.

Mark sighed, then grinned.

"Okay. We have four shovels. We can take turns tossing dirt. Everybody else can grab rocks as heavy as they can lift, and toss 'em overboard. Sound good?"

It was hot and heavy work. Everyone who could handle a shovel—which was all of them except Jenna, Solomon, Emily, and Taylor—took fifteen-minute shifts attacking the pile. Even Teddy was feeling well enough to work.

At first it was just a matter of getting a scoop of dirt onto a shovel and tossing it over the side. But as the day wore on and the pile grew smaller, it was too far for most of them to throw. So one person would toss a load toward the edge, and others would pick up that dirt and toss it over the side.

Some of the rocks were small enough to handle with the shovels, but when they came to a larger one it had to be wrestled loose, and then either lifted or dragged to the edge and kicked over.

Both Solomon and Taylor ended up "helping out," Solomon with rocks the size of baseballs, and Taylor with smaller ones. They both enjoyed tossing them as far as they could and seeing them roll down the hill.

That used up the rest of the morning, and went into the afternoon. As they worked they got a better idea of what they were facing in terms of larger rocks. It didn't look good, but Mark insisted it was not impossible. Facing a logistical engineering job he thought he could tackle, he had become a convert to the idea of getting across the mountains one way or another. He enlisted Dave and Marian in converting the U-Haul truck into a bulldozer.

"My idea is to take out two of the armor panels from the truck," he said. "Then I'll weld them into a wedge shape and attach that to the front. Maybe I can shove the biggest ones aside." He looked dubiously at the front of the truck. "And maybe not."

The thing Mark fashioned was not elegant, but it looked sturdy. Whether it was sturdy enough to move the two largest rocks remained to be seen.

First he had stripped away all the front grillwork on the U-Haul, making an ugly beast that seemed to be snarling at them. He propped up the two pieces of armor and welded them together, then welded two steel braces between them to give the structure strength. When he was done he had a plow blade eight feet wide. It was designed to deliver brute force to rocks, and it only had to move them about ten feet.

By the time it was done, all the dirt and smaller rocks that had to be moved were out of the way. The labor force was exhausted, sweaty, and filthy. Dinner was served while Mark regarded his creation from all angles. They all stood to one side and Mark fired up his wood-burning engine and slowly eased the front of the truck into contact with the first rock. This was the smaller of the two, standing about three feet high and about six feet in its longest axis. The blade kissed the rock. Mark looked out at his audience.

"Here goes nothing," he said.

Unfortunately, he was almost accurate. The truck's engine revved up and whined at a higher pitch. Smoke belched from the vertical stack.

The rock moved, cutting a rut in the asphalt. Everyone cheered. In all, the rock moved about six inches. Then the truck stalled. Mark hit the starter and revved the engine again. The truck stalled. In all, Mark tried six times to move the rock. Each time the truck stalled.

Mark hunkered beside his truck, using a stick to draw things in the dirt and muttering to himself about torque, compression ratios, and other considerations. He was not a happy man.

"Can we break it up?" Marian asked. Mark sprang to his feet.

"Sure, if we had some dynamite. I didn't think to pack any."

"Nobody's blaming you, son," Bob said. Mark wasn't buying it.

"I could probably cobble together some explosives from common household chemicals," he said. "But I'm not sure I remember just how to do it. I'm not real happy messing with explosives when I've never—"

"I absolutely forbid it," Emily said, reverting to protective-mother mode.

"I remember some stuff," Marian said. "But I wouldn't want to mess with it, either, without someone who knew more than I do."

"Could we break it up any other way?" Nigel wanted to know.

Mark blew out a breath.

"It would be a lot harder than you imagine. That's very hard rock. That's a damn *big* rock. I only have one sledgehammer. I don't know if it would last long enough for this job. But if it did . . . it might take days."

Other ideas were tossed around, but none seemed promising. After a while Dave cleared his throat.

"Maybe we used the wrong vehicle," he said.

It took another two hours to remove the blade from the U-Haul and mount it on the Escalade. It involved taking off the front bumpers, fenders, and hood. The Escalade was looking like it had driven through a war zone, with hardly one surface that wasn't dented or scratched. And, of course, it was filthy. When they had the blade mounted it looked even more warlike.

"*Sorcerer,*" Dave said, regarding it. Marian laughed, and they had to explain it.

"That movie about those trucks carrying dynamite over mountains and rope bridges. Good movie."

"I wish I had some of their dynamite," Mark said.

Dave's reasoning had been simple, but persuasive. The SUV was four-wheel-drive and the U-Haul was not. It had a bigger engine. And as Mark admitted, the improvised wood-burning engine simply didn't have the muscle of a sophisticated Detroit mill. But the remounting went smoothly, as something you do for the second time usually does.

When they were ready to go the sun had dipped behind the hills to the west, and there was not much daylight left. They had cleared everything out of the Escalade. It only remained for Dave to start it up and drive it toward the rock.

"Wish me luck," he said, and Karen leaned in the window and kissed him. He dropped it into the lowest gear and eased it forward until the center of the plow blade touched the edge of the jagged rock. Then he slowly began to give it the gas. The big vehicle's engine purred quietly at first. He watched the tachometer as the needle moved slowly up.

The rock moved. First it was only a few inches, and then it slid a foot or more. This time there was no cheering; everyone was holding the celebration until the rock was over the edge of the cliff.

The rock moved another foot, and then all four wheels on the Escalade began to spin. Smoke billowed from under it, and the smell of burning rubber filled the air.

Dave backed off on the accelerator, and the rock stopped moving.

"Easy does it," Bob said. Dave nodded, and started to push again.

Two more times the tires lost traction. Each time Mark and Gordon swept loose dirt from the road in front of the tires, and each time they bit again.

Dave was hooting in triumph when Mark raised his fist in the air, indicating that the rock had moved enough for the vehicles to get by. But he wasn't going to let the damn thing go that easily. He gunned the engine again, and the rock went to the edge, teetered, and rolled over. Everyone was standing on the edge cheering as the boulder crashed through the underbrush. Dave was the only one who couldn't see it, but the sound was wonderful. He had grown to hate that damn rock.

"One more to go," Mark shouted, and ran to the other boulder. He used a tape measure to figure out how much it needed to be moved so they could get by. It came to about ten feet. He made a mark in the dirt showing where it needed to be, and hurried back to Dave.

"That was great, but you probably shouldn't do it again."

"I probably shouldn't have done it that time."

"No, we needed something to cheer about. But be careful, okay?"

"I will be."

He approached the second rock, which was about the same size, maybe slightly bigger. He felt sure he could move it. The only problem might be in the rock's shape. The side where he had to push it was slanted a bit, and he was worried that the blade would just slip up and over it.

But Mark signaled thumbs-up as he watched the blade contact the rock. Dave signaled back, and started to push.

It seemed the bottom of the rock was smoother than the first one had been, as it was not gouging out ruts as deep as the first one had. The tires smoked once, but Dave backed off and they regained traction.

Mark was standing near the front of the truck, watching. As the rock got closer to the line he held his arms out wide, indicating how far it had to move. After a few seconds he moved his hands closer.

When there was only a foot to go the rock seemed to dig in and stop, so Dave pressed a little harder on the accelerator. The rock moved, and then there was a shriek of metal and suddenly the Escalade lurched up and forward. It was very quick, and the next thing he knew he was climbing the rock. The front wheels were in the air but the back wheels were still digging in, and suddenly meeting no resistance.

The Escalade leaped up, to the sound of tearing metal. Dave was jolted so hard that for a moment his hands came off the wheel and his head bumped the ceiling. He took his foot off the gas, but the car's momentum was carrying it up and over the top of the rock. He hit the brakes, hoping it wasn't too late. The front end slammed the ground hard enough to bang his head against the steering wheel, and for a moment he couldn't see anything. But he knew he was still moving. He began to skid toward the edge of the cliff.

He probably would have gone over, but one of the front wheels had been broken from the axle and immediately dug into the dirt, providing a lot more resistance than just the brakes. The front of the Escalade dropped over the edge, hung there a moment . . . and then the movement stopped.

Dave held his breath, not daring to move.

He felt blood trickling into his eyes. Outside the car, and a little behind him, someone was shouting.

"David! Don't move!" That was Karen. He was slowly getting his wits about him. He turned slowly in his seat and saw his wife. Standing beside and a little behind her was Addison. Karen was holding her hands out to prevent their daughter from moving forward, and he realized they were standing on the edge of the cliff.

"I won't," he said. He did move, though. He looked out his window and saw nothing. He looked down and saw that the front of the Escalade was over the precipice. The lip of the cliff was about even with the back edge of the door beside him. He would be able to open the door and step out carefully, and be safe.

If the vehicle didn't tip over the edge.

"Everybody!" That was Gordon's voice. "Come to the rear of the car. We need to hold it down. Just in case. Dave, don't move yet."

"I won't," he said again.

While they organized that, he felt his face for any broken bones. His nose was bleeding, but it didn't feel broken. There was more blood coming from his forehead, but the gash he felt wasn't deep.

"Okay, Dave, we're putting weight on the back. Can you open your door?"

He slowly opened the door and looked down. He would be able to swing out, holding on to the door frame, and reach safety with a bit of a stretch.

If he was very, very careful.

"Addison, get back," Karen was saying, as she reached out to him. He saw that his daughter was crying, and he tried a smile. Then he realized he probably looked pretty ghastly, with his bloody face.

Karen grabbed his hand and pulled, and he swung out and put one foot on the dirt. Then the other, and then one step forward. He immediately fell to his knees. He thought of kissing the ground, but decided that would be too melodramatic. Instead, he found himself laughing as Addison and Karen knelt by his side.

"That was more excitement than I was expecting," he said.

"Well, I never liked that car anyway."

Dave had had a few minutes to recover. Mark had promptly attached a chain to part of the Escalade's rear chassis and pulled it back from the brink, fearful that it might still fall over. As he did this, the broken front wheel came free and bounced down the hillside. The big SUV now sat there, grievously wounded.

"Can't fix that," Mark announced, to no one's surprise. "You know, it actually might drive on three wheels, it has a lot of ground clearance. But I'd have to work on the brake system, and—"

"Forget about it," Dave said. "I'd actually thought of proposing we leave it behind, anyway. It's a big waste of gasoline which we could use in the scooters. The truck already has all our cargo, and there's room for us on the bus. Besides, we don't figure to be traveling all that far. It's sort of Lake Elsinore or bust, isn't it?"

No one disagreed. If they were turned away from there, Dave

supposed they would try to keep moving south on the 15, toward San Diego, but he held out little hope they would get there, or be accepted when they arrived. It wasn't something he would say out loud, not wanting to worry Addison, but that was how he saw it.

They drained the Escalade's gas tank into some of the empty gas cans. Dave thought the moment called for something dramatic, like pushing it over the cliff, but knew that was stupid. Just because the world had gone to hell didn't mean they needed to further vandalize it.

And he discovered a late-blooming affection for the impractical old beast. It had taken his family though holocaust and riot, had performed faithfully and efficiently in spite of its many wounds.

Maybe the thing to do would be to shoot it in the head, like an injured horse.

But they did nothing. They pushed it to the side of the road so it wouldn't block any other travelers. They hitched the horse trailer to the back of the U-Haul, but Ranger could easily walk to Lake Elsinore. It was all downhill. They moved on.

It was getting dark when they rounded a last bend in the road and came to a lookout point. Far down below them was the lake, and the towns of Lake Elsinore and Lakeland Village, surrounding the lake on four sides. The lake itself was almost rectangular, and a lovely blue in the pale evening light.

And there was something that already seemed amazing to them. There were lights. It was one-hundredth as bright as it would have been a few months ago, but the lights were clearly electrical, not lanterns.

"San Onofre," Dave said.

"Must be," Bob agreed. It seemed that some power was still coming over the lines from the nuclear plant on the coast.

"Go down there now, or in the morning?" Rachel asked.

"I don't think it's wise to approach them in the dark," Marian said, and everyone agreed. So they looked over the terrain and picked a spot slightly back from the overlook, as it looked easier to defend. The road was quite narrow there. They parked the bus sideways across the street, leaving only a narrow gap at each end, and kept the truck behind that. They pitched tents and made dinner. He didn't know about the others, but Dave was exhausted. He fell asleep almost at once.

They posted guards both ahead and behind. Dave had the second shift, and Karen woke him at midnight. He had slept through the alarm.

"Want me to take your place?" she asked. "I wasn't sleeping well."

"No, we'll stick to the schedule. Just give me a minute."

He got into his clothes and for the first time since last winter felt the need of a jacket. He didn't know whether it was the altitude or because it was later in the year, or both, but there was a chill in the air. Karen had brought him a thermos of hot coffee and he drank some of it at once. It cleared his head a little.

"You sure? You don't dare fall asleep."

"I won't." He was a veteran of night watches by now, and had taught himself a few tricks that kept him awake.

"It's me," he said quietly, as he came close to the spot where he knew Teddy was concealed. They had chosen it carefully. It was on the cliff side of the road, the east side, where it had been blasted through a ridge about fifteen feet high. There were a few scrubby trees growing from the side and on top, several large boulders, and three or four cracks in the rock big enough for a man to hide in and obtain some protection from gunfire. The place where Teddy should be was also chosen to give him a field of fire if he needed it. Dave couldn't see him.

"I'm here," Teddy said, and flashed his light on and off quickly. Only then was Dave able to pick him out. The young man was about six feet up, leaning down and offering his hand. Dave took it and climbed up beside him. There was barely room for the two of them.

"See anything?"

"Couple of rabbits, running fast. Maybe a coyote. Quiet night"

Teddy handed him the walkie-talkie, and left. Dave settled himself into the niche in the rock. There were places he could have sat down, though none would have been really comfortable, but he knew that comfort was the enemy of alertness. The handmaiden of sleep, if he was allowed to wax poetic.

He looked around. Because of the curve of the road, he could see just the front half of the bus, not quite a hundred yards away. He checked his pockets for spare shotgun shells. He had a few dozen, which he hoped were a lot more than he would ever need.

Then he settled down to wait.

CHAPTER TWENTY-NINE

The man came up the road at around two in the morning. The moon had moved higher in the sky, but was still coming from over Dave's shoulder; he was completely in shadow. The guy was wearing black. He had a gun in his hand. He was tall and skinny, almost skeletal. Maybe a tweaker, a meth addict. Or maybe just a hungry man looking for food. Dave clicked the radio signal for "intruder approaching."

The guy was moving quietly, staying close to the rock wall on the other side of the road. He got far enough around the curve to see the rear end of the school bus. He quickly pressed himself against the rock wall and looked carefully around. This man was a scout of some kind.

Scouting ahead was an entirely reasonable thing to do if you were seeking a safe path for a peaceful party of refugees, like Dave and his group. Traveling at night, sneaking around, didn't strike Dave as quite so reasonable. A night reconnaissance was more in keeping with a raiding party. Dave aimed his shotgun, and waited.

After a minute or two, the man backed away, and when he was out of sight of the bus he turned around and walked rapidly back down the road.

Dave made the signal for "all clear," and relaxed a little. Almost at once he heard someone hurrying toward him from the bus. He quickly flashed his light. He saw that it was Marian, and she was carrying her military rifle. He couldn't remember what it was called, but he knew it was serious firepower.

"One man, dressed in black," he whispered. Then he described the man's actions.

"Scout," she said. "He's going back to get reinforcements."

He gave her a hand up.

"The plan is, I'm going to station myself here because I have a little experience in situations like this. You're to go back and join the others."

"I'm staying right here."

"Your family needs you, Dave."

"And Gordon and Taylor need you. Your son is only four. He needs a mother. You're the one who should go back."

She didn't have any argument to go against that. She sent a series of signals.

"I'm not going back, either. I've told them that I'll buzz once if the guy comes back again. We'll draw down on him, take him to the bus if he surrenders. Kill him if he shoots."

"Okay."

"I'll buzz twice if more people come. Then I'll buzz the number of people we see. We'll let them get past us. Then we'll play it as it goes. If they start shooting, we shoot them. If the people in the bus start firing, we shoot. If it's my judgement that we should shoot first, we shoot first. You have a problem with that?"

"Not at all." Dave's heart was pounding so strongly he hoped she couldn't hear it.

"You're probably scared. No need to hide it. I'm scared, too. But I think I should be in command here. Any problem with that?"

"Not even a tiny problem. You're the boss."

She nodded, and he saw her teeth when she smiled.

"We'll get through this," she promised him. He was glad she was so confident.

It was half an hour before they came. Dave had settled down, but the adrenaline started pumping again the minute the first people came into sight from down the road. They were all dressed in dark clothes, but it was a motley crew. There were guys with big beer bellies, and others who were thin. There was a lot of black leather. Sleeveless vests were popular. Some hair was long, and some heads were shaved. Two of them were probably women, though it was hard to be sure. They were all armed. Some carried pistols and others had rifles and shotguns. Some carried a gun in each hand.

Marian tapped Dave's arm. When he looked at her, she opened her palm five times. Fifteen. He counted, and that was close enough. He nodded, and saw her depressing the alarm button.

They were all sticking to the rock wall on the other side of the road, and they were led by the first man, the scout. He moved more slowly when he approached the spot where he had first spied the bus, and everyone bunched up close to him. They were no more than thirty feet away from Dave and Marian. She whispered in his ear.

"We're not going to wait. These are killers. We shoot first. You with me?"

Dave nodded. His throat was too dry to whisper.

"Wait until I shoot," she said. "Fire for no more than five seconds, then get down, take cover. Got it?"

Dave nodded. Marian picked up a rock the size of a baseball, slowly stood up, holding her rifle in one hand and the rock in the other. Then she threw the rock. It hit the stone wall about ten feet above the group, and tumbled down the side of the hill along with a shower of smaller rocks.

They all turned and started firing above them, where the rock had impacted. They were shouting and shooting. The noise was incredible. All of them had their backs to Dave and Marian.

Then Marian started firing into them, about one shot every second. She seemed to be picking her targets. Dave fired one shotgun round into the crowd, then another, and then another. He thought he saw two or three flashes coming from the bus, but everything was happening too fast, so he couldn't be sure of much.

One thing he was sure of was that some of the intruders were down on the ground. Some were screaming, and some were still.

"Get down!" Marian told him, and he did. He crouched behind a rock as bullets began to impact all around him. Rock chips flew and he felt some of them hit his skin, but there was no pain. He thought he was too pumped to feel it.

The people on the road were shouting, and some were still screaming. Dave risked lifting his head a little as the incoming fire died down. He saw two men crouching low and running toward him. He swung his shotgun toward them and fired two rounds. One man went down hard, the other turned and ran, hobbling.

"Shoot again!" Marian yelled, and he saw her standing and

placing her shots again. He stood up. At least five people were
down, and the others were fleeing up the road, away from them
and toward the bus. A few snapped off shots behind them as
they ran, but they were not aimed.

When the survivors were about halfway to the bus, four
lights came on and gunfire erupted from several of the bus windows. Dave saw the intruders in silhouette, pinned in the bright
light, probably blinded, disorganized, shouting, not knowing
which way to run. He saw three of them go down in rapid suc-
cession. One stumbled to the side of the road and dropped off.

"Hold your fire," Marian said. "We might hit the bus."

Dave had already figured that out. Besides that, he was out
of ammunition. Hands trembling, he got a handful of shells
from his pocket and reloaded. Even with all his caution, one of
them slipped from his hands and vanished into a crack in the
rock below him. When the magazine was full again, he turned
and saw the remainder of the gang coming back toward them.
One of them was walking rapidly backwards, firing as he went.
On the back of his jacket were the colors of a motorcycle gang
that featured a large wheel and a grinning skull. He couldn't
read the name of the gang.

He fired a shot at the man, missed, and fired again. The
lights ahead suddenly went out, and for a moment he couldn't
see much. He heard booted feet pounding the pavement below
him, and then they were gone.

He and Marian were surrounded by the smell of gunpowder.
Below them one man was still screaming, and another moaned.
His vision was coming back, and he counted six bodies below,
only one of them moving, the screamer.

Marian was saying something, and Dave had to lean closer
to her to hear. His ears were ringing from all the noise.

"We have to go down there, but we better wait a minute.
What I mean, this cross-fire ambush probably won't work a second time. They know where we were hiding, they might come
up behind us."

"You think they'll come back?"

"Depends on how many didn't come the first time. Most
biker gangs have more than fifteen members."

They waited, and for a while the only sound was the man's
screaming. That faded away after a few more minutes. He was

either dead, or in shock. Then, from down the road, they heard motorcycles start up. The engines were unmuffled, the way outlaw bikers liked them.

"Uh-oh," Marian said. "We may have to run for it. Don't assume anybody down there is dead. If we have to run—"

"Wait a minute."

Marian was silent, and they listened to the sound of the motorcycles moving away from them. Soon they could barely be heard.

"They're running away," he said.

"Time to move, then. They may be going for reinforcements. I'm going to need a little help."

That was the first time Dave realized she had been wounded. She was holding her hand to her side, and blood was oozing out between her fingers.

"It's not bleeding badly," she said. "I think it was just a graze. It might even have been a piece of rock. You're bleeding from the ear and shoulder, you know."

He had been aware on some level of a nagging pain, but nothing serious. Then he touched his ear and it all came to throbbing, pulsing life, both the ear and the shoulder. The ear was on fire, and he felt like he had been hit in the shoulder with a baseball bat.

"It hurts like hell," she said. "I can't put any weight on my right leg."

"Okay. Should I lower you down?"

"I think that's the best idea."

He managed it, though it hurt his shoulder. She gasped a few times, but never cried out. If she could do it, so could he; he vowed, though he wanted to curse and holler and just generally complain about his pains.

The screamer had gone silent. Marian had one arm over Dave's shoulder, and a pistol in the other hand. Dave used his free hand to keep his shotgun trained on the screamer as they approached him.

It wasn't necessary. The man's left leg was hanging by a thin strip of flesh, and his intestines were spilling from his belly. Dave fought back nausea.

"I did that," he said.

"Don't get your panties in a twist. He was coming at us, shooting at us."

"Yeah, I know. I guess you have more experience in this than I do."

"Actually, this is the first time I've killed someone."

Dave felt like laughing, but was afraid he couldn't stop once he got going. Marian was their veteran, the ex-soldier. Her tactical training was the best they had, but he wouldn't have felt quite so safe in the gun battle if he'd known she had never killed.

"Actually, I have killed someone," he said. He didn't know why, it just seemed the right moment.

"Really? You'll have to tell me about it someday."

"Maybe."

He was hurrying as fast as he could, but they were carefully watching each body for movement. The ones in front of their hideout were all clearly dead, except for the screamer, who was still bleeding but clearly would not survive.

They began to pass more bodies. One was feebly trying to crawl away. He was leaving a bloody trail behind him.

"Watch his hands," Marian said. The man wasn't holding anything, but there was a Glock semiautomatic with an extended magazine near his feet. Dave picked it up while Marian lifted the man's shirt to see if he had any weapons squirreled away. The man rolled onto his back. He was gasping for air and blood was leaking from his mouth.

"My impulse is to finish him off," Marian said. "But I don't think I can."

"I think he's going to die, anyway. It looks like a bullet went through his lung."

"These guys were killed by firing from the bus," she said. "Unlikely we hit any of them at this distance."

Dave was wondering if she was feeling shock or remorse for all the killing they had done. He himself was feeling nothing for them. But he agreed with her. He wouldn't shoot this unarmed man in the head or the heart.

"Let's get the fuck out of here," Marian said.

When they were approaching the bus one of the headlights mounted on the side came on briefly, then switched off. At once Lisa and Elyse and Nigel—the medical team—came hurrying around the back of the bus, followed closely by Karen and Addison and Gordon.

"She's injured," Dave told them.

"Just a flesh wound, I think."

"Both of you, come on around behind the bus." Gordon took over supporting Marian and Karen rushed to Dave's side. After a quick hug from her and his daughter, they all got off the battlefield. Dave was glad that the nearest corpse was at least thirty feet away. The dead were just shapeless lumps lying in the road.

Marian was taken into the bus, while Elyse worked on Dave's injuries by the light of a Coleman lantern.

"I think you lost a little bit of ear here," she said. "This is going to sting."

Dave talked to take his mind off what Elyse was doing.

"Anyone hurt here?"

"No," Karen said. "By the time we switched the lights on they were so disorganized and panicky they didn't get many shots off. I heard some bullets hitting the side of the bus."

Addison was holding back tears.

"I was so scared I didn't even shoot, Daddy. I just ducked down behind the wall there and I couldn't stop shaking."

"I was shaking, too," Dave said. "Ouch! That . . . Okay, okay, you warned me. How much is gone?"

"Just a little piece. You'll never miss it."

"Easy for you to say."

"But you did shoot, didn't you, Daddy?"

"Yes, honey, both of us shot. They were coming at us, and . . . and we'll talk about all this some other day."

Marian's wound turned out to be a ricochet. Lisa extracted a mangled bullet, what she said was probably a .45, from her hip. It had hit the edge of the bone and gone downward, but it wasn't deep.

They sent Gordon down the road and up on the crest of the hill, not to lie in ambush this time, but to come running back if he saw anyone approaching. From his position he could see almost half a mile downhill. Dave suspected they would hear any counterattack before Gordon saw anything. He expected they would come on their bikes, but it was possible they might try to sneak up on foot.

Then there was a dirty chore to take care of. They intended to continue on down the hill in the morning, if that was possible. But there was the matter of the bodies.

Dave was part of the party that moved the bodies. He doubted that any of these men had been good men before the disaster, was sure that most if not all had been violent before. But he had killed some of them. He would never know just how many, and didn't want to know, but he couldn't just leave them lying in the road, and he couldn't let others clean up his mess. He joined Mark and Bob and they ventured once more beyond the relative safety of the bus.

They approached each body with caution, weapons pointing at them. It turned out there were nine, not including the one Dave had seen falling off the slope on the side of the road. They never found him.

All but one of them were dead. They pulled them to the side of the road and behind some shrubs. Mark had to pause for a moment to throw up; one of the bodies didn't have much of a head left, and then there was the one Dave had thought of as the screamer, who was almost cut in half.

They came last to the one still living. He was able to raise his head as they approached, and he held his hands out to his sides to show he was not armed.

"You fuckers," he said, weakly. "You shot me."

"Where are you hit, son?" Bob asked him.

"I'm gut-shot, you bastard. My boys will get you for that."

"I don't think you're in a very good position for making threats," Bob said. "How many of you are there?"

"None of your fucking business."

"Do you want to live?"

The man looked up at them uncertainly, then he was hit by a spasm of sharp pain. He turned onto his side and curled into a fetal position. Dave trained the flashlight down at him and looked closer.

"He's got a real big wound there. I don't think he'll make it."

"Damn you," the man moaned. "there's a hospital down there at the lake. You got to get me to it."

"We can't," Mark said. "We won't move at night. We're worried there are more of your boys down that road."

"Listen, it looks like most of us are dead. There was only three women stayed behind, at a clubhouse a mile down the road. I don't know how many you killed . . ."

"Nine," Bob said. Not counting you."

"Nine? *Fuck!* How did you—"

"Because you are stupid," Dave said, suddenly angry at this pathetic specimen. "Come on, guys, we've got to get him back to Lisa. What's your name?"

"None of your business."

"Well, sorry, but we don't have a stretcher and we can't spend any more time out here in case your friends come back. So we'll have to pick you up."

Dave took his feet and Bob and Mark each lifted him under an arm. The man howled, then lapsed into rapid panting. It looked like he had lost consciousness.

Lisa examined him quickly, and shook her head.

"There's very little I can do for him."

"He said there was a hospital down there."

"Yeah? Well, if we move him tonight—"

"He also said they had a clubhouse down the road," Mark said. "There's no way we're going to drive past that tonight."

Lisa was obviously frustrated, but had grown used to that, to some extent. As a doctor she was only interested in saving lives, it didn't matter whose life it was. But she couldn't argue that they should risk all of their lives to save this man, who had tried to kill them.

In the morning they got an early start, since no one had slept. They fired up their burners, and as they were warming up Mark set out on one of the scooters to scout ahead. He reported back that the clubhouse the injured man had spoken of appeared to be a tavern, a small building perched on the edge of the cliff overlooking the lake. The views from inside must be spectacular, he said, but he had not approached it closely.

"I didn't see any activity. No motorcycles parked outside. No cars, no people, no nothing. I think they've split."

"We'll be careful anyway," Bob said.

"Naturally."

They set out, the bus in the lead, the truck following with Lisa and the wounded man in the back, Addison bringing up the rear on her horse.

There was no sign on the place. It was an uninteresting little concrete-block building with few windows on the street side. There was a large gravel parking lot, with nothing in it but an overflowing Dumpster.

"What do you think?" Bob asked Dave. "Drive on by? It doesn't look like they have any way to chase us."

"They could get a Harley through those doors. I think we need to check it out. I don't want anybody coming up on us from behind." Dave was uneasy about Addison's riding behind them. Now that they had cleared the way, others could make it across the mountains in cars.

"You're right. Let's you and me do it."

They approached from the side that had no windows. Gordon, on the roof of the bus, had his sights trained on the front door. They kicked the door open. Bob peered into a single big room that had been trashed as thoroughly as if a frat party had been going on for a year. Open cans had been kicked into corners. Liquor bottles had been smashed. Filthy sleeping bags were crumpled on the floor and on the bar.

There was someone lying on his back on one of the tables. Dave aimed the shotgun at him as he walked up, but there was no need. The table and the floor around him were covered in dried blood.

"He hasn't been dead long," Bob suggested.

"Wounded last night, I'll bet. Bled out."

A rat poked his nose out of a clutter of empty cans and sniffed the air. Dave looked away. And in the corner behind him he saw a large stack of wooden cargo flats in shrink wrap, with cans of food visible. There were hundreds of cans, maybe a thousand, things like corned beef hash, Spaghetti-Os, and fruit cocktail.

"They didn't attack us because they were hungry," Dave said. "They've been eating well."

"You think they stocked up before the stores ran out, or robbed?"

"My guess would be robbery. It would be their style."

"You want to take any of this?"

"I'm tempted, but I'm still worried about them coming back. And, come to think of it, wouldn't it be looting?"

Bob looked away, then back, with a sheepish expression.

"I'm ashamed of myself. I guess it's easy to get into the attitude of 'If it ain't nailed down, it's mine.'"

"If it makes you feel any better, I thought if it, too. Looting the looters, that doesn't sound all that bad to me."

"Little doubt of that."

"And furthermore, if we were out of food, I'd take every can."

They stepped out of the building and gave the all clear. Lisa had been watching. She got down from the back of the truck and walked toward them.

"He just died," she told them.

They didn't spend a lot of time mourning the dead biker, but Dave wished he had at least told them his name.

"Do we want to leave him here, or take him to the bottom of the hill?" she asked.

"I'd say here. There's another body inside."

The three of them wrestled the body through the doors and, kicking aside the layers of trash, arranged him on a table next to what they presumed was one of his buddies. Lisa looked around at the boxes of food, and they could see her struggling with the same problem they had talked about. In the end she faced her father.

"Did you come across any medical supplies? Any liquor?"

"We didn't think to look."

So they rummaged around. They didn't find any bandages, not even a Band-Aid, but they did find a stash of prescription pills, many of which Lisa could use, and a box of military syringes full of morphine. Lisa almost jumped up and down in delight. She insisted they take all of it, and no one had the slightest objection. She was almost as happy to find an unopened case of half-gallon bottles of vodka, and another of Scotch.

"Absolut and Glenfiddich," Bob said, admiringly holding up a bottle.

"Is that good?"

"They stole only the very best, my darling daughter."

"Well, you won't get to drink any of it unless I come across a whole lot of regular alcohol. Vodka should sterilize a wound nicely."

"All I ask is that you pass the Scotch under my nose once a day," Bob said. "And to be allowed to gaze at the bottles."

CHAPTER THIRTY

They started out again, steadily down the winding road. This time Dave and Karen were in the lead, on their scooters. Addison was allowed to follow on Ranger as long as she kept around five hundred yards between herself and her parents. They took it slowly, particularly through the cuts that had been blasted through the hills, where the road narrowed considerably into perfect spots for an ambush. There were a few driveways off to the right. All of them were blocked with chains or cars, but they saw no people. Then, for a mile or more, there was nothing but the road and the drop-off.

They came to a turn that was not a hairpin, but a long circle that took them through 180 degrees. They were getting down to the level of the lake. There were trees on each side of them, and then a walled community with just the tops of the roofs visible on the other side.

Ahead of them, a roadblock.

Concrete road dividers had been placed across the road so that it was possible to drive through them in a zigzag pattern, but only at about five miles per hour. While you did that police would be firing on you from concrete-and-sandbag bunkers on each side of the road. A large sign warned that remote control mines were embedded in the roadway. There were two police cars behind the barrier, and a large tent.

"I think we'll wait right here until the others catch up with us," Dave said.

"Good idea." They shut off their motors and rested the scooters on the kickstands. Karen removed her helmet and stood looking at the barrier ahead.

"That's what we have to get through," she said.

"Doesn't look exactly like a rolled-out red carpet, does it?"

"They have to take us, David. We have nowhere else to go."

"Then we better make ourselves irresistible."

Two police and three civilians were behind the concrete barriers, holding their weapons. Addison had caught up with her parents, dismounted, and led Ranger to a patch of grass, where she hobbled him. No one behind the barrier made any move to come forward and contact them. Addison looked anxiously at her parents, but said nothing. Dave thought she was still a little shell-shocked from the battle last night.

Fifteen minutes later Bob in the bus and Mark in the truck arrived, pulled up close behind them. The drivers got out.

"Should we walk over there, or drive?" Mark wondered.

"I'd say drive, but as soon as they show any nervousness, we stop and get out."

"Unarmed," Dave said.

"I think that would be wisest."

Dave and Karen handed their weapons to Mark, who stowed them in the back of the truck, then they boarded their scooters and Addison mounted Ranger, and the whole ragtag party moved slowly forward to meet the cops until one held up his hand.

"You folks will have to turn around and go back to where you came from."

Bob and Mark were standing with Dave, Karen, and Addison. Bob looked down at the ground for a while, then turned toward the vehicles.

"Everybody out," he called. "Turn off the engines. Don't bring any weapons."

Lisa was first with her two teenage children, then Rachel, who joined Mark with their twins, and little Solomon, who looked around with the same wonder he brought to any new situation. Marian and Gordon came next, Gordon holding four-year-old Taylor. Last was Teddy, helping Jenna, who was getting around better but still needed crutches. Emily was too sick to get out of bed.

The officer was a young man in his late twenties. His black hair was cut short under his broad-brimmed hat. His eyes were tired and showed a lot of strain. He regarded them and handed his shotgun to a female officer standing just behind him. She took it, and looked at them with a face that was devoid of expression. The officer in charge folded his arms in front of him. A clear posture of rejection, if Dave was any judge.

Bob had been elected to do the talking. He looked the officer in the eye.

"My name is Bob Winston. This is Dave Marshall and his wife, Karen, and daughter, Addison." He went on to introduce Jenna and all the members of his biological family. "You're not wearing a name badge, Officer. Could we know your name?"

"I'm Officer Lopez."

"Could we have your first name?"

"I don't think that would be wise. My orders are to turn anyone around who comes down from the hills. I don't like the job, but it's—"

"I have to tell you, Officer Lopez, that we won't be turning around. We're not defying you. It's just that we *can't* turn around. There's nothing for us to go back to. We were forced out of town by the big fire, I suppose you heard of it?"

"The smoke covered us for days. Yeah, we know about it. And I'm damn sorry, but you're not the first people from L.A. who want to move in with us. There have been thousands of them. We can't handle them all."

"That's the same story we got from all the towns near the coast. People are starving in refugee camps back there."

"So I've heard. I can't do anything about that."

"Of course not. What are you doing with the people who come down along the interstate?"

"We're stopping them. Turning them back."

"I see. What about the ones who won't go back? Do you shoot them?"

Officer Lopez looked offended.

"Sir, you need to turn your vehicles around—"

"They're camped out just north of town," the female officer said. The man turned to look at her and he didn't look happy, but he didn't stop her.

"We don't let people starve. We don't have a lot, but we feed them, once a day. They don't have anyplace to go, either."

"There is a big camp north of town," the male officer admitted. "Worse comes to worst, I guess you could come through and stay there. But we can't admit you to the town. We have to look out for our own."

"I understand that, Officer, and I understand that you are following orders. But is there any possible way to speak to the ones who *gave* the orders? Can we present our case to them? The city council, the mayor, or whatever?"

Officer Lopez said nothing. Dave thought again that was a good sign. Bob didn't let the silence grow.

"My daughter Lisa is a doctor. She has spent all her time since the quake and until we left town tending to injured people. Could you folks use a doctor?"

Again, the man said nothing, but the woman looked interested. She glanced at the man in charge, but didn't say anything.

"Addison here has a horse. I'm betting that you find horses useful these days, with no gasoline for farm machinery."

"Can it pull a plow?"

"Ranger can do anything," Addison piped up. "He's smart, and I can teach him to pull a plow or a wagon."

"My son Mark is an engineer. He converted the bus and the truck to burn wood or coal. He can fix anything, and he can build anything."

"We've converted a few vehicles ourselves," the man said.

"You have anyone who can improve them?" Mark asked, stepping forward. "I've got a lot of ideas to make them more efficient."

"That's not something I know anything about. Look, Mister . . ."

"Bob."

"Look . . . Bob. I can't promise you anything. I've spent the last week on the northern town line, I guess you could call it a border now. I've been turning people away, and it about killed me."

"Me, too," said the woman.

"The children . . . Okay, you don't need to hear my problems."

"Officer, I'd be glad to listen to any of them."

"Look," he said, clearly frustrated. "I'm surprised you made it down here at all. Nobody comes down the hill anymore. We haven't had to turn anyone away for days."

"And why is that?" Bob wondered.

"Because of the Overlords," the officer said. "That's a motor-cycle gang we used to tangle with. They've been happy as pigs in shit. They took over the roadhouse up there a month ago. At first they were only robbing travelers, taking everything they owned. They'd let the people walk down. But lately nobody at all has come through."

"You figure they're killing them?"

"That's what I think. They've raided some of the homes around here. Killed some people. We're planning to go up there and try to root them out, but they're well armed. They've got the high ground. I don't really know if we can take them at all."

"There's not as many of them as there were," the woman said.

The man smiled for the first time.

"Weirdest thing. Last night—early morning, I guess—five of those fuckers came roaring up. I wasn't here, but the way I heard it, they were yelling something."

"Way I heard it," the woman said, "they were yelling about surrendering. Giving up. Something like that."

"I didn't hear that. Anyway, they ran right over some trip-wires we set out at night, attached to some Claymore mines. Just blew the hell out of them. Four of them died right there. One of them's still alive, I hear, but he's not gonna make it."

Lopez stopped, and frowned.

"Wait a minute. Did you folks . . ."

"They were running from us," Bob said, calmly. "They attacked us, and we killed ten of them. There's nobody left up there."

The officer frowned even more, and called another officer to come over. They drew back a little and talked quietly, and the other officer hurried to his motorcycle and started it. He headed up the hill.

"If he finds what you say he'll find . . ."

"Do you think we could get an audience with your city council then?"

"I'd say it's a good possibility."

The motorcycle officer had returned with confirmation of their story, Officer Lopez had made a radio call, and they had threaded the concrete maze into town before they were halted by a train stopped on the tracks. That was amazing enough, but the nature of the train was even more unusual. It was composed entirely of open hopper cars heaped with coal, and pulled by a dusty black open-cab behemoth that seemed to be leaking steam from every seam. It belched and bellowed and gasped.

It had stopped with the first hopper car blocking the road, the engine just beyond it facing south. Painted boldly on the side of the cab was the number 3025. Addison got down from the horse and started walking toward a man in striped coveralls who was standing on the ground contending with a frozen bolt with a wrench as long as his arm.

"It's Mr. Henrikson," she said over her shoulder. "The man we talked to at Travel Town. Hi, Mr. Henrikson." The man looked up. He was sweaty and his face was almost black with coal dust. He frowned for a moment, then his white dentures showed through the darkness in a big smile.

"Why, I remember you, young lady. You're . . ."

"Addison."

"Of course, Addison, how could I forget such a lovely name?"

She blushed, and was clearly pleased. Mark came hurrying up.

"My God, man, is that thing going to explode?"

"Well, I sure hope not, friend. I was hoping to make a few more trips."

"I can't believe you got Number 3025 working."

"You know this engine?"

"Sure. She's a magnificent old beast. You guys have worked a miracle."

Henrikson hadn't seemed to like Mark much at first, but now he warmed to him.

"Well, between you and me, she's a cantankerous old beast, too. She breaks down every fifty miles or so, but we keep her going. Bubble gum and duct tape, mostly."

Mark and Dave gave him a hand with the wrench, and the combined efforts of the three got the bolt loosened and then removed. Henrikson peered down into a chamber, shook his head, and poured a can of something into it. As they worked he told them about his recent adventures. This was the first shipment of coal.

"First two were food. Government surplus stuff, crackers and cheese and powdered milk, bags of rice, flour, sugar. Wouldn't be surprised if some of it was laid down back in the fifties, when everybody was digging fallout shelters. Most of it's stale as hell, but edible."

Dave was amazed at how his spirits were lifted at the sight of the old train and its engineer. Somewhere, someone was doing something on a level higher than the strictly local, even if they hadn't seen much evidence of it.

They were escorted to a high school. City Hall had been damaged and was unsafe, they were told, so the city council had relocated to the school gymnasium. The start of the school year had been indefinitely postponed.

They had been informed that there was a waiting list of several weeks to get a hearing on an application for admittance to the community, and all those people were waiting in the camp north of town. They had been moved to the head of the line by the intervention of one of the councilwomen.

"Any of them can do that," Lopez told them. "Mostly they've done it when personal friends show up from L.A. or San Diego. Councilwoman Ortiz was real impressed with how you handled the Overlords up there. I told you they came raiding in the night. In one of those raids her sister and brother-in-law and their child were killed. I'd say you've got her vote wrapped up."

"How many are on the council?"

"Five."

"And how many votes do we need? All five?"

"Just three."

They gathered in the parking lot to talk it over before entering the gym.

"I guess it's obvious, but I'll point it out, anyway," Bob said. "This . . . this tribunal will determine our fate for some time to come. Think of it as the most important job interview of your life."

"It's not right," Lisa said. "I'm inclined to throw my lot in with those people in the camp. Why should we be treated any different than them?"

"You're absolutely right," Bob said. "It's *not* fair. And if you want to do that, I will respect your decision. But here's how I see it. If we are not admitted to this community, I will submit quietly. Then we can talk about whether to go to the camp, or try to go south. But if we *are* admitted, I intend to devote myself not only to the welfare of my family, which has been almost my only concern for many months now, but to the whole community, which includes those in the camp.

"I'm assuming that this town is trying to come back to the point where they can take in those less fortunate than themselves. I assume that about *all* the other towns that have turned us away. It's been the only way I can get through the day, hoping that people are not solely protecting themselves, but trying to reach a position where they can provide for others, too. If that turns out not to be the case, if no one here is trying to make things better for those outside, then I will join you, Lisa, and stay in the camp."

Bob paused here, and wiped away tears. Dave was moved, too, as Bob had spoken out loud the thing that had been gnawing at him for a long time, and had been first brought out into the open by his daughter. He desperately wanted a home, but he didn't want to live behind walls while people died outside.

"I intend to do whatever is needed to provide food and shelter to not only all of you, but to those outside. If it means digging an irrigation ditch with pick and shovel, I will do that. If it means stoop labor, I will do that. But the way I see it, I can only do that on this side of the fence. Yes, I want food and security, but I hope I have the strength of character to give up those things if the work I'm doing here is only going to benefit a small group of people. If anyone else has a better idea, I'm eager to hear it."

There was a silence, finally broken by Teddy.

"All I can say is, I think you should do all the talking, Dad."

There was laughter, and Bob grinned, but he was shaking his head.

"I have been running off at the mouth, haven't I? But I'm afraid I'm all talked out. I think we should all speak up for ourselves. But we do need a spokesman, and I appeal to the Fearless Leader of our defunct writing team. Dave?"

"Yaaaay!" Jenna shouted, and Addison took up the cheer.

Dave could not recall anything he had ever wanted less than to have the responsibility for the whole group, but he knew that sometimes when a job is thrust upon you, you just have to do it.

"I am confident we'll get through this," he told them. "I'll do what I can. Lopez says we already have one vote. I agree with Bob that we should all speak up. But we should speak up for each other, okay? Any other suggestions?"

"Try to be positive," Rachel said.

"Without too much ass-kissing," Teddy suggested.

"We need to look strong, and confidence is always a good thing," Marian said.

"And tell the truth," Dave added. "If what we are and what we've done isn't good enough for them . . . well, then they're not good enough for us."

The five members of the council sat behind an ordinary folding cafeteria table, on folding chairs. Behind them were the flags of the United States and California. In front of them were several rows of folding chairs, on which the family was invited to sit.

Councilwoman Barbara Ortiz, a Hispanic woman who looked to be around fifty, sat at one end of the table, smiling at them. None of the others were smiling.

Next to her was Edgar Kovacs, a balding man of around sixty, dressed in the first suit and tie Dave had seen in a long time. He did not look, in Dave's estimation, like an ally.

Melanie Gold was also sixtyish, with her gray hair in a tight bun and her mouth in a prim line. She reminded Dave of a particularly harsh elementary-school principal he had known, not fondly.

She was the chairperson, and briefly introduced the others. She herself was a lawyer, Kovacs was a real-estate agent, and Ortiz owned a boat dealership.

At the other end was Pablo Martinez, the second Hispanic and the youngest-looking on the panel, late thirties or early forties. He owned a chain of five restaurants strung out along the valley. His expression was neutral, impossible for Dave to read.

And last, between Martinez and Gold, was a very obese man in a T-shirt, shorts, and flip-flops. When Gold started to introduce him he interrupted her, named himself as Stewart Jankowitz, and described himself as a "Net designer, business analyst, blogger, and rabble-rouser." It sounded like the man saw himself as an iconoclast, who might resist going with the crowd. Dave didn't know if that was good or bad for his family.

He noticed that not one of the five was in a profession that was in demand at present. There was not much work for lawyers or real-estate agents or the sellers of pleasure boats, and none at all for a Net designer and blogger. The times must be lean for restaurant owners, too, though maybe not so bad for cooks. What work there might be for a "rabble-rouser" was anyone's guess.

Dave wondered if this would work for them or against them. Three of the family, including himself, were totally useless in their previous professions as comedy writers. Rachel had been a reporter. Gordon was a teacher. Lake Elsinore probably had plenty of them, and even so, school was out for a period hard to determine. Teddy was a social worker. In the current state of things, there would probably be little need of that.

Seven of them were minor children, one of them mentally challenged, though five were teenagers qualified for heavy labor. Two had been stay-at-home mothers.

Only Lisa and Mark had what everyone would agree were valuable skills. Marian, as a military veteran, could probably do police work well.

That seemed to him the sum total of their human assets. Add in the two vehicles, the supplies they had left, and the horse, and it still didn't look that promising.

He looked at the panel facing him. Momentarily casting himself as a jury consultant, he added it up as one for, one possible, and three probably against.

It didn't really feel like a hearing. More like a court-martial.

He introduced himself and everyone present. He was about to go on when he was interrupted by Councilwoman Gold.

"Thank you, Mr. Marshall. I'd like to make a short opening statement, so that you know what's going on here.

"None of us are happy to be sitting in judgement of refugees. We are sympathetic to them, but the sad fact is that we are overwhelmed. They keep flooding south from the cities of the Los Angeles metro area. Everyone from Corona to San Bernardino seems to be heading our way, or has already arrived. Most of these people have nothing.

"I hope you understand that we feel we have to protect ourselves."

"Yes, ma'am, we do." But Gold wasn't finished.

"I think you can understand, then, that we are extremely worried about being attacked. The people in the camps are getting less-than-subsistence rations. So far they have been mostly peaceful—"

"Because they're too weak and worn-out to stand up for themselves," Jankowitz put in. Dave tentatively put him into the "for" column, based on the outburst.

"Possibly," Gold conceded. "I don't know how to remedy that."

"By giving them something to do."

It was easy to see that this wasn't a new debate. Jankowitz was for "the people," the great mass of the desperate. Dave felt sure that Gold was not on his side.

"Mr. Marshall," Ortiz spoke up. "I'd like to know how you and your family feel about the people outside. Not so much the reasons why *you* want to get in, and why we should let you, but how you feel about the others we aren't letting in."

Dave was glad they had discussed it. Without knowing how Ortiz felt about the question, he felt he had to follow his own advice and tell the truth.

"Obviously as an outsider I don't have a vote here on any matter. And we don't know much about your situation other than what you've just told us, so our opinion isn't formed by much information. We do understand your fear. We've felt it many times ourselves. But I can tell you that, much as we want to become a part of your community, we don't feel that we are special. I will plead our case, but if we are admitted, we will be on the side of those who want to help those who *aren't* admitted. We all agree that our best bet would be to do everything we can to turn those refugees into allies with work to do, instead of barring the door and letting them get hungrier and angrier every day."

"Hear, hear," Jankowitz shouted.

"Stewart," Gold protested, "we agreed this is not to be a debate, just a hearing to decide what to do with these people."

"I'm not debating. Just agreeing. You know where I stand."

Gold frowned at him, but went on with her statement.

"Right or wrong, we have adopted a policy of admitting new members to our community only in exceptional cases. You stand before us today, and we want to get to know you a little better before we make our decision. Now, we know about the horse and the doctor and the engineer, and that's all to the good."

Dave noticed the horse came first on the list. Wouldn't it be something if the damn animal, which he had seen as a necessary evil and a pain in the ass for much of the trip, made a difference in this hearing.

"Don't forget what they did to the Overlords," Ortiz put in.

"Yes, I'm sure we're all relieved about that, though as an officer of the court I can't entirely approve of taking the law into your own hands. When this is all over and things get back to normal that might have to be investigated."

Dave saw Edgar Kovacs give her a slightly startled look. *In other words,* Dave thought, *thanks, and you're under arrest.* He began to wonder if Attorney Gold was in serious denial about how long it might take for things to get back to normal. Was she expecting to be back at work negotiating contracts and divorces and writing wills in the next few weeks?

"Ms. Gold," Dave said, "I hope you don't think we're trigger-happy. We did what we had to do, just as you are doing at your borders. I hope your police officers and volunteers never have to do what we did . . . but you may. All of us will be haunted for the rest of our lives by that night of killing."

"I certainly didn't mean to imply—"

"Yes, Melanie, I think you went a little too far there," Kovacs said. "I want to personally thank you, all of you, for wiping out those scum. We've always been a peaceful town, a good place to live, and I believe deeply in the concept of law and order. But there is very little order now, and law seems to be inadequate to meet the situation."

Gold was glaring at him. Dave knew he had made an enemy, but he was pretty sure she had been against them from the start. He looked over at Bob, and his friend gave him a tiny nod.

But was Kovacs on their side?

"All right, I apologize," Gold said, obviously just to regain the floor. Already Dave hated her. "If we can get back to what I wanted to know at the beginning . . ." She looked around at her colleagues and no one objected. "Fine. Maybe you can all tell us about yourselves. What you have done, what you might bring to this community."

Dave looked behind him, and saw Teddy step up.

"I'm Teddy Winston. I'm twenty-eight, the youngest of Bob and Emily's children. I bicycled from San Diego to Los Angeles to join my family, and it was not easy. I am a social worker, with expertise in drug rehabilitation. I can also function as a scrub nurse." He went on with a few more biographical details. He did not mention that he was gay. Dave had wondered if he would. It was nobody's business, but might count against them if any of the five were prejudiced.

To Dave's surprise, Karen decided to go next.

"I'm Dave's wife, Karen Marshall. This is my daughter, Addison. What I was best at before all this happened was shopping, I'm afraid. Our family was reasonably well-off, and I lost track of what was important in life. I have gotten a new appreciation for real values. I know how to work hard, and I held a lot of different jobs when we were struggling. My wonderful daughter, Addison, is one of the brightest students in her school, and if there's anything she doesn't know about horses I can't imagine what it is. Addison, do you want to say something?"

"No, Mom. You've embarrassed me enough." She gave the panel a small smile. "I just want to say, I'd like to live here." Dave put his arm around his daughter and held her tightly against him.

Lisa went next. She spoke awkwardly, giving the bare-bones details of her medical education, residency, and practice, listing the hospitals where she had worked. Nigel and Elyse stood by her side. Nigel was quiet, calm, and articulate, mentioning his 4.0 grade point average and his ambition to be an architect.

"Give me a hammer, a saw, a few tools like that and I can build anything. I know how to fix pipes and work with electricity. My dad . . ." He paused and looked at the floor for a moment. "My dad taught me to be a pretty good fisherman. That's about it, I guess."

Elyse put on a brave front, but she didn't have that many manual skills, other than being a good cook. And, of course, the recent training both siblings had received as hospital orderly, nurse, and even surgeon's assistant.

Mark spoke confidently for both himself and Rachel, but Dave noticed that Gold was starting to look impatient, and

Kovacs seemed to be about to drift off. They were probably as exhausted as his family.

When Mark paused, Gold seemed about to speak up, but was interrupted by Martinez, the restaurant man.

"That's all very impressive, Mr. Winston," he said. "I'm sure you could be very useful to us. But like Melanie said, we already know about your being an engineer, and about the doctor. I'd like to hear from some others. You, for instance, Mr. Marshall. What do you do for a living?"

Here we go, Dave thought. He took a breath, and dived in.

"I'm a writer. In fact, Jenna and Bob and myself are all writers."

This didn't get much of a reaction. In fact, Martinez frowned. In Southern California, where everybody has a screenplay they would be happy to show you, writers were thick on the ground. Very few of them had ever had anything published or produced. Even this far from Hollywood, being a writer cut very little ice.

"What did you write?" Jankowitz asked, not sounding very interested.

Jenna spoke up for the first time.

"Me and Bob and Dave, plus two others, Dennis Rossi and Roger Weinburger, wrote *Ants!*" she said. Jenna had never been as ambivalent about the quality of the show as Dave and Bob had been. She had actually liked it.

And a strange thing happened. Melanie Gold smiled.

"You're kidding me," Jankowitz said.

"Nope. Every episode."

"I loved that show," Martinez said. "We used to watch it as a family, me and my wife and the kids."

"One of the few you *could* watch with your family," Kovacs said, nodding.

Jankowitz burst in: "Remember that episode where that scientist's shrink ray made 'em both the size of termites? And the termites chase 'em through the woodwork, and catch 'em, and take 'em to their queen? And the queen turns out to be—"

"—Queen Latifah!" Kovacs laughed. "And those termite suits, those were crazy, I about busted a gut."

"Well, we didn't design the suits," Bob said modestly.

"But you wrote it. How do you come up with those wild ideas? No kidding, you really are the writers?"

"They wouldn't dare lie about it," Martinez said. "I've got the whole series at home on DVD. Their names would be in the credits."

"I assure you we're not lying," Dave said, trying to keep a straight face.

"Oh, I didn't mean anything. Like he said, why would you lie about something so easy to check out? Say, I wonder if you'd mind autographing my DVDs, and I'll bet my kids would really enjoy . . ." He trailed off, coughed nervously, and looked down at the table. Dave knew he had just remembered that the writers and their families were more or less on trial at that moment. It would be a little embarrassing to hunt them down in the refugee camp and ask for an autograph.

The whole panel sobered quickly. It looked to Dave as if none of them were really sure which way their colleagues were going to vote. Gold was no longer smiling, and she had had nothing to say about favorite episodes. He had been thinking that maybe that goofy show might make the difference between admission and refusal, but now he wasn't so sure.

Dave glanced at Bob, and he was making a hurry-up motion. He thought Bob was right. Let's wrap this up, there was not much point in more testimonials.

"Ms. Gold, if I may . . ." Gold gestured for him to go ahead. "I think you all know us well enough now. Though I'm proud of our show"—he cringed inwardly; *liar!*—"and I'm glad you enjoyed it, we all realize that being comedy writers doesn't really bring a much-needed skill for surviving after this apocalypse. Neither does being a housewife, or a social worker, or a teenager, or a retarded child. But if I may be so bold, neither does being a real-estate agent or a Web designer."

"Touché!" Jankowitz cried out, cheerfully.

"I guess the only thing I want to emphasize here at the end is that we cleaned out that rat's nest hanging over your town. We didn't do it happily, and we didn't do it for your town, but we *did* do it. I expect to have nightmares about that for many years to come, but there are plenty of other things that have happened lately to give us all nightmares, and there are probably more to come. Officer Lopez told us he expected to have to assault that biker gang soon, and he wasn't sure they would be successful.

We had some luck but we were also alert and prepared. I just ask you to think about that.

"We want to join you, but if you turn us down we will accept that, and do what we have to do. We don't know yet whether that means moving on to the south, or stopping here in your refugee camp. But I want to say again, I think isolation is a bad thing. I fear that you all may discover that, in a very ugly way, if you try to keep all those people out of your town for much longer. I'm not sure you can do it, against a mob of angry, hungry people. I'm sure you have guns, but remember, so do many of them. I think it's an untenable position, and once they understand, really *accept*, that the government is unlikely to arrive soon and feed and house them . . . well, I'm sure you get the picture. I think our only hope is cooperation, all of us pulling together, including the people who have nowhere else to go.

"Thank you."

The council adjourned to another room, and everyone came up to Dave for a hug or a pat on the back. He was far from sure he deserved any of it. Where did he get off telling these people what they should do? He didn't know them, didn't know the community, didn't know the refugees.

He did feel he had said what he needed to say, and that it had been the right thing to say. But deep inside he was ashamed to admit just how deeply he wanted to be let in, just how badly he needed to stop, let down his guard a little, stop worrying every second of the day about protecting his family.

After the round of congratulations, everyone sat around without a lot to say. As the minutes dragged by he wondered how lawyers stood it, waiting for the jury to come back with a verdict.

It was only twenty minutes, but it seemed much longer. At last the door opened and the five people filed back in. They didn't resume their seats, but came around the table and, one by one, extended a hand.

"Congratulations," Ortiz spoke for all of them. "You're accepted."

There was no wild cheering, but a few shouts. The atmosphere wasn't of celebration, but relief, and a sense of solemnity.

They all trooped outside and stood in the parking lot beside their vehicles, and looked out over the lake. How valuable water had become, Dave reflected. Without it, most of the land they had traveled through would revert to the desert it had been when Junipero Serra had arrived in 1769. Yet here they stood on the shores of the largest natural lake in Southern California. They could see its flat blue expanse from where they were standing. With the water from the lake, anything was possible.

Dave noticed Barbara Ortiz standing near him.

"You don't have to tell me if you don't want to," he said, "but if it's not a secret, I'd like to know how the vote went."

"I won't tell you who voted yes or no," she said. "But it was three to two."

So they were in, and by the skin of their teeth. Dave looked out over the lake again.

There was a lot of work to be done.

EPILOGUE: From the Journal of David Marshall

There was a lot of work to be done.

I wrote those words four months ago, on the completion of my account of our journey from Hollywood to Lake Elsinore. I didn't begin it until we had settled into our new home. There was no leisure time to write during the journey, and almost none in the first months after our arrival. But I'm a writer, and a writer writes, if at all possible. I squeezed out ten minutes here, five minutes there at the end or the beginning of the long days of labor.

I wrote it in the third person because that's what I'm used to, and also because it helped me distance myself from the events, treating it all as fiction rather than the awful reality it was.

I have not added to the account for almost four months, since bringing the narrative up to our arrival at Elsinore, because I am not by nature a diarist, and because life has steadied enough that little of real interest happens on any particular day. It would be a pretty boring diary. My life now is mostly routine. Daily entries would consist of how many feet of ditch I dug, how many bushels of plums or peas I picked, what the weather was like, how badly my back ached at the end of the day. The concerns of a farmer, which is what I am.

But today is exactly one year since Colonel Warner died, which is when it all began for me. It seems like a good time to sum up what has happened here and what we have learned happened elsewhere, pieced together from unreliable sources, since our arrival.

We never asked, and never found out who voted for us and against us. We later became friends with Barbara Ortiz, but none of the others. No one ever said whether or not our writing of that silly sitcom influenced anyone's vote. I like to think it did, simply because it's such an amusing idea, that something so critical could be decided by something so trivial. I like to think that our battle with the Overlords got us one vote— Barbara's—that Addison's horse got us another, and *Ants!* got us the third. I may never know, and that's fine with me.

Another thing we never found out was if Ranger could pull a plow. We never had to. What ration of coal comes to town— the lion's share goes south, to San Diego—is used in burners to power tractors and other farm machinery, which are put to work as quickly as Mark and some others convert them. Though they can burn wood or coal, they are very inefficient, and we don't have enough of either fuel to spend on moving fertilizer to the fields and moving harvested crops out. So the unskilled among us hump those things on our backs, like coolies. (It turned out most of the population was classified as unskilled, as their former areas of employment were not necessary to survival.) Our horses can pull the weight of a hundred coolie-back loads on the flatbed wagons we cobbled together. Ranger took to drayage without complaint as if he'd been doing it all his life.

Everywhere we turned we came up against limits and shortages.

Mark and his team could have made more wood burners more quickly, but they soon ran out of acetylene. He says he'll be able to make more. Someday. In the meantime we just worked harder, to make up for the lack of mechanical help that had, over the last century, turned agriculture from one of the most labor-intensive jobs in the country into one of the least.

Only at harvest time, and only for certain crops, had large numbers of pickers been needed before the Collapse. Did you know that potatoes used to be harvested by machines that didn't even need a driver? The harvesters were guided by GPS, entirely robotic. Now, potatoes are once more harvested by a lot of people with shovels and buckets. Did you know they used to keep only those of a certain size, the size that appealed to shoppers in the markets? Now, every potato is eaten. No potato is thrown away for a rotten spot; the spot is carefully cut away and fed to pigs.

It takes a lot of labor. Luckily, labor is one thing we have plenty of.

I could give a million examples, but what's the point? Things that were in abundance are now rare or totally unobtainable.

Acetylene is only one thing of thousands of things we need, and will have to either do without or make for ourselves for the foreseeable future.

And yet we are eating, and that's all that counts.

So, to bring things up to date, I suppose I should start with my family.

Bad news first:

Emily died. It happened only a few days after our arrival. All through the trip we were worried sick about the roving gangs of pillagers, and as the Overlords showed us, with good reason. But in the end it was influenza that got her. It has been almost nine months now, and we all think of her every day. Her children are getting on with their lives, each in their own way, but something has gone out of Bob. He works fiercely, and doesn't speak much.

I doubt anyone will ever know how many died from the flu. It swept through town, and through the refugee camps, and at least a thousand died in just this little valley. It took the youngest and the oldest, the most weakened by not enough food.

The elderly got a double medical whammy, in that many of them had been kept in reasonable health by medications for heart and blood-pressure trouble, and many other ailments. Lack of drugs and unaccustomed exertion made heart attacks almost as common as flu deaths.

One "epidemic" is no longer a problem: obesity. The only fat people you see these days are the ones who must have weighed three hundred pounds or more before the Collapse, and they're on their way down. In fact, anyone who *stays* fat is viewed with the deepest suspicion, and is certain to have his rations cut. One man was beaten almost to death when a huge hoard of food was found in his basement.

Those of us who have survived are definitely a healthier bunch than we were.

Jenna lost her leg. It was even more of a surprise than Emily's death, to everyone but Lisa. She kept telling us that Jenna wasn't out of the woods, that with the primitive treatment and aftercare she had received anything could happen. Like the virulence of the flu, another thing we had largely forgotten about in the modern world was just how hard it could be to avoid and control infection. It took us all unaware.

One good thing was that Lisa didn't have to operate with no anesthetic. She had done several of those when the strong dope ran out at Cedars, and no one who has ever done that wants to do it again. It was as pain-free as such a thing can be.

The other good thing is how well Jenna has coped. She has to be the most positive personality I've ever met. "Glad to be alive," that's her attitude. If she dwells on her gang rape, she has never shown it. And she hobbles cheerfully through the day on her crutch, having rejected all the wooden legs she has tried. She expects to get a "modern" prosthetic one day, and I suspect she will, but it might be a long time. Meanwhile, she is in charge of one of our day-care centers, looking after the youngest children—under six; everyone else works—while the parents are in the fields.

Teddy has not managed to reconnect with Manuel. He has made two trips south, attempting to enter Mexico, but the border is fortified on both sides now, and they are serious about it. Communications are still quite haphazard even within the U.S. There are bulletin boards everywhere, thick with hand-printed pleas and photos, people trying to find each other. There is an area where people can look across the border, close enough to see faces. Manuel has not shown up there. Karen and I believe Manuel is dead, but Teddy continues to hope, so we hope with him.

Even more problematic is Bob's son Peter and his family, who were living in England and unable to return. The Winston family has not heard anything from them since the Collapse. It could be the miserable state of communications. But letters find their way across the oceans, and the continent, though it can take many months, so there is hope there, too.

For the other absent Winston son, George, the news was mixed. He and his family had managed to leave Manhattan, which was now apparently as much a ghost town as Los Angeles. Fire had been a problem all over the country, in cities and croplands, and several fires took out a great deal of New York City. Once started, they were terribly hard to stop if there was any wind at all. The fuel load in dense central cities was very high, and in the Great Plains there was little to stop a windblown fire if trucks could not get to it soon. The usual solution for putting out a fire was to pray for rain.

George and his family had made it to friends in the Catskills, where they spent a very hard winter with little food. One of their children died of pneumonia. That was all Bob would tell me. He had received only two letters from his son, the last informing him that they were heading south, along with what must have been a gigantic migration from the Northeast. We all knew their prospects of being welcome there might be bleak.

We have heard nothing from Roger or Dennis.

The only other news of distant relatives was good news. Karen's brother and his family are doing well, though like everyone else they are on short rations because of the number of refugees to feed. Which they do without complaint, genuinely good Christians that they are. Our invitation to join them is still open. I have no idea when such a trip might be practical, and I'm not even sure I want to go now.

Why? Because we are all appreciating something we didn't even know we were missing: a sense of community. And, all things considered, we are doing well. Certainly a lot better than many of the places we have heard of.

The earthquake was measured somewhere between 9.3 and 9.8. This is the difference between being the largest quake ever recorded, and the second-largest. It only matters to seismologists and record keepers, I guess. Those of us who went through it just know it was horribly big. We were lucky that the tsunami it generated moved away from California for the most part, though coastal communities to the north got six-foot to fifteen-foot waves and many died. The worst loss of life was all the way across the Pacific, in Hawaii, the Philippines, Japan, and China. New Guinea and Australia also got hit. No one seems to know what happened on many of the other Pacific Islands. Many of them have still not been heard from.

I can sum up my feelings about the situation in other countries succinctly: I don't think about them. I am aware of the reports of mass starvation in many parts of the world, like Japan. I know that in some Asian and African countries people are doing better than you might expect, as they were never very mechanized in the first place. They didn't have to go back to the eighteenth century; they were already there. Their agricultural problems tended to be in the area of converting from crops grown in massive amounts for export—such as coffee and tea and sugar—to crops to feed their own people.

It's not that I don't care about the suffering of people in other countries. I do care. But there are equally bad situations much closer to home, and I can't waste my time fretting about conditions in Australia or China. They have to handle their own problems. My concerns have narrowed to the United States, with some thought spilling over into Canada and Mexico. Everywhere else is a million miles away.

In the U.S.A., in Canada . . .

It was a terrible winter. No one knows if it was one of the worst on record; no one was gathering data and correlating it. But everyone agrees it was one of the worst. All through the Midwest and Northeast winter came early and stayed late. People ran out of heating oil and coal early, and had to travel farther and farther to chop wood. They cannibalized their homes to keep a fire burning to heat one room. When spring finally came it thawed the bodies of those who had died by freezing, or had starved and then frozen. Again, who knows how many? The body count is still going on now in early summer, and the fragmentary reports we get from back there hint that the total will be in the hundreds of thousands, or even millions.

The big question now, for those east of the Rocky Mountains, concerns how much acreage can be planted and harvested before winter closes in again. Last year's crop in the nation's breadbasket was basically not harvested at all. Vast quantities of corn, wheat, soybeans, and other staple crops rotted on the ground, where it was a banner year for field mice and prairie dogs. There was no shortage of hungry mouths and willing hands, but by the time most people realized the size of the agricultural crisis it was already too late to do much about it. The great masses of people were too far away to get to Kansas or

Nebraska or Iowa, and there was no transportation to get them there. Even millions of people in the field would probably not have been enough to make a serious dent in what was out there to be picked or scythed by hand, and then getting the crops out of the fields was an even bigger problem. In my mind I see endless lines of Americans, trudging down car-free interstates balancing plastic tubs of wheat and corn on their heads. That happened, and will have to happen again this fall, only there won't be nearly as much to harvest, because plowing and planting that much land by hand is even less likely to be done efficiently on a large scale than harvesting was.

One disaster follows another, in a relentless parade.

While much of the rest of the country was freezing, we got what we always get in a Southern California winter: rain. In a typical year just about all our precipitation comes in the months of December, January, and February. But there really seems to be no "typical year." It's usually too little, or too much. Particularly after a really bad summer-fire season, when the burned areas tend to go sliding down into the canyons. This year we had heavy rainfall, and I'm sure that large portions of high-elevation Los Angeles are now in lower Los Angeles, probably including what's left of my old house.

We hill dwellers used to curse heavy rain, and look anxiously uphill all winter. But as a new lowlander, I see it as the boon that it is. Lake levels are high, as are newly built runoff tanks that collect from rooftops all over town. We'll need every drop of it to get our crops through another hot, rainless summer.

Great battles have been fought over water in the West, with guns in the early days, later in the courts. Lake Elsinore is a large body of water, and as such, there are people who covet it. It's a constant worry.

They can't steal it, not anymore. As in the Old West, if you need water, you have to control the land it sits on or flows through. Southern California stole *plenty* of water before the Collapse, from anyone and everyone who had any. But to do that, you need huge engineering projects to siphon it off from your neighbors. Thirsty people in Arizona—and there are plenty of them, we know—can't pipe our water to Phoenix; they would have to come here and take the town. That land is ours, we're sitting on it and don't intend to give it up. The good news is that, to take it, you would need an organized army, and none has shown up. Raiding parties would accomplish nothing. What would they do? Fill their canteens and leave?

But we do worry about organized invaders, large numbers of desperate people who will risk death on the chance they can kill us or drive us away so that *they* can be the ones in control of our most vital resource.

When I say army, I very much include the ones that formerly fought our wars for us, in American uniforms. We are well organized, but we could never stand up to an assault by a modern army with tanks, helicopters, and aircraft. But the regular army has no choppers, very few tanks, and not nearly as many troops as it used to have. The National Guard is disbanded. Everyone just went home. We have seen no signs of the regular army but we do know they have suffered from mass desertions, too.

Neither Canada nor Mexico shows any signs of wanting to invade us, and without an external threat, what good is a standing, professional army? To keep things orderly? We're doing that ourselves, thank you.

And for that matter, what good would occupying our land and kicking us off do anybody? We are farming it as well as anyone could, and we don't hog it. We send what's left after our own short rations to the people around us, who are on even shorter rations. No train passes through here that we don't add a boxcar full of food we can ill afford to spare, destination San Bernardino or San Diego.

We no longer have hungry barbarian hordes at our borders, simmering with rage at us as they spoon up their thin daily gruel and imagine us sitting down to tables groaning with food. We got rid of the refugee camps by the simple expedient of taking them in. Not all at once, and not without trouble, but the last camp was emptied three months ago. It was a simple equation. The more willing hands we had, the more land we could plow and plant, the more ditches we could dig, the more manual pumps we could power. There was work for everybody. Even small children could pick bugs off the plants. And once people joined the workforce, once they *belonged*, they would fight alongside us to defend it all, instead of against us to take it away.

But still we worry. There must be an army out there somewhere, doing something. It's all classified, covered by the State of Emergency. We get reports over the radio, when it's not being jammed. Someone is doing the jamming, someone still wants to keep us in the dark about the extent of the disaster and what's being done—or not done—about it. We all believe we should never underestimate the damage that can be done by a papershuffler in a bunker in Washington or Sacramento who dreams up some project involving our water. Whether our old governors or new warlords who might arise, they are going to be in for a surprise if they come to take our land and our water. We will fight.

The San Onofre power plant seems to have done what it was intended to. According to a local man who used to work there, it shut down during the quake, cooled off, and awaited further instructions. We know they got it back online because we get the power from it. When the wind blows from the west our Geiger counters show no increased radiation.

Not so from the northwest. The Diablo Canyon reactors were hit by the tsunami and melted down, like the reactors after the big earthquake in Japan. It's not a good idea to go within five miles of it at all, and everything from Morro Bay to Vandenberg to San Luis Obispo is evacuated, too hot to live in for long. We get elevated levels when the wind blows down toward us. It's not something we like much, but there's nothing to do about it except take our iodine tablets and learn to live with it.

Our new world is so . . . spotty. We have been reduced to pumping water with stationary bikes providing the power, and yet for an hour a day—on most days—we get electricity from a nuclear power plant. The lion's share goes south to San Diego, naturally, with some going to the coastal communities, but we get a little time each day to recharge our batteries. You can't call it rolling blackouts, because we're black more than we're light. Maybe rolling illumination. We're frugal with it, as we are with everything. We get an allotment of kilowatt-hours, or whatever they call them, and there's a committee that decides what they're most needed for.

We haul our picked vegetables into town on horse-drawn carts, and yet we can determine the position of those carts within a few yards with GPS units. Those satellites are still up there and they should keep working for a while.

We log on to the Internet at night . . . by the light of kerosene lanterns. Yes, the Net is still out there, though more like it was in 1992 than what we had come to know. We have seen so much destruction in the Southland that it's easy to forget that, in most of the country, much of the infrastructure is still intact. The servers are still there, and so are the phone lines and fiber-optic cables and cell-phone towers. There is only enough power to run a fraction of them, but that will change, has already changed in the last few months. But though the hardware is there, most of the software was lost. E-mail addresses, Facebook pages—almost all Web pages of any kind—all were wiped out and they are hard and slow to reestablish. Most of what has come back is bulletin boards of one kind or another. People search through the millions of postings, trying to locate lost family and friends. It is slow, censored and interfered with by the government, and not well organized. The techies who might fix it are, like everyone else, mostly worried about planting and getting in the next harvest. Cyberspace will have to wait.

So as of now, paper mail is the most reliable way to communicate. Not the postal service. If it exists, we've seen no sign of it. No, you hand your mail to travelers headed where you think the addressee might live, and hope for the best. Most new arrivals these days are carrying a sack of letters, and all departures.

The Internet was never reliable, and now it's even more suspect, but still better than nothing. I think that those who run what is left of the army have decided that even though they can't physically control us at the point of a gun, they can try to keep us in the dark by patrolling cyberspace. We have learned that soldiers guard the large radio stations and the few TV stations that have come back on the air, and the few operating cell towers, and all content is censored by the government. The State of Emergency, you see. The big national political question these days, and the only one I am interested in, is will the SOE ever end? It's a golden opportunity for those who favor a strong state to take over completely, in the name of protecting us. There are still many, many people, including many in positions of power, who believe this nightmare was visited on us by some outside entity. You know who they are. The usual suspects: commies, the Arabs, the Jews, the Chinese.

People are still also blaming the CIA, the Republicans, the Democrats, the Rockefellers, international bankers, the oil companies, and a secret defense department lab (ouch!), but you don't hear that on government-controlled media. Those particular paranoids are confined to the pirate radio stations and what we're calling PUV Web sites that are thriving in spite of jamming and cyber warfare. PUV stand for pop-up-vanish, because they appear from nowhere, send out millions of e-mails, and then fade into the cyber forest. It's sort of like dropping leaflets from a fast-moving airplane. Most of the messages are destroyed, but some get through.

So all news is still suspect. But was it ever very different? I've realized I didn't trust Big News or Mom & Pop Blog news much even before the Collapse. I just didn't worry about it. I didn't think about it as much.

Somewhere out there, people are working to build natural-gas pipelines and convert power-generating stations. Diesel locomotives are being converted to coal. It doesn't happen overnight, but things are starting to move again, mostly by train. We get two trains coming through every week, and not all of them are old steam engines now.

America has lots and lots of both gas and coal. There are still nuclear plants in operation. In the Pacific Northwest they seem to have plenty of hydropower. Hoover Dam is still in operation, though we don't get any of their output.

Regular power generation will happen again.

There are many words that have taken on a whole new meaning, and the most radical of these is probably conservation.

Our household used to be quite proper and correct conservers. All our appliances came with the yellow sticker on the side telling us how much energy they saved. We had solar panels on the roof. We limited our water use, even in nondrought years, with low-flow toilets and showerheads. We only watered the yard at night.

(Granted, the Escalade had a carbon footprint that was bigger than King Kong's, but the Mercedes wasn't so bad, and I was lobbying hard for a Prius, or even a Volt.)

We recycled, we had all the big plastic bins for glass, cardboard and paper, metal, and plastic. When you think back, how smart was it to make the recycling containers out of plastic? Why not metal? Why plastic bags at the supermarket? Why two pounds of plastic packaging for every two pounds of stuff you were actually buying? Why plastic bottles instead of glass? Now that all the petroleum is gone—and *all* our miracle plastics came from petroleum, don't forget—it seems such a gigantic waste.

But everything we did was a waste. We wasted huge amounts of energy, physical resources, and most of all, oil.

Now it's gone. Now we are learning what conservation really means.

Did you ever visit what we used to call a "landfill"? Vast mountains of garbage being crushed by a fleet of bulldozers, to be covered with a layer of dirt and, eventually, a golf course. Paradise for seagulls, a stinking eyesore for everyone else. A treasure trove for future archaeologists, who will surely scratch their heads over the megamiddens of disposable diapers. *Didn't they have cloth? Soap? Water?*

I don't know where Elsinore's trash used to go, but today we have a dump. It's quite small, the size of a couple city lots, and contains mostly the plastic packaging from our rapidly dwindling supplies of pre-Collapse consumer goods, those few items we can't find another use for. Plastic bottles have obvious uses. Tin cans can be flattened and used to line our wooden aqueducts.

Other than that plastic packaging, we don't throw anything away.

We don't waste a watt of electricity. We don't waste a pint of water. Most of it can be reused. We process sewage. Did you know human waste, what they call "night soil" in Eastern countries, can be used as fertilizer? It's smelly until you mix it with charcoal and dry it, but you get used to it. I have taken my shift carrying night soil, without complaint.

As for food waste, there is none. None at all. What we used to call "leftovers" are invariably consumed at the next meal.

We are raising pigs because they will eat anything, they have large litters, and you can use every part of them except the squeal.

We are raising chickens because they can fend for themselves.

We recognize that raising meat animals is not the most efficient way to feed ourselves, but what the hell. We don't do a lot of it. Most of our meals are vegetarian, of necessity. If we get one scrawny chicken per month it's a feast. In addition, my family has eaten and enjoyed deer, squirrel, rabbit, raccoon, and possum. Yummy!

The result is that we now produce enough fruit and vegetables to feed our community. Not gorge ourselves, mind you. But everyone is getting the Recommended Daily Allowance, and it's well-balanced. We will soon be harvesting corn, and some wheat. Next year should be even better, if we have a good—that is, heavy—rainy season. And after the RDA, we even export food. That's a real accomplishment.

Of course, it doesn't hurt to be doing all this in California, where the weather is mild and sunny, and just about anything will grow, year-round. We also grow in greenhouses.

I'd hate to be trying to support a community in Maine or North Dakota.

One year is a good time for summing up. It also strikes me as a good time for looking ahead, to the limits of our poor abilities to do so.

Have we learned anything? Certainly in the short term we have.

Our community has found its way, through horrible loss and privation, to the fabled Ecotopia espoused by conservationists, by "Green" people.

We have sustainable agriculture that doesn't rely on chemical fertilizers.

We have an energy-use policy unimaginable a year ago.

We don't pollute our precious water, and air pollution is negligible . . . though that will change as we burn more wood and coal, which is especially dirty. Nothing to do about it right now, but Mark is working on it.

We have a sense of community that, in most of the country, was as extinct as the family farm.

Most astonishingly, we have what is a virtual communism, without ever having set out to do so. There is no money anyone trusts, so no real rich and poor. People still own property, their homes, some land, but most of the countryside around here was owned by the state of California, the federal government, or large corporations. Theoretically they still own it, but just let them come and try to take it, particularly the agribusiness companies. They'd better bring a lot of weapons to enforce their deeds. We are well armed, we know how to make gunpowder, and we reload.

It might be very different elsewhere. And our dreams of holding on to the land could prove to be pipe dreams. Big corporations very well *may* raise mercenary armies. Time will tell. My hope is that most of them, and their stock shares and land titles and bonds and mortgages, are as worthless as federal greenbacks, useful for starting kindling in your fireplace.

But . . .

The country is fragmented. It hardly seems reasonable to call it a country at this point. We don't know if that is good or bad, but most of us feel we must come together.

We have a distant government that lies to us routinely, habitually, brazenly, and it is quite clear that those who feel they ought to be in charge would like to clamp down on us all and see the chaos of the Collapse as a golden opportunity. There are hordes of restless, homeless, hungry people out there, and if a demagogue with access to television, radio, and the straitjacketed Internet were to come forward, it would be easy to scapegoat communities like ours, no matter how much free food we send to San Diego.

That is a worry for another day.

But I keep wondering . . . we have learned a lot in the short term, but how about five years from now? Ten years, twenty? The question before the jury is, are we an inherently wasteful species?

There is no lack of energy here on this planet. The disruption was caused by how deeply we were invested in petroleum. We were given no time to convert, and things collapsed. But there is coal, natural gas, and hydropower. There is enough coal to last a very long time. It's dirty, but I don't doubt that now that we have to, we will find ways to use it cleanly. The dams are still there, and some are generating again. Pipelines are being repaired. There are hydrogen, fuel cells, solar power, wind power. Only coal is abundant enough to take the place of crude oil, but anything else will help us pull ourselves up by our bootstraps.

What I want to know is, will those millions and millions of cars sitting idly in every garage and on every curbside in America soon be converted to burning wood, coal, gas, or hydrogen, and get back on the road again? Will we once more have traffic jams, roads bumper-to-bumper with single-passenger vehicles? Will we use coal technology to flood the world with unnecessary plastic again?

The jury will be out for a while on that one. I'm hoping we have learned a permanent lesson, and will be more sensible and moderate in the future.

But I'm not putting any money on it.

I have kept this manuscript in a safe-deposit box at the bank. Boxes are about the only services they offer now, as financial transactions are pretty much in abeyance until someone comes up with a currency that everyone can trust. Things still change hands, contracts are still drawn, but their terms are expressed as barter, swaps, rentals.

The box is free; just go ask for two keys from Harvey Wilkerson, the man who used to run the bank and is now a common laborer like me. I intend to keep this account in the box for a very long time, possibly forever.

Karen has asked me if I intend to publish it someday. The answer is no. I doubt there will be much of a market for stories of the Collapse. Everyone has a story of how they survived. Some of them are epic, and horrible, far worse than anything we endured. Who in this brave new world would want to read mine? I'm sure that, in ten or twenty years, someone will write the Great American Novel of the Collapse, like *Gone With the Wind* did for the Civil War, *The Grapes of Wrath* for the Great

Depression. I won't be the author of that book. I didn't see enough of it all, and my story is only middling awful.

There's a second and more compelling reason why I don't intend to seek publication. I'd have to take out the beginning. I realize that my account of how and why this all happened would surely be drowned out by the incredible babble of conspiracy theorists, that I would sound like just one more nut. But I worry that Colonel Warner's name might alert some National Security computer, and I remember what happened to him. I could change his name, I could fictionalize the circumstances and the location where the assassination happened, but why take even that chance? No, this account goes into the vault and stays there, a family heirloom to be shared (and probably disbelieved) only with my descendants, and those of the Winstons.

Speaking of descendants . . .

Addison is a year older, and has blossomed in a way that I suppose makes any father proud and terrified at the same time. Boys come calling, lots of boys. I see them flirting with her in the fields, and she flirts right back. My only hope is that she remains as levelheaded and picky as she was before the Collapse, but I'd be a lot happier if her birth-control pills hadn't run out months ago. Of course I want grandchildren . . . but not yet, Lord, not yet!

But there will soon be a new arrival. In about four months Addison will have a little brother or sister. Karen has never looked prettier, or happier. At night I put my ear to her baby bump and, among the stomach gurgles, hear the kid kicking around in there. If there's a more wonderful feeling, I don't know what it is.

Life goes on.

Until two months ago, leisure time was a fond memory. Saturday night was just like any other night, and Sunday was just another day. We worked from dawn to dusk every day of the week, no holidays.

Then the city council decided we were doing well enough that we could set aside Sunday mornings. Those who were so inclined attended church services, which had been happening all along, on Sundays after sundown, for the very devout. Those of us not inclined found other things to do. Sleeping late was a popular option. Then, starting at noon, we would work until dusk again.

Last month we started experimenting with letting Sunday be a true day of rest. So far, we're doing well with only six workdays a week.

With more leisure time than we have had since the crisis began, romance is not the only thing beginning to flourish again. There are the arts. A great deal of it is what we used to call crafts: quilting, knitting, carpentry, and the like, combining pleasure with usefulness. But there has already been one dance performance by a local troupe, and last Sunday I saw a man painting on canvas. Songs are being written and performed, dances and other gatherings are being held.

And the theater has once more staggered to its feet and trotted out onto the boards to beguile and amuse. I'd like to say that the first performance of the fledgling Lakeside Repertory Company was something like *Hamlet*—after all, what could be more appropriate in a community called Lake Elsinore?—but it wasn't.

It is with a crazy mixture of horror and pride that I report the inaugural selection was three episodes of *Ants!* I'm not going to take this as a sign that civilization will eventually rebound, only that television will.

The first two acts were adaptations of two of the most popular episodes, and the guys we recruited to play the parts were quite good, and even looked like their television counterparts. The third act was an entirely new episode, cobbled together by Jenna and myself with a little reluctant help from Bob. (He came up with three good jokes, and actually smiled twice, which by itself made the effort worthwhile for me.)

The response was uproarious, delirious, all out of proportion to the quality of the material, but I don't care. It reminded me of a scene from a Preston Sturges movies, *Sullivan's Travels*, where labor-gang prisoners were taken into a church to see a Disney cartoon. Laughter lightened their burden for a while. That's worth something.

It is now Monday morning, the kerosene in my lamp is running low, and my only pencil is worn to a nub. When the sun comes up I will take this down to the bank and seal it away, a time capsule to be opened when I or my descendants deem it safe. I send you greetings, descendants, whoever you are. Don't make the same mistakes we did.

Monday mornings are my shift at the northern border of the community, so my day will begin there, scanning the horizon for threats. Later, it will be harvesting, which I like more than plowing or planting, and infinitely more than composting and ditch-digging. I'm learning carpentry in the hope that I can get on the crews building elevated aqueducts, but I'll need to get a lot better. And, next Sunday, I will sit down with Jenna and Bob and write another episode.

There's a lot of work to be done.

ABOUT THE AUTHOR

JOHN VARLEY is the author of the Gaean Trilogy (*Titan*, *Wizard*, and *Demon*), *Steel Beach*, *The Golden Globe*, *Red Thunder*, *Mammoth*, *Red Lightning*, and *Rolling Thunder*. He has won both the Nebula and Hugo awards for his work. Visit his website at www.varley.net.

> "This is well-crafted science fiction written by a master."
> —*SFRevu*

FROM

JOHN VARLEY

ROLLING THUNDER

Lieutenant Patricia Kelly Elizabeth Podkayne Strickland-Garcia-Redmond— otherwise known as Podkayne—is the third generation of her family to set foot on Mars. Her grandfather Manny was one of the first colonists. So Poddy has some planet-sized shoes to fill. That's why she's joined the Music, Arts, and Drama Division of the Martian Navy. Though some may say her voice is a weapon in itself, Poddy passed the audition. And now she's going to Europa, one of Jupiter's many moons, to be an entertainer. But she's about to learn that there's plenty of danger to go around in the Martian Navy, even if you've just signed on to sing.

PRAISE FOR THE NOVELS OF JOHN VARLEY

> "One of science fiction's most important writers."
> —*The Washington Post*

> "[Varley's] conclusion to a trilogy begun with *Red Lightning* and *Red Thunder* demonstrates his skill as both raconteur and master of science-based fiction." —*Library Journal*

varley.net
facebook.com/AceRocBooks
penguin.com

M1259T0213